Trouble

Samantha Towle

Other Contemporary Novels by Samantha Towle

The Storm Series:
The Mighty Storm
Wethering the Storm

Paranormal Romances by Samantha Towle

The Bringer

The Alexandra Jones Series:
First Bitten
Original Sin

CONTENTS

For those whose pain went unnoticed...
You were never alone.

Prologue

Mia

"I'm so sorry, Mia. He didn't make it."

My lips feel numb as I say the words, "He's dead?"

Dr. Solomon touches my arm, his expression grave. "Yes. I'm so very sorry."

The muscles in my face are frozen – solid. Which is probably a good thing because I don't want him to see what I'm truly feeling.

Elation. Relief. Complete and utter relief.

Oliver is dead.

I want to laugh.

"Mia, are you okay? Maybe you should sit down."

I feel Dr. Solomon's hand on my arm, guiding me to sit on one of the plastic chairs in the waiting room.

I can't believe Oliver's dead.

I can feel the relief bubbling up inside me.

"Could I have some water?" I ask Dr. Solomon.

"Of course."

He leaves the room, and I'm grateful for the moment alone.

Oliver is dead.

I'm free.

Free.

I wrap my arms around myself, hugging tight.

In exhilaration? In comfort?

Maybe both.

I guess I should feel something in the form of grief that my father is dead.

But honestly I don't. I really and truly don't.

And I'm glad about that.

Happy.

Then I feel something form on my lips.

Something that hasn't happened to me in a really long time; not for real anyway. A smile.

I touch a finger to my lips.

There it is; an honest to god smile.

I hear movement by the door – Dr. Solomon.

I force the smile away and relax my features to neutral.

Dr. Solomon takes the seat beside me and hands me a plastic cup filled with ice water. The cold against my fingers makes me shiver.

He puts his hand on my shoulder and squeezes it in comfort. He probably thinks I'm shivering from shock.

I want to push his hand off. I hate people touching me. I hate men's hands touching me.

"Is there anyone I can call?" he asks.

He's asking this, but he knows there isn't anyone. Oliver was my only family.

I shake my head.

"Are you going to be okay?" he asks, releasing his hand from my shoulder, resting it back in his lap.

I glance up at him and nod.

I can't speak because if I do, I'll quite possibly tell that I'm going to be more than okay.

Not really what I should be saying minutes after finding out that my father has just died, but it's the truth. For the first time in my life, I can honestly say that I'm really and truly going to be okay.

Chapter One

Mia

Eight months later…

I push an errant strand of hair back with my hand. Setting down the roll of tape, I survey the boxes piled around me. For the last few days, I've been boxing Oliver's things to give to Goodwill. It's been eight months since he died of a heart attack, but trust me, I wasn't hanging onto them out of any sentimentality. I was just putting off having myself near anything of his, but now the house has finally sold after being on the market for six months, so everything has to go.

I feel no sadness. Nothing. Just relief that he's gone, and then a big black void of emptiness. I've felt this exact way from the moment I found out he'd died.

How ironic it is that he died of a heart attack? The great Oliver Monroe, respected and revered heart surgeon, dies from a heart attack.

I like to think of it as divine retribution.

The only one who could have saved him was himself. Maybe punishment does eventually come to those who deserve it. I need to believe that because it's the only thing that's keeping me hanging on.

You know the saying 'from bad to worse'? Well, my situation is kind of like that, but more like 'from worse, to a diluted version of worse, but still shit nonetheless'.

I moved out of my home—it's a joke for me to call it that. A home is somewhere you feel safe, but I hadn't felt safe in this house for even a moment.

I woke up one night, panicked and terrified from a nightmare. I thought Oliver was coming to get me, but then I suddenly realized that I was no longer trapped; that I could leave this place that closeted my nightmares.

So the next day, I put the house on the market and bought an apartment close to school and close to my boyfriend Forbes.

We started dating a month after Oliver died.

The instant I'd realized I was free of my father, I went a little wild. Well, wild for me. I went out to bars drinking, something I had never been allowed to do before.

I didn't really know what I was looking for, or what I was hoping to find … but that was when I found Forbes.

Or maybe he found me.

We met in a bar. He approached me, offered to buy me a drink. He was charming. I was flattered. No one had ever paid me attention the way Forbes had that night. Like everything I said mattered.

I fell into him like he was a vat of melted chocolate, but I later found out that Forbes is more like quicksand.

Dating quickly morphed into Forbes becoming my boyfriend.

My first boyfriend.

My first everything.

I was happy. Exuberant.

That quickly changed.

Four months ago I discovered that I had gotten myself into a relationship with the exact same man as my father when Forbes backhanded me during a disagreement.

Really, I should have seen it coming. Forbes is the epitome of Oliver, except instead of being a doctor, Forbes is well on his way to becoming a successful lawyer.

Everyone loves him. He's stupidly handsome. Smart. Charming. You know the type.

I should have known that, behind closed doors, the similarity to my father would be akin there too.

Cold-hearted. Physically and emotionally abusive.

Why do I stay?

Because it's all I know.

All I have ever known.

Like a bee drawn to honey, I was drawn to a man like Forbes because the life he offers is the one I'm used to.

It's easy to be worthless to someone, but to matter to someone … well, I think that would be harder.

I'm not playing for sympathy here. My life is what it is. I live it. There are people out there who are far worse off than I am. Children living with famine and loss, and dying every single day without reason and cause. So yes, I can cope with the occasional beating.

I do believe that everyone has a pain and coping ability that is individual to them, and if you want to feel sorry for yourself because of the hand life dealt you, then that's your god given right—I won't judge you for that.

I spent a long time crying my heart out because of the life I had. Then the tears dried up, and I got up and carried on.

I live to my worth. That's what Oliver taught me.

And there are good times. Little rays of sunshine on a bleak, cloudy day where Forbes shines through, reminding me of why I care about him.

Until the next time he splits my lip or cracks my ribs.

I don't love Forbes. I tell him I do because he wants to hear it, but really I don't.

In the beginning, I thought I did, but what did I know of love? I'd never been shown it to know what it was. It had taken me a while before I realized that what I felt for Forbes was nothing more than my own feelings being reflected through my utter desperation to be loved by someone.

Forbes showed me affection in the beginning—so I, of course, gorged like the needy person I am.

The one lesson I've learned is that if I were ever blessed to fall in love in the future, I would be able to tell it from my own wants and see it for the real thing.

Not that I ever see love happening in my future.

I'll be with Forbes until the day I die. Which could be sooner rather than later. One wrong hit is all it takes. Then I'll be with my mother.

I never knew my mother. She died when I was a baby. Oliver wouldn't talk about her. I've never even seen a picture – he got rid of all traces of her when she died. All I know is that she was called Anna and that she died in a car accident four months after I was born.

I've often wondered if that was why Oliver hated me so much. Because I was here, but she wasn't, and I reminded him of her.

I have her painted in my mind like an angel. She's one of the things that got me through the hard years with Oliver. I used to imagine how life would have been if she were still here. Would he have been the way he was? And if he were, I know she would have taken me away with her.

I know, because it's what I would have done, and I have to get that from her. Oliver didn't have one speck of goodness inside him, so it has to have come from my mom.

Thirsty, I head downstairs to the kitchen. The sound of my bare feet slapping against the tiles haunts me. Shivers run across my skin, fighting horrors to the surface.

Taking a deep breath, I close my eyes and calm myself before walking on, quietly this time. Before going to the fridge, I turn the TV on to fill the space with noise. I pull a bottle of water from the fridge, unscrew the cap and lean back against the counter.

My cell starts to vibrate against my butt.

I pull it from my pocket. I don't have to check the screen to know who it will be; Forbes. I don't have any real friends, not ones who call me anyway.

Growing up, I'd kept my distance from other kids. I'd wanted friends, desperately so, but I couldn't let anyone close because of the way Oliver was. It wasn't a risk I could take.

After a while, I'd become the weird kid. The loner.

I could have changed that when Oliver died, but I didn't see any real point, and even less so when I met Forbes. He isn't exactly big on me having girlfriends. He likes control, and I'm easier as a solo project.

"Hey," I answer.

"Hey babe, how much longer are you going to be?"

He's in a good mood. Thank god.

"Not too much longer. I just have the attic to finish, and then I'm heading home. That just leaves Oliver's office to do tomorrow."

"Shall I come over tonight?"

No.

"Of course." I force bright and bubbly into my voice.

"I've missed you these last few days," he says quietly down the phone.

"I've missed you too." *Not once.*

"We'll make up for it tonight."

Oh god.

"Can't wait."

"Great, I'll come over at eight."

"I'll make us dinner."

"I love you, Mia."

"I know. I love you too." *I hate you.*

Oh a sigh, I hang up the phone, shove it back in my pocket and head back upstairs to make a start on the attic.

"Hey." Forbes envelops me in a hug of expensive cologne and rich cotton.

Forbes is very handsome. Blond hair, six foot, built like a linebacker. He's the all American boy, and physically, we suit each other. I'm blonde and slim, though Forbes often tells me I'm overweight. And I'm short. Five three to be exact. It puts me a severe disadvantage when things get rough with Forbes. Not that I ever fight back. Fighting back only makes things worse. I learned that lesson a long time ago.

He leans down and kisses me firmly on the lips. I taste the alcohol on his breath instantly. He's been drinking.

My stomach sinks.

I used to love Forbes kisses in the beginning. Especially the alcohol free ones. I remember how I couldn't wait to have the feel of his lips on mine. Now, it's the last thing I want.

Don't get me wrong; Forbes doesn't need alcohol to set him off. He just ignites quicker when he's been on it.

Forbes follows me into the kitchen, keeping hold of my hand, which is unlike him. He's not usually tactile in private. Only in public, or when he wants sex.

I wriggle my fingers free from his to grab the pan handle so I can stir the sauce bubbling on the stove.

He frowns, then steps away, moving to the fridge.

He gets out a beer but doesn't offer me a drink. Forbes doesn't think women should drink beer, especially from the bottle. He says it's unladylike to do so, but I drink it when he's not around. He thinks I have it in the fridge for him, and I let him believe that.

He comes over and leans with his back up against the counter beside me. I turn the heat down to let the sauce simmer. I'm making Pasta Norma. Simple but delicious. Our old cook, Mrs. Kennedy, showed me how to make it. She used to teach me how to cook when Oliver wasn't around. I missed her a lot when she left. Oliver had let her go when he'd overheard her questioning me about the bruises on my arms.

"I was thinking I should move in here." Forbes words drop into the air like oil in water.

My hand freezes around the pan's handle.

No. No. No.

"What do you think?"

I have to tread carefully here.

Keeping a neutral face, I turn to him. "I thought you enjoyed living with the guys?"

Forbes lives in a huge rental house two blocks over from here with four of his frat buddies.

"I do, but it's loud. They're always partying, and I need quiet to work. You know how it is. That's why you live alone, so you can have peace to study."

Actually no. I live alone because I have no girlfriends to room with, and I would never, ever want to live with a man again. Especially not you.

Taking the spoon, I start stirring the sauce again.

Unable to stop my next words, I try to get them out as gently as possible. "Don't you think it's a bit soon? I mean, we've only been together seven months."

The length of pause tells me just the level of anger we've reached.

And it's not good. Not good at all.

"Don't you want to live with me?" His voice doesn't sound hurt. Just angry.

Stupid, Mia.

Stupid. Stupid. Stupid.

"Of course I do, I'm just thinking of you. I don't want you to feel tied down too quickly." I'm speaking quickly, but it's pointless. I know this.

"Bullshit." He shoves the pan back off the heat, and grabs a hand full of my long hair, tangling his fingers into it. He moves behind me and slowly pulls my head back toward him. "Would *you* feel tied down if I moved in, Mia?"

"Forbes, *please*," I say, swallowing hard.

"Answer me!"

"No, of course I wouldn't."

"Is there someone else you want to live with, Mia? Another guy? Are you fucking someone else?" His hand is tightening on my hair, pulling the roots. My eyes water from the pain.

"No, of course there isn't. There's only you I want to be with. I love you."

I hate you.

"I don't believe you! You've been fucking someone else,

16

haven't you?"

He turns me around and slams me up against the fridge. Pain bites up my back.

"No, I haven't. I swear." I'm breathless, and my mouth is dry. A tear runs down my cheek because I know what's coming next, and there's nothing that I can say or do that will stop it from happening.

"If you've done nothing wrong, then why the fuck are you crying?" His face is in mine. I can tell from his eyes that he's gone. The nice Forbes that arrived has stayed at the door.

He yanks me forward, then slams me back hard against the fridge again. My teeth clatter together as my head makes impact.

"I'm c-crying b-because I don't want you to hurt me." The words wobble from my trembling lips.

I don't want him to hurt me – that's what I say. It's a stupid thing to say because that's all he ever does, and it's not about to change because I say the words.

"C-crying," he mimics, letting out a sharp laugh.

Then his face darkens and I know exactly what's coming next, so I close my eyes and brace myself.

I feel the familiar hard sting of his hand hitting my face.

A sharp tang of blood flows into my mouth.

Happy. Think of happy things, Mia.

The feel of the sun on my face. The scent of the flowers I keep in my window box. Lowering the roof on my car on a warm day, loving the way the wind feels as it blows through my hair. I'm a bird. A bird flying free in the sky...

Music. Think of a song, Mia. Sing it in your head while you fly away...

"Be a shame to waste those tears of yours." Forbes slaps me across the face again. "Keep crying, Mia. And I'll keep giving you a reason to cry."

I'm not crying anymore, but that doesn't stop him. Nothing ever stops him. Forbes is done when he's done.

So I fly away to a safe place. One filled with happiness.

I come to, unsure of how much time has passed.

I'm alone on the kitchen floor.

Picking myself up, I get to my knees. The tiles are hard and unforgiving against my shins. My head is throbbing, and pain is radiating down my side. I hold my hand to my ribs. Not broken, just bruised. I've had broken ribs before, so I know how bad they feel. I clutch my hand around my ribs in an attempt to contain the pain as I get to my feet.

Seeing the heat is still on the stove, I move quietly to turn it off. The click of the knob echoes loud in the silence. I freeze. Making myself invisible is what counts right now. I don't want to attract Forbes' attention.

Turning my head, I see him in the living room, through the crack in the door. He's sitting on the sofa, beer in his hand, staring down at it.

I know what will come next. We play this role regularly.

Moving lightly on my feet, I open the door carefully and slip down the hall, heading straight to the bathroom.

Closing the door quietly behind me, I pull the first-aid kit from the cabinet, then check my face in the mirror.

No bruises. Forbes doesn't usually hit me hard enough in the face to leave a bruise, just like Oliver didn't.

People question bruises on the face.

I check my lip. Spilt on the inside. Caught on my tooth.

I down a couple of Advil to take the edge off the pain in my ribs, then get some antiseptic cleaner out and work it onto a cotton swab.

Pulling my lip forward, I dab the antiseptic against the cut. "Shit," I whisper.

A tear of pain leaks from my eye. I rub it away on my forearm.

When I'm done, I throw the cotton swab away in the trashcan, close up the first aid kit up, and put it away.

With care, I lift my shirt so I can examine my ribs. My skin is red and swollen. There will be a bruise showing in a few hours. A bad one.

Movement in the doorway catches my eye.

Forbes.

I freeze. My shirt drops from my grip, covering me. Covering what he did to me.

"I did that to you." Regret is in his voice. Tears in his eyes.

I hate you.

"God, I'm so sorry, Mia." He rushes me, grabbing me, pulling me against him.

He doesn't care that I wince from the pain in my ribs. All he cares about right now is himself. All he ever cares about is himself. Making Forbes feel better, no matter the cost to me.

"I'm so, so sorry, Mia. So sorry." He's pressing kisses over my face, along with his insufficient words.

His tears wash against my skin. They make me feel angry. Used. Weak. Consumed.

"I'm okay," I whisper.

Scripted. My life is one big goddamn script.

"It'll never happen again. I promise you. I love you so fucking much, Mia. I just get so jealous of the thought of you with another guy, and I've been under so much pressure lately, with my dad and…"

I switch off to his empty excuses and apologies, just ensuring I speak in all the right places.

"It's okay, Forbes. It's going to be okay."

"I love you," he breathes. "I can't lose you. I don't know what I would do without you."

I feel his mood shift, and I know what's next. It always happens after he beats me.

His hand moves to my jeans and he starts unzipping them, slipping his hand inside, and into my panties. "I love you so much, Mia. Let me make this better. *Please.*"

I close my eyes and nod my assent.

I don't fight him on this. I don't fight him on anything.

So I close my eyes and let Forbes strip my clothes from me. I let him have sex with me against the wall because it's all I know.

And as wrong as this sounds, a part of me craves to feel good. To feel loved. Even if it is fake … but for this moment, here, listening to Forbes tell me how much he needs me, how there's no one like me, how he could love no other—I can close my eyes and pretend that it's real; that I'm being loved in the way I can only dream of.

When Forbes is done, he carries me through to my bedroom.

Lifting the cover back, he lays me down and climbs in behind me, pulling me up tight against him. His arms cage me in.

"I love you," he whispers. "I'll never hurt you again. Never."

I close my eyes, and force the words out, "I love you too."

After a time, I feel Forbes' breaths even out, so I slip out from under his grip.

I walk into the dark kitchen, not bothering to turn the light on, and open the refrigerator door. The light glows through the room. I stare at the contents, pain and self-loathing stabbing like needles in my skin.

I just want to escape. I want to be free.

Free again, like I was the day Oliver died.

I felt like a giant that day. Like I could do or achieve anything.

But all I've managed to do was replace Oliver with Forbes. What does that say about me?

It says that I'm screwed up. Damaged.

Things I already know.

And I can't get away from Forbes. It's not like I can just break up with him. Women like me don't get to break up with men like Forbes.

I'm only free when he says so.

And he won't.

I know this because I'm ideal for the life he wants.

I'm pliable. Controllable. Visually, I look the part. I come from money, and I have the right breeding as I overheard his father telling him once. I'm training to be a doctor, a surgeon like

Oliver was. It wasn't my chosen career path, but Oliver told me I was going to be a surgeon, so I'm going to be a surgeon.

All of these attributes work perfectly for Forbes.

Men like him choose a woman like an employer chooses candidates for jobs—cold and methodical. Love has nothing to do with it, even though Forbes probably makes himself believe that love is a part of it.

Then one day, in the not too distant future, I'll become Mrs. Forbes Chandler. We'll have kids, and Forbes will continue to beat on me regularly as an outlet for his anger and failings.

On the outside, we'll have a perfect marriage. And behind closed doors we'll be everything that could be wrong with a marriage. Day in and day out I'll wear the façade. I'll be the perfect wife to Forbes just like I was the perfect daughter for Oliver to parade around.

Then degrade and beat senseless the moment the doors to our house slammed shut.

Forbes has never asked about my past. Never questioned the scars that mar those secret parts of my body.

I remember being so afraid the first time we made love. Afraid he would ask about them, but he never did. Part of me was relieved but disappointed.

I encouraged myself to believe that he hadn't asked because he didn't want to make me feel uncomfortable, or upset me by highlighting them.

Truth is, he didn't ask because he didn't care. My scars probably validated that I was exactly the right girl for him.

Maybe he saw it in me the second our eyes met in that bar that night.

Like knows like, right?

Reaching into the fridge, I start pulling out food, setting it on the counter.

Leaving the door open for light, I turn to the cabinet to get more food. When I'm sure I have enough to see me through, I tear off the foil from yesterday's saved chicken. And I start eating.

I'm sitting on the floor, sweat dampening my skin, my hands sticky from food. My stomach full and aching, my back pressed up against the door. Surrounding me are empty food containers and wrappers.

Knowing I can't sit here all night, I get to my feet. My stomach aches under the pressure of gravity.

I'm uncomfortable. I feel sick.

I relish the feeling.

I tidy the mess. Containers in the dishwasher. Wrappers pushed to the bottom of the trash can, so Forbes won't see them. Not that he'd question it, but better to be safe. I try never to leave a reason to set his anger off.

I wash my hands clean. Then go to the bathroom and lock the door.

I leave the light off. I don't want to risk catching a glimpse of myself in the mirror in this moment.

Kneeling before the toilet, I lift the seat.

Fingers poised by my lips, I push back, and make all the hurt go away.

Chapter Two

Mia

I'm back at Oliver's house to finish packing. My last day here. After today, I will never again have to come to this house.

The knowledge is like clean air in my lungs.

All that's left to empty is his office.

I left this room until last because I despise this room.

Oliver always beat me in his office, as though he thought that if he kept it to one room, he could leave this room and lock the door on it when he was done.

That's never been the case for me, but being in here does bring things back full throttle.

Bad memories start to scream out in the silence.

I sit down on the floor and get my iPhone out. Setting the music to play, I place it up on Oliver's desk.

He loved this desk. It belonged to his grandfather.

I should burn it. Just like I should have burned Oliver's body. Cremated him to dust. Make sure he was gone for good.

Unfortunately for me, Oliver had it set in his will that he was to be buried.

He'd already purchased a plot. I also discovered he had bought one for me too.

The plot next to his.

I'd rather burn in Hell than spend an eternity trapped beside him. I've served my time. I'm done.

Reaching for the last flat pack box, I stretch too far, and my ribs ache. I'm sporting a nice black bruise on them courtesy of Forbes outburst last night.

I check my bag for Advil and remember that I took the last of them first thing this morning.

Knowing everything is packed, I start to search through Oliver's drawers in the hope there may be something in here.

I tug on the bottom drawer, but it's locked.

I search the other drawers for a key but find nothing.

Then a thought crosses my mind. Oliver's keys, the ones I was given with his things at the hospital, have a few keys on it that I hadn't found a use for.

I retrieve the keys from my bag, and start trying the three keys. The second one fits, so I turn it, and the lock opens with a click. I pull the draw open, and there's nothing in it, but a manila folder. I take the folder from the drawer and sit down in the chair, placing the folder on the desk.

In the top right hand corner, it has one word – Anna.

Seeing my mother's name on it has me opening the folder.

There are two pieces of paper inside. Both are titled: 'Sawyer, Davis and Smith. Family Lawyers.' Dated: October 12th 1990.

I was born 1990. January 10th is my birthday.

The first letter is addressed to Oliver. I start to read.

No.

This … this can't be right.

Blood starts to pound in my ears.

With trembling fingers, I turn to the second piece of paper and read quickly through the lawyer jargon. I'm getting the basics of what this letter is about.

It's not a letter. It's a contract.

I, Anna Monroe, do decree to cease all parental rights of my daughter, Mia Monroe, giving sole custody to her father, Dr. Oliver Monroe.

I don't read anymore. I don't need to.

My mother didn't die in a car accident. She signed me over to Oliver.

She left me with him. She gave me to him.

Everything starts to fracture around me.

My eyes blur, and my heart starts to hurt in chest.

The letters flutter from my hands, dropping to the desk. I grab the folder, searching it, scrambling to find anything else.

I find one scrap piece of paper at the bottom.

It has my mother's name on it, and an address for a place called Durango in Colorado.

Grabbing the papers and address, I shove them in my bag.

I need to get out of here. I need to talk to someone.

So I head to the only person I have in this world – Forbes.

When I reach his house, I don't bother knocking as I know it'll be unlocked. There's always someone here.

The urge to talk to him about what I've discovered has increased on the drive over here. I just need to air this out. Figure it out. He'll be able to help me do that. Yes, Forbes is an asshole, but he's smart. He's almost a lawyer.

He'll know what these papers mean.

He'll know what to do.

As I walk through the foyer, I see the living room is deserted.

If he's not in, I'll just wait in his room until he gets home.

I run up the stairs to the first floor. Forbes' room is at the far end of the hall. I walk quickly, clutching my bag to my side. The papers inside feel as if they're burning through the leather and onto my skin.

Reaching Forbes' door, I grab the handle and push down, opening it.

And I'm greeted by the sight of Forbes in bed, having sex with a girl – who isn't me, obviously.

I can't really say what I feel in this moment. There's such a myriad of emotions streaming through me, but I do know the one emotion I feel with absolute certainty is relief. In what context I'm just not sure.

Funny.

Oliver dies, I feel relief.

Forbes cheats, I feel relief.

Not really the natural feeling one should have in these kind of situations.

Does this mean I'm free of Forbes?

The words are right there on the tip of my tongue. Of all the things I could say to him at this moment in time, that is the one thing I want to ask most.

It takes Forbes a moment to see me standing here in his doorway as he's too busy getting his rocks off. The surprise is evident on his face, but it quickly morphs into the cold, blank expression I'm familiar with.

The girl is facing away from me. All I can see is a mass of brown hair curtaining her face as she is on her hands and knees being screwed from behind by my boyfriend.

She has no clue I'm here, watching, feeling utterly emotionless by the whole thing

And Forbes says nothing. Just holds my eye as he continues to have sex with her.

"Yes, God! Forbes!" she screams out, making me jump. Forbes actually smiles.

"Harder! Fuck me harder!"

She really does seem to be enjoying herself. More than I ever have with him. Maybe that's why he hits me. Maybe I don't do sex right. He was my first. Has been my only.

"Yes! Right there!" she continues to scream.

You'd think he'd stop and try some lame attempt of *It's not what you think, Mia.*

But he doesn't say a thing.

Then again, you'd think I'd say something; any normal girl would if she caught her boyfriend cheating on her. She'd probably be the one screaming right now.

But then Forbes and I don't exactly *do* normal.

He has all the power, and I'm just dragged along for the ride.

Continuing to have sex with this girl, and keeping his eyes on me, his smile changes to a smirk. Then a fire ignites in his eyes. It's new. I've never seen this look on him before, but then I've never seen him having sex with someone else before either.

But there's something in the way he's looking at me right now that terrifies me. He looks empowered, like he's finally got me exactly where he wants me.

Chills creep down my spine like spiders.

"Oh god, I'm coming! I'm coming!" the girl screams, totally unaware of what is transpiring right now between Forbes and I.

Leave Mia, now. Go!

Tearing my gaze from his. I take one step back. Two. And then I'm gone, fleeing down the stairs and out of there.

I toss my bag into the foot-well and I'm back in my car, driving away.

Vision blurred, I wipe my eyes and realize that I'm crying.

Why? I'm not entirely sure.

I drive to a convenience store, park my car way in the back, go in and buy as much food as I can carry in my arms. Potato chips, candy, cookies, ice-cream – anything I can lay my hands on.

I get back in my car, open up the food and start eating like I always do. Eating is probably too nice a word for what I'm doing – I'm gorging.

When I'm done, the feeling of my stomach tight and bursting, relief momentarily fills me. Then I look around at the empty wrappers and containers and the sick, dirty, guilt feeling washes over me.

I stuff the wrappers in the bag and look around at the lot. There's no one around, so I walk toward the trash can and dump the bag in it. Then I skirt quickly to the cluster of trees by the edge of the store and hide myself from view as I brace my hand against one of them. I push my fingers down my throat, emptying my stomach.

I get back in my car, clean my hands on a wipe, and put a breath mint in my mouth.

Finally feeling in control of my emotions, I start my car and head for home.

I don't know Forbes is there waiting as his car isn't parked up front—maybe that was the point; he always likes to have the upper hand. When I see him under the alcove by my door, I try to run, but he grabs my arm, dragging me back. "Oh no, you don't."

I can smell perfume on him.

And sex.

The sex I just saw him having.

He didn't even shower.

Just finished screwing his bit on the side and came over here. Or maybe I'm his bit on the side. Maybe she's his girlfriend.

Forbes yanks my keys from my hand and unlocks the door. He pushes me into my apartment.

I stumble, but quickly correct my footing. For some reason, in this moment, it's important to me that I don't fall in front of him.

Moving back, I press up against the back of the sofa and grip the top of it with my hands.

I'm not really sure what I expect of him in this moment, but I need to prepare myself for the worst.

He places my keys on the table by the door and leans back against it, folding his arms across his chest. I watch his muscles flex. In the beginning of our relationship, I used to love how strong his arms looked. How safe they made me feel.

Now all I see is the power behind the pain. The fear they make me feel. The same fear that I grew up feeling because of a man exactly like him.

I don't want this anymore. I don't want to feel this way.

Not now.

Not ever again.

It's like clarity. Like my light has finally come on.

Why now? I'm not sure. But it has, and it's like a weight off my shoulders. I'm never going back to how my life was. Whatever it takes, it stops now.

That knowledge pushes my backbone up. I stand a little straighter.

Forbes' eyes are trained on me.

"Is she your girlfriend?" I ask, making sure to keep my voice clear and steady, even though my heart is beating so hard in my chest it's almost painful.

He looks surprised. Of all the things I could have said, I don't think he was expecting that. I wonder what he was expecting me to say.

"No. That privilege is all yours," he replies through tight lips.

"Do you fuck her often?"

His eyes narrow. "Watch your mouth, Mia."

"Sorry." I smile, sweetly … antagonistically. "Do you have sex regularly with her?"

"No, she's new."

New?

"There have been others?"

"Yes." He smirks. It hurts more than I was expecting.

Tears squeeze at my eyes. Not because of his betrayal, or the beatings, but because I'm angry with myself. Angry for being so goddamn weak.

"Have you used condoms with them?" He doesn't with me.

"Yes."

Thank god. I'm still going to get tested.

I can see the anger increasing in him. It tells in the dark of his eyes. The taunt skin across his cheekbones. The clenching of his fists by his sides.

My questioning is annoying him.

He actually has the audacity to be annoyed in this situation. But then, can I really expect any more from him?

Normally, when Forbes is this way, I will do anything to appease him. Anything to calm him. But right now my sole aim is to anger him more.

I don't know why, or what I want out of this apart from him gone from my life for good, but I will do whatever it takes now to make that happen.

I tilt my head to the side, appraising him as I ask this question. I'm genuinely interested to know the answer because honestly, it doesn't make sense to me.

"Forbes, you wanted to move in here with me. Wouldn't that have slightly hampered your ability to have sex with other women?"

"No." He's smug in his statement. And it makes me feel less than worthless. He folds his arms across his chest. "It's just simply time for us to move onto the next stage in our relationship. But my extra-circular activities will remain the same."

God, I knew he was a cold-hearted bastard, but now I'm seeing a whole brand new bastard. I guess there are more sides to Forbes Chandler than I had realized.

I wrap my arms around myself. I need to feel some form of warmth. "So you have these girls and me. Why?"

He smirks. "Because I can. And there is no separate now, Mia. You will be a part of it too."

My expression drops. "What?" The words wobble from my lips.

I'm pretty sure I know what he's getting at—not that I know much about sex, but I'm not dumb. I just don't want to believe it. He's never shown any interest in anything like that before. We've always had straight forward vanilla sex. He's never even taken me from behind like he did that girl.

"You. Will. Be. A. Part. Of. It." He addresses me as though speaking to a child. "You'll let me fuck them here in *our* apartment whenever I want. You'll sit out here and listen to me fuck them. And sometimes..." He steps closer. "You'll participate."

No. No. No. No!

Hell no!

"I don't think so." *Is that me speaking?*

His features tighten. He takes a step forward. I can see his hands twitching by his sides.

I sidestep around the sofa.

"You will do as I tell you, Mia. You're mine to do with as I want."

The belt cracked across my behind.
"Who is in control here, Mia?"
"You are, Daddy."

I lift my eyes to his face. Forbes might be handsome, but he's never looked uglier than he does right now.

"Do you hit those girls like you do me?"

I see surprise flicker across his face.

Even though we are both very clear on the fact that Forbes hits me … I've never actually said the words out loud before. They feel odd to have said, but also *empowering*.

"No," he answers, his voice cold.

And the empowerment I held so briefly dissipates and I want to cry. The ugly type of cry.

He beats me because he can.

Because I allow it.

Because I'm weak.

"Why me?" I ask. I know why, but the sadistic part of me wants to hear him confirm it.

He moves closer until he is right in front of me.

I don't move this time. I stand my ground, even though my legs are shaking to the point that I'm surprised I'm actually still standing.

If my act of strength surprises him, he doesn't let it show. He leans down, getting in my face. His hot breath burns my skin. I can still smell that girl on him.

I want to vomit.

"Because you're mine, Mia." His voice sounds like a hiss. "You belong to me. You're my other half. My little … easily controllable … fucked-up other half."

31

I might have known this already, but that doesn't stop it from hurting. I hide the burning flinch of pain I feel because I don't want him to have the pleasure of knowing.

He lifts his hand.

I flinch.

This pleases him.

Touching my cheek with the barest of touches, he runs his fingers across my skin and tucks my long hair behind my ear.

"You really are beautiful," he murmurs, brushing his fingers through my hair and down my back. Then he roughly grabs a hand full of my hair, yanking my head back. My eyes water from the pain.

"You and I are the same, you know." His voice is low and vengeful. "Pretty on the outside, but all kinds of fucked up on the inside. I wanted you, Mia, for the same reason you wanted me. Because like knows like. The abused becomes the abuser. Or, in your case, the abused just stays abused."

A veil lifts from my eyes. How did I not see it before?

Stereotypical pattern.

Forbes has lived my childhood. To what degree, I don't think I'll ever know. But he's lived through the pain.

Did his father beat him too?

I suddenly feel awash with sadness for him. An ache for the child he was. For the childhood that was stolen from him as mine was.

Then I look up at the man before me, and that sorrow instantly turns to rage. White hot rage.

He knows how it feels, yet he does it to me.

He could have stopped the cycle. Just loved me. I would have loved him back without question. I would have given him all of me. My heart. Together, we could have healed each other.

But instead, all he gave me was a co-dependent, hate fueled, abusive relationship.

And now I'm just left with an empty chasm, lined with that hatred, and bitter resentment.

I open my mouth to tell him this … then it hits me.

I could have walked away … maybe not walked, but run. I *should* have run.

The simple truth is that I took the only way I knew … I carried on being the old me. The one who Oliver created, instead of trying to find a new Mia. The real Mia.

Because I was afraid to try.

Anger for my own failings burst in my chest … swelling … compressing me from the inside out. I feel as if I'm going to explode under the pressure.

I somehow manage to find my voice. "I want you to leave."

Cruel laughter bursts from him. "You breaking up with me, Mia?"

It takes everything in me, but I force myself to meet his eyes. "I'd say I've got good reason to, wouldn't you?"

He grabs my face, pinching my cheeks hard, then shoves my head back. He wraps his hand around my upper arm, yanking me straight back to him. I collide hard with his chest.

"So, let me get this straight – I get to smack you around whenever I feel like it, but the moment you catch me with my dick in some cheap slut, you're apparently done?"

I wince from the pressure of his fingers digging into my arm, but I speak through the pain. "It's got nothing to do with you having sex with that girl. This is me finally waking up. Something I should have done a long time ago. I won't continue to be your punching bag, Forbes. And I definitely won't become your whore."

He laughs in my face. His voice chilly, he says, "You've been my whore from the moment I met you."

"What happens when you dress like a whore, Mia?"

I bit my lip through the lashing, unable to speak through the pain.

"Answer me!"

My body jumps from the force of his voice. Sweat trickled down the side of my face, like the tears I wanted to shed. "I-I get treated like o-one, D-Daddy."

"Exactly right. You're finally starting to learn."

Something in me snaps.

I stare hard into Forbes' eyes. "I'm no one's whore! Now get the hell out of my apartment! I'm done with you!"

Rage engorges his features, making him barely recognizable. In all this time, I've never seen him this angry, this far gone.

I should be terrified. I'm not.

"Done with me?" he spits in my face. "You think it's that fuckin' easy? I'm going nowhere! And neither are you!"

He slams his lips against mine at the same time as he restrains my hands by my sides. The next thing I know, my back is pressed against the wall, his body hard on mine, caging me in.

I'm trapped.

I feel his quick erection dig in my hip, and my senses instantly tell me where this is going.

My heart plummets.

Oh god, no. Not this. Anything but this.

I've been degraded, humiliated and beaten. But never raped. He's not taking this from me. I have to fight back.

The laughable thing is, I don't know how to fight back.

Fear is bubbling my blood, adrenaline spiking my senses, so I do the only thing I can think of. I bite down on his lip until I taste blood.

"You fuckin' bitch!"

He slaps me hard. I expect it, but not the punch that follows.

My head ricochets off the wall. Pain explodes everywhere. Light swims my vision.

Forbes grabs me and lifts me off my feet, then slams me up against the wall. I cry out from the pain it sends hurtling through my already bruised ribs.

Shoving my skirt up, his hand goes down my panties while his other pins my throat, squeezing hard.

Fingers press painfully into my flesh. One violating me. The other stealing my breath. Yet all I can think is: *Why did I wear a skirt this morning? Why didn't I pick pants? If I'd picked pants, it*

would have made this harder for him. Maybe gave me an out.
Something so small can define how a situation goes.
I will probably never again wear a skirt.
Something small. Insignificant.
But it matters to me.
I can feel myself shutting down. I close my eyes tight.
Warmth. Music. Flying free in the blue sky...
Safe. I'm safe.
"I'm going to fuck some sense into you," he hisses in my ear. "You need teaching a lesson."

"Come to my office, Mia. It's time for a lesson."

Forbes' fingers roughly and painfully pull out of me, dragging me back to the now.
For a spilt stupid second, I think he's changed his mind—that maybe he isn't going to do this.
Then he reaches for the zipper on his jeans.
In this moment, it's difficult to say what I feel. Realization, mainly. This is really going to happen to me. He's going to take from me the last shred of dignity I have.
Only if I let it happen.
Stop this, Mia! Stop being weak and fight back! You stop this, and there will be no more pain. No more hurt. Ever.
Forbes is struggling with his zipper. He moves off me, just a fraction, but I take full advantage of that fraction. Using courage I didn't know I had until now, I bring my knee up as hard as I can and slam it into his balls.
A sound like garbled agony emits from him.
His hand drops from my throat, releasing me as both his hands go to his crotch, holding the pain I just created.
Now you know how it feels you bastard.
I slide down the wall, gasping for the air I so desperately need.
Forbes staggers a little to the side, face lined with pain, then he drops to his knees.

Now, Mia, go!

I'm moving. Running through my apartment. I grab my keys off the table, and I'm out the door, flying down the stairs.

I don't stop to look behind.

The street is quiet. No one around. I unlock my car in the race toward it. Slamming the door shut, my hand shakes as I try to get the key in the ignition.

Shit! I can't get it in.

Out of the corner of my eye, I see Forbes come stumbling out of the building, hand still holding his crotch, and I don't know if it's sheer luck driving this moment, but the key suddenly punches in.

I turn the ignition, shift into gear, and slam my foot down, getting me out of there.

Reaching the end of the street in a matter of seconds, I turn left and race off down the street. I feel wet on my hand as I push my hair off my face. Pulling it back, I find it smeared with blood.

I take a quick glance in the rear-view mirror.

My eyebrow is split open and the blood from the wound is running down my face, dripping onto my clothes.

"Shit," I wince, instantly feeling the pain from the knowledge.

I need to clean it up, but I can't stop. Not now. I can't risk Forbes catching up with me.

Because he will, undoubtedly, be coming after me.

I press my sleeve against the cut to soak up the blood and press down harder on the gas, firing me onward.

Before I know it, I'm on the I-90 with absolutely no idea where I'm going.

I have nowhere to go.

No friends to turn to. No family.

There's only me.

I drive down the I-90 for an undetermined amount of time. I'm just staring ahead, foot on the gas pedal, putting as much distance between me and Forbes as I can.

It starts to rain, so visibility becomes poor, and my eye is starting to shut. It isn't easy driving as I am, but with the rain pouring down, I'm going to have to pull off.

The thought of stopping terrifies me, but at the moment, I don't have a choice.

A few minutes later, I see a sign for a service station coming up in a mile.

When the turn comes up, I pull off and follow the road round.

I park my car into the lot just outside the service motel. Shutting the engine off, I check my doors are still locked, then I examine my eye in the rear-view mirror. It's looking bad.

I reach into the glove compartment and get out the hand wipes I keep in there. That's when I spot my handbag sitting in the foot well where I'd dropped it earlier. Relief fills me.

I've got money.

There's no way I can go back to my apartment. When Forbes gets bored of looking for me, that's the first place he'll go to wait. Looks like this motel is going to be my bed for the night.

I lift my bag onto the passenger seat. The papers about my mother are still there. I gently touch them with my fingertips.

My cell starts to ring, making me jump.

Forbes.

With trembling fingers, I cancel the call and switch my cell off.

I clean my face using the hand wipes. On closer examination, I see the cut is really deep. I'll need to tape it. What it really needs is stitches, but I'm not up for stitching myself at the moment, and going to the ER is out of the question.

I can live with the scar. It's not my first.

There should be some tape in the first-aid kit in the trunk of the car. Always prepared. That's me. I could do with an icepack. I'll see what the motel has.

I grab my overly large sunglasses from my bag and put them on to cover my eye. I don't care that it's raining. I hang my bag on my shoulder, open the door and step into the bouncing rain.

Popping the trunk, I get the first-aid kit and shove it in my bag before I head to the reception of the motel.

The female, a middle-aged clerk barely looks at me as she checks me in, which is good because I must look a complete state wearing sunglasses, soaked through to my panties and blood on my clothes.

She hands me over a key card with barely a word, so I thank her and head straight to the room. Stopping on the way, I grab a can of soda from the machine. It'll work as a makeshift icepack.

I open the door, and I'm greeted with the stench of stale air freshener. Walking into the room, I shut the door behind me, locking it. I remove my sunglasses and put them in my bag, which I drop on the bed as I sit down. The mattress is hard and uncomfortable. I rest the cold can of soda against my eye using one hand. With the other, I curl my fingers around the edge of the bed and grip the comforter.

Then I just let go. I cry the tears I've needed to cry all night.

I've no clue how long I sit here for, crying, but when I'm finally dried eyed, I go to the bathroom and strip my clothes off.

The urge to eat and purge is overwhelming right now, but fear of going back outside keeps me in the room.

Fear is driving my every decision right now.

I wash my blood stained shirt in the sink and hang it to drip dry over the towel rail. I turn the shower on hot and climb underneath. I just need to get the stench and feel of Forbes off me, then I'll be okay.

I'll be okay.

Tears sting my eyes at the reminder of what just happened to me. A lump lodges in my throat, sticking there like dry wood. I suck in a deep breath to stop the tears from starting again as I pick up the hotel soap to wash myself with. When I feel as near to clean as I'm going to, I grab a towel and wrap my hair up. Then my body. I hate that I can't brush my teeth. I'll have to buy a toothbrush and paste in the morning.

I go back into the room and get the first-aid kit from my bag.

I clean the cut using an antiseptic wipe, then tape it up. I take a couple of Advil from the kit and swallow them down.

I really don't want to put the clothes I was wearing back on, but they're all I have to wear. I leave my panties off and just put my bra back on, wrapping the towel around my waist.

Climbing back onto the bed, I tuck my legs underneath me as I stare down at my bag.

The 'Giveaway Mia' contract and my mother's address are still in there.

I can't believe that she's alive. More so, that she signed me away. Just like that. With the press of a pen to paper, she was no longer my mother.

How does that even work?

The mix of emotions I feel is confusing. I'm angry. No, I'm raging. She has been out there all this time while I had to endure growing up with Oliver.

She abandoned me.

She left me with him.

Did she know the kind of man he really was? The person she was actually leaving her child with? Did she willingly just walk away leaving me there with that monster of a man?

I have to believe she didn't know because the thought that she did is just too painful to consider.

I can't think about it now. I don't want to think about it.

Too much has happened to me today. I can barely process it.

I need to sleep.

Pressing all thoughts from my mind, I straighten a leg out, and using my toes, I push my bag off the edge of the bed. I switch the light off and climb under the covers.

Closing my eyes, I listen to the sound of the distant traffic on the interstate, trying to focus on that.

I wonder if Forbes is looking for me. What if he finds me here?

On that thought, I get out of bed, grab the heavy chair from the desk, and drag it over to the door, propping it up underneath the door handle. I should have hidden my car behind the motel instead of leaving it upfront, but I'm not going out there now to move it.

Then again, I'm too far out of Boston. Forbes won't think I'll have gone this far. I never leave Boston.

The thought makes me sad.

I've never left Boston. Not once.

The life I had existed within the city limits. While my mother lived a whole other life, without me.

Climbing back into bed, I turn the TV on using the remote control and focus on the screen instead of focusing on what is going on in my own mind.

Inside my head is not a place I want to be right now.

Chapter Three

Mia

I wake feeling disorientated. My head is throbbing, and I can hear a television on.

I realize I'm in the motel room I slept in last night.

Yesterday's events come flooding back. Forbes tried to rape me. He sexually assaulted me. My mother – she's alive. She signed me away. She left me with Oliver.

My heart and stomach start to ache, painfully.

Then I make the mistake of rubbing my eyes. "Shit!"

I press my head back into the pillow and ride out the wave of pain, and grief until it all settles into a dull ache in my chest.

I don't move again until my bursting bladder forces me out of bed. When I'm done using the bathroom, I check my eye in the mirror.

Jesus, it's bad. Swollen and black and my eye is bloodshot to hell. No amount of cover-up will conceal this.

Guess I'll be wearing my sunglasses for the next week.

I drop a couple of Advil to take the edge off the pain, and go back to bed. Resting my back against the headboard, I start channel hopping. I'm trying to focus on the television, and ignore the noise and questions in my mind, but it's not working.

I know I need to decide what the hell I'm going to do. I can't just stay here in a motel room, off the I-90, in god knows where. But I can't go back to my apartment either. Or Boston for that matter. Forbes will be waiting for me.

So what do I do?

I could go to Colorado and find my mother.

No way. She abandoned me. She left me with Oliver.

But you don't know her reasons. You know what Oliver was like. How terrifying he was. What if she had no choice but to leave?

I bang my head back against the headboard. *"Goddammit! No!"* I mutter into the silence.

This goes on for a while. But no matter which way I argue it in my head, I won't rest or be able to move forward until I know why she left me. It will eat away at me.

Maybe finding my mother will finally help me figure out who I am. Give me closure or something. And I have the free time. School is out for summer break. The time could help me figure out what to do with my life, and finding her might help me find myself.

Since Oliver died, I've just carried on with the life he set for me. This is my chance to break free and change things.

I don't even have to go back to Boston if I don't want to. Yes, I have my apartment there, but that's not going anywhere, and I could eventually sell it—shit! Goodwill is coming today to collect Oliver's things.

I dive for my bag and get my cell. I turn it on and ignore the notifications of texts and voicemails from Forbes. I place a call to the lawyer who is handling the house sale.

Voicemail. Too early for anyone to be in the office. I leave a message, explaining that I've had to leave town for a few days, and asking if they can arrange for someone to be there to let Goodwill in the house.

I hang up and turn my cell off. The last thing I want to do is hear any of Forbes' cruel words.

With a plan in hand, I dress quickly, cringing that I have to wear yesterday's things. I need to make a stop and get some new clothes and underwear.

I tie my hair into a ponytail, put my sunglasses on, and check out of the motel.

In my car, I tap 'Durango, Colorado' into the GPS.

Wow. Okay, so this going to be one hell of a long drive.

I consider for a moment flying to Colorado, but then I decide I want to leave no trace for Forbes to follow. Not that I think airports give out that type of information, but Forbes can be very persuasive when he wants to be, and I just don't want to risk leaving him a way to find me.

I know he'll look for me.

Forbes is not the kind of guy who gives up easily on what he thinks belongs to him. And he definitely believes that I am his.

I get back on the road and drive for a few hours before I need to stop for gas. While in the station, I ask the attendant if there are any malls nearby. No malls, but he tells me there is a Walmart a few miles away.

Perfect.

I follow his directions to Walmart. I stock up on jeans, t-shirts, tank tops, pajamas, underwear, toiletries and more Advil. I also grab a pair of ballet flats. And a gym bag to keep all my new things in.

Heading for the checkout, I pay for my items, making small talk with the cashier.

I've just left the store, bags in hand, when I realize I haven't gotten a hairdryer. My hair is a nightmare—thick and holds water like a sponge. It was still damp this morning from washing it last night.

I'm just about to head back inside, when the hair salon next door catches my eye. Before I even have a chance to think, I'm walking toward it, then I'm seated before a mirror as a woman called Shirley asks what I want to do with my hair today.

I blink. "Oh, uh…"

My eyes drift around at the many pictures of hair models on the wall. Then I realize what I want. I want to look different.

"I want you to cut it all off."

Did I just say that?

"All?" She looks at me as though I've lost my mind. I probably have.

I have great hair. It's blonde, very thick and very long, but now I just want it gone. I want to look different. I want to start my new future, with a new me.

"Yes. I want that style." I point at a picture of a woman with short hair. It's a pixie style.

She looks so pretty…

So happy…

I want to look like that.

Shirley tilts her head to the side, assessing me in the mirror. "Well, you definitely have the bone structure to carry it off." She smiles. "Right, let's get your hair washed. Give you time to change your mind."

"I'm not going to change my mind."

I sit down at the basin and lie my head back into the sink.

"You okay to remove the sunglasses, sweetie?" Shirley asks.

I freeze.

It takes me a moment to gather the courage to reach my hand up and slowly slide them off.

I hear her gasp of breath, and I'm thankful that I can't see the expression on her face.

"Sit forward, sweetie. I forgot to put a towel around your shoulders."

I do as she asks.

Shirley slips a towel around my shoulders, then I feel her hand gently squeeze my shoulder.

It feels like support. Solidarity.

It brings a lump to my throat.

Maybe she knows what it's like to get a black eye. It's not the pain on the outside that does the damage; it's the effect that bruise has on the inside that does the worst kind of damage.

The black eye heals. The pain never does.

"Right, lay yourself back," Shirley says. "Let's make a new woman of you."

An hour later and I'm back in my car. My purchases on the backseat. The new me in the front.

I tilt the mirror to look at my new hairstyle. My bangs sweep across, hanging in my eyes a little, and it's just long enough to tuck behind my ear, but it is short.

I look completely different, just like I wanted.

Suddenly, laughter bubbles up and out of me. I'm laughing, and I have no clue why, then without warning I burst into tears.

I'm laughing and crying. What the hell is wrong with me?

Maybe I'm having some kind of breakdown.

A woman walks past my car, giving me an odd look, and I realize I must look like a crazy person, sitting here laughing my head off with tears streaming down my face.

I dry my face with my hands, start my car up, and begin my long drive to Colorado.

Chapter Four

Mia

It's early evening.

Two and a half very long days since I drove out of that Walmart parking lot, but I'm finally here, driving across the city limits and into Durango.

I'm stiff, tired, hungry and beyond crabby.

Apart from two nights spent in horrid motel rooms, all I've done is drive. Thank god for the radio is all I can say. I've spent entirely way too long in my car – more than any person ever should.

It's my own fault. I could have taken a little longer to get here, but I've been on a mission to put as much distance between me and Forbes as possible.

I just need something to eat, then I want to lie down on a comfortable bed and sleep for a week at least, then I'll put my big girl panties on and go to this address that I have for Anna Monroe and find out if my mother still lives there. After that…

I have no clue.

I'm leaving that one down to fate.

Sticking to the main road, I follow it into the center of town. I lean forward, which stretches my back out nicely, and peer through the windshield to take a look around.

It's a really pretty place. Quaint with a homey feel to it. I can see why someone would want to live here.

Why my mother would want to live here.

Lifting my eyes to the skyline, I see the backdrop of the mountains.

Wow. Stunning.

Leaning back in my seat, I catch sight of a diner. It looks nice and clean. I'll grab a quick bite to eat here, then find a hotel.

Checking the road is clear, I pull across and park up front the diner. I put my sunglasses back on before exiting my car. My black-eye is still looking noticeably bad.

Locking my car, I stretch my aching body out, then make my way toward the diner.

I push the door open and step inside. Glancing around, I see a lot of the booths are already taken, so I'm praying they can seat me right away. I'd skip eating tonight if I could, but I've not eaten much these last few days, and I can feel the toll it's taking on my body.

A girl walks over to greet me. She is about my age, but half a foot taller with long straight brown hair.

"Hi, welcome to Jo's. I'm Beth, I'll be your server. Just a table for one?" she asks, glancing behind me.

"Yes. Just me." I smile awkwardly. I hate the discomfort that comes with eating alone.

Beth grabs a menu from the hostess stand, and I follow her over to an empty booth at the back of the diner. She places the menu on the table in front of me as I slide in the booth.

"What can I get you to drink?" Her pen is hovered over her notepad.

"I'll have a diet coke, please," I answer while my eyes make quick work of the menu. I just want to put my order in so I can eat quickly and drive to the nearest hotel. "I'd like to order my food now if that's okay?"

"Of course." She smiles. "What would you like?"

"Cheeseburger and fries." I was never allowed to eat this kind of food growing up. Oliver wouldn't allow it, and of course, Forbes has an issue with it. He says the sight of a woman eating a greasy burger is disgusting. Or maybe just the sight of me eating one is what disgusts him.

This is the kind of food I eat in private. And now I'm about to eat it in public.

Freaking thrilling.

Tragic, I know, but nonetheless true.

"Sure." She takes the menu from me. "Your food will be ten minutes. I'll be right back with your coke."

"Thanks. Um, I was wondering … if you could help…"

She gives a curious look.

I twist in my seat a little to look at her. "I literally just arrived in town, and I need a place to stay, so I was wondering if you could recommend a decent hotel?"

Her eyes appraise me, taking me in from the sunglasses on my face to the sneakers on my feet. It makes me feel uncomfortable and tense. I paste a smile on my face as I tuck my feet back under the table.

"Golden Oaks," she says, putting the menu under her arm. "It's the best hotel in Durango by far. It's just up in the mountains. A bit further out than most, but well worth the journey."

"How far is the drive?" The last thing I want to do is spend more time than necessary in my car.

I notice her watching my mouth, and realize that I'm pulling on my lip with my finger and thumb. I do it when I'm uncomfortable, or nervous. Which is often.

I lay my hand on the table.

"It's just a fifteen minute drive – ten if you drive fast." She grins, tilting her head to the side.

I let out a little laugh. "Do you have the address or street name? – For my GPS," I explain.

"Sure." She scribbles on the notepad in her hand, then tears off the piece and hands it to me.

"Thank you."

"No problem." She smiles, brightly. "I'll be right back with that drink."

I've just eaten, quite possibly the best burger I've ever had in my life, and now I'm back in my car, following the directions my GPS is telling me.

I'm feeling pretty proud of myself. There was a point back at the diner when I felt the pressing urge to overeat once I started in on the burger—stress catching up with me and trying to take control—but I held myself together and contained the urge. I ate what was on my plate, paid my bill and left.

That was a big achievement for me. I've never eaten food like that without purging it straight after.

Leaning forward, I glance around through the windshield.

Where in the hell am I?

All I'm seeing is nothing but road.

And trees.

And more road.

Lots and lots of winding road, going up and up, taking me further into the mountains.

I glance at my GPS checking the route. Yep, I'm definitely going the right way, and according to this, I should be there in a few minutes.

Only I'm still seeing nothing, and I already passed two other hotels on my way up here. I'm really starting to regret not stopping at one of them. I'm sick of driving, and I don't want to be staying in the middle of nowhere, but Beth from the diner did say it was the best hotel here, so on I go.

A few minutes later I see a sign for Golden Oaks. *Hallelujah*! I actually do a little mini air-punch, I'm that relieved.

I catch site of the hotel from the main road. It looks pretty, and the backdrop of the mountains makes it seem even prettier. I'd probably appreciate it a whole lot more if I weren't so bone tired.

I take the turn as directed, and pull onto a long driveway. Tires crunching over the gravel, I drive on until the foliage disappears and the hotel opens up in front of me.

It's smaller close up. Pretty. And totally perfect.

I look around for designated parking, but there is none, so I pull up alongside an ostentatious red mustang which is parked on the grass just off the driveway. It looks like the type of car one of Forbes douchey friends would drive.

Forbes.

A shudder rolls through me at the mere thought of him. I've made sure not to think of him once in the past few days. Keeping my phone turned off has really helped with that.

Grabbing my handbag off the passenger seat, I get out of my car, and stretch out again. My body feels as if it's seizing up. I just need to lie down on a soft mattress for a very long time. I'm really hoping the beds here are comfy because the last two motel beds have been horrendous.

Moving around my car, I pop the trunk and get my bag out.

The first thing I notice about this place is how quiet it is. Nothing but the sound of birds chirping in the background. Peaceful.

And perfect.

This place is starting to feel pretty close to heaven right now.

As I walk past the Mustang, I glance down at it and see that it has flames painted along the side.

Oh my god. This car is a definite penis enhancer if ever I saw one. I let out a snort of laughter and cover my hand with my mouth.

Stopping at the walkway leading up to the reception, I take a look around.

The hotel is a large wooden cabin style hotel, set on stilts which run down one side where the hill rolls down into what looks to be huge grounds. As I glance down, I see the building also goes down the side where the stilts round it. Maybe that's where the owners live. Large windows reflect out onto a wrap around porch up top. Lanterns light the front, giving it a warm glow, and there is a pretty garden at the bottom by the walkway up to the hotel. As I move toward it, the fragrance from the wide mixture of plants invades my senses. I stop and inhale deeply, letting out a contented sigh.

50

I walk up the steps and onto the porch toward the reception so I can get checked into this place.

A bell tinkles when I push the door open. I step inside and find the place deserted.

It's just as pretty in here as it is outside. A dark oak reception desk is situated directly in front of me. To my left is an open sitting room complete with huge unlit fireplace, and there are three plush sofas situated around the room.

It looks so homey. I have a good feeling about this place.

"Hello? Is anyone there?" I call out.

I don't hear anything for a moment, but then I hear, what sounds like an elephant bounding up stairs.

Then, quite literally, the epitome of everything a girl like me should stay away from walks through the door directly behind the reception desk.

Lean. Tall. Tattooed – one of them covering the full of his arm. Dark brown hair, long, but not ponytail long; surfer boy long and hanging in his eyes.

Taking me in, he sweeps his hair back revealing eyes the color of maple syrup. I have the sudden urge to eat pancakes.

This guy is gorgeous.

Masculine...

Strong jawline...

Everything about him screams male.

He looks like sin.

Like hot, dirty, incredible sex.

Jesus Christ! Where did that come from? I never think of men and sex—or sex with men—in that way.

I realize I'm staring at him, so I open my mouth and speak.

"Hello." I moisten my dry lips with my tongue.

Tattooed Adonis says nothing.

He stares at me like I'm an alien who just landed on this planet – like he's not quite sure what to do with me, or why I'm here.

Maybe I made a mistake coming here. Maybe they're closed for the season, and Beth got it wrong.

51

I'm ready to back up and leave when he speaks. His voice is as deep and manly as I'd expect it to be. It sends shivers coursing over my skin.

"How can I help?" he asks.

How can he help? This is a hotel, right? I'm tempted to step back outside and check the sign again.

"I, uh, need a room." I move closer to the counter. "Beth, the girl at the diner in town? She sent me here. Said you'd have a room available."

He stares at me for a long moment. I'm just starting to wonder if I've got something on my face, when I see he's actually staring at my sunglasses. He's probably wondering why I'm wearing them at night. Well, rather this than have him staring at my black eye.

He looks down at the desk in front of him. "We do. How long do you want to stay for?"

I almost sigh in relief that they've got availability. The last thing I want to do is get back in my car.

How long do I want to stay for?

"Um…" It's my turn to look down. I shift on my feet, thinking.

I need a while to give me time to find my mother. And if I do find her, then I'll need time with her.

If she wants to see me that is.

I wonder how long they rent rooms for. Looking up, I say, "I'm not sure … two weeks?"

"Are you asking or telling me?"

Wow. Okay. He might be good-looking, but he's not very nice. But what do I expect? Forbes is handsome—more in a classic way than this guy here—and he's the biggest asshole of all.

Pulling on my lower lip with my finger, I swallow, then fold my arms over my chest, and steel my voice. "I want to stay for two weeks, and I'm asking if you have a room available for that long?"

He looks down at the booking sheet, then looks up. His eyes

flicker past me before coming back to my face. "We do. It's one hundred and seventy five a night."

It's certainly a lot more expensive than the last two motels I've stayed at, but it's far nicer, and it's not like I can't afford it, courtesy of Oliver's tainted money. And honestly, right now I'd pay anything to be able to sleep in a comfy bed.

"That's fine," I say.

He gives me a narrowed look, then draws a line across the book in front of him. He reaches into a drawer, returning with a sheet of paper which he slides across the desk and puts a pen beside it. "Fill this out with your name and home address."

I pick up the pen.

Should I put an incorrect address like I did at the last two places I stayed? I don't want a trace back to me in case Forbes is looking for me. And tied together with my name, he'd know it was me that has been here.

But then I'm not staying just one night like those other places. And it would look suspicious if I lie about where I live, and this guy finds out.

I decide to go with the truth and write my real home address and cell phone number down. Forbes won't be looking for me way out here. I'm half-way across the country. Two thousand miles from home.

When I'm done, I hand the form back to him. My fingers accidentally touch his. Warm, rough fingers. Yet gentle. They feel good.

Deceptive.

Because men's hands cause pain. They give hard, sharp slaps. They give black eyes. Grabbing, clutching, never-ending pain…

I pull my hand back quickly and wrap it into my other.

Face prickling, I look into the living area, imagining the fireplace lit. I can almost feel the warmth on my face if I just close my eyes.

"I just need your card details and we're done. Your card won't be charged until you check out." Tattooed Adonis' voice snaps me back to the now.

"Okay."

I get my card from my purse. I hold it out for him to take, but he ignores me and instead starts fussing with one of those card devices. Then he hands it to me without casting a glance my way.

"Put your card in…"

I do as asked.

"And now your PIN."

When I'm done, he takes the device back from me, eyes still off somewhere else.

I watch him with interest as he stares at the little electronic gadget.

He really is gorgeous. The more I look at him, the more handsome he becomes. I have never seen someone who is as physically attractive as this guy.

I bet he has women tripping over themselves to be with him. And I think he knows exactly how good-looking he is. I can see it in the confident tilt of his stance, and the air of indifference he exudes.

He removes my card from the machine, then hands it back to me. I slide it in my back pocket.

I see him get a key from a hook on the wall.

He steps out from behind the counter. "This way."

I reach down to grab my bags, and with much effort, hoist them to my shoulder.

They feel way heavier than they did five minutes ago. Must be knowing I'm one step closer to a bed … one step closer to sleep, that has really set the fatigue in.

"Here let me get those for you," Tattooed Adonis says, his hand reached out toward me.

Is he being nice to me? Why?

He wasn't being nice a few minutes ago, and he has barely given me a glance. And in my experience, men are only nice when they want something. I have nothing to give this guy.

Retracting his hand, he scratches his head and frowns at me. "It's my job to carry your bags. We're not the kind of establishment that has a bellboy," he says, then grins. A boyish kind of grin.

Oh, right. Stupid Mia.

I lift the bags from my shoulder and hand them to him. My body sighs in relief. "Thank you." I smile.

A weird look passes over his face, then he frowns again. Slinging my bags over his shoulder, he strides off down the hall.

Okay, mood swing much? Nice one minute, moody the next. But then, aren't all men like that? Some more than others.

I'm practically jogging to catch up with him, then Tattooed Adonis comes to an abrupt stop outside a door half-way down the hall. I have to catch myself from running into the back of him. He unlocks the door and goes in the room, turning the light on, and setting my bags on the bed.

I try to step inside the room, but I can't. My muscles are frozen.

Being out there alone in the reception with him was okay because it's a public place. But this … I can't walk into this room alone with him. He could trap me.

The lock clicks.
I turn around.
Oliver is dangling the key from his hand. His belt in the other.
"Time for a lesson, Mia."

My eyes search tattoo Adonis' jeans. He's not wearing a belt.

What difference does that make? He wouldn't need a belt to hurt me. There are other ways to hurt someone. Many other ways.

Why did he go in the room?

To put your bags in your room. To do his job.

This guy isn't Oliver or Forbes. He's just some guy who works at a hotel. He's not going to hurt me. Not all men all cruel.

I'm safe here. This is a hotel. There are other people staying here.

Actually, come to think of it, I haven't seen another soul since I arrived. Only him. And there was only one other car parked up outside when I arrived. The Mustang – the penis enhancer – which could be his car.

Oh god, is that his car? Am I alone in this hotel with him? *That's his car, and I'm alone in this hotel with him.*

Chills shiver down my spine. I try to take in a deep breath, but my lungs won't allow it. Panic is gripping my chest like a vice.

It's okay, Mia. Calm down. There could be people in the other rooms. It's evening. They could be settled in for the night. Or out and returning later. Just because there isn't another car parked outside, doesn't mean a thing.

Tattooed Adonis turns around. He tilts his head to the side, giving me a questioning look.

Can't blame him. I am standing in the hall, acting like a complete weirdo, on the verge of a panic attack.

His eyes move down my body. Why is looking at me like that?

All my senses kick into high-alert.

I wrap my arms around my chest and straighten my back, trying to look taller and more confident than I could ever hope to be.

I *can* take care of myself now. I'm stronger than I used to be. I kneed Forbes in the balls and got away, didn't I?

Tattooed Adonis walks toward me. My urge to bolt becomes compelling.

I am not weak. I am not weak.

I'm a strong woman.

I force myself to keep steady, and step back to give him space to pass by.

Tattooed Adonis towers over me. I knew he was a lot taller than me—not that it's hard being that I'm pocket sized—but it's so much more noticeable now he's closer to me, and surprisingly, his closeness isn't freaking me out as much as it should.

"Your key," he offers.

I take it from him.

"Breakfast is served between seven and eight-thirty," he

states before walking away. Stopping, he adds, "And we don't do evening meals, but there are plenty of restaurants nearby."

"Are there any other guests staying here?" I have to ask.

He stops and turns back. "No. Not until next week. Until then, it's just you and me."

I'm pretty sure my heart just died in my chest.

Me. Alone. Here.

With him.

No. No. No.

I can't do that. I am stronger than I was, but that's pushing myself to far too soon.

"Don't worry it's totally safe out here," he says. I'm guessing it's the look on utter panic on my face prompting this. "We have a great alarm system, and I have a shotgun. You know, just in case."

A gun.

God, no.

"What would happen if I pulled this trigger, Mia?"

I squeezed my eyes shut as I felt the cold metal press against my forehead. I could feel my body begin to sweat.

But I held myself together. Made sure not to cry. If I did, it only made him angry.

"I would die, Oliver."

The gun pushed harder against my head. "Oliver!" he yelled. "You know to address me only as sir or daddy! How many times do I have to tell you this? How many lessons will it take?"

Shit. Shit. Shit.

I'm so stupid.

The gun retracted.

"I'm s-sorry, s-sir—d-daddy." My voice was shaking as hard as my body because I knew what would come next.

And my fear was confirmed when I heard the familiar snap of his belt.

"I'm totally kidding. I don't have a gun here." The sound of

Tattooed Adonis' voice brings me to the now.

I need to be sick. Fear and bad memories are creeping across my skin, standing every hair on end.

I'm trying to stay calm. Stay normal. I don't want to freak out in front of this guy, but it's getting increasingly hard.

He lifts his hands in a gentle gesture. "No guns. I promise. No need for them, like I said, it's a safe place."

Breathing in through my nose, I pull on my lip and tuck my short hair behind my ear.

"Are you okay?" he asks, taking a step forward.

No.

Be strong. Stay here. You can do this, Mia.

"Yes. I'm fine."

His stare on me is curious. Can't blame him. I am acting like a nutball.

"Okay, well if you need anything, just press reception on the phone in your room and it'll bring you straight through to me." He turns to leave. "Goodnight, Mia."

"How do you know my name?"

Looking back, his eyebrow lifts. "I got it from your details when you filled the booking form in."

He smiles. It's a really nice smile. Warm. Friendly. It eases me some.

"Oh, right. Yes." I laugh, feeling a little stupid. "What should I call you?"

He smiles again. "Jordan."

I turn to face him. "Is this your hotel, Jordan?"

He laughs. It's a deep, manly sound that makes my stomach do somersaults. "No. My dad's. He's away taking care of my Grandpa at the moment, so I'm holding the fort."

"Oh, nothing serious I hope?"

"No, just a minor op, but he's off his feet for a few weeks, so Dad's gone to take care of him."

I nod. "Well, thank you. Again." I smile at him as I back up and quickly retreat into my room.

I lock the door behind me and fall against it.

Deep breaths, Mia.

This is going to be okay. And apart from his snippiness before, Jordan does seem like a good guy.

Yeah, but so did Forbes.

I grab the chair I just spotted by the dressing table, drag it over to the door, and push it up under the handle.

Doesn't hurt to be safe.

Turning, I take the room in for the first time. Really pretty. A four poster bed dressed in soft beige linens rests against the back wall. A large window is situated to the side, and on the far wall there are double glass doors. I go over to the doors and push the drapes back to peer out. I can't see much; just the porch and the moonlight pouring over trees in the distance. I'll check it out in the morning.

I double check that the doors are locked, then close the drapes, including the ones on the windows.

I stand in the middle of the room. The silence chills me, and my mind starts to overwork again.

Fear curdles inside and poisons me.

And I can't stop myself from walking straight to the bathroom, kneeling down in front of the toilet, lifting the lid, and purging.

Chapter Five

Jordan

A few hours earlier...

I climb out of bed. Removing the condom, I tie a knot in the end and toss it in the trashcan. Grabbing my jeans from the floor, I start to pull them on.

"Stay in bed with me." Shawna's hand sneaks out from under the cover and grabs hold of my hand, tugging on it.

I pull it free. "Can't. I've got work to do. And I need to get this bed made up."

That's a lie. There's not a lot to do here at the moment. We need guests to create work, and currently there aren't any, so the world won't end if this bed stays unmade for a while longer. I just don't want to stay in bed with her and cuddle.

Because that's what she's asking. She doesn't have to say the exact words. I just know when it reaches this point with a woman.

And that's when I'm done.

I'm not a cuddler.

I fuck.

The end.

She knows this. I told her right before we started having sex how it was. Like I tell them all. It's just a shame they don't bother to listen, regardless of how heavily I highlight the fact.

Guess it's time to put the brakes on this little thing we've had going. Shame. She was pretty good in the sack.

I'm just pulling my t-shirt on when she climbs out of bed.

I watch her walk toward me. I might be about to call time on her, but that doesn't mean I can't appreciate her fine body – legs that go on forever, and tits that are definitely not real. Still, I wasn't complaining when I had them in my mouth ten minutes ago.

She presses herself up against me. Arms snaking around my waist, she starts to kiss my neck. "I want to fuck again," she murmurs against my skin.

Tempting as that is, just knowing what's going on inside her head—the words 'Jordan' and 'boyfriend'—keeps my boy at bay.

You might think I'm a bastard for just having sex with her and then calling time, and really that wasn't my intention when I crawled into bed with her an hour ago. I'd thought there were a few more times to be had.

Until she wanted to get cozy with me.

I usually end these things in a much nicer way, but trust me, it's crueler to let her leave here thinking I'm going to call her again when I'm not.

I'm always honest, if nothing else.

Reaching behind me I take hold of her hands. Pulling her free from around my waist, I squeeze her hands, then let go.

I step back from her. "Look, Shawna, it's been great an' all … but I'd say we're done here."

She pauses. Frowns. Then gets this crazy look in her eyes that some chicks get when they realize you're ending things with them.

The stage five clinger look.

"Done?" Her voice has gone screechy.

Fuck.

I really didn't have her pegged as stage five clinger material when I met her. Guess I got that plenty fucking wrong.

I could really do without a crazy chick moment right now.

Here we go…

"Shawna…" I rub my forehead, and drive my fingers into my hair, pushing it back. "We both knew what this was from the beginning. I was clear on that. It was never gonna last longer than

61

a few weeks, and we're already well past that."

"It's been a week, Jordan."

Fuck, is that all? Feels way longer. Definitely time to get rid of her.

"Look…" I put on my best 'sensitive, but I'm still ditching your ass' voice. "It's been fun, Shawna. You're fun. But it's time to move on."

With a look straight from the devil, she grabs her clothes from the floor and starts yanking them on.

"Fun? FUN!" Her screeching is actually hurting my ears. "I thought we had something really great here! I thought you really liked me!"

See what I mean?

Never.

Fucking.

Listen.

"When did I say that? Oh yeah, never. I thought you were hot, and I *definitely* wanted to have sex with you – multiple times. But feelings never came into it. Not once. And no fuckin' way do I want a relationship."

Ouch. That was probably a bit harsh.

She steps close and pokes me in the chest with her fingernail.

Fuck, that hurt. Her nails are sharp. They felt good when they were raking down my back, but now, not so much.

"You're a fucking bastard!" she yells in my face. "And you're going to spend your whole life lonely and miserable!"

Wow, so original – like I haven't heard that line before. Why do all women say that exact same thing when you're blowing them off?

Trust me, I'm not miserable. Far from it.

Seeing what my dad's gone through … loving Mom, then having to watch her die … seeing how my dad is now … an empty shell of the man he was…

That's misery.

I'm never putting myself through that. I'll stay as I am, thanks.

When it comes to women, I put my dick in and keep my heart out. It's the easiest way.

I lean down, close to her face. "Shawna, you knew from the beginning I wasn't in for anything more than a fuck, so don't act all shocked and shit on now. You knew exactly who you were getting into bed with."

Why do all women think they can change me? I'm unchangeable. When will they get this?

"Fuck you!" she screams. She actually screams at me.

Jesus Christ, I cannot stand dramatic women. Nothing turns me off quicker … well, apart from cuddling.

"Isn't that the point?" I smirk, stepping back. "You want to fuck, and I don't." I sweep my arm out in the direction of the door. "Don't let the door hit your ass on the way out, sweetheart."

I'm not usually this much of a dick, but honestly, she's getting on my last fucking nerve.

Shawna looks as if she's ready to pummel me to death. Bending down, she grabs her heels, shoves her feet in them, and grabs her purse from the nightstand.

"You're going to regret this," she hisses.

"Not likely."

"Asshole!" She pushes her way past me, and stomps out the room, slamming the door behind her.

I hear her heels clattering down the hall, then the main door slams shut. A minute later, her car engines revs loudly, and spinning tires kick up against the gravel.

Well, that went well.

I run my hands through my hair, then go and grab some clean sheets from the linen closet.

I strip the bed and have it remade in two minutes flat.

Can you tell this isn't my first rodeo?

I have sex in the hotel rooms because I don't like to share my bed. I want to go to sleep without the scent of sex lingering from the last girl I hooked up with. And for some reason, the girls I hook up with seem to think it's romantic to have sex in a hotel room.

Couldn't be less so in my opinion.

But they think that, so it works well for me. This is when living at a hotel comes in handy.

I bundle the dirty sheets up in my arms to take to the laundry room.

Guess it's time to find a new fuck buddy. First things first, though. Shower, then food.

I'm starving.

I'm just biting into my sandwich when the phone rings. Putting it back down on the plate, I grab the phone off the wall, quickly chewing and swallowing down my bite. God, that's good. I make a great fucking sandwich.

"Golden Oaks," I say, cleaning sandwich off my teeth with my tongue.

"Jordan, it's Beth."

I sit back down in my seat. "Beth, I know it's you. I've known you my whole life, so it's safe to say I recognize your voice on the phone."

She laughs. "Fair enough. Anyway, I'm just calling to let you know I've sent a tourist up your way."

"Ah, great thanks. You're good to me."

"I know I am. Too good. And Jordan, the tourist is a girl. And she's pretty, real pretty. So just try to keep it in your pants, okay? Your dad needs the business, and screwing the guests, then screwing them over, just doesn't bode well with that."

"Jesus, Beth! One time. One fuckin' time it happened! And she never told me she was married."

"One!" She laughs. "Angry husband's aside, I can count off the top of my head at least ten women you've had hissing at you this past year, and it's only July."

"Ten? Come on that's a bit of an exaggeration."

She laughs, once. "I was being kind with that figure."

I do quick math in my head.

Okay, maybe she's right.

"Whatever," I mutter. "I'm actually a little insulted you think women leave here with not one good word to say after a ride from Jordan Matthews."

"Don't talk about yourself in the third person, it freaks me out when you do that. And yes, once you stick your dick in a woman it doesn't end in a song of happiness. You're awesome at the wooing. Just not the ending."

"I don't woo. We're not in the nineteenth century. I fuck. And I'm awesome at it. Hence why women keep coming back for more. And can you stop talking about my dick? You're actually starting to turn me on, and that's freaking *me* out."

"Ugh, god! Okay, we'll end the conversation here. Just leave the pretty tourist alone."

"You seem overly pushy on this one. Are you warning me off for another reason? Maybe because you want her for yourself?"

"Jordan Matthews!" she scolds, making me laugh. "One, she's not into girls. I could tell. And two, she's *too* pretty if you know what I mean."

"No. I really don't," I deadpan. "There's no such thing as too pretty."

"Yes, there is. There's the kind of pretty that comes with a warning label. This girl is trouble. Look, I have to go. The diner's busy, and Mom is shooting me daggers from up front. Just be good, for me. And if not for me, your dad. He could really do without the hassle after everything that's happened."

My back stiffens.

Her stark reminder is like a sharp slap in the face. Probably one I needed.

"You're not saying anything … did I overstep the mark?" she says softly.

"No." I sigh. "You said what I needed to hear. I'll be good, I promise."

"I'm only looking out for you because I love you, you know

that."

"I know. And you're the only woman who can say that to me without sending me running."

"That's because I haven't slept with you."

"And that is because you, Beth Turner, are one smart girl."

"Yeah. That, and the fact I'm a lesbian."

I chuckle. "Well, yeah. That too."

Fifteen minutes later, I hear a car pulling up the drive. It'll be the hot tourist.

I'm going to show Beth that I'm completely capable of keeping myself in check around a pretty girl.

I am not ruled by my dick.

And anyway, just because Beth thinks she's pretty doesn't mean I will.

She could be fuck ugly. Or at the very least, a butter face.

Nah. Who am I kidding? If Beth thinks she's pretty, then I definitely will. We have the same taste in women.

A few minutes later, I hear the bell ring on the main door. Showtime.

I haul my ass out of the chair and start to make my way upstairs. As I'm climbing, I hear her voice call out.

"Hello? Is anyone there?"

"Jeez, give me a minute," I mutter.

I take the rest of the stairs two at a time, quickly moving through the office, out to the reception desk, and…

Fuck me.

Fucking. Fuck. Fuck.

The *hottest* chick I have ever seen in my life is standing before me.

The.

Hottest.

Ever.

Beth calling her pretty was an understatement. A massive understatement.

She's stunning.

And I'm so completely screwed.

It's weird though because I usually go for tall girls. I like long legs, but this girl is tiny. I'd give her five-three max. At six-two, I'm almost a whole foot taller than her. And her tits are smaller than I usually prefer.

Her hair is blonde and short. Pixie cut. She kind of looks like Tinker Bell. I usually dig long hair on chicks; something to wrap my hand around while I fuck them.

But this girl, who is pretty much the opposite of everything I usually go for, has made my dick as hard as stone just by looking at her.

Never. Happened. Before.

I usually need them to be naked, or to at least have a little hands on action first.

She's like the world's best visual hand job.

Seriously, I think if she just lays a finger on me I'll jizz my pants, and that hasn't happened since seventh grade when I was with Katie Harris in the sports closet. Two tugs and I was done. Not one of my finer moments, but in my defense, Katie was the first girl to touch my cock.

I'm just thanking my good luck right now that this reception desk is high enough to hide the massive boner I'm sporting.

"Hello," she says. Her tongue darts out to moisten her lips.

Jesus, she has the sweetest looking mouth. The kind of cherry red lips you want to suck on. The kind of lips I want to see sucking me off.

I only wish I could see her eyes. Eyes are my other thing aside from legs. I like them big, but she's wearing huge ass sunglasses. I hate it when women do that. It's sunny, you wear sunglasses. Not at eight in the goddamn evening.

Realizing I haven't spoken a word in reply, and have done nothing but stare at this girl for an insane amount of time, I find my voice and ask, "How can I help?"

There are a few different ways she could answer that question. One involves her telling me to bend her over this reception desk and…

"I, uh, need a room."

Jesus, her voice is as sweet as light molasses.

My dick twitches, pulsing hard against my, now, incredibly tight jeans.

I need this hard on to disappear.

I can do this. My dick does not rule me. I'm in control here.

Think of being some chick's boyfriend, Matthews. The stage five clinger from earlier…

And there you go. Down boy.

Hot girl steps close to the counter and sets her bags to the floor.

She smells good. Like a mixture of vanilla and expensive perfume.

I want to lean in close and inhale.

And possibly lick her.

She moistens her lips again before speaking. It's really distracting. "Beth, the girl at the diner in town? She sent me here. Said you'd have a room available."

I pull my eyes from her lips and stare into those ugly ass sunglasses. All I get is my own reflection back. Which is not a bad thing, I just really want to see her without them on.

I wonder if she'd be offended if I reached over and pulled them off?

Clearing my head and throat, I say, "We do. How long do want to stay for?"

"Um." She tilts her chin down and shifts on her feet. "I'm not sure … two weeks?"

Two weeks. This is just the kind of money we could do with right now. If I can keep my hands off her that is.

"Are you asking or telling me?"

Wow, I sounded like a complete asshole then.

She looks uncomfortable.

And I feel like shit.

What the hell is wrong with me?

Her hand reaches up and starts to pull on her lower lip – it's actually kind of hot watching her tug on that lip. It's definitely turning me on again. Okay, so *again* is probably the wrong word since I haven't been 'off' since I laid eyes on her.

Letting go of the lip that I most certainly want to suck on, she folds her arms. "I want to stay for two weeks, and I'm asking if you have a room available for that long?"

Forcing my eyes from her, I look down at the booking sheet.

Like I have to check. Of course I have a room free for two weeks. We don't have another booking coming until next week, and that's the Perry's who stay every year for their anniversary. I just needed a reprieve before I do something stupid, like hit on her.

God, I want to hit on her. So bad.

Clear your head, Matthews. No hitting on the hot tourist.

You can do this.

Right. I'll put her in Lakeview. It's the most expensive room we have. And the nicest. The kind of room a girl like her should stay in.

And judging from the flashy Mercedes I can see parked outside, I'm guessing she can more than afford it.

Also, it's the one room I haven't had sex in. Not that it matters in regards to her, but Mom and Dad spent their first night as a married couple in Lakeview. That's why I steer clear of it.

"We do," I say. "It's one hundred and seventy five a night."

"That's fine," she replies. She doesn't even blink.

Like I thought. Loaded. I wonder if it's Daddy's money, or maybe she has a husband?

She doesn't look old enough to be married, but who knows the ages of women nowadays. Earlier this year, I banged a chick who looked twenty, but she was thirty. The marvels of plastic surgery.

I give a quick check to her ring finger. Empty.

Picking up a pen, I mark out the week. I pull out a booking

form from the drawer for her to fill out her details, then slide it across the counter to her, putting the pen I was just using beside it.

"Fill this out with your name and home address."

She picks the pen up. I notice her hand is trembling. Odd. Is she nervous, or afraid?

Not a damn reason she would have to be afraid, so I'm betting on nervous.

Now why would a hot girl like her be nervous around me? Only one reason. She wants a piece. They always do.

Hey, I'm not an arrogant ass. I'm just aware of how I look. And most women like how I look. Okay, *all* women like how I look. It's the hair and tattoos. They like the bad boys, and I'm bad. What can I say?

But this girl is not worldly. I can tell. This one is inexperienced, hence the nerves. Maybe she's a virgin.

Nah, she can't be a virgin looking like she does.

She finishes filling out her details and hands the paper back to me. Her fingers brush mine in the exchange. She snatches her hand back like touching me is a big no-no.

Odd. Women usually can't wait to get their hands on me.

I glance down at her name on the paper in my hand.

Mia Monroe.

Huh. Like Marilyn Monroe, but not.

I didn't just say that out loud, did I?

I cast a glance at her. She's staring off toward the living room.

No, don't think I did. Thank fuck for that.

"I just need your card details and we're done. Your card won't be charged until you check out."

"Okay." She bends down to her bag. I take the opportunity to lean over the counter and check her ass out.

Nice. Real nice.

I shouldn't have looked because I'm getting hard again.

She comes back up with her card in hand.

I key the amount in and hand the card device to her.

70

"Put your card in … and now your PIN."

I take the device back and wait for it to ring through.

When it's done, I pull her card from the machine and hand it back to her.

I notice she takes care not to touch me this time.

She shoves the card in her back jean pocket. For a moment, I actually wish I was that card.

I grab the key for Lakeview and step out from behind the counter. "This way."

She reaches down for her bags and sluggishly lifts them to her shoulder. That's when I realize how tired she looks.

Here I am checking her out like a total douche, and the girl is exhausted. I feel like a complete tool. My mom raised me better than this.

"Here let me get those for you." I hold my hand out to take her bags.

She hesitates. Her fingers curl around the handles, gripping them tight to her.

What does she think I'm going to do, run off with her stuff?

Retracting my hand, I scratch my head. "It's my job to carry your bags. We're not the kind of establishment that has a bellboy." I grin so not come off as an asshole. She is a paying guest after all.

Her death grip relaxes and she lifts the bags from her shoulder, placing them in my hand.

"Thank you," she says in that sweet voice of hers.

She doesn't talk much, but when she does … it's *effective*.

Then she smiles.

I called her stunning before. I take it back. With that smile, she's nothing short of beautiful.

I don't think I've ever referred to a woman as beautiful before. Now, there's a first.

If she can look this beautiful with those huge hideous sunglasses covering what I imagine is the best part of her face, then I can only imagine how she looks without them.

And how she would look under me.

Naked.

I sling her bags over my shoulder and stride off in the direction of Lakeview.

You can't have sex with her, Matthews.

My dick, of course, disagrees. Yeah, my dick is absolutely positive that I could screw this chick for two weeks straight and not get bored once.

Who am I kidding? I'd get bored after a week. I lasted that long with Shawna, and she had a huge rack and legs that went on forever.

But even with those assets, she was nowhere near as hot as Mia Monroe.

Hot or not. I don't have the staying power. And right now, money is more important. And proving a point to Beth, of course.

I come to a stop outside Lakeview. I unlock the door, turn the light on and go inside, setting her bags on the bed.

When I turn back, I see she's still standing out in the hall.

Everything about her body language screams tense. My eyes flicker to her hands. They're trembling again.

What is wrong with this girl? I thought it was because she was hot for me, but no, it's not that. It's something else.

She wraps her arms around her chest and straightens her back up.

With care, I walk toward her. She steps back to let me pass.

"Your key." I hold it out to her, leaving a distance between us.

Freeing a hand, she takes it from me.

And now it's me making sure not to touch her in this exchange. Even though I want to, something tells me that right now I shouldn't.

"Breakfast is served between seven and eight-thirty." It's on me to make breakfast tomorrow as it's Paula's day off. Paula is both our cleaner and our cook. She's worked here ever since I can remember.

"And we don't do evening meals, but there are plenty of restaurants nearby," I add, remembering the remainder of my spiel.

"Are there any other guests staying here?" Her voice sounds small.

I turn back to her. "No. Not until next week. Until then, it's just you and me."

The look on her face throws me for a loop. She looks terrified.

What the hell? Jeez, it's not like we're the Overlook Hotel.

"Don't worry. It's totally safe out here," I feel compelled to say. "We have a great alarm system, and I have a shotgun. You know, just in case." I wink as I laugh.

At the mention of a shotgun, her body stiffens and she looks like she's about to bolt.

Or puke.

Okay, I'm guessing *that* was the wrong thing to say.

"I'm totally kidding, I don't have a gun here."

That's a bit of a lie. We do have guns. My dad used to be a cop, so he still has shotguns, and rifles for hunting. I know how to shoot. I'm pretty good. Dad taught me when I was a kid, but I think it's best if she doesn't know that.

I lift my empty hands, palms facing, placating. "No guns. I promise. No need for them. Like I said, it's a safe place."

She pulls on her lip again. Then runs her fingers around her ear, tucking her short hair behind it. I see that her hand is trembling again.

"Are you okay?" I take a small step forward.

"Yes. I'm fine."

She doesn't sound it, but I don't press it. It's none of my business.

"Okay, well if you need anything, just press reception on the phone in your room, and it'll bring you straight through to me. Goodnight, Mia." I step back, ready to leave.

Her brows knit together. "How do you know my name?"

Damn, I should have called her Ms. Monroe, but something about her feels familiar like I should always be calling her Mia.

And now *I* sound like a stage five clinger.

73

Awesome.

"I got it from your details when you filled the form in." I smile.

"Oh, right. Yes." She laughs a little sound, and it hits me straight in the chest, leaving a tingling fullness there.

What the hell?

"What should I call you?" she asks.

There are a million different ways I could answer this, none of them clean.

I lean my shoulder against the wall and push my hand into my pocket. "Jordan."

She turns and mirrors me, wrapping her arms around herself.

"Is this your hotel, Jordan?" My name sounds amazing on her lips.

I let out a laugh. "No. My dad's. He's away taking care of my Grandpa at the moment, so I'm holding the fort."

"Oh, nothing serious I hope?"

"No, just a minor op, but he's off his feet for a few weeks, so Dad's gone to take care of him."

She nods her pretty head. "Well, thank you. Again." She smiles once more before disappearing into the room.

The door shuts. I hear the lock click.

I lean back against the wall.

So I have a *very hot, nervous one minute, friendly the next,* chick on my hands who I cannot have sex with under any circumstances.

Should be interesting.

Feeling unsatisfied … but satisfied that my only paying guest is settled for the night, I push off the wall and head downstairs to feed my other guest.

He's actually more of a resident than a guest. Guests usually leave, but he's been a permanent fixture here for over a year now.

He makes for a great alarm system, but he's slobbery and hairy, and the only one I've ever let sleep in my bed. He's a mouth we could do without feeding, but when he turned up at our door a starving puppy just over a year ago, I couldn't turn him away. So we kept him, and now we have a dog. A huge fucking dog.

I go to the kitchen and get his clean bowl off the drainer. I grab a can of his favorite food from the pantry and empty it into the bowl. *Jesus, this stuff stinks.* I mix in his biscuits just as he likes and call for him.

"Dozer, dinner's up."

I hear his huge paws pound against the floor as he makes his way from our private living room down the hall.

He comes barreling through the open kitchen door and straight into my legs, nearly knocking me off my feet. "Jesus Christ, Dozer!" I growl, steadying myself on the counter.

With a grunt he sits by the backdoor with a dopey look on his face.

"Bulldozer." I laugh, shaking my head.

I pick up his bowl and cross the kitchen. On the way, I grab a beer from the refrigerator.

I turn on the outside light and open the back door, letting Dozer out. I set his bowl on the step, and his nose goes straight in it.

I sit on the step beside him and take a swig of my beer.

"We've got a guest, Dozer, and she's hot, *really* hot, but flighty, so no sniffing round her as we don't want to scare her away. And your ugly mug would definitely scare her."

Dozer lifts his head, gives me a dirty look, and grunts.

"What?" I chuckle.

Then he farts.

"Fuckin' hell, Dozer!" I bury my nose in my arm. "You stinky bastard! I bet you did that on purpose! There's no way you're sleeping in my bed tonight after that!"

I'm trying not to laugh because laughing means inhaling, and that dog's farts are killer. Seriously.

Dozer shoves me hard with his head, knocking me to my side. He starts climbing on me, nudging my head with his wet snout.

"Get off me, you crazy fuckin' dog!" I'm breathless,

laughing, which means inhaling, and now I'm gagging. "Jesus, Dozer, you stink! Okay! Okay! I take it back, you can sleep in my bed! Now get the hell off me!" I shove at him.

Satisfied he's won, he climbs off me and goes back to his food.

Sitting, I pick up my beer. "Crazy ass dog," I mutter, chuckling.

I take another swig of beer, and lean back on my hand. I stretch my legs out and look up at the night sky.

Tonight is going to be a long night, knowing I've got Sex Goddess upstairs, in one of my beds, and there's not a damn thing I can do about it. And the only person I'll be sharing a bed with tonight is Dozer and his farts – awesome.

I bet Mia sleeps in those sexy negligées. The see through kind. Without any underwear.

Goddamn it to hell! It's going to be a long two fucking weeks.

I'm going to have to find someone else to keep me busy for the time Mia's here to ensure I keep my hands off her. Someone uncomplicated and easy. Won't be hard to find. There are always plenty of girls here vacationing with their families, bored and in need of entertainment.

The kind of entertainment I'm perfect at providing.

I'll go up to Mountain Resort tomorrow and find myself a new fuck buddy.

With that thought in mind, I go inside to take a cold shower to get me through the rest of the night.

Chapter Six

Mia

Noise. Someone is yelling.

"Shhh," I grumble, burying my head into the pillow.

Still yelling.

"What in the world…?" I roll over, blinking open my eyes to the dim light coming in through the drapes.

Who is yelling? It's coming from outside.

My heart pauses.

Forbes. Has he found me?

My pulse starts to thrum, setting my body on high alert.

Sitting bolt upright in bed, I listen.

It's definitely a guy's voice … but no, it's not Forbes. I'd know his voice anywhere.

I breathe a sigh of relief, laying back down.

I'm figuring it must be Jordan. I wonder what he's yelling about.

Glancing over at the clock, I see it's 10am.

I reach for the glass of water on the bedside cabinet and take a sip. My throat is sore. I went hard on myself last night.

I look down at my right hand – the hand which helps me purge all of my grief and self-loathing. It's sore and itchy. I rub my finger over the calluses on my knuckles, trying to relieve the itch. They're caused by the catching of my teeth on my skin; years and years of making myself throw up have caused this scarring.

I'm thinking about getting some cream from my bag to ease the itch when I hear Jordan call out again.

Curiosity gets the better of me, so I climb out of bed and pad my way over to the sliding doors, grabbing my sunglasses on the way and slipping them on.

I pull the drapes back, unlock the door, and step out onto the porch.

The first thing I see is the lake. Guess this why it's called the Lakeview room. The view is gorgeous.

Jordan yells again, so unexpected and so loud that I nearly jump out of my skin.

He's a lot closer than I realized.

With a racing heart, I approach the railing and lean over to see what he's yelling about.

My eyes find Jordan about twenty feet from the where I stand. His back is to me. He's wearing black work boots, dark blue jeans, and a short-sleeved black t-shirt that shows the defined contours of his shoulders and arms perfectly.

He lifts a hand to his hair. The muscles in his arm flex under his tattoos as he runs his fingers through the dark strands. *His hair looks so soft...*

An image of me running my fingers through his hair flashes through my mind. I blink myself free.

He turns a little my way, lifting his hands to his mouth, he cups them and yells, what I think is, "Dozer!"

"Everything okay?" I call out.

"Jesus fuckin' Christ!" He spins on the spot hands clenched by his sides. "You scared the shit out of me!"

"Sorry." I step back from the railing, but keep hold of it. My eyes are trained on his closed fists. "I just, uh, heard you yelling. I wanted to make sure everything was okay." My mouth is nervous dry, so I moisten my lips with my tongue.

His eyes flicker down to his hands, then back up to me.

I see his hands relax, and he flexes his fingers out. "Sorry, yeah, I uh..." He looks over his shoulder, then back to me. "I can't find my dog."

He's got a dog? I love dogs. Never had one, always wanted one.

"I let him out earlier, and he's gone. He's never disappeared like this before. He never strays far from the hotel."

He sounds really worried.

"You need help looking for him?" The words are out of my mouth before I have a chance to consider them.

Jordan shoves his hands in his back pockets and looks down at his boots. He seems to be contemplating my offer. So am I.

What the hell possessed me to say that?

Jesus, am I that damaged that the thought of spending a little time with this seemingly okay guy to help him find his dog is so bad to comprehend?

Yes. Yes, I absolutely am.

Freeing a hand, Jordan holds his hair back from his face, tilts his head back, and stares up at me. "Sure." He nods. "If you don't mind."

It's not like I can retract my offer now.

"Of course I don't mind." I smile, ignoring the twinge of nerves in my stomach. "Just give me a minute to change and I'll be right down."

I retreat back into my room, shutting the sliding door behind me.

Standing still for a moment, I close my eyes and take in a deep, calming breath.

I can do this.

Then I open my eyes and quickly change into jeans and a t-shirt. I give my teeth a brush, slip my feet into my sneakers, run my fingers through my hair to tidy it—the beauty of short hair—and slip my sunglasses back on.

I quickly make my way through reception and out the main entrance. I walk around the hotel and find Jordan a little farther on.

I jog over to him. "Still no luck?"

"No." He pushes his hair back, revealing his eyes.

Maple syrup. Stunning.

"He never disappears like this," he reiterates.

"Don't worry, we'll find him. What's his name?"

"Dozer."

Interesting name.

"Where do you want me to look?"

He points to the woods before us. "I've looked everywhere else. He wouldn't normally go in there alone – he's not real big on the woods, but maybe he was chasing a rabbit or something…" he trails off.

He wants me to go in there? With him.

Anxiety clamps down on my chest like a vice.

There's something about the solitude of the woods and Jordan combined that isn't sitting well with me.

Stop being a coward.

"Okay." I swallow. "The woods it is."

We walk quietly side by side heading for the trees.

"What kind of dog is he?" I ask, trying to occupy my overactive brain.

"A Mastiff—*Dozer!*" he calls out just as we break through the trees.

Copying him, I cup my hands around my mouth and call out, "Dozer!"

My voice echoes through the trees, chasing Jordan's echo.

We both listen for a return of sound in the form of a bark, but nothing comes.

We walk on a little farther as Jordan and I continue to take turns calling for Dozer.

After a few minutes of walking and still no sign of the dog, I pick up on the sound of passing traffic.

"Are we close to a road?" I ask.

The look on his face – realization, then complete panic. It makes me panic.

Jordan breaks off in a sprint. I run after him, trying to keep up, but his legs are longer than mine and he's a hell of a lot faster.

I finally catch up to him close to a clearing. He's looking around, frantically calling for Dozer.

I'm seriously out of breath and have a stitch. I'm not the fittest of people.

Bending over, I brace my hands on my thighs as I try to catch my breath.

The sound of traffic is a lot louder up here, meaning we're really close to the road.

Holding my quickened breaths, I stand up straight, and try to focus my hearing on any sound that could be related to a dog.

Nothing.

"How about you go that way," I suggest, pointing to Jordan's right. "And I'll go this way." I tilt my head to the left.

"Okay." He takes a step back. "Just yell out if you find him. I'll hear you."

"I will … and I'm sure he's fine, Jordan."

He nods again, then turns, quickly walking away.

I turn, and start walking. "Dozer!" I call out.

Another car whizzes past.

I walk on a little farther in the silence, looking around for any signs. Then I call out his name again.

That's when I hear a whimper. It's quiet, but I definitely hear something.

My heart starts to beat faster. "Dozer!" I call out again.

A whine.

Following the sound, I move closer to the clearing … and that's when I see him – a huge, fawn Mastiff laid over by a tree.

I run to him, yelling at the top of my lungs for Jordan, hoping to god he hears me.

I drop to my knees beside Dozer. He's panting, chest heaving up and down, his body trembling.

"Oh my god, your poor boy. You're gonna be okay, Dozer." I hover my hands over him, unsure whether to touch him or not. I'm guessing he was hit by a car and crawled his way back here.

"I'm Mia. I've been helping Jordan look for you. He's been really worried."

Dozer lifts his head a little. Big brown eyes stare blankly up at me.

I should check him for injuries.

"Okay, Dozer, I'm not a vet, but I'm well on my way to

becoming a doctor, and my father was a doctor, so I know what I'm doing. I'm gonna check you over, see what's going on with you. That okay? Not that you can answer me…"

Great, now I'm rambling to a dog.

Dozer lays his head back down and closes his eyes, so I take that as a yes.

I push my sunglasses up onto my head so I can see clear to begin assessing his injuries. I don't know anything about dogs, but I'm guessing they don't work much differently than people.

With care, I lay my hand on Dozer's trembling body, and that's when Jordan lands on his knees beside me.

"Shit, Dozer! You okay, buddy?"

Dozer grumbles a sound.

"I think a car hit him," I say.

He stares at me for a long moment. Incredulity, anger and a few other emotions I can't quite grasp pass over his face.

"Motherfucker!" He shakes his head, roughly. "When I find out who did this … fuck!"

I try not to flinch at his anger.

It's not directed at you. He's right to be angry. Someone just hurt his dog.

"We need to get him to a vet," Jordan says with urgency.

But all I can focus on is the anger in his voice, and the physical tension that's vibrating off him. It's taking everything in me not to run.

I need a way to hold my calm.

So I switch into my trained mode, turn every emotion off. It's the only way I can deal.

"Just let me check him over first. See if it's safe to move him." My voice sounds robotic. I hate when I sound this way.

Ignoring Jordan's questioning stare, I run my hands over Dozer, checking for contusions, possible fractures, and internal bleeding.

Dozer yelps when my hand touches his front right leg.

I lean closer, getting a good look at the leg. There's a disjoint in the bone. Definite fracture. Possibly more than one. No blood or signs of protrusion, which is good. It means the bone hasn't broken the skin.

I haven't come across any indication of internal bleeding, so I'd say this broken leg is the worst of it.

"His leg is broken," I say, resting back on my haunches. "There's some swelling around the ribcage, no cracks from what I can tell. I think he's just going to have one hell of a bruise there. I think the car must have clipped him." I glance at Jordan. His eyes are wide on my face, scrutinizing me.

Ignoring his gaze, I look back to Dozer. "We can move him, but getting him back to the hotel and to your car isn't an option. He's too big to carry that far."

"I can do it," Jordan asserts.

"Maybe so, but it'll be really painful for him if you do. Can you go get your car and drive it to the road just up ahead? You can move him from here to there with much less pain to him."

Jordan looks between the dog and me, his brow furrowed. "You'll stay here with him?"

"Of course."

"I'll be back in five." Jordan jumps to his feet in one swift move, and takes off running back the way we came.

"Not long now, boy." I stroke Dozer's ear. "Jordan will get his car, and we'll get you to a vet. You'll be feeling better in no time."

Leaning forward, I take another look at Dozer's leg. I really should strap it up; it'll make it less painful for when we move him.

I glance around, looking for a suitable splint. I spot a stick at just the right length, so I crawl over and grab it.

Using my teeth, I bite and gnaw at the hem of my t-shirt. I manage to get a small tear—thank you cheap material—then using teeth and hands, I pull against the fabric, tearing upward. I stop a good few inches below my breasts. I secure the fabric to my chest by placing my arm under my breasts. Holding the t-shirt in place, I start to tear across.

When I'm done, I have enough t-shirt to cover my breasts,

and enough material to strap up Dozer's leg.

"Okay, Dozer. I'm going to strap your leg up with this stick, and what was my t-shirt."

Brown eyes stare up at me unhappily.

"I won't lie to you – it's gonna hurt, but I'll be real quick, I promise."

Dozer closes his eyes and huffs out a sigh.

I don't think he'll bite me as he's in too much pain, but I'm edging on the side of caution here because he's a huge frigging dog. He could take my hand off.

Carefully, I take hold of his broken leg. He growls, baring his teeth. I pause, his leg in my hand.

"I'm helping, Dozer. Remember that before you decide to sink your teeth into me, okay?"

He makes no other sound. Just huffs out a breath and his lips slacken, covering his teeth.

I take a deep breath, and try again. "I'm gonna have to straighten your leg a little … you ready? Done." He growls again, and I realize it's not at me but at the pain.

"Well done." I exhale. My heart is pounding solid against my ribs.

I pick up the splint and place it against the back of his leg. I grab the material, and start to wrap it around the make-shift splint, tight enough to hold his leg.

When I'm done, I rip the end of it the fabric with my teeth again, giving me a tie. I wrap one side around, then fasten it with the other into a knot.

Setting his leg down, I puff out a breath. "Well done, Dozer." I pat him.

A minute later, I hear the roar of an engine. Assuming it's Jordan, I get to my feet, brushing dirt and twigs from my knees.

"I'll just be a second," I say.

I step through the clearing and into view of the road. The red Mustang from the hotel is coming toward me.

Jordan pulls to a quick stop beside me. He jumps out of the car. "How's he doing?"

"In pain, but he's doing good." I follow behind.

Jordan crouches down beside Dozer. "Hey boy. Gonna get you to the vet now."

He carefully slides his hands under Dozer, then in one swift move, and with minimum effort, Jordan lifts Dozer and stands with him in his arms.

Wow.

That is one huge dog. He must weigh one sixty at least.

Jordan is a lot stronger than he looks. Not that he looks wimpy because he doesn't. Nope. Not at all. Quite the opposite, in fact. He's definitely all man. He's just not muscular in a bodybuilder sense. More in an athletic, defined, toned kind of way. Well, from what I can tell through his clothes, anyway.

Jordan looks exactly how a guy should look … says me and my vastly inexperienced knowledge of men.

The only male body I have ever known is Forbes, and he's built like a linebacker. Complete opposite to Jordan.

But I prefer Jordan's physic. It's just … perfect.

As I stare at him, my mind wanders to fantasy…

Jordan lifting *me* into his arms. Me wrapping my legs around his waist. Him pressing me up against a tree, crushing his lips to mine. His hand moving lower, between my legs, touching me in just the right place…

"You coming?"

Coming?

"What?"

I look up at his face. He's staring down at me. Brow furrowed. Dozer still in his arms.

Dog. Hit. By. Car.

Going to the vets.

"Oh, uh, yes. Yes, I'm coming. With you."

Oh god.

Way to go, Mia. Get turned on from watching the hot guy carrying his injured dog.

This is not me at all. But around Jordan, my state of normal no longer seems to exist.

Maybe that's not such a bad thing.

With embarrassment flooding my cheeks, I jog on ahead to the car.

Reaching it first, I open the passenger door, and pull the seat forward, giving Jordan access to the backseat. It's a two door car, so Jordan could have a task getting Dozer in, but he manages it with minimal fuss.

"I'll sit in the back with him," I say, hand on the car roof, foot in the door, ready to climb in.

I see Jordan's eyes making quick work of my torn t-shirt. They settle on my face. He frowns.

My black eye. Shit.

I slide my sunglasses down covering my shame.

"You fixed his leg up." His eyes are still on my face.

"I did."

"Thank you."

Ducking my head, I climb in the backseat and sit in the small space that Dozer isn't occupying.

Jordan shifts the seat back to its place, then closes the door behind me and makes his way to the driver's side.

I put my seat belt on, then carefully lift Dozer's head and rest it on my thigh.

"You're gonna be just fine, Dozer."

I press my hand against his chest and begin timing his heartbeats. I want to make sure he's doing okay, but I also to keep myself busy. I need something to focus on right now.

Jordan spins the car around. I feel the quick acceleration pushing me back into the seat as he speeds us off in the direction of the vets.

Chapter Seven

Jordan

Who the fuck is this girl?

Checking Dozer over … sounding like she knows what she's talking about … fixing up his leg…

And that black eye.

I've never felt as angry as I did when I saw that. And trust me, some fucker just ran my dog over, so take it that I'm pretty fucking angry about her black eye.

That's the reason she's been wearing those sunglasses since she arrived. And the way she covered it up when she finally realized I'd noticed it … that bruise was no accident. Someone did that to her.

It's probably why she was so nervous around me last night. She's so tiny and sweet and kind. How anyone could ever hurt her is beyond me.

The way she took care of Dozer … the way she's still taking care of him … Jesus, my poor fucking dog.

When I find the bastard who did that to him, he's going to be eating through tubes—just like the guy who gave Mia that black eye.

Dozer might eat way too much, and take up all the space in my bed, but he's family. I don't have much of that left nowadays. I can't lose him too.

"How's he doing?" I ask over my shoulder.

"His breathing is a little labored."

I cast a quick glance back. "What does that mean?"

"It means drive faster."

I slam the pedal to the metal.

A few minutes later, I'm skidding to a stop outside the vets.

Jumping out of the car, I yank the seat forward and lean into the back. Mia shuffles forward and moves Dozer with her, bringing him closer to me.

I lift him into my arms.

Fucking hell. My body groans under his weight. He seems to weigh twice what he did when I picked him up back in the woods.

I shift Dozer against my chest, evening out his weight, and move as quickly as I can toward the vets. Mia is right behind me.

She overtakes and pulls open the door. I dash through.

Spotting the receptionist, I head her way. "My dog's been hit by a car – he needs help."

The receptionist rounds her desk. "Follow me."

I follow quickly behind her, down a hall and into a room. A middle aged guy in a white coat is sitting at a desk working on a computer.

"Dr. Callie, we have a dog who has been hit by a car."

The vet glances up at us, then gets straight to his feet. "Place him on here." He points to an examination table.

Dozer flinches when I set him on the table. "Sorry, buddy," I whisper.

"What is his name?" Dr. Callie asks, plugging a stethoscope into his ears. He presses it to Dozer's chest.

"Dozer." My voice sounds rough, so I clear my throat.

"I kept a check on his heart rate on the way here."

I turn at the sound of Mia's voice. I didn't even realize she was still behind me.

She keeps her focus on Dr. Callie as she speaks, "It stayed steady at sixty bpm. About five minutes ago, his breathing became a little labored. He has a chest contusion, not severe from what I could tell upon examination. And his front right leg is broken – possibly a mild fracture. I strapped it up the best I could with what I had."

And I'll say it again – who the fuck is this girl?

She sounds confident, a little mechanical—just like she did

88

back at the woods when she was checking Dozer over. Nothing like the quiet, sweet, nervous girl who came into the hotel last night.

Dr. Callie looks up, removing the stethoscope from Dozer's chest. He takes it from his ears and hangs it around his neck. "Vet or doctor?" he asks Mia.

I wait, suddenly *very* interested to hear her answer.

"Med student," she answers quietly. "Second year."

And just when I thought she couldn't possibly get any hotter...

Dr. Mia Monroe.

Yep, she just went up a million notches on the hottie counter.

I've got doctor (Mia), patient (me), sex scenarios running through my mind on warp speed right now. All of them awesome.

Dr. Callie turns from us and walks over to a metal trolley. He picks up a syringe.

I shudder. I fucking hate needles.

My mom was constantly being stuck with needles while she was going through treatment.

The treatment that didn't save her.

Dr. Callie walks back toward Dozer, syringe in hand. "Great job on the leg." He directs his words to Mia, then looks at us both. "I'm going to need you both to wait outside now."

"Are you going to stick that in Dozer?" I nod at the needle in his hand.

"Don't worry, it's just to sedate Dozer. It won't hurt him."

Liar. Needles fucking hurt.

I take a step closer. "Look, I just need to know ... is he going to be okay?" My voice suddenly sounds small. I'm reminded of how I sounded in the hospital when we found out the treatment hadn't worked. That mom was going to die.

A lump forms in my throat. And my eyes start to water. A dog. I'm getting emotional over a fucking dog.

I clear my throat.

"He's going to be fine." Dr. Callie smiles kindly.

The receptionist holds the door open for us. For the first time,

I notice the name badge on her uniform – Penny.

"If you want to wait up front in the reception area, I'll come and let you know how Dozer is doing as soon as I can," Penny says.

I follow Mia to the door. Stopping, I turn back to Dr. Callie. "Take good care of him."

He nods.

Penny closes the door behind us, staying in the room.

I stare at the door. My eyes start to water again.

Stop acting like a pussy, Matthews.

"Shall we sit?" Mia says from behind me.

Pulling in a deep breath, I blink my eyes clear and turn around.

The first thing my lowered eyes make contact with is Mia's bare stomach.

Flat, soft creamy skin that is just begging to be licked. I lift my eyes, and of course, I have to check her tits out.

If she just raised her hands above her head, I'd totally get a view...

Jesus Christ. What the fuck is wrong with me?

She ripped her t-shirt to help Dozer, who is currently being treated by a vet because he was hit by a car, and here I am checking her out like a sex-crazed idiot.

"I owe you a t-shirt." I point to the bare skin I was just staring at.

She glances down. Her cheeks flush red, and she wraps her hands around her mid-section, covering herself. "Don't worry about it. It was just a cheap Walmart shirt."

She drives a Mercedes and wears Walmart? This girl makes no sense at all.

"You sure?"

"I'm sure."

With a brisk nod, I turn and walk past her toward the reception area.

I know she's behind me, so when I reach the seats I step aside and allow her to sit first before taking the seat beside her.

See, I'm not a total douche. I can be a gentleman.

I lean forward, resting my arms on my thighs. They're still aching from carrying Dozer. This move puts me real close to Mia. She smells just like she did last night—vanilla.

No one should smell this good. It makes functioning difficult. Or not *functioning*, if you catch my drift.

I can't remember ever being this hot for a girl before. Just my fucking luck that I can't touch her.

"Thank you … for what you did for Dozer," I say. I don't look at her. If I want to keep my thoughts clean, then it's a good idea to avoid as much visual contact as possible.

"No problem."

Her voice is so soft, just as I imagine her skin feels. Soft and warm, and I bet she's really tight…

"I like dogs," she adds. "All animals, in fact. They're a whole lot nicer than people."

There's a sudden sadness to her voice, and I can't help *but* look at her.

Her lips are downturn, and I notice she's still wearing those god-awful sunglasses.

"You can take the sunglasses off, you know. There's only us here, and I've already seen what you're hiding behind them."

Her whole body stiffens.

There's a long pause where she does absolutely nothing. I'm not actually sure that she's still breathing. I wonder if I've said the wrong thing. Gone about this the wrong way?

I don't want to upset her.

Why? I'm not actually sure. It's not like I'm usually concerned with a woman's emotional goings on. But with her, something is just … different.

She lifts her hand to her face and slowly slides the sunglasses off.

I watch her slender fingers tremble as she turns the arms of the sunglasses in and sets them on her lap, hands covering them.

Then I notice that she has these sore looking calluses on the knuckle of her right hand. I notice them because they look out of

91

place with the rest of her soft, flawless skin.

Maybe she has eczema or something.

I lift my eyes to her face.

Her eyes are closed. The bruise so very evident.

Anger pulses inside me again, so fucking fierce that I could punch a hole in the wall and still not feel clear.

I clench my hands in my lap. "The asshole that did that to you…?"

She bites her lip and looks away.

The caveman inside me is beating his chest right now, ready to beat the shit out of the asshole that did this to her. No woman should ever go through that. Especially not her. *Definitely* not her.

"I can hurt him, Mia. Just say the word and it's done."

I hear her sharp intake of breath. Wide, blue eyes meet mine.

Jesus, she's breathtaking. Even with the black eye.

Her eyes are as stunning as I knew they would be. They're the color of the water of a caldera.

After high school, I went traveling with some buddies—it was before my mom got sick, and I had to come back home. We were in Lombok, an island in Indonesia, and we had trekked out to Mount Rinjani. There was a caldera there. The water stays hot permanently, due to the volcanic activity, and is so purely blue. All filtering shades rippling together to make the most amazing shade of blue you will ever see.

Mia's eyes are the exact shade of blue as that water.

Breaking our stare, she begins examining the sunglasses in hand with her eyes and fingers as if her life depends on it.

I don't think she's going to say anything, and I have no clue what else to say.

"No one did this to me. It was just an accident."

Her words are softly spoken, but I feel like they've just punched me in my chest.

I shake my head. "People don't hide accidents like you're hiding that black eye. And the very fact you said it was an accident just confirms to me that someone did this to you."

Her eyes snap up to mine. There's an unexpected fire in

them. I like it. Means there *is* some fight in her.

"So what if someone hurt me. What business is it of yours?"

Wow, that stung. Why did that sting?

I grit my teeth and lean back in my seat. "You're right. It's not my business."

Her anger instantly disappears. So quick, it surprises me.

"God, I'm so sorry. That sounded—I don't—" She shifts in her seat, her fingers pulling on that plump lower lip. "I don't mean to come off like a bitch. I really appreciate your offer, but hurting ... *him* ... it's not necessary."

I turn my head and stare her straight in the eyes. "It looks necessary from where I'm sitting."

Her hand drops back to her lap. "Violence never solves violence."

This asshole blacks her eye, yet she thinks that way. She's either a fucking angel, or really stupid. From what I've already seen of her, I'm going with angel. I hope she doesn't prove me wrong on this.

"Maybe not." I notice her eyes are on my mouth, so I swipe my lower lip with my tongue. "But trust me, it's the only language that scum, like the bastard who did that to you, understand. And it'd make me feel a whole lot better knowing that me teaching him some manners would mean he'd keep his fuckin' hands off you."

Seriously, once I was done with him, he wouldn't even breathe in her direction again. I want to hurt this asshole badly. About as badly as I want to be situated between her thighs.

Why? I barely know this girl. Is it because I want to fuck her more than I've ever wanted to fuck anyone before.

No, it's not that. So what the hell is it?

I glance at her, and see that her eyes have filled with tears.

Shit, don't cry. I don't do crying chicks.

"Look," I start to speak quickly to stave off her tears, "I'm just saying that if you want me to hurt him, I will. Call it my way of paying you back for taking care of Dozer. If you don't, you don't. No big deal."

Biting her lip, she nods. A tear falls from her long lashes, splashing onto her jeans.

My chest starts to feel tight. *What the fuck is that?*

I look away, giving her privacy as she swipes her fingers under her eyes to dry them.

And also so I can rub this fucking ache out of my chest.

"Mia, I just want you to know that not all men are assholes."

What. The. Fuck?

Not all men are assholes? Jesus Christ, Matthews. Yes, we are. There are just varying degrees of male assholeness.

I'm an asshole. One who would never raise his hand to a woman, and I fucking abhor men that do. But I have absolutely no problem in hooking up with a chick, then walking away from her the second my cock is out of her.

Case in point – whatsername from yesterday. See, I can't even remember her name. That's how big an asshole I am.

Weird thing is ... I don't want Mia to think I'm an asshole. I want her to like me.

It's the whole damsel in distress thing. Has to be. And the way she took care of Dozer before, so gentle with him. Frigging amazing.

It's doing fucked up things to me.

I risk a glance and her wide, glistening, bright blue eyes are blinking back at me. Long lashes bat against her cheekbones.

Jesus, she's beautiful.

She licks her lips and presses them together. My eyes fall to them.

I want to kiss them.

Her.

Everywhere.

Run my tongue over every inch of her silky soft skin.

I bet she tastes like vanilla. Tastes exactly like she smells.

I want to spread her legs and bury my head between her thighs. Lick her until she screams my name. Then push my cock deep inside and fuck her until we both lose our goddamn minds from the pleasure.

94

I might not have test driven her yet, but I just know that sex with Mia Monroe would be *that* good. I have a sense for these things.

Yes, I know it's totally inappropriate for me to want this at this exact moment, but people look for comfort in difficult situations, right?

And Dozer would understand. That dog is as horny as I am. He's just about dry humped every piece of furniture we own. I once caught him going at it with the wooden table in the garden. Poor bastard was so desperate to get off that he risked splinters. I really should get him laid.

Holy shit. Dozer's a virgin.

Now that's just not right.

I swear to God right here and now – get Dozer through this and I promise the first thing I'll do is hook him up with the hottest dog I can find. Not that I know anything about hot dogs … yeah, I caught that, I'm as funny as I am good-looking. But I think a fancy dog like a poodle or something would work for Dozer.

"So, Jordan…" I seriously dig the way she says my name. "Dozer is an unusual name for a dog. Where did that come from? He sleep a lot?" Her lips work on a smile, and my dick pulses in response.

She's after a subject change, and I can go with that. I let out a laugh and look away before I do something stupid like pull a Dozer and try to dry hump her leg.

"Yeah, he sleeps tons, but that's not where it came from. Dozer was a stray. Found him at our door one night when he was a puppy. He was starving, so we took him in and fed him. We put out fliers, but no one claimed him, so we kept him. In the first week he stayed with us, he broke a shit load of stuff—ornaments, plates, glasses, even a window."

I laugh again, remembering how pissed my dad was when Dozer jumped head first at the living room window trying to get at a bird on the porch. Shattered the window.

"Basically, Dozer broke everything he touched, and my dad said he was like a bulldozer taking down everything in his path, and it just kinda stuck. Ended up being shortened to Dozer, because he can be a little dozy at times." I smile, then I glance in the direction of the hall. "I've just always thought of him as invincible, you know."

"He's going to be fine, Jordan. It's just a broken leg—well, not *just* a broken leg, because broken legs are incredibly painful, I just meant—"

Her face has gone red. She's flustered. Cute.

"I know what you meant." I smile.

A small smile touches her lips. "Aside from his leg, I really don't think there is anything else to worry about." She touches my arm with her fingers. It's a gentle touch, almost imperceptible. But even still, my blood turns to molten fucking lava at the contact.

She withdraws her hand. A look of surprise on her face.

You're surprised, sweetheart? Well, you're not the only one.

With the hot lava flooding straight to the main man, I talk to distract myself from my impending boner. "So you're a doctor," I say, just remembering that. How the fuck did I forget that?

Hell, she's a living, breathing wet dream.

"Training to be," she says quietly.

"Where?"

She slides me a glance. "Harvard."

Harvard. She's beautiful *and* incredibly smart.

There's isn't anything that's less than perfect about her. Except for the douchehole of an ex.

"Ivy League – nice." I nod, impressed.

She shrugs her shoulders in response and looks to the floor, kicking her sneakers together.

So, she's from Boston. Interesting. I don't remember seeing that on the form she filled out last night, but then I was too busy eye-fucking her to notice where she was from.

What's she doing way out here then? I'd say vacation, but women rarely vacation alone, and they *always* take pre-planned trips. Turning up at Golden Oaks like she did … this was an unplanned trip. And I'm guessing it had something to do with the asshole who marred that perfect face.

"So, are you originally from Boston?"

I see her hesitation. Her whole body has stiffened again.

"Yes," she says on a breath. "Lived there my whole life."

"What you doing way out here in Colorado?"

She shifts in her seat, tilting her body away from me. "I'm trying to, um…" She clears her throat. "I'm here to find my mother."

Didn't expect that.

"You adopted?"

Did I mention I have no filter?

She shakes her head. "No, my father—I lived with my father. My mother left when I was a baby."

"Shit," I say. "So your dad … he's okay about you been out here alone searching for your mom?" *And why hasn't he kicked the cocksucker's ass who hurt her?*

"My father is dead."

Shit. Guess that answers my questions. But what surprises me is the lack of emotion in her voice about her dad being dead.

Losing my mom was horrendous—beyond horrendous. I adored my mom. If I lost my dad … well, my world would implode.

"Sorry to hear that." It's a crap thing to say, but really what else *is* there to say.

"Thank you." Emotionless again. Weird.

I twist in my seat to her. "So your mom lives here?"

She brushes her golden hair from her eyes. "Apparently so. I have an address, but it was from over twenty years ago. Whether she still lives there or not, I'm not sure."

I nod in agreement. "What's your mom's name? I've lived here my whole life. If she's still here, I might know her. If not, my dad will. He used to be a cop. He knows everyone."

She sucks her top lip into her mouth. An image of me doing exactly the same plays a scene in my head.

"Anna Monroe. Well, that was her married name. I don't know her maiden name."

I rake through my brain for an Anna. The only person I can think of is Annie Parker, and she's only a few years older than me. Has a mouth like a vacuum cleaner. Good memories.

"Sorry." I shake my head.

"It's okay." Her smile is sad.

"Hey, how about I look up the address on my phone? See if she still lives there?"

"Would you? I never thought to do that. Thank you." She reaches into her bag and pulls out a ratty piece of paper, then hands it to me.

I get my cell from my pocket and type the address and the name *Anna Monroe* into the search engine.

What comes up makes my heart drop for Mia. I almost don't want to tell her.

"Anything?" God, she sounds so hopeful.

I glance up at her. "The address you have for your mom is now home to a grocery store."

"Oh."

Jesus, I can literally feel her disappointment like it's my own.

My chest feels tight again. Seriously, what the fuck is that? I rub at my sternum with my fingers.

"The houses must have been leveled for the store to be built," I say. "I'm sorry."

"Don't be. It's not your fault." She takes the piece of paper from me and holds it in her hand.

She smiles, but it's forced.

She looks so lost. So sad. It's painful to see.

"I can help you find your mom, if you want?"

What the fuck! Have I lost my mind?

I don't spend time with girls outside the bedroom. Apart from Beth, and that's only because she plays for the same team as I do.

If I spend time with Mia, I know what will happen. And I can't get balls deep with her.

Yes, I might have spent the last five minutes imagining her flat on her back, and me pounding into her like a jackhammer, but I'm not a complete bastard.

I may not know the full story, but it's clear this girl has been through the wringer with the asshole who gave her the black eye, and now she's searching for her mother. The mother who abandoned her when she was a baby.

Mia might be the hottest girl I have ever seen ... okay, *she is* the hottest girl I have ever seen in life, and the sweetest. And I'm so horny for her that my dick actually hurts. It motherfucking hurts.

But the girl's got enough to deal with.

And me spending an invariable amount of time around a hot girl that I cannot put my dick inside ... it's just not possible.

I might as well be in prison.

Or hell.

That's it, I'm in hell.

This is payback for the chick I banged who was married.

Okay, I lied before. I totally knew she was married when I tapped that.

"Would you?" She sounds hopeful. "I mean, I wouldn't know where to start, and you know the people in this town, so you'd know who to speak to."

"Sure I will." *That's it. Keep talking dickhead. Keep digging that hole deeper.* "Like I said, I owe you for what you did for Dozer."

"You don't owe me anything, Jordan. I wanted to help you."

She said my name again. I'm toast.

"And I want to help you."

And I want to help you. Jesus, I'm such a lame ass pussy.

It's official. I've lost my fucking mind.

Then she smiles. It's wide and bright and dazzling, and like a sucker punch to the chest. And ball sack.

My life has just got seriously hard.

Kind of like the permanent state of my cock while around Mia Monroe.

Chapter Eight

Mia

I can't believe what has just happened.

I just admitted to Jordan—a guy who I barely know—that Forbes hit me. And I also told him about my mother. The mother who abandoned me. The mother who I drove across seven states to try and find and she doesn't even live at the address I have anymore.

I'm so stupid.

Why didn't I check this before I drove across the country in a lame attempt to find her?

But what was I going to do? Go back to my apartment and make threesome with Forbes?

I don't think so.

Jordan must think I'm a real mess. And an idiot.

He'd be right on both counts.

I think it's best if I just get out of here. I'll go back to the hotel, grab my things and go … where?

I'll just find another hotel, and then I can figure out my next move.

I just hope he doesn't tell anyone what he already knows about Forbes hitting me. Why would he? He doesn't exactly seem like the gossipy type. But then he did say his dad used to be a cop. What if…?

No, I would have to report it myself, and I don't really think the local police force are going to be concerned with a stranger in town who happens to have a black eye.

But I do need to leave. Right now.

I'm just about to get to my feet, make my excuses and run the hell out of here, when he says, "I can help you find your mom, if you want?"

What? He wants to help me find my mother?

A few minutes ago, he offered to kick the crap out of Forbes, which practically floored me, and made me teary. No one has ever offered help like that to me before. And for help to come from a man makes it even more astounding, and poignant.

And now this…

Help me find my mother…

It's beyond kind.

He would be giving up his time to help me. Why would he do that?

Maybe because he really is a good guy, Mia.

I can feel myself starting to choke up with his kindness, so I hold my voice as steady as I can. "Would you?" I can't help the hope in my voice. "I mean, I wouldn't know where to start, and you know the people in this town, so you'd know who to speak to."

And now I'm babbling. Great.

"Sure I will," he says. "Like I said, I owe you for what you did for Dozer."

He's helping me because I helped him. Even then, is that such a bad thing? It doesn't make him a bad guy.

"You don't owe me anything, Jordan. I wanted to help you."

"And I want to help you," he says. His voice sounds so warm and wonderful that I can't help the goofy smile that spreads across my face.

"Then thank you. I would love to take you up on your offer to help me."

"Good." He smiles.

He's so lovely.

And so good-looking.

I suddenly have the urge to reach out and touch his face.

I clamp my fingers together, pinning my hands to my lap.

We're silent for a moment before Jordan speaks.

101

"I wonder how much longer they're going to be with Dozer?"

I glance at the clock like that's going to help. "I'm sure they won't be much longer. They're probably x-raying his leg for the break, and I imagine his chest as well to make sure none of his ribs are broken."

He's smiling at me.

"What?" I say, a little self-conscious.

"Nothing." He shakes his head. "You just sound really different when you're talking doctor stuff. You sound like…"

"A doctor?" I grin.

"Yeah." He laughs. "A doctor."

"Well, I'm not quite there yet … if ever," I add quietly.

"And why's that?"

I glance across at him, unsure what to say, or why I even said what I just did. Then Jordan's eyes lift, looking over my head. They quickly flick back down to mine, then lower to my sunglasses. I hear footsteps heading our way, so I lift the glasses and slide them on as I mouth a silent thank you to Jordan.

He nods lightly, then gets to his feet, as do I.

"How he is?" Jordan asks Dr. Callie.

"He's doing really well. He's still asleep under anesthetic, but he'll come round soon. His leg is broken, like you diagnosed." He directs his gaze at me, then back to Jordan. "The problem was the bone was fractured in two places, so I had to set it with pins to get the break to heal straight."

"But he's okay?" Jordan asks, concern lacing his voice. It tugs at my heart.

Dr. Callie smiles. "He's fine. I've set the leg in a cast. He'll need to rest it up and come back in about six weeks to have the pins removed. But he's going to be back to himself in no time."

"When can I take him home?"

"He's in recovery at the moment. I want to keep him here for the rest of the day just to keep an eye on him. You can come back later today to collect him."

"What time?"

Dr. Callie looks at his watch. "Say, four thirty, and he should

102

be fine to go."

Penny comes over to us. "If you could come with me, I just need to take a few details from you," she addresses Jordan.

"Sure," he says.

I'm just about to follow Jordan to the reception desk, when Dr. Callie stops me. "Great assessment you did earlier. The strap on his leg was really good work. You're going to make a fine doctor." His smile is genuine. Shame I don't feel it.

I don't want to become a good doctor. I don't want to be what Oliver created.

I dip my gaze. "Thank you."

"Well ... best of luck with the rest of medical school."

"Thanks." I nod.

"Right. I better get back to it."

I watch his retreating back, then I turn to Jordan and walk over. He's just finishing up.

"Ready?" he asks.

"Yes."

I follow him out to his car. "You hungry?" he asks once we're in the car.

I touch my hand to my empty stomach. "A little."

"To be expected. You did miss breakfast."

"Sorry about that. I don't usually sleep so late, but I was really tired. I hope you didn't go to any trouble."

"Nah." He shakes his head. "Let's go grab some lunch."

He pulls away from the vets, onto the street, then starts fiddling with the radio.

I slip my sunglass off and glance around the car, taking it in. I've never been inside a Mustang before today. It's a really nice car. Pretty cool. I know I said yesterday that it's a penis enhancer, but knowing Jordan now, I really don't think he would need any help in the enhancing department. Not that I've seen anything to know, but he's just so confident and this car suits that about him. It reflects his confidence and charm.

"This is a really nice car," I comment.

Settling on a station, he rests his hand back on the wheel.

"Thanks. I won it."

"Won it? Like on a car lottery or something?" I tease.

Jordan lets out a laugh. "No, cards. I won it in a hand of poker."

"Wow. That must've been some hand," I say impressed.

Taking his right hand off the wheel, he flexes his fingers out between us. A grin akin to the devil appears on his lips. "Oh, you have no idea, babe."

Babe? Holy shit. Is he…?

Did he just flirt with me?

No. No way.

Even still, my cheeks heat.

Pretending his words have absolutely no effect on me, I clear my throat. "You like to play cards?"

"I used to." There's something off about his tone. It instantly makes me curious.

I'm not usually nosy. I don't ask people things because I don't want them to question me in return. But he knows about Forbes, and something about Jordan makes me want to know more about him. I feel like I could sit and listen to him talk for hours, and not once get bored.

"Used to?" I question.

I watch his fingers tap restlessly against the steering wheel. "I used to gamble a bit. I liked to play cards. After my mom died it, uh … it got a little worse."

"Your mom died." I press my hand to my chest. "God, I'm so sorry, Jordan."

He bobs his head. "We've both lost a parent. Guess we have that in common."

"Sucky thing to have in common," I say.

Well, it's not like I can tell him the day Oliver died was the best day of my life.

He would never understand.

"Yeah it is," he says quietly.

"How did she die? If you don't mind my asking?"

He shakes his head, eyes fixed ahead. "Lung cancer. Stage

four. Never smoked a day in her life. I was away, traveling with some buddies out in South East Asia, when I got the call from Dad that she was sick. I came straight home. She had surgery … chemo … it didn't work."

His shoulders lift on a heavy sigh. "After she died I, uh … well, life got a little hard. Crazy, you know?"

A glance. I catch the sad in his eyes before he looks back ahead to the road. "Then I had a wakeup call, and I cleaned up my act. And here you see, the brand new, almost responsible me." He sweeps a hand down himself, smiling, but I can tell it's forced.

And that's when I see the broken in him. Not broken the way I am, but there's definitely something. He looks as if he's carrying a heavy burden of guilt over his mom.

I twist in my seat so that I'm looking at him. "Well, I didn't know the before you Jordan, but this Jordan is incredibly kind."

He laughs, but it's more of a scoff. Self-deprecating.

"Yeah, kind. That's me."

"I think you are. And well, uh, that counts. To me." I pull on my lip, taking a deep breath.

He glances across at me again, and our eyes more than meet. They connect.

My skin flushes. My mouth dries. Heartbeat erratic.

I have the sudden and very pressing urge to lean over and kiss him.

Breaking his gaze, I turn face front and start picking at imaginary lint on my jeans. We don't speak again until we pull up outside the diner.

I put my sunglasses on and get out of the car.

"I ate here last night," I comment over my shoulder.

"I know."

I whip around, and my muscles lock with tension. "How do you know that?" I know my voice is sharp, but I can't help it.

He frowns a little. Resting his hand on the roof of the car, he says, "Beth, the waitress who served you last night, she's a good friend of mine. She called ahead to let me know you were coming."

"Oh, right." Way to overreact Mia.

Running my hand through my hair, I laugh, but it sounds off. "Makes sense why she recommended your hotel then, being your friend an' all. Of course she would. Not that it's a trashy hotel or anything because it's not. It's great. The best hotel I've ever stayed in."

Jesus Christ. Stop talking. Now.

I really need gagging while I'm around him.

Jordan chuckles. He makes his way around the car toward me, with what looks to be a plaid shirt in his hand.

"Thought you might want to wear this." He nods toward my bare stomach.

God, I can't believe I forgot that my t-shirt was all torn up. Not like me at all. I'm usually very aware of my state of dress. I had to be because of my father.

And Forbes.

I immediately cover my mid-riff with my arms. Then free one to take the shirt that he's now holding out to me.

"Thanks," I say, pulling the shirt on. It smells masculine. Woodsy. It smells of him. I don't think I'll ever want to take this shirt off again.

Stepping close, he pulls the shirt together and starts to do up the buttons. "I don't want people to think I've mauled you," he says low, with a smile.

I feel it in every single part of me.

I can't move. I'm just staring at him, watching his eyes trace each button up as he does them, while reminding myself to breath.

Deftly, he soon reaches the top. His eyes lift to mine.

I try not to notice that his breathing has ratcheted up a little, like my own has. Or that his hand is lingering on the shirt, close to my chest, even though the buttons are all done.

I gulp. "Thanks," I whisper, my voice breaking on the word.

With a nod, he steps back from me. "Come on, let's get you fed."

Pulse galloping, I follow Jordan into the diner. He doesn't

wait to be seated, just bypasses the empty hostess station, so I follow behind, still feeling a little off balance from the whole buttoning of the shirt.

He motions for me to sit first, so I slide into the booth. Jordan sits opposite me.

I see Beth walking toward us. She looks between me and Jordan. A frown mars her pretty face.

She doesn't look happy to see him here with me, and I start to wonder if they're more than just friends. I also don't like how the thought of them together is making me feel.

Jealous.

Uneasy.

Jealous.

"Hey you." She ruffles his hair.

"Watch the hair!" He bats her hand away, laughing.

She gives his shoulder a shove. "Don't worry, you still look pretty." Her eyes dart to me, then back to him.

"Beth, how many times do I have to tell you that men are not pretty. We're hot. Gorgeous. Fuckin' awesome. But *not* pretty."

Looking at me, she rolls her eyes. I can't help but laugh.

Jordan grins at me.

I feel that as well. Mainly in my southern region.

"Beth, you've already met Mia." He gestures to me.

"I have." She smiles. It appears genuine which helps a little with my concern.

"Thanks again for the hotel recommendation," I say.

She looks at Jordan again, but he's looking at me. Her eyes come back to me. And I notice curiosity and possibly a little humor in them.

It makes me curious.

"No probs." She smiles again. "I didn't expect to see you in here today," she says to Jordan.

His face shifts to a sullen expression. "Some fucknut hit Dozer with their car."

"Oh my god!" She claps her hand over her mouth. Sitting down next to Jordan, she forces him to shift over. "Is he okay?"

Jordan nods in my direction. "Thanks to Mia he is."

I can feel my cheeks heating. "I didn't do anything, not really."

"Yes, you did." He gives me a look, before turning to Beth. "She checked him over for injuries and saw that his leg was broken, so she tore up her shirt and strapped up his leg. Mia's training to be a doctor," he informs her.

"Wow," Beth says, looking at me.

I shift uneasily in my seat. I'm not really comfortable with this conversation or attention. I don't like the focus being on me.

"Guess that explains why you're wearing one of Jordan's shirts," she adds with a grin.

My face instantly fires. "Oh, yes." I look down at it, fidgeting with the buttons and trying to hide my face.

"We good to get some food? Mia hasn't eaten anything since last night," Jordan says, changing the subject. I'm guessing he can sense my discomfort at the whole shirt conversation. "She missed breakfast helping with Dozer, so I brought her out for lunch while I wait to go pick him up."

She nods. "Absolutely. So Dozer's gonna be okay?"

"Yeah. He's gonna be fine."

"Good." She pats his shoulder and gets to her feet. "Let me get you both something to eat. Sounds like y'all need it. Your usual, Jordan?"

"Yeah."

"Mia, what can I get you?" She looks at me.

I grab the menu off the table and quickly scan it. "I'll have a chicken salad sandwich and a diet coke, please."

She smiles. "Cool. Won't be long."

I watch her walk away to the kitchen. Jordan shifts across the bench, so he's back opposite me, putting him directly in my eye line.

He rests his hands on the table, tilting his head, and stares at me. It's then I realize I'm pulling on my lip again. I set my hands in my lap.

"You do that when you're nervous." It's not a question.

108

I nod.

"You're nervous now. Why?"

I lift my shoulders, looking anywhere but him. "I'm not really sure."

He leans forward, clasping his hands together. "You don't need to be nervous around me, Mia."

I meet his warm gaze. "I know." I nod.

"Good." He smiles and relaxes back. "I've been thinking about finding your mom, and how to go about it." He picks up a pack of sugar from the holder and starts playing with it. "I thought we'd be best starting with the basics like Google, White Pages, Public Records, that kind of thing."

"Sounds like a good plan."

Of course it does. Any plan would sound good to me because I have no clue how to search for my absent mother.

Putting the sugar down, he pulls his cell from his pocket. "Okay, let's get started."

"Now?" My gaze snaps up to his.

"No time like the present … unless you'd rather I wait?"

"No. Now is fine." I force a smile, knowing how stilted my voice sounds.

"If you're sure."

"I'm sure." I'm pretty certain my voice sounds harsher than I mean it to. I'm just afraid. I want to find my mother, but fear of the unknown is suddenly clouding that.

Jordan looks at me with confused sympathy on his face.

I look at him until I can no longer bear it. I hate sympathy.

Turning my face, I stare out of the window.

"Okay." He exhales. "I'll start with public records."

"Sure," I mumble. My hands feel fidgety, so I wrap them around my stomach, which is turning over.

I can feel myself coming undone.

"What was your mom's name again?"

"Anna Monroe."

More typing from him. More fear and panic from me.

I don't think I'm ready for this. My legs are itching to take me out of here.

I need to leave. I need food. I need to be alone.

Jordan exhales a loud breath, bringing my attention to him. His brow is all scrunched up in thought. He looks really adorable. And suddenly all of my attention is on *him*.

"I checked your mom's name against Colorado and New Mexico with us been so close to there, I thought it worth a try, and it's brought up ten Anna Monroe's. None in Durango. But three are in neighboring towns. One in Montrose. One in Gunnington. And the other in Farmington, New Mexico which is only an hour away. So I think they are the best to start with."

He places his phone down on the table and runs his hand through his hair, meeting my eyes, which are fixed on him.

Seeing the warmth in his maple eyes sets my heart beating like a kick drum.

"We can download the full reports on them, addresses and the like. I'll do it when we get back to the hotel."

I like how he thinks of things I wouldn't. I would never have thought to check New Mexico.

Fear aside, I'm so glad he's helping me. I think I'll locate her much quicker with his help.

"Thank you for doing this for me."

"Seriously, stop thanking me. I only do things because I want to. And I want to help you, okay?"

No one has ever spoken to me or treated me like he does. Like I'm a person who matters. That I count for something.

It makes my heart feel warm and alive in a way it never has before.

I've known Jordan for such a short time, but that time just feels irrelevant when I'm sitting here with him.

It's scary. But a good scary.

I like it. I like him.

"Okay." I smile.

Chapter Nine

Jordan

I told Mia that I'm cleaned up from the person I used to be. That I'm responsible now. Yeah, right. I don't gamble anymore, but…

If she knew the reason why I'd stopped gambling, she would think I was the lowest of the low.

I try to be responsible, try to keep out of trouble, but it just seems to follow me everywhere I go. Or maybe I just attract it.

No maybe about it. I absolutely do.

Even after everything that has happened, I still bring shit to my dad's door.

I hook up with a married woman, thinking solely with my dick, and the pissed off husband shows up at the hotel.

I was beyond relieved that Dad was out when he turned up. Even though he found out about it later, I was glad he was out of the loop. I don't want him getting into any more shit because of me. He's already lost so much at my hands.

Not that he'd ever say that. He would never blame me a day in his life. Dad never makes me feel like a disappointment, but I know I am.

Thankfully, the angry husband fiasco didn't culminate into a kick-off—and that was thanks to Beth and her ability to calm angry men down.

But I can't keep doing shit like that.

Problem is, I don't know how to be good. Gambling's out of the question, so women it is. I need to keep my mind busy when I get the urge for the tables, which is often.

Fucking helps with that. So I fuck often.

I just have to be careful of the women I choose to screw as I don't want anything I do coming back on my dad.

So, definitely no married ones. And no guests at the hotel – meaning no Mia Monroe.

My list of reasons to stay away from her just keeps growing. She's a guest at the hotel. She has more baggage than JFK. But mainly, because she is too damn good for someone like me.

Nothing good could come of Mia wrapped around me. Well, something good would come of it—pun totally intended—but after the physical high, reality would bring me crashing back down to earth.

She deserves better than I could ever give her.

And I'm doing well, I think. I've been around her for a good while now. Yeah, I know what you're thinking, it's been less than a day in her company. But trust me, this is some kind of fucking record that I haven't tried to hit on her.

My only slip up was in the car earlier when I flirted with her. But that was nothing compared to how I usually go for it.

I just couldn't resist. And the look on her face … so goddamn cute. Her cheeks turned pink, and she looked surprised and embarrassed. You'd think no one had ever flirted with her before, but looking like she does, I find that *very* hard to believe.

We're back at the hotel, and I'm in the kitchen making us some coffee. After we'd finished lunch at the diner, there was still an hour to kill before I have to pick Dozer up, so I brought Mia back to the hotel and downloaded the info I found. I printed the details off while Mia went to change out of her torn t-shirt.

She gave me my shirt back before she went to change. I'm not ashamed to say I smelled it once she'd walked away.

It smelled amazing. Total jerking off material.

Seriously, if Mia Monroe were a bottled scent, I'd spray it all over my pillows. And my clothes. Hell, I'd spray it on myself.

When she came back from changing, she was freshly showered, and her hair was still a little damp, vanilla scent floating around her. She was wearing a pale pink tank top and ass hugging jeans, and my cock nearly sprang from my jeans. She looked fucking gorgeous.

It took me a good few minutes to get my head working properly before I could sit down with her and start looking over the details. She'd seemed quiet while I talked her through what I'd printed off, so I left her sitting outside on the porch, thinking she maybe needed a few.

Hence the reason I'm in here making coffee.

I figure she'll just be processing things. I can't begin to imagine how it must feel to know that your mom abandoned you.

I've never been abandoned, but dying mothers I have down to pat.

My real mom, Abbi, died in childbirth. She had a heart problem that they didn't know about, and the stress of giving birth to me killed her.

She wasn't married to Dad. They were young, in a steady relationship, but my dad hadn't kept it covered, so nine months later it was hello Jordan.

After Abbi died, Dad raised me alone with the help of my grandpa. When I was two, Belle, my step-mom who I always refer to as mom as she's the only one I ever known, came back to town, and her and dad got back together. Dad and Mom were childhood sweethearts. Mom left town to go to college, but Dad stayed here and went to the police academy. Before she left they broke up, and that was when he met Abbi and had me.

Mom died four years ago, and he hasn't looked at another woman since.

Dad has had such a rough time in his life. He's lost two women he loved. I think losing both of them has killed his faith in love. Totally understandable.

And that's why I stay single. I only bother with a woman when I need to get laid.

The phone starts to ring. "Golden Oaks."

"Hey son, how you doing?"

"Hey Dad, I'm good. How's Grandpa doing? He driving you crazy yet?"

He laughs. "Of course. You know your Grandpa. How are

things at the hotel?"

"Yeah, good. We've got a guest staying at the moment. She's here for two weeks."

"She?" Silence. "You've got a woman staying there right now?"

"Yes, Dad." I sigh.

"Is she alone?"

"Yep."

"How old is she?"

"I don't know, around my age, maybe a few years younger."

"Does she have a boyfriend?"

"Jesus, Dad." I sigh again. "I don't know her relationship status—" *A lie.* "—because I don't need to. I'm not gonna touch her, okay? She's not my type."

That one is a small lie. Mia isn't my usual type. She's so much more.

"Every girl is your type, Jordan."

"Not every girl!" I scoff. "I would never sleep with an ugly girl. Jeez, give me some fuckin' credit, Dad."

"Jesus, Jordan, do you have to cuss so much?"

"Yes, I *fucking* do."

How do parents have the ability to turn you from a grown ass man into a teenager in the matter of seconds?

"So, she's ugly then?" he says, starting in again.

"Who?" I play out.

He lets out a loud sigh. "The girl you have no intention of trying to get into bed."

"Well … no, she's not what I would call ugly…"

He laughs. Loudly.

It really pisses me off.

"Look, I know you think I'm a fuck up, and I know that's my fault, but I am fully capable of keeping my hands to myself. I'm staying away from this girl. She's a guest. End of."

"Whoa, calm down, son. First off, I do not think you're a fuck-up. You hear me? I just worry about you. Parent's privilege. I just want you to be happy, but you always seem to look for

114

happiness in all the wrong places. More so recently."

This is getting a little deeper than I like. I don't do deep. Especially not with my dad.

I lean my arm against the wall and rest my forehead on it.

I blow out a breath. "I'm fine, Dad. I'm happy. Look, I have to go. Say hi to Grandpa for me, will you?"

"Sure." He sounds resigned, and I'm glad. I don't want this conversation to go on any longer than necessary. "Take care, son. Speak to you soon."

I hang up the phone, then realize I forgot to tell him about Dozer's accident. Whatever. I'm not in the mood to call him back right now. I'll tell him later.

I take our coffees outside. Mia is sitting at the table. Her sunglasses are off, and she's leaned back in her chair, head tilted, staring up at the sky.

I watch her for longer than I should.

Her head comes up suddenly, and she catches me staring.

Acting like there is nothing weird about me staring at her, I smile and walk over, putting her coffee on the table in front of her.

"Thanks." She smiles up at me, and it feels like I just got punched in the chest.

That is seriously starting to drive me crazy. Not the smiles … no, those are awesome. It's my reaction to them that's pissing me off. My reaction to her.

I take the chair across from her. Settling back, I take a sip of my coffee and set it down.

"Any idea where you want to start?" I nod at the papers in front of her.

Mia takes a sip of coffee, her eyes watching mine over the brim of the cup. "I thought maybe I would start with the Anna that lives in Farmington. That's the largest town, right? Because I thought if I were her and I was getting away that's where I would go. Or maybe go to another state altogether, so I'd be harder to find."

Her lips downturn. I feel a pang of … I don't know. All I do know is I really don't like to see her sad.

"Think positive, Mia. Start with what we have and go from there."

Her eyes lift. "You're right. I'll drive out there tomorrow—"

"*We*," I emphasize.

I could really do without going to Farmington. I've avoided that place like the plague since what happened with Dad. But I can't let her go there alone. And the likelihood I'll see anyone I don't want to see, during the day, is slim to none.

The likes of me only come out to play at night.

Mia places her cup down. "You don't have to come with me. You've helped me enough already – and you have the hotel to run."

Leaning back, I cross my leg over my other and rest my ankle on my thigh. "If you haven't noticed, we're not exactly busy. You're my only guest, so call this the all-inclusive package." I grin so that it doesn't come off as creepy.

She laughs.

Good sign.

Her eyebrow lifts, and she starts pulling on that damn lip again. "So … what does this all-inclusive package entail?"

Hmm. She's flirting with me. Interesting.

Very. Fucking. Interesting.

"Nothing specific. It's more of a try and see kind of thing."

"Right." She hasn't taken her eyes off me.

I'm really liking the direction this is going. I shouldn't, but I can't help myself. I have Mia's interest, and I'm not letting go until I know what it means.

My breathing has picked up, so I take a quick sip of my coffee to cover it, but don't take my eyes off her.

"But part of that package does mean I'm coming with you tomorrow. I really don't think it's safe for you drive out there alone."

A little frown dimples between her brows, and a fire lights in her eyes. It's sexy, but I know I've pissed her off. I had this going in a good direction, but I just had to open my big mouth and ruin it.

She folds her arms across her chest. It pushes those perfect tits of hers up; tits that I'm trying really hard not to look at.

"Jordan, I drove across seven states alone to get here. I can manage a drive out of town." She sounds pissed off, and her lip has jutted out. I can't help but chuckle.

She's so goddamn adorable. I'm tempted to throw all caution to the wind, and take her face in my hands and kiss those beautiful lips of hers.

"I get it," I say, covering up a smile. "You can take care of yourself. But just humor me. Remember, I grew up the son of a cop, I know about the bad side of women driving alone long distance. Jeez, just knowing you did that to get here makes me feel like I'm going to break out in hives. And that wouldn't be pretty. You don't want to be responsible for making me look ugly, do you? Like the kind of ugly that scares small children." I pull a face, and she smiles.

I'm playing, because I don't want to knock the self-confidence and independence she so clearly needs to exert—the confidence that bastard took away from her the instant he laid a finger on her.

But I also can't let her go there alone.

She looks down at the table and runs her fingertip along the groove. I've already gotten familiar with the face she pulls when she's thinking something over, and she's wearing that look right now.

She lifts her head, looking at me intently. "I don't want to be the one responsible for spoiling that nice face of yours, so … okay, you can come."

"You think I have a nice face?" I tilt my head to the side, grinning.

Of course, I caught that. And of course I want to know the answer. Mia is the only woman I've ever had to question as to whether she finds me attractive or not.

She's so hard to read that it's impossible to tell what she's thinking most of the time.

It's fucking with my head, to say the least.

Her face has gone as red as I expected it would. I've never met a girl as shy as she is.

I've never met a girl like her, period. She's so different. Unassuming of anything, mainly herself. She has no clue just how fucking awesome she actually is, but I want her to know. I just wish I knew how to tell her.

"Uh, um, well…" She runs her fingers through her hair, and keeps her eyes fixed on the coffee in front of her. "You have a nice face. You know, as faces go."

"I'll take that as a compliment." I smile. But what I actually feel like doing is breaking into a fucking dance. "You have a nice face too, Mia. *Really* nice."

I hear her quick intake of breath, and I notice the flush on her chest. She's affected by me.

A-fuckin-men!

"Thank you," she says quietly, biting down on a smile.

"You have a serious problem with that."

"What?" Her eyes flick up to mine, the warmth instantly dying.

I hold off the frown I feel knowing why she reacts like she does – suspicious of what I say and do. But it doesn't mean I have to like it. What that asshole has done to her, how he has broken her confidence … and I don't even know the half of it. I'm just praying that the black-eye was the whole of it and nothing more.

"Saying thank you. You say it all the time," I tell her.

"Oh. Good manners … they were drummed into me." The light heartedness in her voice doesn't match the look in her eyes.

If I hadn't been watching closely, I would have missed how her eyes dimmed, but I didn't, and now it's stirred an uncomfortable feeling in my gut.

There is more—more than the black-eye from the douchebag ex of hers. And now I'm fucking fuming.

I want to know the rest … *need* to know so I can help her. But I can't ask her outright, I don't want to upset her like I did before, so I'll just have to wait until she's ready to tell me.

If ever.

"You don't need to use good manners around me." I lighten my voice, trying to bring her back from wherever she's gone. "If you haven't noticed, I don't have any."

She gives a half-smile. "I don't know, you seem to be pretty well mannered around me."

I raise my eyebrow. "I cuss. A *fuck* of a lot."

She laughs. The sound eases through me.

"You do cuss a lot, but I find it refreshing."

"My cussing is refreshing? There's a new one. You'll have to tell my dad because I'm pretty sure he'd disagree. Apparently, cussing in front of guests is a big no-no," I say with mock-confusion, lifting my shoulders in a shrug.

I don't know what it is that sets her off, but she throws her head back and starts to laugh. A real honest to god belly laugh. And it's just such an awesome, beautiful sound that I can't help but laugh too.

Clutching her stomach with her hand, she attempts to catch her breath. She sweeps her bangs back.

Her blue eyes are glistening.

She looks like poetry. Like the sky on a hot summers day. Like the ace in the hand I need to win.

Okay, I'm guessing you get the picture.

She looks beautiful.

"You're funny." She smiles. "You make me laugh."

Hold up. Clarification needed. I don't mind being the class clown, but not the village fucking idiot.

"Funny ha-ha, or funny peculiar?"

She leans forward, elbows on table, chin in hands as she purses her lips. I feel like I'm being appraised. I can't say a woman has ever looked at me this way before. Or left me hanging on a question. I feel a bit rattled, to be honest.

"Funny ha-ha," she finally says.

Well, thank fuck for that.

"You're quick, straightforward, and you don't mess around. It's refreshing."

"Now, if I didn't know better, I think you were calling me common…" I tease.

She drags her lip back with her teeth and her eyes flash me a look. It's seriously hot.

"You're anything but common."

"I'll take that as another compliment."

"It was meant as one." I notice that her voice has dropped a few octaves lower. That her breathing has hitched slightly and that the flush is back, curving the tops of those amazing breasts of hers.

There's a tangible heat moving between us. It's taking everything in me right now, to hold back and not make a move on her.

Fuck, I want to make a move, and the way she's looking at me…

She wants me.

Trust me, I know one thing well, and that's when a woman wants me. And Mia wants me.

I meet her eyes again, and I'm swiftly reminded of the bruise on her face.

Crash and burn.

She's too fragile.

She's been through too much. I'm not the kind of guy she needs.

Shoving the chair back, I get to my feet. Mia's eyes dart up. I'm pretty sure I see a flash of disappointment in them. It both, buzzes and sours my mood.

Fucked up, right?

"Time for me to pick Dozer up." I glance at my watch as though to confirm this fact to her.

"Would you mind if I came along? I'd really like to see how he's doing," she asks in that sweet ass voice of hers.

It invades my head like a physical presence.

I want to say no because I could do with the time to clear my mind of her, and what I want to do with her … to her.

I even open my mouth to say no. But, of course, I say yes.

One look into those stunning blue eyes of hers and all my sense flies out the window.

Then she smiles, and I'm fucking done for.

I can't even blame this one on my cock as he hasn't even shown up for the party.

The drive to the vet is quiet. Mainly because I can't think of a damn thing to say to her. This is a foreign concept to me. I'm never without something to say to a woman, but right now I'm rattling around inside my head trying to understand what is happening here.

Why is Mia affecting me so much?

Maybe it's because the unknown is eating away at me.

Putting the sex aside—yes, I did just say that, unbelievable, right? See this is what she's doing to me. The thing is, I actually like talking to her. She's smart. And fun. I'm hot for her, *and* I want to spend time with her.

Never. Happened. Before.

And I don't like it.

This girl is going to slowly drive me crazy, I can feel it.

Maybe I should just have sex with her and get it over with, be damned the consequences. She's definitely hot for me; I could tell before. Maybe if I just…

"—wasn't that the turn for the vet?"

"What?" I come to at the sound of Mia's voice.

"I think you just missed the turn to the vet." She points over her shoulder.

I cast a quick glance behind me, and see that I have indeed missed my turning because I was thinking about her.

"Shit, yeah," I mutter.

I check the road is clear and spin the car around, heading back the way I just came. I take the turning and pull up outside the vet.

There's no one behind the desk when we enter the building, so I ring the bell on the desk.

Penny appears from behind a door. "Hello again." She smiles brightly. "Dozer's all ready for you. If you want to take a seat, I'll bring him right out."

I sit down beside Mia, but I feel restless. I'm not exactly sure what it is that's making me restless. Maybe it's because I'm hyped up on sexual tension.

"Are you okay?" Mia asks.

I follow her eyes to my tapping foot.

"Oh, yeah, fine."

"Are you worried about Dozer?" She smiles softly and touches my arm with her hand.

My body electrifies from her touch. I can barely think straight from the heat burning my skin.

Seriously, what the *fuck* is that?

"Who?" I mutter.

She looks confused.

I open my mouth, but close it when Penny comes out with Dozer. "Here he is."

Dozer limps toward me. His leg is in a cast and he has a pissed off look on his face. He's wearing one of those huge cones around his head.

I have to bite back a smile. Poor bastard. He's really been through the wringer.

"Hey, buddy." I walk over to him and crouch down. "How you doing?"

He grunts and scuffs the cone against my shoulder.

"How long does he have to keep this on for?" I stand up, taking his leash from Penny.

"See how he goes. Dr. Callie only put it on as he was chewing at the cast."

"See Dozer, leave your leg alone and the cone can come off."

He gives me a dirty look, then yanks his leash from my hand and limps over to Mia.

I watch them, the way she welcomes him over, no fear. Dozer is a big dog, and people are usually wary of him, but not Mia. Not even when he drops his huge head on her lap, awkwardly shuffling around with the cone, drooling on her jeans. She doesn't falter, just gives him the attention he wants.

Dozer is never this friendly with people he doesn't know. Generally, he gives them a wide birth. He's always been that way, and I've put it down to whatever happened to him to make him land on our doorstep.

But Mia did care for him after his accident; she showed him a kindness that most people don't have in them. It will have pre-warmed him to her, and Mia is hard not to like. I know that all too damn well.

I watch her scratching his ear, cooing over him, and he's freaking soaking it up. Lucky bastard. What I wouldn't give to have her hands on me right now. Seriously, I'd take an ear scratching if it meant her touching me.

A broken leg is starting to sound quite appealing at this moment in time.

Mia suddenly lifts her eyes from Dozer to me like she can hear my thoughts, and catches me staring.

Her blue eyes peer curiously into mine. I know I should look away, but I don't...

I can't.

A smile slowly lifts her lips. The light coming in through the window, behind her, frames her perfectly. She looks like an angel. The most beautiful thing I have ever seen.

Punch. To. The. Chest.

I feel like I can't breathe.

"If you can just sign these forms for me, and settle up the bill," Penny says, pulling my attention from Mia.

"Sure," I say, rubbing at my sternum.

If this keeps up, I'll be having a heart attack way before my time.

With a nod, I follow her over to the reception desk. I hand Penny my credit card, trying not to think of how the hell I'm going to pay it off after these vet bills drain it, and sign the two forms she hands to me.

I glance over my shoulder, and catch Mia staring at me. She's definitely checking me out. My ass to be exact.

She looks away when she realizes I've caught her out.

I can't help the happy fucking glow I feel. I'm grinning like a stripper at a frat party.

After I've finished signing forms, and spending money I don't have, Penny gives me a small bag containing Dozer's medication.

"These are for his pain. Give him one, three times daily with food, and we'll need to see him back here in a month's time to check how that leg's healing. Only give him a light dinner tonight as his stomach will still be tender from the anesthetic. You can take the collar and leash home with you. Just return it to us when you have time."

"Thanks, I'll bring it by tomorrow."

I make the appointment for four weeks time, and slip the appointment card into my wallet along with my credit card. I shove the medication in my pocket as I make my way back to Mia. Dozer is still making doe eyes at her.

Even my dog is crazy about her.

Not that I'm crazy about her.

No fucking way.

Absolutely not.

Never. Ever.

"Ready?" I reach down for Dozer's leash.

Turning his head, he knocks my hand away with that huge cone he's wearing and puts his leash in his mouth, holding it out for Mia to take.

Nice, Dozer. Blowing me off for a chick. I think he forgets who feeds him.

Taking the leash from his mouth, she rubs his head.

She gazes up at me, a smile pushing the corner of her mouth. "Is it okay with you if I walk him out to your car?"

"Doesn't look like you've got much of a choice." I grin in the

124

direction of Dozer's wagging tail. "I think you've got an admirer."

She giggles. It's one of the sexiest sounds I've ever heard.

"Well, Dozer wouldn't be a bad admirer to have, but I think I'm just a new face to get some attention from. Not that I imagine you ever struggle for attention," she says to Dozer. "Handsome boy that you are … aren't you … yes, you are." She smooshes his face in her hands, and I actually find myself jealous of my dog.

I'm jealous of my dog.

I really need to get laid.

"Let's go." I shove my hands in my pockets, then head for the door and out to my car.

I help Dozer in the back seat. Turning, I find Mia hovering behind me as he settles himself.

"Should I sit in the back with him again?" she asks, biting her bottom lip.

Jesus, I want to bite that lip. Lick it. Suck it. Fuck it.

I see Dozer's head lift, and his ears prick up. "Nah, he'll be fine. You'll have more room up front here next to me."

"Okay … if you're sure."

I see Dozer's head drop on a grunt.

I hold a smile back as I watch Mia walk around the car and climb in the passenger seat. But as I'm getting in the car, I can't resist giving Dozer a smug grin.

Honestly, the look he's giving me right now … I think if he could flip me off, he would.

Yep, you lost that round, Dozer.

I turn the ignition, feeling pretty satisfied with myself that I've got Mia sitting up front with me…

Then it hits me.

I was just in a pissing contest with my dog.

There are no words.

No. Fucking. Words.

I put the car in drive, heading for home.

I'm actually starting to think Mia has got some magical power, and that's what's making me act out of character. Like

125

voodoo or some shit.

It has to be. There is no other logical explanation for the massive pussy I'm turning into.

All I need to do is get myself away from Mia for a few hours, stick my dick inside some chick, and I'll be back to myself in no time.

Except I can't tonight with Dozer being hurt.

Tomorrow.

Definitely tomorrow.

I'm going to go and pick up the hottest chick I can find, and bang her – multiple times.

I'm going to fuck Mia Monroe right out of my head.

I'm happily smiling to myself at this idea, when that annoying Taylor Swift song "I Knew You Were Trouble" starts to play on the radio.

I'm just about to turn it off, when Mia starts to sing along softly, so I leave it playing.

Jesus, her voice is one of the sweetest sounds I've ever heard.

I listen to her the whole song through. My skin is practically vibrating when she's finished. Who knew that song could sound so good?

I reach over and turn the radio down.

"You like Taylor Swift?"

"What?" She blushes. "Oh, yeah, she's okay. I just really like that song. Probably not your kind of music though, huh?"

"Not really." I smile.

I want to touch her so very fucking badly in this moment.

"I'm sorry," she says quietly.

I quick a glance at her. "What are you apologizing for?"

"For singing. I do it sometimes without realizing. I know I have the worst voice ever, and it must have really hurt your eardrums listening to me." She laughs, but it sounds unnatural, forced. Not like that awesome sound I heard earlier.

Another quick glance. I notice her body language is off. Her hands are wrapped around herself, almost in protection.

Tension prickles me like knives.

"Who told you that?" The asshole ex told her. I really want to punch that prick in the face. Repeatedly.

She glances down at her jeans and start picking lint off them. I can feel her drawing into herself and away from me. I don't like the feeling one goddamn bit.

"Oh, no one told me. I just have ears, you know?" A shrug, another fake laugh.

"Well your ears are off. I think you have a great voice, Mia. Really awesome. I enjoyed listening to you sing."

I can feel her eyes on me, so I meet them. I'm yanked in and speaking before I realize.

"What are your plans for tonight?"

What the hell am I doing?

Surprise flickers through those gorgeous blues. Then she lifts her slender shoulders and tilts her head. "Oh, uh, I was just gonna grab some dinner, then read myself to sleep."

"You wanna have dinner with me?"

Why can't I stop talking?

Mia's eyebrow lifts, and the way that sounded *finally* reverberates inside my head.

Jesus that sounded like I was asking her out on a date.

I don't date. Ever.

What am I doing? Asking her to eat with me when a minute ago I was planning a 'fuck Mia out of my head' strategy.

Rectify! Rectify!

I swallow down, hard. My eyes now fixed firmly on the road ahead, I moronically stammer out, "I, uh, just meant that I was gonna be cooking myself some dinner, so I can make extra for you if you want? Or not. Whatever."

Smooth, Matthews. Real fucking smooth.

There's one of her long pauses before she speaks. "That would be great, Jordan. Thank you." Her voice is so stilted and quiet that I don't even risk a glance to see the expression on her face.

Someone kill me now. Please.

I hear Dozer snort a sound in the back.

I'm half tempted to turn around and tell him to piss off, but I'm guessing Mia already thinks I'm a moron, so I skip it.

Instead, I reach over and turn the radio back up to fill the awkwardness. And let's just say, the drive back to the hotel is as quiet as the ride out.

Chapter Ten

Mia

Why do I feel so disappointed?

I didn't want Jordan to ask me to dinner, but when he corrected his offer, all I felt was disappointment. It's stupid. I'm stupid.

Of course he's going to offer me dinner. He's a nice guy. I know he said the hotel doesn't provide evening meals, and he's probably being polite because I'm the only guest, but I can't let him feed me for free. I'll have to make sure he adds the cost of the meal to my bill. I'm sure he will anyway, but I'll have to make sure.

Look at me, crushing on the first guy who's nice to me. It's ridiculous, even for me.

I just need to concentrate on what I'm here for—finding my mother, getting some answers, and moving on with my life. Starting fresh.

We're back at the hotel now. I'm standing by the archway watching Jordan as he settles Dozer onto the sofa. He even turns on the TV for him.

I have to suppress the smile I feel. And the zap of attraction that hits me.

He really does think the world of Dozer. He's a lucky dog. Minus the car hitting him, that is.

I follow Jordan through to the hotel kitchen after he's finished settling Dozer.

I take a seat on a stool by the kitchen counter.

"I'm not the best chef…" he says over his shoulder, heading

for the refrigerator.

"Sounds promising," I quip.

I'm surprised at my own boldness. This isn't natural for me, and not how I speak around men at all. I'm always guarded, thinking over my words before I speak.

I had to be. One slip up could cost me badly.

But with Jordan it's easy to slip because everything with him feels natural.

He turns slightly, looking affronted. "Hey! I'm not bad. I make a mean Green Chili. I'll get the ingredients in and make it for you another night, but for tonight, just name anything you want—that I have the ingredients for—" he grins, "and I'll make it."

Feeling lightened by his banter, I shrug. "I'm easy. Whatever you want is fine with me."

His brows lift. He turns his body fully around to face me.

Easy. Not the best word to use, Mia.

See this is what happens when I don't consider my words. Verbal diarrhea.

"N-not that I'm *e-easy.* Just easy about the food, you know," I start to stammer. "J-just not fussed, easy to please."

His brow lifts higher, and he's grinning.

I want the ground to swallow me up. Now. Please.

"Easy to please. Got it." He turns his attention back to the fridge.

I'm such an idiot. I really shouldn't be let out around people.

Jordan starts pulling food out and placing it on the counter. Eggs, tomatoes…

"So, 'easy to please', will a Spanish omelet be okay?"

I can't help the laugh that escapes me. "A Spanish omelet will be perfect."

He gives me a smile before turning back.

"You want any help?"

"Nah, I got it. You want something to drink? There's beer in the fridge, or wine if you want?"

"Beer's great." I hop off the stool and go over to the fridge.

"You want one?"

"Sure."

I grab two bottles.

"Opener is in the drawer." Jordan points to the drawer with the knife he's using to chop the tomatoes.

I falter in my step, my chest tightening, legs stiffening. My eyes hazing.

Shit.

Oliver trailed the knife across my collar bone and over my shoulder.

"Where did you get this from, Mia?" He held up the top I'd bought myself the day prior. A beautiful, low cut, strappy top, which I had hidden in the back of my closet. I was hoping to wear it when Oliver was at the hospital. I bought it because of the colors. It made me think of summer. I felt warm and happy when I tried it on. I wanted to keep hold of that feeling, so I bought it, even knowing the risk.

"I b-bought it, sir."

"Did I give you permission to buy this?

I hung my head. "No."

He moved closer to me. "This is a whore's top! Designed to get the attention of boys! Is that what you want, Mia? You want the attention of boys?"

"No, Daddy."

He held the top in front of me as he shredded it with the knife.

I wanted to cry. Over a top. But that top had made me feel happy. For that fleeting moment, I had felt happy, and he'd taken it away again. Like always.

"Take off your sweater, Mia."

My eyes snapped up to his. "W-why?"

"Don't question me!" he roared. "Just do as I say!"

My body shaking, I lifted the sweater over my head. Leaving me in my bra, I held my sweater, fingers clutching it, against my stomach.

Fear was roiling inside me.

131

Oliver walked behind me.

I squeezed my eyes shut.

I heard the knife being placed down on his desk, then the snap of Oliver's belt as he removed it from his pants.

My stomach dropped hollow. No matter how many times it happened, the fear was always the same.

"You've disobeyed my rules, Mia. You've been a bad girl. What happens to bad girls?"

I swallowed past the fear that was drying my mouth and shaking my insides. "They get punished, sir."

I braced myself, gritting my teeth.

I felt the lash of the first hit on my back. Stifling my screams, I bit down on my lip until I tasted blood.

"Jesus, Mia! Are you okay?"

A worried Jordan is standing before me. I feel something running down my chin. I press the heel of my hand against my mouth. Blood.

I bit through my lip.

"God, oh, I, uh – it was an accident."

An accident? Yeah, because normal people bite their lips and draw blood all the time Mia. Perfectly normal. He won't think anything is off there.

Saying nothing, Jordan takes the beer bottles from my hands and places them on the counter.

That's when I realize my hands are shaking.

"Sit up here." He pulls a stool over. I climb onto it, my legs suddenly feeling like jelly. He opens a drawer, then comes back with a first aid kit.

God, I'm such a screw-up. Now I'm zoning out and biting my own lip open. Awesome Mia. Way to go.

"Sorry," I mumble as he starts to dab at the blood with a wipe. Antiseptic. Stings a little but I'm used to the sting – years of using the stuff will do that. "I'm such a klutz."

I'm trying not focus on Jordan's nearness, or how my skin tingles when he touches me. Or how amazing he smells. Or that I want him to kiss me.

Right now.

More than anything.

Yes, that's what I'm thinking about in this screwed up moment.

Normal is something I will never be. I figured that out a long time ago.

"Stop apologizing," he says softly, meeting my eyes. "Just tell me what happened back then."

I hold my gaze steady. "Nothing happened."

"Nothing happened? You zoned out completely. Where'd you go?"

I look away, focusing on the wall behind him. "Nowhere special. I'm sorry."

He sighs. His warm breath blows through my hair. His exasperation should bother me, but all I can focus on is the way his nearness is making me feel right now. And that's alive.

I can't ever remember feeling this alive before.

"Seriously, stop saying you're sorry. You have nothing to be sorry about. I'm just worried about you." He presses the wipe against my lip. "Were you thinking about what your ex did to you? How you got the black-eye? I know that traumatic events can sometimes be triggered by the smallest thing, causing blackouts and that kind of thing."

My body freezes. Muscles stiff.

I shake my head.

It's the truth because the real screwed up in me happened long before Forbes came into my life. Forbes was just the rain after the tornado.

"I'm fine," I say, probably a little too harshly. I don't mean to be this way, but I just can't talk about it. Not with him.

Not with anyone.

Removing the wipe, he steps back and rakes a hand through his hair. I can tell he's frustrated, and I'm the one frustrating him.

All I ever seem to do is frustrate and anger men, but that's also all I know. Kindness confuses me. Throws me for a loop.

An angry, frustrated man makes more sense to me.

"I know you don't know me well, but you *can* trust me. You can talk to me and tell me anything. I won't judge … honestly, I'm no one to judge." His gaze sweeps the floor, then meets back with mine. His eyes are honest and clear. "I might be able to help you."

Even when he's frustrated, he's kind. I don't know what to do with that.

But I do want his help. More than anything I want to trust someone. I want to trust him.

I open my mouth to let the words spill out. But I can't. The broken in me can't be fixed.

"I'm long past help." I shake my head, hating that I let that slip out. "I appreciate it – you – everything you've done for me. But really, there's nothing to talk about." I slide down off the stool.

"Thanks for the clean-up, but I'm going to skip dinner. I'm feeling pretty tired."

"Mia…"

Ignoring the plea in his voice, I'm out of the kitchen and running to my room.

Chapter Eleven

Jordan

I lift my hand to knock on the door, then retract it and step back.

I'm standing outside Mia's room, wondering if I should knock on her door or not.

It's a fairly simple act. I lift my hand. It makes contact with the wood. I knock. She opens the door.

Simple, right?

So why am I thinking it over?

Because after last night, things don't feel so simple anymore when it comes to Mia. Not that I've been coasting down easy street from the moment I met her, but this is just way out of my territory.

I have no clue what to say to her. And I *always* know what to say to women.

I suppose, I could just act like it never happened.

Yeah, because that wouldn't be a totally shitty thing to do.

Maybe I can just let her know if she ever needs to talk to me about anything, I'm here.

That's it. I'll do that. I'll knock on the door, tell her breakfast is ready, ask her what time she wants to leave to go to Farmington, and subtly mention that I'm here for her.

Easy.

I lift my hand to the door, and suddenly see a flash of Mia's face from last night.

The look on her face. She was completely zoned out. Somewhere else. And the way she bit into her lip … I have honestly never seen anything like it.

I'm not afraid to admit that seeing her like that frightened the shit out of me.

What could have made her get that way?

I'm guessing things are way worse for her then I'd first thought. More than just the douche ex giving her that black eye.

I got that when she said she was beyond help and ran out of the kitchen like her feet were on fire.

In that moment, I wanted to go after her. Help her. I almost did. But I stopped myself.

Why? Because I knew if I did, I would be crossing the line into something else.

I would be getting in deep with her.

I don't do deep. I *can't* do deep.

Fucking? Yes.

Touchy feely? Huge no-no.

I back up, lean against the wall and drive my hands through my hair.

I'm exhausted. I hardly slept last night. I had Dozer and his broken leg in bed with me, leaving me with an inch of mattress to sleep on. My lack of sleep had absolutely nothing to do with Mia's freak out last night. I might have thought about it a few times. But not much. I was just trying to figure out what her fuckhole of an ex could have put her through. And all thinking about it did was rile me up.

So then I thought happy Mia thoughts.

I thought about having sex with her in multiple different ways. And I imagined what those sweet lips of hers would feel like to kiss.

How she would taste.

How all of her would taste…

Her skin…

Her tight, hot pussy…

Fine. I spent all of my night either worrying about Mia, or thinking about all the ways I want to do her.

Mia was on my mind all goddamn night.

Happy?

Cause I'm fucking not.

Fuck this shit.

I push off the wall, arm raised with the purpose of banging on the door, when Mia suddenly opens it.

"Shit!"

"Jesus!"

My arm is still raised mid-air, and my heart is pounding like a motherfucker.

Mia's eyes are on my raised arm, her breaths coming in quick, chest heaving.

Fuck, her tits look great in that top.

And I'm staring.

Eyes avert. I lower my arm to my side.

"Sorry," I say at the same time as she does.

I lift my eyes to hers and grin. Her eyes smile at me.

"I just—"

"I was—"

She laughs.

The sound is so fucking sexy.

I want her. I can honestly say I have never wanted anything more in my life than her. My cock is throbbing. It's a pleasure/pain thing.

Pleasure at the sight of her.

Pain that he can't get in her.

I think he's dying of thirst. He needs to bathe in the fountain of Mia.

Am I experiencing sexual frustration? Shit … I think I might be. So this is what it's like. It's pretty torturous. How the hell do monks survive? I know for a fact that I'm not going to last much longer without getting laid.

"You go." She gestures.

What?

Oh yeah, we were talking. Kind of.

I push my hands in my pockets and shift on my feet. "I just came to let you know breakfast is ready, and also to see what time you wanted to head out to Farmington?"

"You still want to go with me?" She looks surprised.

"Of course. Why wouldn't I?"

Her eyes drop to her feet.

I follow her gaze down, wishing her legs weren't covered in denim right now. I see she's wearing a pair of flip-flops and that her toenails are painted pink.

Is it strange that the sight of her feet is turning me on?

Yeah, well if it is, I don't care. I want to push her back onto the bed, take those flip-flips off, then her jeans, and lick my way down her sexy instep, all the way up those gorgeous legs until I reach home.

"Because … well, uh…" Her soft voice pulls me back to her. "Because of last night."

I frown. I can't help it. "Nothing's changed." *Everything's changed.* "Last night … it's your business. If you want to talk about it, I'm here. If not…" I lift my shoulders. "I'm still here."

Jesus, could I sound any more like a woman? I'll be growing a vagina if I keep this shit up.

A smile touches the corners of her lips.

Our eyes catch, and I almost flinch from the pang that flashes across my chest.

That shit is getting on my last goddamn nerve.

I only get it when I'm with Mia.

Maybe it's…?

No.

No. Fucking. Way.

"Are you ready to eat now?" I blurt out.

She looks a little taken aback at my abruptness. "Yes."

"Okay. Good." I turn and walk down the hall.

I was short. I didn't mean to be, and I know I'm having mood swings like a hormonal teenager, but I just can't seem to control my emotions around her. My head is all over the goddamn place.

I hear the door click close behind me, then the gentle sound of flip-flops slapping against her feet.

The sound is like a beat inside my chest.

I'm out on the terrace before she is. It's a warm morning, so I thought she might like to eat outside.

I set the table already. I called Paula last night and told her not to come in today. There's not much that needs doing, nothing I can't do myself.

It has absolutely nothing to do with the fact that I like being here with Mia. Alone.

Nothing at all.

"You mind if I eat with you?" I check as she takes a seat.

She's still a guest here, and I have to remind myself of that. Even if I am letting myself get a little entwined in her life.

Her smile is a puzzled one. "No, of course not."

"Cool." I start to back away toward the door. "What would you like to drink?"

"Coffee would be great."

I head in the kitchen. I have the food already on a tray, so I just add the coffee pot, cream and sugar.

"I made a few things," I say as I come back outside. "I wasn't sure what you would like, but last night you said you were easy to please…" I grin as I put the tray of waffles, pancakes, bacon and toast down in the middle of the table.

"You made all of this … for me?" She gulps. Her eyes are glittering.

A feeling yanks inside my chest like the pulling of puppet strings. I shift uncomfortably.

"Yeah, well, you are a paying guest." I shrug.

Her face falls. "Yes, of course." Her words are quiet, but they've affected me more than if she had yelled them at me.

I'm such a fucking idiot.

"Shit, that sounded…" I take the seat across from her. "I don't make breakfast like this for everyone."

Actually, I've never made a breakfast like this for anyone in my life before, come to think of it. I don't do breakfast for the guests. Paula or Dad do. And if I did, they'd be lucky to get a bowl of cereal.

"You haven't?" Her eyebrow lifts in disbelief.

"Nope. Scouts honor." I tap two fingers to my temple.

"You were a boy scout?"

"Lasted a day." I grin. "But it's the truth about the food. I just broke my breakfast virginity with you."

Her cheeks turn deep pink.

Too much?

Like I care. I want her. Bad. Fuck everything I've said these last few days about staying away. I can't. I'm not holding back with her anymore. There's something here with Mia, and I have to find out what it is.

Our gaze holds for one beat … two…

She looks away to the food. "The waffles look really yummy. Well, it all looks yummy. And the pancakes look … delicious, and the toast is…" She's stumbling on her words. It's cute to watch.

"Toast," I finish for her with a chuckle.

As if on cue, her cheeks flush again. She starts to chew on the inside of her lip. Watching her do that makes my cock pulse and my heart race.

"You should eat. You missed dinner last night." I push the tray toward her.

She pinches her lower lip between her thumb and forefinger. "I am quite hungry."

Tentatively, she reaches out and picks up a waffle, putting it on her plate.

I sit and watch as she pours maple syrup on the waffle, then lifts it to her mouth and takes a bite. Her eyes close on the food, and the small moan that escapes her stands my guy to attention.

Fuck. Me.

It sounds exactly like the moans I spent most of last night imagining her making.

I shift in my seat, tilting my body from her view, then cross my leg over the other to hide the boner I'm now sporting.

I dig into the pancakes and start piling them up on my plate.

Dozer trots over and lies by my chair, giving me the doe eyes.

I take a pancake off my plate and give it to him. When I look up, Mia's gazing at me with a smile.

My chest starts to ache again.

"This is a good waffle," she says, tearing off another piece and putting it in her mouth. "Am I okay, to give Dozer some?" She gestures to my greedy ass dog who has swallowed the pancake I just gave him whole, and is now eyeballing the food in Mia's hand.

"Sure." I smile.

"Here, Dozer." She pats her leg, holding out the rest of her waffle to him.

Dozer is over there quick flash. Taking the waffle, he swallows it whole, then lays his head on her knee, gazing up at her for more.

And that's how the rest of breakfast goes. Dozer having Mia's full attention while she continues to feed him her breakfast, in-between feeding herself.

And I sit here watching. Like the third fucking wheel.

Seriously, this is getting out of hand. I'm getting cock blocked by my dog. Dozer and I are going to be having a serious man to man chat.

I'm feeling pretty relieved that we'll be out of here soon, and I'll get to have a little one on one time with her.

Yes, I'm completely aware of how pathetic I sound. You don't need to tell me.

"Thanks for breakfast," Mia says, wiping her mouth on a napkin. "It was delicious." She rises from her chair, handing me her plate. I put it on the tray.

"Are you sure you've eaten enough? Dozer had most of it." I nod at him, passed out on the floor, content with all the food he's had from her.

"I'm good." She presses her hand to her stomach indicating that she's full.

I don't know how she can be after the small amount she ate, but then she *is* only a tiny thing.

"You want a hand clearing away?" she offers.

"Nah, I'm good. I'll just dump them in the kitchen and wash

them later. You ready to head out for Farmington now?"

She pauses by the chair, her fingers gripping the edge of it. "Sure." She smiles.

It's one of her forced smiles. I've gotten pretty used to recognizing them over the last couple of days.

I lift the tray, balancing it on my forearm. "We can go later if you want?"

She contemplates this for a moment, then shakes her head. "No. We should go now." Her eyes meet mine. "If I don't, I'll chicken out."

Chapter Twelve

Mia

"My car or yours?" Jordan asks.

I look between his Mustang and my Mercedes.

The Mercedes that Oliver bought me two years ago. The day after he'd broken my arm.

Apparently he didn't mean to do it. It was an accident.

It didn't feel like an accident.

The car was supposed to be an apology.

All it did, all it *does*, is remind me of my weaknesses. Remind me of my life before now. Of every single beating before and after it.

It reminds me of him … *them*.

"Yours," I reply. "If that's okay?"

"It's more than okay." Smiling, Jordan pulls his keys from the pocket of his jeans.

"I'll pay for gas," I say as I walk toward his car. I don't want Jordan to think I'm taking advantage of his kind nature.

He stops by the hood, the smile quickly changing to a frown. "No way." He shakes his head.

"Of course I'm going to pay for the gas you're using to do me a favor." I open the door and slide onto the leather seat.

The car dips as Jordan folds his tall, lean body into the car. "No way. I'm not taking any money from you for gas. End of." His tone is forceful.

Instinctively, my shoulders pull in. The feeling of defeat washes over me.

Then out of nowhere, something spikes in me. Adrenalin

floods my bloodstream, kicking my senses to life.

I know it's only a small thing, and I know Jordan is trying to be kind in his own way … but I'm really tired of men telling me what to do and how things are going to be.

And I'm even *more* tired of the fact that I let them.

Well, no more.

I open the car door, climb out and shut the door behind me—a bit too hard—and head toward my car.

I know it looks like I'm overacting, but I've spent my whole life under-reacting. I need to start behaving like the woman I want to be, and this is me starting. Maybe it's not the right way, but I'm new to this, and apparently my words don't seem to work with Jordan, so I'm trying actions.

I hear his door open, and the sound of his confused voice follows me. "Mia, are you okay?"

"No." I toss the word over my shoulder.

My body is trembling with nerves, but I hold firm.

"What's wrong?" He sounds worried. I hear his door shut on a clunk.

I turn as I walk. "You. I don't do well being told what to do."

Wow. I can't believe I just said that! That was awesome!

Face forward, I keep heading for my car.

"Okay…" He sounds confused. "And where are you going?"

"To Farmington. Alone."

I hear his frustrated growl, then the sound of jogging footsteps over gravel heading my way.

I'd be lying if I said my heart wasn't in my stomach. Or that my pulse is beating so loud it's all I can hear.

I've just got my car door open when his hand comes on the door from behind me, holding it shut.

I bristle. He's close. Millimeters away I'd say.

My body reacts with fear … and lust.

Quite an abundance of lust, in fact.

I know I find Jordan attractive—okay, I've got the serious hots for him, but the level of desire I feel right now is off the charts. I've never felt anything like it. It's coming off me in

144

waves.

I'm all weak knees and wet panties. I've never felt this turned on before. One minute I'm pulling up my big girl panties, and the next I'm more than willing to drop them for him.

To say I'm confused is putting it mildly.

Getting back to my task at hand, I push all my confusing lusty feelings aside, take a deep breath in, square my shoulders, and turn around.

And … he's smiling.

No, he's grinning.

There's something else in his eyes. I think I know what it is because it more than likely mirrors my own eyes right now, but I could be wrong.

I'm not exactly the most experienced when it comes to men.

And Jordan and me right now? Not a good idea. No matter how sweet, funny, and gorgeous he might be. Yes, he is the epitome of sex. So freaking hot. I bet he's amazing in bed. I can only imagine what he looks like under those clothes of his…

I hear a low chuckle, and it snaps me out of my sex thoughts. I realize I've been ogling his body like a pervert.

Great. Just great.

My face flushes bright red. "Something funny?" I snap.

"Nope." Shaking his head, he flashes me a glimpse of his white teeth.

I tilt my head to the side with my hands on my hips. "So, why exactly are you laughing at me?"

His eyes flicker down my body, then back up again. I feel it, like he's just run his hands all over me.

"For a tiny thing, you sure can be feisty."

Arguing the tiny part would be a moot point because I am vertically challenged. But a 'thing'? Hmm … I don't think so.

I fold my arms over my chest and straighten my back. "I'm not a *thing*."

He eyes me for a long moment. His face suddenly a blank canvas. Then he leans down and says close to my ear, "Bad choice of words. You're right. You are most definitely not a thing. You, Mia … are most definitely a woman."

My stomach jolts, and I can't help the gasp that escapes me. I press my thighs together.

From the laugh and cocky look on his face, he totally knows the effect he just had on me.

It annoys me.

And turns me on.

In equal parts.

Smiling, he runs a hand through his hair. "Fine. We'll do this your way. You can pay for the gas."

What?

What were we talking about again?

Oh, yeah. Paying for gas.

Wow. Well … that was easy.

I've never in my life won an argument. And that instantly makes me suspicious.

I narrow my gaze on him. "Why are you giving in so easy?"

"Why are you questioning it?"

"Because … uh … because…" *Because this isn't life as I know it.* "Because the men I know don't back down so easy." *They don't back down ever.*

Sorrow flickers briefly in his eyes. I hate the way it makes me feel.

Exposed and vulnerable.

The two things I really do not want to feel right now.

"Men you *knew*, Mia," he says. "Not me. And surprisingly, I can compromise. Not all the time, so don't go getting used to it." He grins. "I just don't want to spend the next however long disagreeing with you over this when I know I'm gonna end up giving into you anyway."

"Because?"

Taking a step back, his arms fold over his broad chest.

"Because you're a hard girl to say no to."

Oh. Okay then.

I suddenly feel lightheaded.

And light-hearted.

"So are you going to take this win and get back in the car?" He sweeps a hand in the direction of the Mustang. "Or are you going to stand here all day being stubborn about it?"

I bite the smile that's forcing its way onto my lips. "Well, I'm not one to gloat." I throw him a smug grin as I walk past him, destination Mustang.

He's quiet behind me. I only know he's following from the crunch of the gravel under his feet.

"Did you know you swing your ass when you walk?"

What?

I stop, shocked that he's just said that about my ass. And also a little turned on hearing him talk about my ass.

Turned on. Again.

Jesus.

I didn't actually know that I swing my ass when I walk, but that's beside the point. I scowl at him over my shoulder. "And your point is?"

"No point. Just an observation." He holds his hands up in surrender, and his eyes crinkle from the smile on his face. "It's kinda cute is all."

"Cute?" I frown, ignoring the pull I feel for him in my lower half. "I'm not cute."

"I never said *you* were cute. I said your ass-swinging was cute." He gives me a wicked grin.

My face goes beet red. Embarrassed, I start walking again, ignoring his soft laughter behind me.

By the time I've reached his car, I'm feeling out of sorts. Vulnerable, edgy...

Horny.

Totally not how I expected to be feeling this morning. Jordan just seems able to throw me off kilter at any given notice. I've never known anyone like him.

And today, things between us have shifted. I'm not really sure where to, or what's going on, but something is definitely different between us.

We get in the car at the same time. I buckle up as Jordan

turns the ignition. The engine is rumbling, ready to go, but we don't move.

I look across at him.

His head is tilted my way, his deep eyes staring at me, and he's wearing an expression I can't decipher.

"What?" I ask, feeling self-conscious. I push my short strands behind my ear, feeling myself heating under his stare.

He shakes his head, blinking himself free. "Nothing. I'm just really digging this assertive side of you." A smile. Then he looks behind him and sets the car in reverse.

I'm left reeling.

Jordan digs me.

He *digs* me.

And just like that, the cold block of ice I carry around in my chest melts.

Jordan does most of the talking on the drive to Farmington. I think he's doing it to keep my mind busy, and off what I'm going to Farmington for.

I was good until we got about ten minutes away from Farmington. I broke out in a cold sweat, and when we crossed the city limits a few minutes back, my heart went into overdrive. I'm pretty sure a panic attack is on the horizon.

It takes me a moment to realize the car has stopped.

"Are we here?" My eyes are wide and alert like a rabbit.

"A block away. I thought you might want a moment to yourself before we go to her house."

"It might not be her."

I look at him. I know there's an edge of desperation in my eyes and voice.

"It might not be," he says slowly. "But if it is?"

I shrug, forcing a casualness I don't feel. "Then I've found my mother."

We both stare ahead, sitting in silence.

"You ready?" he asks.

"Yeah."

Jordan turns the engine on and pulls back out onto the street. A few minutes later he pulls up front a red brick house.

I turn to him. "Will you come with me?"

He smiles. "Already was."

Taking a deep breath, I slip my sunglass on and climb out the car.

I hesitate at the top of the walk. Jordan takes my hand and tugs me forward.

Reaching the door, Jordan doesn't let go of my hand as he leans across me and presses the bell. The scent of his aftershave momentarily soothes me.

"What do I say?" I whisper.

"Just ask if Anna Monroe lives here, and we'll go from there."

Meeting his eyes, I nod.

Then I hear footsteps in the hall. A figure approaches the door. My body freezes. Jordan gives my hand a reassuring squeeze.

"You're okay. I'm here," he whispers softly.

The door opens, revealing a Chinese lady.

Nope. Not her.

Is it strange that I feel relief at this thought?

There's definitely not a trace of Chinese in my pale skin, blonde hair and blue eyes. Unless she's not Anna Monroe.

I just need her to confirm this, and then I'm out of here.

"Can I help you?" she asks, eyes moving between Jordan and me.

"I was, um—" I clear my throat. "I, um…" *Why can't I get my voice to work?*

"Does Anna Monroe live here?" Jordan's voice come from beside me.

She blinks from me to Jordan. "Yes," she answers slowly.

"Would it be possible to speak with her?"

"And you are…?"

"Sorry. My name is Jordan, and this is Mia."

She shifts on the spot, crossing her arms over her chest. "I'm Anna Monroe."

I exhale the breath I didn't realize I was holding, and then I'm out of there. Turning, and pulling my hand free from Jordan's, I run down that path away from them both.

I know it's wrong for me to abandon Jordan, but I can't stop my legs from moving.

My heart is pounding. Blood is roaring in my ears. And all I want to do is eat.

And throw up.

I really need to throw up.

Climbing back into the safety of Jordan's Mustang, I yank my sunglasses off, and sit on my hands, trying to steady my heart and calm the war raging on inside me.

Jordan gets in the car a few minutes later. He turns to me. "So … she's not your mom."

"What gave it away?"

I'm at an impasse at the moment. I either laugh or cry. I really don't want to cry in front of Jordan, so laughter it is. It bursts out of me. I know I'm probably coming off as a little crazy, but I can't seem to stop, or find the will to care.

When I finally regain control of myself, wiping my eyes dry on my hands, I find Jordan staring at me with an expression on his face that I've never seen before.

No one has ever looked at me like he is looking at me right now. Like he cares. *Really* cares.

He relaxes his gaze, a wicked grin sliding onto his lips. "You seem to be taking the disappointment well."

His smile has me laughing again.

"Sorry, I abandoned you back there." I gesture, still a little breathless from my crazy laughing.

"No worries. Come on." He starts the car. "Let's go grab some lunch."

Food. Not a good idea for me right now.

"I'm not hungry." I put my seatbelt on.

"Well, I am. You can watch me eat." He flashes me those whites of his, and I'm too dazzled by him to disagree.

We end up in a coffee shop that Jordan seems to know well. Apparently, this place make the best Key Lime pie in the world.

I'll have to take his word on it because eating right now is not a good idea, not while I'm with Jordan. I'm afraid that if I start, I won't be able to stop, and then I'll end up exposing a part of myself that I *never* want anyone to see, especially not him.

"Guess it was a waste of time coming all the way out here." I sigh.

"Depends on how you look at it."

I rest my elbow on the table and prop my chin on my hand. "And how would you look at it?"

He leans back in his seat. "That it's one less Anna Monroe on the list. Narrows the odds. Leaves us with two. So that's a fifty/fifty chance on the next one we pick being your mother."

Or neither are her.

"And I'm getting to eat the pie I love. I'd call it a lose/win."

"Do you assess everything that way?"

His eyes darken. "Not everything." His lips lift with a flirtatious tilt as he leans closer, over the table. He lowers his voice. "Only things that I know are a sure thing. And when I *really* want something ... I get it."

Gulp. Heat infuses my skin, firing off my pulse.

The waitress interrupts our moment, arriving with our coffee and Jordan's pie.

I'm relieved.

And disappointed.

He was absolutely, definitely flirting with me then.

I'm not complaining. It's nice to have someone as gorgeous as Jordan flirt with me. I guess what bothers me is that I don't know what it means for him. Or more so, what I want it to mean for me.

"How's your pie?" I ask, watching him dig into it like it's god made.

"So good," he murmurs through a mouthful. The sound is as delicious as he looks. "You wanna try?" He holds out a pie-filled fork.

I shake my head.

"You're missing out on the best pie you'll ever taste." He waggles the fork in front of my face.

Laughing, I shake my head again.

He grins and puts the fork in this mouth, letting out an over-exaggerated groan of pleasure.

For a split second, I actually wish I was the fork.

I have serious issues.

I pour some sugar in my coffee. "Thanks for coming with me today. It really means a lot."

"We're friends. Friends help each other out."

"We're friends?" I tease, unable to help the smile that's crept on my face.

He lifts a dark brow. "Hadn't we already established that?"

I bring the cup to my lips and blow on the hot coffee. "I don't think it had been confirmed, no."

"Well, consider it confirmed." He digs his fork in his pie, eyes smiling. "We're friends."

With benefits?

Holy cow, I can't believe I just thought that.

"Well, well … Jordan Matthews. Didn't expect to ever see you here again."

I turn my head and see a guy about Jordan's height and build, shaved head, arms sleeved with tattoos, heading in our direction.

My eyes move beyond him, and see two other guys walking behind, both tall and skinny.

From the corner of my eye, I can see that Jordan's whole

demeanor has changed. His body is rigid, tense.

The air instantly prickles with discomfort, and the sound of Jordan's fork clattering to the plate makes me jump.

"Turn the fuck around and walk away, Donnie," Jordan hisses, the level of anger in his voice surprises me.

Donnie lets out a laugh. He grabs a chair from the empty table by us and sits down, his front to its back.

On closer inspection, I spy a tattoo on Donnie's neck. It says *Fuck You.*

Nice

"That's no way to greet an old friend," he says.

Jordan laughs a hollow sound. "That's the last thing I'd ever refer to you as."

"You're breaking my heart here, Matthews." Donnie slaps a hand over his chest before moving his gaze to me. "And who do we have here?"

The way he looks at me sets alarm bells ringing in my head. I'm familiar with the look. I've seen it before from Forbes.

I curl my fingers together in my lap.

"Don't answer that." My eyes shoot up to Jordan's. He stares at me for a long second, trying to convey something in his eyes that I can't quite grasp.

He turns his head to Donnie. "Don't fuckin' talk to her again, or I'll—"

"You'll what?" Donnie tilts his head to the side. "What ya gonna do, Jordan? Set your daddy on me?"

Jordan's jaw sets rigid. "Your issue is with me," he grinds out. "So say whatever the fuck it is you need to say, then fuck off back to your cave, you sorry piece of shit. Just leave her out of it."

Donnie lets out another laugh. "Jeez! Easy now. You must actually like this chick. Never thought I'd see the day. Isn't your motto 'fuck 'em slow, leave 'em fast'? Gotta say though, can't blame you with this one … she is *fuck hot.*"

"Like your girlfriend was," Jordan bites out.

Donnie's face goes hard like granite, and for a moment I

think he's going to hit Jordan.

Instead, his eyes slide back to me. He gives my body a full perverse perusal. It makes my stomach turn. "Bitch, when he's done with you, you pay me a visit, and I'll show you a good time."

Jordan jerks out of his chair, causing it to bang to the floor, bringing mine, and every eye in this place, to him.

"I said, leave her the fuck out of it!" Jordan is bristling anger.

Donnie slowly gets to his feet, shifting his chair aside.

A glance to his friends tells me they're standing too. The situation feels dangerous. My insides start to tremble with the possibility of what's going to happen.

"Let's go." Jordan's harsh voice comes my way as he jerks out a hand for me to take.

I look at Donnie who is staring hard at Jordan. I slip my hand into Jordan's, allowing him to pull me to my feet.

The instant my skin makes contact with his, I feel the true level of Jordan's anger. It's rolling off him in waves and seeping straight into me.

Surprisingly, I don't feel afraid. I don't worry as to what will happen when we leave here, and I'm alone with him. What I actually feel right now is something I've never felt before.

I feel safe in his hands.

I know without a doubt that Jordan won't hurt me. And I know unequivocally that he won't let anything happen to me.

Jordan pulls on my hand, leading me through the coffee shop, away from Donnie, and toward the exit.

"How's your dad doing nowadays?" Donnie calls out.

Jordan stops abruptly. I crash into his back. His hand tightens around mine gripping it to the point of almost pain.

"Heard he lost his badge. Real shame that, quality fuckin' pig that he was."

Jordan turns, putting me behind him.

Donnie and his buddies are in the middle of the coffee shop now. Only a few tables parting them from us. I can tell from their stances and body language that they are itching for a fight. And

154

by the way Jordan is bristling beside me, it seems like he's going to give them one.

"I bet you really wanna hit me right now, don't ya?" Donnie smirks. "How does this sound – I'll let you have the first hit. Just you and me, one on one. Whaddya say? Winner gets your girl."

Donnie tilts his head my way, the look in his eyes repulsive.

He thinks he's affecting me. He's wrong. I was raised by worse. But he is affecting Jordan. I can feel how tightly wound he is.

Jordan pushes his hand into his jean pocket, then presses what feels like car keys into my palm.

I look up at him, confused.

"Go to my car," he says with a low voice. "Get in and lock all the doors. If I'm not out in five minutes, drive straight back to Durango. Don't go to the hotel. Go to the diner, to Beth."

I curl my hand around the keys. "And then what?"

"And then…" He shakes his head slowly.

Self-preservation is telling me to do what he's saying and leave this coffee shop, but I've never been very good at listening to my self-preservation.

"I'm not leaving here without you." I lift my chin and put my hand on his arm.

I'm purposely and willingly touching a man filled with anger. That's a really big thing for me. Huge, in fact.

Jordan's eyes flare, but it doesn't deter me. "Don't give him what he wants. You don't have to fight this guy."

His eyes close as if he's in pain. "You don't understand."

"Are you gonna stop whispering sweet nothings to the hot piece of ass, and let us get this over with?" Donnie cracks his knuckles.

Jordan's eyes leave me, and go straight to Donnie, hardening on him.

I see the other patrons heading out the back door.

"Leave now or I'm calling the police!" a shaky female voice, assumedly the waitress, says from behind us.

"You do that, sweet cheeks," Donnie laughs. "I'll be done

155

with him before they even arrive."

Ignoring everyone else, I keep my focus on Jordan. "Jordan." He looks back to me. "I might not understand, but I don't need to because I know that violence never solves anything. It won't solve whatever *this* is."

He stares down at me. I can see a war raging in his eyes.

After what feels like forever, he exhales. "Okay."

I nearly cry out with relief when he takes my hand and shifts the car keys back to his.

"Not today, Donnie." He turns, walking away, taking me with him.

"What? You're leaving! You're a fuckin' pussy, Matthews! A motherfucking pussy!"

My heart is beating so hard, afraid that Donnie won't simply let Jordan walk away from this and that he'll come after him.

Jordan pulls some bills from his pocket and drops them down on the counter as we pass by the wide-eyed waitress. "I'm real sorry for the trouble, ma'am."

Then we are of out of there.

I glance over my shoulder to see if Donnie is following us. He's not.

Jordan squeezes my hand, pulling my attention back. "He won't follow us. Despite his bravado, he's a fuckin' pussy. He challenged me in there because he wants an audience. He wants me to hit him first so he can get what he thinks is his revenge."

I don't question what that revenge is. Jordan will tell me if he wants to.

We're back at the Mustang in record time. He unlocks it, letting me in.

I've just clipped my seatbelt when I hear the sound of Jordan yelling. Seatbelt off, I'm back out of the car just in time to see Jordan's fist connecting with the wooden fence by the parking space. "FUCK! Motherfucking fuck!"

Normally, in a situation like this I would be paralyzed by fear, but not with him. My feet carry me toward Jordan without a second thought.

He's standing with his forehead pressed to the fence he just beat on and his hand clutched to his heaving chest.

"Are you okay?" I ask softly.

"I'm fine."

"You don't look it."

"Well I am."

"Can I take a look at your hand?"

"Why?"

"Because you just punched a fence and the med student in me wants to make sure it's okay."

He tilts his face in my direction. The look on his face is hard. His eyes cold. The warmth I'm used to gone.

"I don't need *you* to fix me, Mia."

I feel my face flush under the harsh sting of his words.

Clearing my suddenly full throat, I say, "I'm not trying to fix you. I just want to make sure you haven't broken any bones. Nothing more."

His eyes close on a long blink.

Stepping away from the fence, he moves toward me and holds his injured hand out.

I take it in my own, ignoring the rush of sensation I feel, and begin checking his hand, making sure he hasn't broken anything.

"All fine." I look up at him a few moments later. "It's just going to be swollen and bruised for a few days. Could do with some ice on it, and we need to clean that out." I run my fingertip over the small graze on his knuckle.

I lift my eyes to his, finding Jordan already staring down at me with dark eyes. The air instantly shifts. My pulse quickens. Fireflies swarm my stomach, setting my insides on fire.

And what do I do?

I release his hand and step back, putting space between us.

I might not be afraid of Jordan, but I know what anger and sex combined can mean to a man.

Not that Jordan and I will be having sex. I just don't want to confuse an already confusing situation.

He flexes his fingers out. "All you seem to do is fix us

Matthew men up." I notice his voice sounds gruff.

"I don't mind." I shrug.

"Mia…" He rubs his good hand over his hair, exhaling heavily. "I'm sorry I lost it just then. There's just a real big ugly history with me and Donnie. It's no excuse, but it was either that fence or his face. And better the fence, right?"

"Right." I smile. "But I don't think the fence would agree with you." I poke my index finger through the hole his anger has left in it.

Jordan's body starts to shake with silent laughter. His eyes smile at me.

I let out a little laugh. "Do you want to talk about it?"

His humor quickly dissipates. He stares at the ground for a long moment. "No," he says, lifting his head. "Right now, I just wanna get drunk."

It's pretty early to be drinking … but what the hell. I can call day drinking part of the new me.

"I could go for that." I smile.

"That's my girl." He grins.

His girl?

His girl.

We drive back to Durango and head straight into town where the bars are. Jordan says he'll leave his car there and pick it up in the morning, so we'll be getting a cab back to the hotel when we're done.

I've never done anything like this before – going to a bar in the afternoon with the intention of getting drunk.

I'm kind of excited. Okay, I'm freaking thrilled. I feel like a rebel.

Sad, but true.

Jordan has brought me to a bar aptly called 'The Bar'. I'm

sitting at a table in the back. Jordan's gone to get us some drinks. This round is his.

The next is definitely mine.

He comes back with four shots in his hands, two beer bottle under his arm. I guess we're starting big.

"Tequila," he says, putting two of the shots down in front of me.

I've never tried tequila, but what the hell. This is the new Mia. The new Mia could be a tequila drinker.

I pick up one of the shot glasses, but his voice stops me. "Salt first."

Taking the seat across from me, Jordan picks up the salt shaker from the table.

"Hand," he says.

I hold my right hand out to him.

When he takes hold, my body instantly fires on all cylinders, the traction heading straight to the right parts of my anatomy.

He pours a line of salt on the side of my hand and says, "Lick."

Jesus Christ. That sounded really hot.

I could really get into this tequila drinking. Especially if I get to hear Jordan talk to me like that.

Doing as told, I lean my mouth down to my hand and lick the salt off.

Jordan's eyes haven't moved from me. I see them flare the moment my tongue touches the salt.

I may or may not make the most of the moment, taking my time licking the salt from my hand.

I kind of like the affect it has on him.

When the salt is safely in my mouth, dissolving away, Jordan says in a really hoarse voice, "Now, drink the shot."

I pick one of the shot glasses up. Glass to my lips, I down the tequila.

"Holy crap!" I'm breathing fire. I place the back of my hand to my damp lips, my eyes watering from the burn.

Jordan laughs. "Chase it with the beer, it'll take the edge off.

I forgot to bring the lime over."

I take a big mouthful of beer.

My eyes are still watering, so I run my fingers under them catching the leaks.

"Not a tequila drinker?" He grins.

I shake my head. "This is the first time I've had it."

"And what do you think?"

"Tastes like crap." I grin. "But it does the job. Am I drinking alone?" I nod at his untouched drinks.

He shakes his head, then makes quick work of his own salt licking. He throws back his shot with far more ease than I just did.

Glass down, his eyes smile brightly at me.

I lean back in my chair, taking my beer bottle with me, and start picking at the label. "You look like a seasoned pro at that."

"The tequila?"

"Hmm." I nod.

"I'm a hard liquor man. What can I say." He grins and picks the salt shaker up. "You want another hit?"

I flinch. He notices.

"I meant the salt, Mia. Do you want another hit of salt for your next shot?"

I shift, embarrassed. My face burns with my shame. "Uh … yes." Biting my lip, I hold my hand out to him.

Instead of pouring the salt, Jordan encases my hand in his. Normally I would feel intimidated by this, but with Jordan, I don't. His hold feels safe, gentle … kind.

For the first time in my life, I'm with a man who literally has me in his hand, and I don't feel fear.

Instead, I find myself feeling connected to another human being in a way I never thought possible.

Releasing his hold a little, he turns my hand over and runs his thumb over my palm. It leaves a delicious trail of sensation in its wake.

My emotions start to tilt on their axis, and straight in his direction.

Lifting my eyes, Jordan's gaze instantly captures mine. Without moving his eyes from me, he runs his fingers to my wrist, guiding my hand to the side.

He slides his hand back along mine. Palm to palm. His fingers gently rest against my pulse point.

I can only hope he can't feel that it's practically beating the blood out of my body.

Tilting the salt shaker over our joined hands, he runs two lines of salt. One on mine. One on his.

"Do you mind if I…?" He tilts his head in the direction of our connected hands.

Unsure of the question, I raise a questioning brow.

"The salt?"

Still lost, I just nod my head, not wanting to come across as stupid. Hoping that by agreeing, I don't end up looking stupid.

Then Jordan does something that I will forever remember as the most insanely intimate moment of my life.

And his question makes perfect sense when he leans forward and licks the salt from my hand. Slowly.

Holy. Crap.

Head still lowered, he looks up at me through long dark lashes with a look that turns me to mush.

"Your turn."

What? He wants me to lick the salt from his hand?

Holy Jesus.

This is a really sexy thing to do. I'm not sexy. I have no clue how to do sexy.

No, come on, I can do this. New Mia here. I can lick salt from Jordan's hand. No big deal.

Taking in a breath, I lean forward and sticking the tip of my tongue out, I lick the salt up onto my tongue.

All I can taste is him. The salt doesn't even register. And now I'm begrudged to drink the tequila and take away his taste in my mouth.

"Drink," he says, his voice sounding husky.

Glass to my lips, I tip the shot back at exactly the same time as he does.

His hand leaves mine.

I'm left feeling bereft without his touch, dizzy from the alcohol, and wondering if that just actually happened.

My hands start to fidget of their own accord. I reach for my beer.

"Second time easier?" Jordan asks, sounding completely normal as though we haven't just licked salt of one another's hands. Or maybe this is just what normal people do. What do I know?

Clearing my throat, I force a casualness I don't feel. "Much easier."

He smiles.

I start in on my beer label again.

"So…" he says.

"So…"

"I guess I should explain about earlier, what happened in the coffee shop."

"Only if you want to."

He gives a tight-lipped smile. "You remember I told you I used to gamble?"

I nod.

His eyes lower. "After my mom had died, I went off the rails. I'd always liked to play cards … but this went further. I was playing, gambling way more than I ever had. I was winning for a while, then the losing streak kicked in. I kept trying to make back what I lost, but before I knew it, I'd run up a massive debt that I had no way of paying back."

"You owed the money to Donnie?"

He laughs a humorless sound. "No, Donnie's just the hired monkey. I owed money to the guy he works for – Max. I used to regular a few places in Farmington to play, then I got involved in a poker ring that Max ran. There's not much in the way here for card players like me. Like I was," he corrects. "But over in Farmington … there's plenty for a seasoned player." He leans close, elbows on the table as he scrubs his hands over his face.

162

He folds his arms on the table, looking down. "I'm just real sorry that you got pulled in it back there, Mia."

That's why he didn't want me to tell Donnie my name. He didn't want those horrible people knowing who I am. He was trying to protect me.

Something about that touches me.

"It doesn't matter. I'm just glad you're okay now." I put my beer down. "Do you still owe the money? Is that why he was trying to pick a fight with you?"

If he does, I'll pay his debt. It's not like I can't afford it. He's been so good to me, helping me with the Anna stuff, and I can finally do something good with Oliver's money. Helping Jordan would count as something good to me.

"No, my debt was paid." He scrubs his hand over his face again. "My dad. He used the money from my mom's life insurance."

Oh. Right.

Now I know where his guilt comes from.

I try to conjure up something worthy to say, something to make him feel better, but I come up with nothing. So I say the only thing I can, "I'm so sorry, Jordan."

He takes a long drink of his beer. Drying off his mouth with the back of his hand, he shakes his head. "Don't feel bad for me. I don't deserve your kindness." His eyes close on a long blink. "Do you remember I told you that my dad used to be a cop?"

I nod and take a drink of beer.

"Before the debt was paid, before my dad knew about any of it, the gambling and how deep in I was, I was out one night in town. Not in this bar," he adds like that would have some bearing on his story. "I was out drinking with some buddies of mine, and later on in the night I was … uh, leaving the bar with … a girl." He scratches his cheek, looking uncomfortable.

I ignore the unpleasant twist in my stomach brought on by the knowledge of Jordan leaving a bar with a girl he more than likely wanted to have sex with.

"We were headed to get a cab, when I was jumped by Donnie

163

and a couple of his guys. It was meant to a warning beating because I hadn't paid up, but I made the mistake of fighting back, instead of just taking it – I'm not one to take a beating." He shrugs. "And I … mid-fight, to antagonize him … kind of told Donnie that I'd had sex with his girlfriend."

"Had you?"

"Yes."

Stomach twist. "Oh."

"It was a one-time thing. A mistake." He sighs. "But after telling him … well, that was when Donnie pulled out a baseball bat."

"Dear god." I wince, closing my eyes, feeling his pain as if was my own. I know how bad beatings can be. Especially when a weapon is involved.

"Anyway." He drags his hand through his hair. "The girl ran back to the bar while it was happening, got my friends out to help me, called the cops…"

I see the rest in his eyes. "Your dad?"

"Yeah. He lost his shit when he saw the state they had left me in. The bastards had fucked off the second they heard sirens, but my dad didn't let up. He eventually found Donnie a couple of blocks over, and…" He lets out a long sigh. "…he beat the shit out of Donnie—who was unarmed by this point. He'd dropped the bat running. My dad hurt him. Really hurt him. Left him in a bad way."

Jordan's eyes search out mine. "You gotta understand, Mia … my dad … he's not violent by nature. It's just not who is. He's a great guy – *really* great. The best. And he deserves a kid better than me. It was just … well, Mom hadn't long since passed, and I'm his only child. I guess he just lost it when he saw me."

I nod, letting him know I understand. I only wish I'd had a dad as caring and protective as Jordan's.

"Dad was suspended pending investigation." He leans back in his chair and rubs his eye. "After the investigation, he was found guilty and stripped of his badge and gun. He can't ever work in law enforcement again – courtesy of my fuck-up." He lifts his bottle in mock-cheers, then presses it to his lips and tips his head back.

"Did anything happen to Donnie for what he did to you?"

Jordan lets out a hollow laugh. "He got a twelve month suspended sentence."

"And you still had to pay off the debt you owed?"

"Yep. Just because Donnie and his boys kicked my ass, didn't make the debt with Max go away. So dad lost out again. Bailed me out plus 'interest'. I started attending Gamblers Anonymous and got clean. I still attend the meetings now." His eyes seek mine out as though it really matters to him that I know this. "And now we're flat broke, trying to keep a failing hotel afloat, and Donnie is still out for my blood for what my dad did to him. And because I screwed his now ex-girlfriend." He gives a weak smile as he puts his bottle down.

Ignoring the third ache of pain I feel at Jordan's crass words over his past sexual activity, I lean forward, placing my arms on the table. "I really am sorry this happened to you."

"It didn't happen to me. Everything that happened was my own fault. I fucked up my life and took my dad down with me."

"Your life is not fucked up, and you definitely didn't take your dad down with you."

"It is. And I did. I'm not a good person, Mia." He shakes his head, leaning back in his seat.

I can feel him withdrawing from me. I don't like the way it feels.

"You've been good to me," I press.

He lets out a hollow laugh. "You're probably the only person on this planet who can say that." His eyes fix me with a stare. "And I haven't really done that much for you, Mia. Not really." He looks away from me. "There's nothing good about me, *believe me*."

"I think there is a lot that's good about you," I push back. *So much. Too much.*

His eyes come back to me. Dark and angry. "Did you not hear what I said before? I completely screwed everything up. I

165

fucked up my dad's life."

"No. Everything your dad did was his choice."

"As a result of my actions." I can see his anger rising.

This is normally the point where I back down, give in, and agree – not that I would have ever argued this far. But with Jordan I know I can, and I'm not backing down. Not this time.

"Everyone is responsible for their own actions."

"I fuck random women all the time. I use them for sex, then discard them like trash."

My breath catches in my throat, and a jealousy I shouldn't feel hits me with a harsh wallop.

Jordan grabs his beer and takes a long drink. His eyes don't leave mine for a moment, almost like he's daring me to look away, but I don't … *I can't.*

His confession just doesn't fit with the Jordan I've gotten to know. But then when do you really ever know anyone?

I, better than anyone, know that.

But the thing annoying me most is the stupid little voice on repeat in my head. The voice that wonders why, if Jordan does what he says he does, hasn't he hit on me?

I hate that I think this. I shouldn't want him to hit on me, but I did … do.

I can feel my skin prickling.

Tapping my fingertips on the table, I swallow down my feelings. "And your point is?"

My response surprises him. I see it in the widening of his eyes.

Trying to hide his surprise, he straightens his back like he's gearing up for round two.

"My point is … I'm responsible for those actions. They're not the actions of a good person."

He wants me to dislike him. Why?

I shrug, forcing a casual I don't feel. Then using his earlier words against him, I simply say, "Depends on how you look at it."

His eyebrows lift.

I've got his attention now.

He leans close, arms perched on the table. "And how are you looking at it, *Mia*?"

God, I totally love how he says my name.

"Well … the way I see it, you're a lose/win. I've known men who do far worse things than just sleep around with lots of different women."

Okay, so Forbes did that too – but that's not going to help make my point, so I'll just eclipse the fact.

His brow furrows. "Your ex?"

I take a deep breath. "The black eye wasn't the first time he hit me." I rub the instant chills from my arms.

I see Jordan's jaw tighten. "How often?" His words come out punchy.

"Um…" I lift my suddenly heavy shoulders, my confidence slipping. Memories slam into my mind. A blur of memories, mixed with two faces.

Oliver…
Forbes…

Slammed up against a wall.
Thrown to a floor.
Pinned to a bed.
Thrown down the stairs.
Hit.
Slapped.
Kicked.
Punched.
Beaten.
Broken ribs, wrist, fingers…
Heart–broken – irreparable.
Worthless.
In pain.
All the time.
It never stopped.

No one ever saved me…

"Mia." I feel Jordan squeezing my hand.

I blink my eyes clear.

"Jesus, are you okay?" His voice is soft, but his jaw is tight.

"Yeah, I … uh." I touch a hand to my face, wanting to cover any emotion showing on it.

"I lost you again. Where did you go?" he asks gently.

Closing my eyes on a long blink, I shake my head and slide my hand from his.

I hear the grind in his teeth as he speaks, "How often did he hurt you?"

Swallowing down my shame, I answer, quietly, "More often than not."

His face freezes. He looks like he's in pain. "Why did you stay?" It sounds more like a plea than a question.

"It's a long story."

"I've got all night … week … year."

"It's not worth going into."

He drives his hand into his hair. "But you left. Came here. What gave you the push?"

"He tried to rape me."

I see my words hit him like a physical blow. He recoils, hands white-knuckle around the edge of the table.

There's this horrible strained pause between us.

I feel sick.

My body has broken out in a cold sweat. Tremors running all over, settling into my stomach, a pit of fear and self-loathing.

I need food. And privacy.

Now.

I curl my fingernails into the bed of my hand, trying to control my urge to leap from my chair and run to the nearest convenience store.

Jordan's eyes have not left my face. A myriad of emotions scrolling through them. I don't want to look at him right now, but I can't seem to bring myself to look away.

"He did *what*?" I don't know if he actually says the words, or mouths them because my ears are ringing with the truth.

I pull my top lip into my mouth, biting it.

I blink once. Twice. "He tried to … rape me."

"Jesus fuckin' Christ," Jordan whispers angrily. Elbows on the table, he drops his head in his hands.

I shouldn't have told him. Why did I tell him?

I shrink back into my seat, wishing to be invisible. Wanting to rewind time.

The atmosphere is awful. The silence painful.

When I reach the point where I can't take it anymore, which isn't long, I push my chair out.

Jordan's head snaps up at the sound of wood scraping wood. "Where are you going?"

"I, uh…" I glance in the direction of the exit.

His eyes follow mine, then flicker back. "Don't go." He blows out a breath, pressing at his temples with his fingers. "I'm sorry, I'm not handling this right … I just—" He shakes his head, leaning close to me. "Jesus, Mia, I just can't handle the thought of anyone hurting you – not like that – not at all."

His words make it hard to breath. They matter to me more than I care to admit right now.

When his eyes rest on my face, they soften. "What can I do … to help you?"

And those squeeze my heart.

"Nothing." I swallow past the huge lump in my throat. "I'm fine."

"I don't buy it. I can see it in your eyes that you're far from fine." A storm rolls in over his features. "Tell me where he lives."

"W-what? Why?"

"Why do you think?"

I tense. "Jordan, I didn't tell you so you'd go beat him up." *Why did I tell him?* "I told you because…" I shake my head. "I don't want you to beat Forbes up."

He frowns. "That's his name – Forbes?"

I realize this is the first time I've spoken his name in almost a week. And I wonder if Jordan knowing his name is a mistake on my part.

I say nothing.

He breaks my gaze and rests his elbows on the table, putting his head in his hands again. Tension is pouring off him in waves.

Tilting his head back slightly, his eyes lift to mine. There's a vulnerability in them that surprises me. "I need to do something, Mia."

"Why?" My words are quiet.

"Because ... I just do." His are soft.

"You are doing something. You're being my friend. That counts for a lot."

"I need to do more."

"No." I shake my head, edging off my seat. "I don't need more. I shouldn't have told you. It was a mistake."

The skin around his eyes tightens. "You're wrong. The only mistake was not telling me sooner." He reaches over and grabs my hand, keeping me from leaving.

I try to ignore the way his touch makes me feel. The ache in my chest of longing for something I never knew I wanted until now.

"I wish you'd told me before now," he adds quietly.

He rubs his thumb gently over the back of my hand. It's an unconscious move on his part but means so much to me.

Men don't touch me gently. Not like this. Not ever.

And he's done it twice in the matter of minutes.

"Have you told anyone else, aside from me, what he did to you?"

My eyes widen in horror at the thought. I'm still in shock that I told him and trying to figure out what that means, let alone tell anyone else.

"I'll take that as a no." He shakes his head sadly. "You need to report this to the police. He can't get away with what he did to you."

"What? No." Panic squeezes my stomach like a vice.

"Mia..."

170

"*No!*" My voice is harsher than I knew I had in me. I rear back, taking my hand with me.

Whatever Jordan sees on my face has him placating, "Okay. No police." He lays his palms on the table between us. "Just do one thing for me…?" When I don't respond, he continues. "Don't keep anything else locked up inside you. You need someone to talk to, someone to trust – that person is me. I won't ever judge you. I will *never* hurt you. And I won't let you down. I might have done some shit things in my past, I might have treated people badly … people who didn't deserve it, but I won't do that to you – *ever*. I promise."

His words are impassioned, his face earnest. "You have me at my word. I won't break it." His mouth lifts into a gentle smile.

I want to believe him. I do.

But it's just not in me to be able to trust. The ability is not something I'm gifted with.

I don't know what to say. So I do what I do best, and avoid. Smiling, I nod and ask, "So, what now?"

Jordan's dark eyes are curious on my face. For a moment, I wonder if he's going to push it further.

He doesn't.

"Now…" he says, rising from his seat, "we drink more tequila."

Chapter Thirteen

Jordan

I never thought I would want to be close to a woman as I do Mia.

But I do. I'm just not entirely sure why.

And even though I am close to her, possibly closer than anyone has ever had the privilege to be, I want more.

I want *all* of her. In every way possible.

The morning after the tequila had worn off, I was worried things would be weird between us.

Not because of what Mia told me had happened to her … fuck, no.

That changed nothing in the way I see her, the way I want her.

The only thing that has changed is how deeply I want to bury my fist into that asshole's face.

I thought I was pissed when I knew he'd hit her. But knowing what I know now, my anger has gone so beyond pissed there isn't even a word for it. All I know is I want to kill a man I've never met, and I'd do it with absolute fucking pleasure.

The look on Mia's face when she told me what he did and how he hurt her … it was shame. Like somehow what happened was her fault.

It made me hurt for her … for me. It's hard to distinguish between the two now. Her pain has somehow entwined with mine.

But that's Mia. She's not a person you meet, then just simply walk away from.

She embeds herself so deep within you, without even meaning to, that you have no choice but to feel her. That's what she's done to me.

And I'm so fucking happy for it.

When I'm around her, I actually feel alive in a way I haven't for a long time. And I'm going to spend every moment I have with her, making her see that none of what happened to her was her fault.

I'm going to make her see herself the way I see her.

Incredible. Strong. Beautiful.

So fucking beautiful.

It hurts to want her in the way I do and not be able to have her. After my brain connected with what I'd told her in that bar about myself, I was worried shitless that I might have lost her.

I couldn't have been more wrong.

Mia doesn't care about any of it – the mistakes I've made. She doesn't look at me different. She doesn't judge me.

She sees more in me.

She sees the real *me*. The Jordan I had long forgotten existed.

The me before the gambling, and the women … before the epic fuck-ups.

I'd spent so long believing I was a bad person. And I couldn't see beyond that, until her.

Sometimes that's all it takes. Just one person to turn everything on its head. Remind you of the person you were.

Mia makes me want to be the person I was before all the shit.

I know I sound like a pussy, but I don't care.

I just want to be around Mia, and continue feeling the way I do when I'm with her.

And I'm finding that I want to be around her more often than not.

Yesterday, Mia and I went into town shopping so she could get some things she needed. This was new territory for me. I've never shopped with a girl. Not even Beth.

It might sound like nothing to you, but trust me, shopping with a girl was a big step for me – huge, in fact.

When she was all shopped out, we had lunch at the diner again. I could see Beth's raised brow and curious looks the whole time we were there, but I didn't leave her with an opportunity to quiz me.

I'm just not ready to discuss this … whatever *this* is.

Our day together was good, considering the big revelations of the night before. We had fun, and the subject of our pasts never came up. Mia didn't mention anything about wanting to go and check out another potential mother from the list, and I wasn't about to push her.

I was just happy to have her there with me.

I told crappy jokes. She laughed a lot. And yes, I might have been trying to win her over with my sparkling personality. I know that my face and body won't simply be enough to win her affection. Mia's going to need more from me, and I want to give that to her. Give her all of me.

When we got back to the hotel, I had chores to do, but Mia insisted on helping me. We worked together with ease.

I cooked her dinner. Granted it was only mac and cheese, but she said it was the best she'd ever tasted. After dinner, we watched a movie in the main living room with Dozer positioned as a chaperone between us.

It was hard being that close to her in the dark and not being able to do a thing. I wanted to kiss her so very fucking badly, but it just never seemed to be the right time to make a move.

I find myself looking for clues in her words and actions, but the instant I get a hint it's gone, and I'm left wondering if I'm just looking so hard that I'm making myself see things that don't actually exist.

I know I'm acting like a chick, analyzing shit – I'm turning into a fucking pussy. And yes, I'm fully aware of how fucking annoying I sound, but this is what she does to me. She has me tied up in all kinds of knots.

Mia is not like any girl I have ever known, and knowing what happened to her makes pursuing her all the more difficult. So I'm left with only one option – if we're meant to happen, we will. Let nature take its course. No taking the bull by the horns for me.

I'm just hoping nature hurries the fuck up because I can feel the clock ticking with Mia.

Of course, I'm still flirting with her. That hasn't stopped. This is me we're talking about. I couldn't stop if I tried. It'd be like asking Dozer not to sniff another dog's ass.

Flirting comes as natural to me as ass sniffing does to Dozer.

And Mia doesn't seem opposed to it—my flirting, I mean. I like the reaction I get from her when I do it. The blush in her cheeks gives me hope for more.

God, I want more.

And right now, I'm desperately trying not to stare at her legs. It's the first time I've seen them.

Thank you hot sun is all I can say.

She's stretched out on a blanket on the walkway over the lake reading a book. Dozer is, of course, with her. Dog's got it bad.

She's wearing a tank and the cut-off shorts she bought yesterday. They sit an inch or so above her knee.

The chicks I know usually wear their cuts-offs so short their ass cheeks show, but not Mia. She keeps tugging them down, like she's uncomfortable to be showing so much skin.

But you know, I find her cut-offs way more sexy than the ass showing ones. They leave more to the imagination, and I know the day I do get to see underneath them, it will have been totally worth the wait because the partial leg I am getting to see is turning me on big time.

She has great fucking legs.

My cock twitches, so I drag my eyes from Mia and focus on steering the riding mower so I can get this damn grass cut.

My cell starts to vibrate in my pocket. "Beth," I answer, tucking the phone between my ear and shoulder.

"Hey … okay, so I have a date tonight." She sounds panicked.

"And this is a good thing or a bad thing?"

"Both."

"Why?"

"Because my date is with Toni Stryder."

"Ah, right."

Toni is a chick Beth has a huge thing for. She's a cool girl who works as a DJ. Very hot. And sadly for all men, she's a lesbian, just like my best buddy.

I'm well aware of how hot Beth is—I'm not fucking blind—but even if Beth didn't play for the other team, it wouldn't make a difference. She's my best friend and the closest thing to a sister I have.

"I ran into her at the grocery store," Beth says, still sounding anxious. "She's got a gig tonight over in Grand Junction, and she asked me to go."

"Are you sure she actually asked you out on a date, and wasn't just asking you to go to her gig?" Beth's been known to misread signals in the past. She's been hurt before – badly. I won't let it happen again.

"Yes, *Dad*. I'm not a complete fucktard. I know when a chick is asking me out on a date. You know, when she says, 'Hey Beth, I was wondering, if after my set, do you want to hang out?' So I ask, 'What, you mean like a date?' And she says, 'Yeah, I mean a date.'."

"Okay, I get it. It's a date," I laugh. "I'm over the fucking moon for you."

"Good, because I need you to come with."

"What? Aw, come on, Beth. You know I dig a threesome with two hot chicks as much as the next guy, but seriously, I'm not having a threesome with you."

"In your fucking dreams, Matthews!" she screeches down the line.

Laughing, I hold my cell away to prevent an ear bleed. Beth has a real set of lungs on her, but I can't help winding her up. She's too easy.

I put the phone back to my ear. "Seriously though, screechy, what do you need me there for?"

"Because Toni's set lasts for an hour and a half, and I don't want to sit in the club on my own."

"So just go after her set is finished."

"I can't. I said I'd watch her play. *Please*, Jordan. I'm really nervous about it. Toni is the hottest chick I've ever met. And she's cool. I'm not cool."

"You're cool, Beth."

She makes a scoffing sound.

"Seriously, we need to work on your confidence."

"Okay, so let's work on it tonight. You can give me pointers on how to act around Toni. This is what you're awesome at—talking to hot girls and being cool. You can make me awesome at it too. And if I start to act like … well … *me*, you can give me a nudge … and I know there will be plenty of hot girls for you to hook up with after you've finished coaching me."

She thinks she's coaxing me by adding that, but I don't want to be that guy anymore. I don't want to be out in a club picking up chicks. I want to be with Mia.

Pressing on the breaks, I stop and look over at her. She's lost in her book. She looks so fucking beautiful. She looks like everything I never knew I wanted.

I cut the engine, taking the phone into my hand.

"Does your silence mean you're considering?" Beth asks, sounding hopeful.

I don't want to let Beth down. And if I go out, it doesn't mean I have to end the night with a girl in my bed. I could just go, then leave after Beth's feeling okay with Toni.

I exhale. "I'm considering. Keep talking."

"Okay … so it's free entry, courtesy of Toni. And I'll buy your drinks all night. Also, it's a paint party, something different."

"What the fuck's a paint party?"

"From what Toni said, paint is sprayed all over the clubbers."

"Sounds awesome."

"Don't be snarky. So will you come? *Please*."

My eyes wander to Mia again, and a thought starts to form … I could ask Mia to come with me.

Mia and me together in a club … dancing … hot and sweaty … our bodies close together…

This could make things happen. Or at the very least, move

177

things on a little bit.

"Okay, I'll come. But I'm bringing someone."

"Yay! Jordan, you are the best effin friend ever!"

"I know," I deadpan. "So what time is this thing?"

Ignoring my question, she asks, "So, who are you bringing? Anyone I know?"

"What time, Beth?"

She sighs at my blatant dismissal. "Toni's set starts at nine. One other thing … can you drive? My car is in the shop."

"Fuckin' hell! So the drinks you planned on buying me all night …?"

"Soda."

I can't help but laugh at her audacity.

"I'll owe you."

"You will. Big time."

"What am I gonna end up doing? Your laundry or something equally gross?"

"I don't know." I switch the phone to my other ear. "But I'm sure I can come up with something good."

"Whatever it is, it'll be worth it for a date with Toni," she says in a dreamy voice. "So come on, tell me who you're bringing tonight? It's not like you to play coy. Am I missing something here?"

"I'll pick you up at eight." And right before I hang up, I add, "And I'm bringing Mia with me."

Chuckling, I push my cell in my pocket and hop down from the mower. That'll give Beth something to chew on instead of fretting over her impending date.

Dozer's ears prick as I approach. He gets to his feet and hobbles over to me. I crouch down to stroke him.

Mia's eyes lift from her book to me. "Hey." She smiles, sitting up.

I suddenly feel nervous. And a little queasy. "Your book good? You looked lost in it."

Turning the book over, she stares down at the cover.

I grin when I see that it is a picture of a half-naked guy

draped over a half-naked chick.

Book porn. Go Mia.

Realizing her mistake at showing me the cover, her face goes bright red. She quickly closes the book and sets it down. Back cover up, naked couple down.

Shame.

"Yeah, it's okay." She looks out at the lake. Leaning over, she trails her fingers in the water. "I wanted to ask … is this water okay to swim in?"

"Yeah," I answer, moving to sit in front of her. "I swim in here all the time. You up for a swim now?"

An image of Mia wearing a bikini flashes through my mind. It's a really fucking great image.

"Oh, not right now." She scores her lower lip with her teeth.

And that's it. My thoughts go to shit. It takes me a good minute just to remember why I actually came over.

Beth. Date. Club.

"So I, uh…" I push my hair out of my eyes. "I came over because I just got off the phone with Beth. She's got a date tonight, and she's talked me into going with her."

Her eyebrow lifts. "Aren't dates supposed to be just a two person thing?"

"Normally. But it's a big deal for her, and her date is going to be DJing at the club, so she'll be alone for the first hour or so. She needs me to keep her company. And Beth is impossible to say no to when she wants something, so I said I'd go and … I was … uh, wondering if you wanted to come along – with me?"

Her eyes widen. I'm not sure if it's shock of the bad variety, or surprise of the good.

"Do you mean, like, on a date?" Her eyes instantly close on a groan. "Did I say that out loud? I said that out loud. Oh god."

I can't help the smile on my face, or the happy in my voice. "Yeah, you said it out loud."

"Oh god." She groans again, covering her face with her hands.

My confidence instantly bolstered, I reach over and pull a

hand from her face. One eye pops open.

"Do you want me to be asking you out on a date?"

Slowly, she lowers her other hand from her face.

My heart is hammering in my chest, waiting for her to put me out of my misery.

"Yes," she whispers.

I tangle my fingers with hers. "Then I'm asking you out on a date."

Chapter Fourteen

Mia

Oh god. Oh god. Oh god.

I agreed to go on a date with Jordan.

What was I thinking?

I wasn't thinking. That's the point. I was looking into his amazing eyes and saying yes before I knew what I was agreeing to.

It was my fault because there was all that talk of Beth's date … I got confused and thought he was asking me out … and me being me, I blurted out what I was thinking, which I seem to do all the time around him, and before I knew it, he was asking, and I was saying yes.

I should back out.

I don't want to, but I should. I don't have the best track record when it comes to men. I'm not a winner picker.

But this is Jordan.

And I'm about eighty-five percent sure I can trust him. He's given me no reason to not. And yes, I know Forbes came across as trustworthy in the beginning, but back then I was naïve and a fool.

I'm not that person anymore. I know the signs to look for, and I see none of them in Jordan.

There's no over the top niceness, which is there in the beginning to hide the monster lying in wait. There's no control in his personality. He is just who he is. If anything, Jordan has been really open and honest with me about his past.

If all he cared about is tricking me and getting me where he wants me – in his bed and under his control – that wouldn't be the way. And men like that are not honest. Not right away, anyway.

Jordan's fun. He makes me laugh. He makes me feel happiness in a way I've never known. I love being around him, and I think I deserve some fun; some happiness and laughter in my life.

And really, it is just one date. It's not as if I'm marrying the guy.

I should just go out with him tonight and see how it goes. I've got absolutely nothing to lose, and we won't be alone. Beth will be there with her date too.

It'll be fine.

Taking a deep breath, I survey myself in the mirror.

I wasn't sure what to wear. Jordan said I shouldn't wear anything I'm too attached to as apparently it's a paint party at the club tonight. I've never heard of that before, but it sounds fun, if not a little messy. But I'm all up for trying new things at the moment.

I'm not really a dancer, and I'm not attached to any of my clothes, so it's not too difficult for me to choose what to wear. It's a really warm evening, so I've decided to wear a white tank top and khaki linen pants. I've accessorized with a cute black and white bead necklace and matching bracelet that I picked up while shopping with Jordan yesterday.

I want to look as nice as possible, but I don't have a lot to work with here. Not much can be done with my short hair, but the style has really grown on me and it looks cool.

I've applied some make-up – mascara, blusher and lip-gloss. I also used cover-up as there is still a trace of yellow bruising around my eye. No hiding the cut on my brow, but it's healing nicely.

I'm just fastening the laces on my sneakers when there's a knock at the door.

My date is here.

A swarm of fireflies takes flight in my stomach. I quickly finish off tying up my lace and get to my feet, taking deep breaths as I approach the door. I open it to a 'more gorgeous than normal looking' Jordan.

He's only wearing a plain black t-shirt and distressed jeans. White sneakers on his feet. Simple, but oh so effective. Jordan makes anything look good.

I can see that he's shaved as his stubble from earlier is gone. His dark hair is in its trademark style. My fingers itch to run through the silky strands.

I can smell his aftershave. Clean and fresh. He smells as gorgeous as he looks; exactly as a man should smell. I have to resist the urge to lean close and inhale.

He runs a hand through his shiny hair. "You look great—" He shakes his head. "—I mean, pretty. You look real pretty, Mia."

I curl my fingers around the beads, holding them like a life support. "Thanks, you too. Not pretty – handsome. I mean you look handsome." God, kill me now.

Jordan chuckles and leans his shoulder up against the door frame. "Are you ready to go? I told Beth we'd pick her up at eight, so we need to set off soon."

"Sure. Let me just grab my things."

I decide against taking a purse with me, so I put my room key, money and lip-gloss into my pocket while Jordan waits in the hall. I let the door lock behind me, then follow him out the hotel and to his car.

He opens the passenger door for me. No one has ever done that before, and I can't help but smile at his gesture. I slip into the seat and watch as Jordan rounds the hood. The way his body moves with such confident ease … it's so attractive on him. I wish I was that comfortable in my own skin.

He climbs in next to me.

There's a quiet unease between us. I know I'm the cause of it because of my nerves at being on a date with him, but I'm really missing the ease we normally have between us. I do want to be on a date with Jordan, I just don't like the pressure it's putting on me … or the pressure I'm putting on myself.

He starts the engine and the radio fills the empty background, but the silence between us is still palpable.

"Are you okay?" His softly spoken words bring my face to him.

I wring my hands in my lap. "Just a little nervous, I guess."

"About?"

"Being on a date." I twist the beads around my finger. "I just … I haven't…" I shake my head, struggling to find the right words to explain my feelings.

"Hey…" He gently touches my chin with his finger.

I love the way his touch feels. I never thought it would be possible, and I'll never tire of him touching me, but I just wish I knew how to tell him. How to express how he makes me feel … how I feel about him. I know I'm not what he's used to, and I know I won't ever be able to be like those women. I'm afraid I'm going to be a disappointment to him.

"… there is nothing to be nervous about. We're just going out to have some fun, dance and get sprayed with paint." He grins.

It's impossible not to smile back.

"There you go." He touches the corner of my smile with his thumb. And those damn fireflies start off in my stomach again, swooping and somersaulting. "Nothing will happen tonight that you don't want, okay?" His gaze is warm on my skin.

I take a deep breath. "Okay."

Beth seems nervous about her date. She has done nothing but talk about it from the moment we picked her up. She's like a bundle of nervous energy, but honestly, I like it. I like her. And Beth's nerves are making me feel a little more normal about my own.

I love the dynamic between Beth and Jordan. The way he never seems to get annoyed or irritated by her incessant chatter about her date with Toni. Forbes would never have let me talk that way, but then I guess Beth is Jordan's friend, not his girlfriend.

I've wondered why they are nothing more than friends as Beth is really pretty and they get on so well, but I had my question answered after five minutes of Beth being in the car when she talked about Toni in the female sense. Turns out Beth is into girls.

A girl who went to my school was a lesbian. She was bullied incessantly because of it. I used to feel so terrible for her, but it wasn't as if I could do anything to help her. I wish I could have, but I couldn't even deal with my own problems, so I had no chance of helping anyone else. I wonder if Beth has suffered any hassle because of her sexual orientation. If she has, then I'm glad that Jordan is by her side because I can imagine him kicking the crap out of anyone who bullied her.

Jordan parks a few blocks over from the club and we start the short walk. The sidewalk is narrow, so Beth is in front, Jordan and I behind.

Because we're so close, our hands keep brushing as we walk. Every time they touch, a jolt of heat flares up my arm. I'm desperate to hold his hand. We've held hands before, always Jordan holding mine, but that was before *this*, when we were just friends. Now things have changed, and it makes holding hands seem like such a bigger deal.

"Fuck it," I hear him mutter, and the next thing I know he's taking hold of my hand.

My heart takes flight, buzzing around my chest.

He leans down to my ear. "Is this okay?" His warm breath whispers over my skin.

Shivering, I turn my head resting my chin against my shoulder, I stare into his eyes. "It's more than okay."

He lifts my hand, bringing me close to his side, and brushes a kiss over my knuckles.

I can hardly take my eyes off him. He becomes more beautiful and more precious to me with each passing second, and it terrifies me.

He's too good for someone like me. Forbes was right when

he said I was nothing. I'm not meant for someone as good as Jordan.

The happiness I was feeling disappears. My stomach drops. I look ahead and find Beth looking over her shoulder at us, smiling.

Then she catches my eye, and her smile vanishes. I quickly look away, and paste on a fake smile, relieved when the club comes into view.

We follow Beth over to the doorman, and thanks to Toni putting us on the guest list, we don't have to wait in the huge line.

I've only ever been in a club one time before. It was with Forbes and his rich douchey friends. That club was a bit nicer than this place, but I actually prefer this club. It looks how a club should look. All dark and grungy. Floor sticky from spilt drinks.

It feels real.

The bass is pumping loud, vibrating up through my feet, and I feel a tremor of excitement at being here; doing something out of my ordinary.

The club is packed; a sea of people. I notice most of the girls are dressed in fewer clothes than me, wearing shorts and cut-off t-shirts. I wish I could wear shorts as short as they are, but the scars on the back of my thighs prevent me from doing so as does my severe lack of confidence.

My good feeling instantly disappears, leaving me feeling dowdy and out of place, and wondering just why the hell Jordan is here with me. A sudden urge to leave so I can hide away and comfort eat myself until I'm sick compels me.

I curl my fingers into my hand, pressing my nails into my skin, trying to expel the urge.

As if hearing my pain, Jordan squeezes my hand. I glance up at him. "Hey, you okay?" he mouths over the music.

With a fake smile, I nod.

He looks at me for too long, suspicion curving his mouth. It feels like he's trying to see deep inside me, and it makes me fidgety, so I look away.

He moves closer. I know he's going to question me further. I feel his body press against my side, and my body goes to war with my mind. I want him close, yet I want him to go away.

I'm saved by Beth, when she comes bounding over.

"Toni's coming out in ten, so let's get a drink first, then we can go see her," she yells over the music.

Jordan steps back giving me space. I almost exhale in relief. I can feel his eyes burning into me, but I can't bring myself to meet his stare.

Smiling at Beth, I say, "Sure. Sounds good."

Beth leads the way to the bar. Jordan is close behind me. When we reach the bar, I stand beside Beth. Jordan comes up behind, hands either side of me, placing them on the bar and caging me in.

My body is fully aware of how close he is and wants him closer. My hands are itching to reach back and pull him to me.

"Drinks are on me, so what do you both want?" Beth says.

"I'll get the drinks," Jordan's deep voice comes between us.

Beth's eyes flicker to him. "No way! Deal was that I'd buy your drinks tonight for coming with me."

"Deal's off. Now tell me what you want?" There's an air of authority in his voice, which I surprisingly like. It has my skin tingling, and other parts of me.

Beth, seemingly unaffected by him, says, "Fine. I'm not gonna argue with you. Saves me a few dollars. I'll have a whiskey and soda – make it a Fireball."

"Mia … what do you want?" he speaks in my ear, his voice deep and breathy. It makes my toes curl.

I feel like he's not asking me about choice of drinks right now. And I know exactly what I want – him.

I turn my head, only to find my mouth now dangerously close to his. And by dangerously, I mean *dangerous* because of my insistent need to kiss him right now. If that's going to happen tonight, then here at the bar is most definitely not the place.

My eyes meet his, just in time to see them darken. He feels it too … wants this … *me*.

My body goes into overdrive.

Quickly gathering myself, I say, "Beer. Bottled. Please." And

I face forward.

Casting a sideways glance, I see Beth smiling happily at us. I'm kind of getting the feeling she likes me with Jordan.

Jordan's hands come from around me. He moves to the side and leans up against the bar to get served. I feel a tap my shoulder, and turn to a smiling Beth. She moves back a little away from Jordan, so I follow.

"How are you finding Durango?" she asks.

I smile, thinking of Jordan—the one thing that I *really* like about this town. "I like it."

"Yeah, it's not so bad. But when you've lived here your whole life, like I have, it becomes a bit boring."

I get that, knowing how it felt to be trapped in Boston my whole life.

"You've never been anyway else?" I ask.

"Sure, I've been away on vacation, but nowhere exciting. I'd love to go to traveling."

"You should."

"Jordan's been traveling."

"Yeah, he told me. South East Asia, right?"

Beth looks a little surprised at my knowing this, which quickly morphs into a smile.

Before I get a chance to consider her reaction, a high-pitched female voice grabs my attention. Mainly, because she's screeching Jordan's name.

I turn to see a very pretty bartender with long dark hair and legs even longer. She seemingly knows Jordan very well if the look on her face is anything to go by as she leans over the bar and throws her arms around his neck.

My stomach tightens into a knot of jealous ire. Stupid, I know, but still there nonetheless.

He awkwardly pats her back, then quickly pulls her arms from around him. She grabs hold of his forearm, keeping him with her, but I watch him remove her hand. She leans in and says something. He shakes his head, which she clearly doesn't like if the pissed off look on her face is any indication.

188

She stares at him for a long moment, then without another word turns away and starts making our drinks.

Jordan turns in our direction. I quickly look away so he doesn't see I'm watching.

"I wouldn't worry about it," Beth says close to my ear. "All women behave like that around him."

"Yeah, but more so the ones he's already slept with." The words are out of my mouth before I can stop them. I clamp my mouth shut.

I can't believe I just said that.

Beth will, without doubt, be aware of Jordan's past when it comes to women, but it's not my place to pass comment.

She lifts her eyebrow. "He has been talking to you. I'm glad, but surprised he told you that stuff. Still, I'll take it as a good sign considering you're here on a date with him. You must really like him." Then she smiles wide. "And he must really like you."

I can't say her words don't affect me because they do. I want Jordan to like me.

"What makes you think that?" I ask.

"Because he's never been *that* honest with a girl before. Hell, he's never been on an actual date before. And if he's telling you all his shit up front, then you must really mean something to him. He must think a lot of you. He wants you to know the truth, and that's a big step for him."

I honestly don't know what to say, so I say nothing.

"Look, I don't know how long you're here for, Mia, and I know Jordan might come off as being a bad ass, but he's not. Not really. When he cares about someone, he cares about them with everything. And he takes, losing someone he cares about, badly."

"His mom?"

"Holy crap! He told you about his mom? Shit, he does like you." She grins and wraps an arm around my waist. The contact surprises me and locks every muscle in my body. It does every time a new person touches me. "Just don't break his heart now that he's finally got it working, please." She laughs lightly.

My insides coil. "I don't think I have the power to do that."

189

"Oh, you'd be surprised," she says, lowering her voice.

I lift my eyes to see a smiling, but curious Jordan walking toward us, hands laden with our drinks.

He hands me my beer.

"Thanks." I smile. His eyes hold mine for a moment before moving to Beth.

"You wanna go see Toni now?" He hands Beth her drink.

"You know what?" Her eyes dart to me, then back to Jordan, a smile creeping across her face. "I'm good. I got this with Toni."

Jordan's brow creases in confusion. "You sure?"

"I'm sure," she says, walking backwards and away from us into the crowd. "You two go have fun." Before turning away, she gives me a conspiratory wink.

Subtle much? I have to hold back a laugh.

"If you need me, call my cell," Jordan calls after her.

Beth waves a hand in acknowledgement before disappearing into the crowd.

Jordan turns to me. "So … it's just you and me."

Shivers and a whole bunch of nerves swarm me. "It is."

"You wanna try and find somewhere to sit?"

"Sure."

I follow Jordan upstairs where he says it'll be quieter and we'll be more likely to find a seat. He's right. We find an empty sofa overlooking the dance floor below.

I sit down first. Jordan sits beside me. My nerves have ratcheted up a couple of thousand notches now because it's just him and me. No Beth as a buffer. I can't think of a single thing to say to him, so I cover it up by continuously sipping on my drink and pretending to be fascinated by all the people in the club.

"You're still nervous." His hand comes up, pulling mine from my mouth. I was playing with my lip without even realizing.

Jordan slides his fingers through mine, holding my hand. My stomach scatters.

I turn my face to him, not realizing how close he is, bringing me almost nose to nose with him. My cheeks heat. I shuffle across the sofa, putting myself up against the arm rest, and I don't deny the nerves. There's no point. Not when he can read me so well.

"Is it me who's making you nervous? Something I'm doing, or just the whole being on a date with me thing?"

I turn my body to him. My knees touch his thigh. "It's not you. It's just being on a date. I've only dated one guy before, and that didn't work out so well for me." Without thought, I touch the healing cut on my brow.

His eyes follow my hand, and they stayed trained on the remnant of my relationship with Forbes long after I've moved my hand away.

His face is impassive, but I know his mind is working. I can see it in his eyes. I'm wondering if all I've done is remind him of the mess I came from … the mess I am … what Forbes did to me … that I carry too much baggage. Have I turned him off me?

"I'm canceling our date," he says.

What?

Panic starts to crawl up my throat.

"Jordan, look, I'm sorry if I…"

"Don't be sorry. And you really do say that way too much. We need to work on that."

I clutch the beads around my neck, needing something to hold onto. "Do you want me to leave?"

His eyes widen with discontent. "What? No fuckin' way do I want you to leave. What I want is for you to relax and enjoy yourself with me tonight, so all I'm doing by canceling our date is taking it out of the equation. If it happens to turn into a date later, then awesome. If it doesn't, then I might be a little disappointed…" He grins to let me know he's teasing. "There isn't any pressure here. I like you – a lot. I think that's pretty obvious. But I want you to *want* to be here with me in the same way as I do you. If you're not quite there yet, then that's okay. I'll wait until you are. However long it takes."

Is he real? I almost want to pinch him to make sure.

He likes me. A lot.

I'm washed aglow with the most amazing sensation – I've never felt anything like it. My heart starts to beat faster than I knew possible without causing a heart attack.

I know I'm staring at him, but I can't stop. All I can see is him, and I forget why I was nervous in the first place. Why I built this whole date up in my mind.

The music quietens to a dull throb. The world shutting out, fading to just us…

Him.

Then all thought is lost, and I just follow what my body is telling me to do.

I press my hand to the side of Jordan's face, absorbing the heat and strength of him. I lean in to press my lips to his cheek. He moves as I do, and my lips graze the corner of his. Heat scores through me, branding me his.

I withdraw, shocked but wanting more. I moisten my suddenly parched lips. A lick leaves me with the addictive taste of him. His aftershave, the soda he's drinking … just everything that embodies *him*.

Jordan's eyes flare with something I'm sure of. I'm sure because I'm feeling it too.

Lust. Desire. Want. And something more. Something deeper.

He slides his fingers into my hair, cupping the back of my head, he rests his forehead against mine.

"I feel the same as you do," I say, my mouth so close to his that if I moved an inch we'd be kissing. "I want to be here with you … more than anything."

He releases a contented breath. It soothes me.

"Should I take it our date's back on?" His voice sounds deliciously husky and incredibly sexy, sending shivers tumbling through me.

"It was never off." I smile.

Chapter Fifteen

Jordan

"Do you want to dance?"

Lifting her shoulders slightly, Mia gives me an unsure look, then turns to look down at the dance floor.

After kissing me, she's been a little more relaxed. If I'd have known that would have relaxed her, I'd have told her to do it sooner.

Maybe it was the break in the ice that she needed.

Problem is, now I can't stop staring at her mouth … her soft full lips … wanting to feel them against mine … fully…

She felt amazing.

And she smells so fucking good.

I'd be content to sit with my nose buried in her neck, inhaling her sweet scent for the rest of the night, in-between kissing that gorgeous mouth of hers, of course.

When she leaned in to kiss my cheek—believe it or not it wasn't on purpose, just a natural reaction to her. I don't regret it for a second because when her lips touched the corner of mine … fuck … if that's what a brief momentary touch of her lips on mine is like, then I can only imagine how amazing it will feel to kiss her properly.

And now, of course, all I can think about is kissing her. It's taking a real effort on my part not to make a move, but I don't want to rush her and fuck things up. That's why I'm suggesting dancing – something to keep my mind occupied.

Though, watching her gorgeous body move on a dance floor will probably send my thoughts back south.

I lean close to her back, looking over her shoulder. "I think the paint spraying might start soon. I'm thinking it could be fun, and we can stop by and see how Beth is getting along with Toni."

She looks back at me, her lips curving up slightly. "Okay."

We both stand. I move aside to let Mia out first. She passes me, and the brush of her body against mine has me holding back a groan.

We've just started walking when I feel Mia's tiny hand slip into mine. I look at her surprised.

But happy.

Really fucking happy.

Her cheeks blush.

This is the first time she's ever held my hand. It's always been me taking hold of hers. I've been making up excuses to justify touching her if only for a second, and now tonight, after a no-touch policy on her part—which I understand knowing what she's been through—she has kissed me *and* is holding my hand.

I know these are big things for her, which makes them big for me. They show she trusts me.

I gently touch her pink cheek with my fingertips. She smiles.

We walk back down stairs, holding hands, in a bubble of our own, and because the motherfucking world hates me … we bump straight into Shawna the instant my foot hits the bottom step.

"Jordan … hi." Shawna slants a smile at me.

Fuck.

There's an unmistakable gleam in her eyes. I've seen it before. Namely when she was naked and under me.

"Hi." My voice is tight. I pull Mia to my side, putting my arm around her shoulders so there's no mistaking who she is to me. "Shawna, meet Mia. Mia, Shawna." I do the polite thing and introduce them, but honestly, it's the last thing I want to do. Introducing the girl I'm crazy about, to the last girl I was doing? Fucking, yay.

"Hi." Mia lifts her hand in a little wave. She's so goddamn adorable. "It's nice to meet you, Shawna."

Shawna's eyes dart to Mia. She falters a little, then makes a quick recovery. Her gaze returns to me, burning me with a laser like effect.

"Well, you certainly weren't lying. You sure don't waste any time moving on and finding a new fuck buddy."

I feel Mia tense under my arm.

"Shawna…" There's a warning in my voice.

"Looks like you've traded down though – majorly. But then, it's not like you can get better than me." Her eyes slice to Mia. "I'm sorry to tell you this, but he's nothing more than overused trash. He'll fuck you, then dump you before you even have a chance to get your panties back on."

What the fuck!

Okay, so she's not too far off the mark with the dumping part … but still, what the fuck!

Talk to me like shit, fine – I deserve it. But not Mia. I won't have her spoken to in this way.

I open my mouth, ready to tell Shawna to piss off back to where she came from, when I hear Mia's sweet voice say…

"Well, looks aside, going solely off your personality here, Shawna, I'd say Jordan has traded up higher than a skyscraper with me. And as it turns out, I'm just in it for the sex – so seems we're perfectly matched. Oh, and I don't wear panties either, so we've no worries on that part."

My mouth falls open. Shawna looks like Mia has just slapped her.

"Okay. Right. Well, I'd say it was nice talking to you, but it wasn't, so … bye." Mia moves out from under my arm, letting it drop to my side. Head held high, she walks away and makes her way through the crowd.

And my eyes are glued to her hot, sashaying ass as she goes.

Holy fucking fuck.

Have you ever watched that scene in Grease, right at the end of the movie, when Sandy turns up looking and acting completely different, decked out in tight black pants. And Danny sees her, and he's … shocked—disbelief of the best kind. Like, *'holy fuck, how did I not know how hot my girl could actually be?'* Then he

195

pretty much chases after her like a dog with his tongue hanging out.

Yeah? Good, so you know what I'm talking about because right now, that's me.

I'm chasing after Mia as if she's the last drop of water on earth, and I'm seriously fucking parched.

I'm ready to break out in song and serenade her with "You're The One That I Want" just to get her attention.

Because angry Mia is fucking *hot*. Like, off the charts hot.

Of course, I already knew she was hot. But this … wow.

Fucking wow.

I have never been as turned on as I am now. My dick is so hard it could pound nails. Thank god it's dark and crowded in here so no one can see my boner.

I finally catch up with her just near the dance floor. Hooking my fingers into her tank top, I reel her back to me.

She turns.

Her eyes are wide, a fire still in them. Her chest is heaving up and down, and I'm literally lost for words. I have a hundred thoughts streaming through my mind—none of them clean—and I can't seem to find one fucking word to start a coherent sentence.

And also, I'm trying really hard not to stare at her tits.

I see the anger in her eyes dim, and the Mia I know is back. "Oh god, Jordan, I'm so sorry. What I just said back there…" She covers her face with her hands. "God, I don't know what came over me. I just … I didn't like the way she was talking about you. It just … it made me so angry. And I don't get angry – ever."

I step into her space. Peeling her hands from her face, I hold them at her sides.

Those huge blues of hers blink up at me with total innocence. "What you did back there was good. You stood up for yourself. Shawna was being a bitch, and she deserved what you said. I'm just sorry she said those things to you because of me."

She shakes her head. "It's fine."

"No, it's not." I dip my head closer to hers. "I'm not happy about the way Shawna treated you just then, but I am glad you got

196

angry. You should get angry more often." *God, she should. She really should.* "But mostly, I'm glad that you got angry over me." *Because it tells me you care, probably more than I deserve.*

"Oh no … oh god! I told her that I don't wear panties," she says, like she's not even heard a word I've said. An expression of horror flitting across her face. "In the middle of the club, I said *'I don't wear panties'*." She searches out my eyes. "I do wear them. All the time. Even for bed." She closes her eyes on a groan. "Stop talking, Mia."

I chuckle. "I never thought for a second that you didn't wear panties." *Just wished, hoped, prayed…*

Her eyes open back up, the look in them surprisingly alert. "Jordan, I know it's none of my business, but … did you actually … go out with that girl? I only ask because … well…" she bites her lip. "She's just not a very nice person."

I wasn't expecting her to say that. I consider my answer carefully before speaking. I'm not going to lie to her, but I'm going to make damn sure I say it in the right way.

"I never went out with Shawna – it never got that far."

"Oh. Ahh," Understanding flickers her eyes. "You just slept with her."

"I've never actually *slept* with anyone. But … we did have sex, yes."

She steps back, moving away from me, forcing me to let go of her.

"I know you told me about what you used to do … with women … and it's fine, I'm not judging you. Not at all. And I know this is only our first date, and I don't have a lot of experience in the dating field … well, when it comes to men in general, but I do know one thing … when I'm with someone, I'm with just them. And I want them to be the same with me. I understand if that's different for you, but if you want to be with other women while we date … then I'm sorry, I'm not the right girl for you."

Eh? I'm not entirely sure where this is coming from. I thought I'd been very clear about how I feel about her, but obviously not, so she needs to know.

And now.

"Mia, I've never really been with anyone to define parameters ... I've *never* had a relationship. I've never dated anyone. You're the first person I've ever had a *real* date with."

She doesn't say anything, her face blank, and I get this sudden ache in my chest.

I feel like I'm losing her before I've even gotten her.

"When I told you about me, the way I was, the way I behaved ... the guy who you just got a glimpse of through Shawna, that is who I was. *Not* who I am *now*."

She wraps her arms around herself in a protective manner. I hate that she feels she needs to shield herself from me.

"What changed?" Her voice is quiet, wavering.

"You." I take the chance and move close to her again, closing my hands around her upper arms. She doesn't pull away. It gives me hope. "*You* changed things for *me*."

She looks away. "You've ... changed things for me too."

"I have?"

She nods, tugging on her lower lip with her thumb and forefinger.

"I see *you*, Mia. Only you." My gaze drops to her lips.

She stops tugging on them, her hand falling to her side.

"This Is Love" by Will.i.am starts to filter in the background. The piano medley eases through the crowd toward us. Mia's eyes lift to mine. My heart starts to kick a beat in my chest. Then the song explodes, like the heat between us, until there's a bonfire of want flaring all around.

Her breathing falters, coming in quick ... her eyes close on one of those sweet, short breaths ... her lips part slightly...

And I know.

This is it.

The moment I've been waiting for since she walked into the hotel.

I lean into her, cupping her cheek in my hand, more than ready to press my mouth to those sweet lips of hers ... and then the noise level around us increases exponentially until my ears are nearly bleeding from the squeals and screams of laughter.

And then I feel the reason for those screams of laughter when paint splatters all over me.

Mia's eyes flash open, her mouth popping to an O.

Motherfucking paint party.

They couldn't have waited like, five more fucking minutes before blasting out that shit!

I run my hand through my hair and look down at my palm. It's streaked with yellow, blue and pink neon paint. Mia's hand goes to her face. She's equally as covered with the paint as I imagine I am. Running her fingers over her cheek, then her forehead, she streaks the colors, mixing them together.

She looks even more beautiful, if possible.

Incandescent.

Exotic.

And incredibly dangerous to my heart.

She looks up to watch the continuing shower of color, shielding her eyes with her hand, and laughing.

And I can't wait a fucking second longer.

I take her face in my hands, and I kiss her. Hard.

There's a tremble in her body. I feel her tense for just a split second, then she relaxes into me and her lips part on a soft moan.

I feel it all the way down to my dick. And let's just say, he's pretty fucking happy about it.

Sliding my fingers into her hair, I cup the back of her head. "Is this okay?" I whisper over her lips.

She nods.

It's the only answer I need.

I kiss her deeper, slipping my tongue into her mouth, needing more of her.

Mia's hands slide up my arms. I can feel the slick of the paint between my skin and hers, and it makes the sensation of her touch even more intense.

Okay, so maybe they're onto something with this paint thing.

She inches up on her tiptoes, looping her arms around my

neck, gripping my hair with her fingers, keeping me with her.

Not that she needs to because I have no intention of going anywhere right now. If ever. But I like that she wants me closer. That she doesn't want to let me go.

I wrap my arms around her tiny waist, enveloping her, lifting her small body against mine. She's so tiny, so fragile, yet so unbreakable.

She's fucking amazing.

Everything I didn't know I was looking for.

I know I'm fucked. She has me now. If there were ever a chance of me going back after this one taste of her, it's gone.

I'm gone for her.

I know she's meant to be leaving in a little over a week's time, but I can't let that happen. I'm going to have to figure out a way to keep her in my life for good. Figure out a way for her to want to stay with me.

Chapter Sixteen

Mia

If a moment could be held in time forever, kept there to revisit and cherished, then mine would be last night.

I would box the memory, tie it tight with a ribbon, and keep it safe for always. Keep it there to open whenever I need to be reminded of a moment of wonderful.

I know for most girls, going on a date with a guy, being taken to a nightclub and sprayed with neon paint, might not be their idea of an evening to cherish.

But for me, it is.

Because it was *my* night. Jordan made everything about me. Focused on me. Cared if I was happy, and if I was having a good time.

Me.

It was like complete freedom while with another person.

I could dance how I wanted to dance. Talk to whomever I wanted to. Kiss who I wanted to kiss…

Jordan.

There was no fear. No control. No anger.

Just happiness.

I have never experienced anything like it, but I want to again…

And again…

And again…

It was like the best slice of freedom cake, topped with whipped cream and sprinkles.

And Jordan was the sprinkles.

We stayed at the club, wrapped up in each other. When the night was over, and it was time to leave, Jordan and I went back to the hotel together in his car, and Beth got a ride home from Toni.

He was perfect. It was perfect. And when he walked me to my door, he kissed me goodnight, the sweetest kiss of all. Then he went to his room.

I showered the paint off best I could, and fell into bed in a cloud of contentedness.

Now, I'm lying in bed, wide awake at the butt crack of dawn, unable to go back to sleep. I'm counting the seconds until I can see Jordan again while recounting every moment of last night—barring the bumping into one of Jordan's previous conquests. I cringe when I think of what she said, and I cringe even worse when I think of what I said to her.

When I hear a knock at my door, I almost leap out of bed in my excitement, not remembering until I'm opening the door that I'm still in my pajamas. I probably look a complete state. I've never really been that concerned with how I look, until him. I only ever dressed and looked nice because it was expected of me by Oliver and Forbes

"Morning." His voice is low and husky. "I didn't wake you, did I?"

God, he looks gorgeous, even at this early hour.

"No. I've been awake a while. Couldn't sleep."

"Me either. I've had this girl on my mind all night."

"Anyone I know?" I hold back a smile.

Dozer comes into view at Jordan's side, all puppy dog eyes at me. Pushing past Jordan, he comes to me.

"Hey, buddy." I kneel down to stroke him.

"You might know her," Jordan says, answering my question. "Blonde hair, blue eyes … beautiful. We went out on a date last night as it happens."

He just called me beautiful.

Beautiful.

Composing myself, I look up at Jordan. "Really?" I say,

playing along. "So how was the date?"

"Well, that's the thing…" He crouches down, stroking Dozer who's positioned between us. His fingertips touch mine. Heat flashes up my arm careening straight for my heart.

"The date was amazing, and I haven't been able to stop thinking about her … or her gorgeous mouth ever since…" He leans over Dozer. Close to me. I suck in a breath. "And the thing is, I really need to kiss her again."

Baboom! The sound of my heart … so loud, I'm sure he must hear it.

"I think she needs you to kiss her too," I breathe.

"You do?" He swipes his lower lip with his tongue.

My insides coil. "Mmm," I murmur.

I close my eyes as he brings his mouth to mine, more than ready to taste him and feel the explosion his kiss creates inside me.

It's only when I part my lips against his that I remember I haven't brushed my teeth.

"Wait," I say against his mouth, pressing my hand to his chest. "I haven't brushed my teeth."

"Shh." His hand goes to the back of my head … holding me … kissing me deeper. Apparently he has no issue with my morning breath. I should, but I really don't want to stop kissing him right now.

All thought is lost when he runs his tongue along my lower lip, then slips it into my mouth. I curl my fingers into his shirt.

His kisses are drugging. I could live a contented life being as high as a kite on him all day long.

He gets as close to me as he can with a hundred and sixty pound dog laid on the floor between us, and takes my face in both his hands, taking full control of the kiss. It's at this exact point that I feel things change between us.

Deepen.

Don't ask me why or how, they just do, and I know he feels it too because of the look on his face when he parts his mouth from mine on a gasp, eyes staring deep into mine.

I know, in this moment, there's an unbreakable connection between us. Something tying us together, irrevocably, and no matter what, I'll never be without him.

"Hi," I whisper.

"Hi." He smiles.

Dozer lifts his head between us, nudging Jordan back from me a little.

I chuckle, and stroke Dozer, giving him the attention he wants.

"So, where was I before you distracted me?" He grins, still looking as dazed as I feel.

"You were telling me about the awesome date you had last night."

"Right, yeah. Well, it was so awesome that I was hoping she'd go on another date with me today."

"You always could ask her."

"What do you think she'd say?"

"Hmm…" I press my lips together in thought. "I'm thinking that she'd definitely say yes."

He smiles wide. "Good, 'cause I've got an awesome day planned for her." He leans across and gives me another quick kiss, pulling back far too quickly, leaving me wanting more.

"You're going to want to wash your hair again." He twists a piece of my hair round his finger.

"What? Why?" I touch my hair where his hand is and feel the strands of crunch. Damn paint.

"Blue, and a bit of pink." He leans over, examining. "It's a good look on you."

"I'll stick with my natural color, thanks."

Chuckling, he gets to his feet. I follow.

"Shower. Then get your cute ass dressed ASAP so we can head out. Need an early start for where we're going."

"Where are we going?" I ask.

"You'll see when we get there. Come on, Dozer. Leave Mia to get ready. I've got some sausages with your name on."

Dozer's ears prick up at the mention of sausages. For a dog

with a cast on his leg, he sure does move quickly.

"Tossed aside for sausages," I croon. "And I thought we had something special, Dozer."

"Just so you know..." Jordan leans his shoulder against the door frame. "I would never toss you aside for some sausage." The glint in his eye is unmistakable.

I flush bright red all the way down to my toes.

Grinning, he turns and starts off walking down the hall. "Oh, and make sure to wear comfortable shoes. And bring something warm, just in case." He calls to me.

"Will do." I close the door behind me, catching hold of my happiness and hugging my arms tight around it.

One thing I'm starting to realize with Jordan is that moments of wonderful aren't a rarity. It seems I might just have more than one great memory with him to keep, and I'm thinking my arms and heart are going to be full of them.

Dressed in jeans, t-shirt and sneakers, and carrying a hooded sweatshirt with me just in case, I'm in Jordan's car, heading to town with him. He still won't tell me where we're going, but I get a pretty good idea of what we're going to be doing when he pulls up outside, *White Rock Jeep Tours.*

"You're taking me out on a jeep tour?" I've never done anything like that before.

"Yeah. Is that okay?"

"More than okay." I run my fingers into the back of his silky hair.

"I do tours for Wade, the owner, mainly in high season," he tells me. "Though, not as much this summer with Dad being away. You're safe with me. I'm an official tour guide." He grins. "Thought I'd take you up to *La Plata Canyon.* It's amazing there, and one of my favorite places to go. Aside from the canyon itself, there are some amazing lakes, rivers and waterfalls. Tons of wildlife … and I remember you saying how much you like animals."

I used to think animals were much kinder than people. Until I met Jordan, that is.

"What kind of animals?" I get a frisson of excitement at the thought.

He takes hold of my hand, moving it from his hair, and kisses my knuckles. "Deer, elk, marmots, juncos. You can usually spot some hawks and eagles. And if we're real lucky, we might even see a mountain lion or a bear."

My eyes widen. "Lions and bears. Sounds cool." I tug on my lower lip. "But if they come too close, we'll drive away as quickly as possible from them, right?"

He laughs, and places his hand on my thigh, squeezing gently. "Right."

He doesn't seem to notice how my whole body freezes, which is a good thing. The freeze is a mixture of surprise, fear, but mostly want. I want Jordan's hands on me.

"Come on, let's get moving."

I get out of the car and follow him over to the shop, tying my sweatshirt around my waist as I walk.

Jordan pushes the door open, and a bell announces our arrival. He lets me through first. A big man with grey hair, is behind the counter, reading a newspaper.

He looks up. "Jordan my boy, how you doing?"

"Good," Jordan says, walking over to him.

They do that manly handshake thing that men do.

"Wade, this is my friend Mia." He introduces me.

Wade's smiling eyes move to me. I know he spots the remnant of my black eye and cut brow.

"Hey Mia, nice to meet you. You been in a fight there, little lady?" He hints at my face.

I instantly freeze, then relax into shutdown, face impassive, the lie flowing easily from my lips. "I had an interesting conversation with a flight of stairs after too many beers."

Wade chuckles. "Yeah, had a few of those myself. Let me just get the keys for your jeep." He pats Jordan's arm and disappears into the back.

I can *feel* Jordan's eyes on me. I know what he's thinking. He's wondering how I can lie so effectively, so easily, without a second thought.

It comes from years of practice.

Finally, I risk a glance at him. The look he's wearing is more confusion, showing in his puckered brow, and sadness in his eyes.

"Sorry about Wade asking … you know," he says quietly. "He doesn't mean any harm. He's just a straight forward kind of guy."

"It's fine." I smile, shrugging it off. It's easy to do because the shutdown on my emotions is still in place.

Leaning down close, Jordan brings his face to mine. "Pretend to the rest of the world, Mia. I understand your need to do that." Lifting his hand, he runs his thumb over my lips. "But don't pretend with me."

I'm shocked to the core by him. All I can do is nod.

He cups my cheek and presses his lips to my forehead, pulling me close to his chest, saying the rest without words.

Every part of me is attuned to him in this moment.

I hear Wade clear his throat. Jordan and I part quickly.

Wade chuckles. "Here you go." He hands Jordan the keys. "I'm lending you mine, didn't think you'd want one of the eight seaters with just the two of you."

"You're sure?" Jordan checks.

Wade nods. "Take her, have fun. She's parked up back. When you're done, just put her back there. If I'm not here, put the keys through the mailbox."

"Will do. And thanks again for this, Wade, I really appreciate it." Jordan reaches over and shakes his hand.

"Anytime, son. Have a good time. Say hi to your dad for me. How is he? Haven't seen him around lately."

"He's good, away at the moment. My grandpa had an operation, so he's there taking care of him for few weeks."

"Let him know I was asking about him," Wade says.

"Will do, thanks."

"Bye," I say, following Jordan to the door. "It was nice to meet you, Wade."

"You too, little lady."

The instant we're out of the shop, I ask Jordan, "How's your grandpa doing?"

Jordan looks at me with warmth in his eyes. "He's getting back to his old self. I called Dad yesterday and spoke to Grandpa on the phone. He was giving me grief, winding me up, so I know he's getting better." He smiles fondly.

"I'm sorry I haven't asked before now. My head just gets a little filled up at times."

"I get it." He touches my shoulder. "Now wait here, I just need to grab something from the car."

I watch him jog over to his car, then pop the trunk and pull out a cooler bag.

"Food for later," he clarifies when he reaches me.

"Did you make a picnic, Jordan Matthews?"

For the first time *ever*, I see a blush in his cheeks. "I might have," he mumbles and sets off walking.

Smiling, and feeling a little … *glowy,* I fall into step beside him and thread my arm through his. "Thank you. I've never had a picnic before."

His look is one of surprise. "Never as in – never?"

"Never." I affirm.

He presses a kiss to the top of my head. "Well, I'm really glad I'm taking your picnic virginity because I make a fuckin' excellent picnic."

I laugh, glad he can't see my face right now as it's gone somewhere close to resembling sunburnt red.

"That so?" I try to sound casual, but it doesn't work. "Well, I have nothing to compare it against, so I'll have to take your word."

"Oh, take my word. I am the best."

Jordan really is gifted with the art of flirting. His innuendos have me blushing like a teenager, and my body firing up like a porn star.

We walk around the back of the shop where I see a big red jeep waiting for us. It's covered in dirt but looks totally cool. My excitement ramps up a couple of thousand notches.

Jordan opens my door, then helps me in as it's so high off the ground and I'm seriously vertically challenged.

My waist and hips are still burning from the feel of his hands as he climbs in the driver's seat. He puts the cooler on the backseat.

"Buckle up, babe. I'm about to take you on the ride of your life." Grinning, he starts the engine, revving it loudly.

Babe.

He called me babe.

I know it's totally stupid, but I can't keep the smile from my face at his term of endearment.

Recovering before he notices that I'm acting like a complete girl, I laugh. "You're a total nerd, you know that?"

He looks mock-offended. "Hey! I'm cool, and you know it."

I roll my eyes, shaking my head.

"Come on, say it … you know you want to. Just let the words out … *'Oh, Jordan. You're so cool and so awesome.'* There's no need to be embarrassed to speak the truth, babe." He gives a cocky grin.

I let out a laugh. "I like how you're adding to it. I'll give you that you play cool and drive an awesome car, but underneath it all is a nerd trying to bust out."

Throwing his head back, he laughs loud. It's deep and manly. And wonderful.

"Wounded here." He dramatically presses his hand to his heart. "Here I was thinking I had you learned to my awesome ways. Guess I'm just going to have to wow you with my amazing tour guide abilities."

"Said like a true nerd." I grin.

We chat with ease while Jordan drives us out to *La Plata Canyon*.

When we reach the canyon, I'm blown away. I've never seen anything like it before. We don't have these kind of places in Boston, and it warms my heart to Colorado. I can see why my mother returned here to live.

My mother.

I haven't thought about her in days. Not because I'd forgotten, but because Jordan has become the focus of my thoughts. When I think of my mother, and how she abandoned me, it makes things hurt. I don't want to hurt. I just want to feel all the wonderful things that I feel when I'm with him.

I know I can't avoid it forever. Finding my mother is what brought me here. But for today, I choose not to think about it.

"This is Lake Creek we're crossing over," Jordan says as he drives us over a wooden bridge. I peer out my window to look below at the water. Pretty.

"And that's La Plata Peak." Jordan points to mountain covered with scatterings of snow. "It's a great place to hike up."

"Looks beautiful," I murmur.

"We can hike up there one day if you'd like? I'd take you today, but we haven't got the right equipment with us."

A promise of more time with Jordan? Um, yes, please!

"I'd like that." I smile.

The drive through the canyon is amazing. Jordan stops often to point out certain things to me. He knows this place so well, and he sounds so enthralling when he's telling me about the canyons history.

We stop and get out of the jeep to go look at Jordan's favorite lake. It's deep in the canyon and the peaks around it are snow-capped. The water is the bluest of blues that I've ever seen, and right in the middle of the lake is a raised rock formation.

I close my eyes and imagine what it would be like to sit out there on that rock, the water all around me.

Complete solitude. Freedom.

Peace. Just peace.

I wonder if the pain in my heart and the haunt in my head would just disappear, and I would finally be free of everything.

Jordan comes up behind and wraps his arms around my waist. His heat surrounds me. I feel safe in his arms.

"Tell me about your travels," I murmur, content.

"What do you want to know?"

"Where you've been."

He snuggles his face into the crook of my neck. "I've been to the Philippines, Indonesia, Malaysia, Singapore, Vietnam, Cambodia and Thailand."

"Wow. That's a lot of places."

"Hmm. My buddies and I wanted to see the world, so we figured we'd start with South East Asia. Backpacking, working as we went, fitting in as much as we could – we stayed in a lot of dives." He chuckles. "But I didn't care, I just wanted to see the world." He eases out a breath. It's hot on my skin, flowing through me, setting my stomach to tumult. "We were about to head off to India … when I got the news about my mom."

"I'm so sorry, Jordan." I wrap my arms around his, holding him. "Do you ever think you'll travel again?"

"No."

"Why not?"

He moves his nose up my neck, inhaling. It does crazy things to my body. "You smell so fuckin' good. Like vanilla."

I know he's evading, but it's hard to care in this moment. Tingles run south, and I can feel my panties getting damp. "I use vanilla body wash." My voice sounds breathy. Not like me at all.

He breathes me in again. "It smells amazing." His hand frees, smoothing down the flat of my stomach, and he hooks a finger into my belt loop, pulling me against him.

I can feel him against my back, and my body starts to react, instantly lighting up … wanting to feel more of him … feel more of *this*.

"I love this lake," he says close to my ear, his breath tickling and arousing me. "It reminds me of the caldera I saw at Mount Rinjani."

"Where's that?" asks the totally unworldly me.

"Indonesia." Placing a hand on my cheek, he turns my face to him. "You have the exact same eye color as the water there."

My mouth dries. "I do?"

"Hmm." His gaze moves to my mouth. My tongue darts out to moisten my suddenly dry lips.

His eyes flare. "Are you hungry?" he asks.

I'm not entirely sure that we're talking about food right now. "I'm hungry," I say in a voice that doesn't sound like mine. It's all breathy and sexy.

Without another word, Jordan crushes his mouth to mine, his tongue instantly in my mouth. I turn in his arms. He pulls me hard against him.

I like the way it makes me feel. Protected. Wanted. He makes me feel sexy and desirable. Everything I've never before felt.

Our kiss quickly turns heated and desperate. I wind my fingers into his hair, pulling it, keeping him with me. He must like it because the sound he makes in my mouth is more than encouraging. He cups my behind and lifts me off my feet. Instinctively, I wrap my legs around his waist. I don't even realize we've moved until I feel my back press up against the jeep.

His kiss is urgent, mirroring my own. I'm shocked by my reaction to him … how much I want him, but I'm confused—confused by the lust that is urging my body to pull him closer, yet the fear telling me to push him away.

Would he stop if I did? Do I want him to stop?

No.

Not yet.

"God, Mia," he says against my mouth. His hand moves up my side, cupping my breast over my t-shirt. The instant he touches me, my nipple hardens. I moan against his mouth.

His hand is moving under my t-shirt, lifting it, and his fingers are running inside the cup of my bra, and I'm thinking yes … *god, yes!* He pulls down my bra, taking my bare breast in his warm, rough hand, running his thumb over the hardened peak…

I want him so much…

Then I feel him harden against me. His erection pressing against my girl parts…

And a flash of Forbes, pinning me to that wall, trying to rape me, takes away everything with it.

"I'm going to fuck some sense into you. You need teaching a lesson."

Jordan's hand suddenly becomes Forbes' hand. And there's no pleasure. Just fear. Pure unadulterated fear.

And panic.

I'm panicking. My muscles locking with the fear controlling me.

I'm going to be sick.

"Stop. *Please,* stop." I'm breathless, pushing at his hand.

I need him off me, now.

Jordan removes his hand from my t-shirt instantly, putting it onto the truck above my head. "Jesus, I'm sorry. Mia, are you okay?" He searches my face. "Tell me you're okay? Shit, I moved too quick. I wasn't thinking. I'm so sorry." He's shaking his head.

"It's okay, I just … I wanted…" I can hardly catch my breath. "I think … I just … I can't. Not right now. I'm so sorry."

"Mia, no…" He rests his forehead against mine. "You don't have to explain. You never have to explain to me. And don't *ever* be sorry. I'm the one who's sorry. I just got lost in you for a moment there, but it won't ever happen again." His tone is vehement, full of promise. "From now on, I follow your lead. We go as slow, or as fast as you want."

The sound of his voice, his words, calm me – soothe me like nothing I've ever known.

"Okay," I breathe.

It takes me a moment to gather myself, but when I do, I take his face in my hands. "You're the best person I've ever known, Jordan."

He stares into my eyes for a long moment. "Ditto, babe. Ditto."

Chapter Seventeen

Jordan

I've completely screwed things up with Mia.

Not surprising as this is me we're talking about. I started thinking with my cock instead of my brain when I had her pressed up against Wade's jeep.

She felt so fucking amazing against me, and I wanted her so bad, but then she start panicking, her fear was palpable.

And I felt like the world's biggest asshole.

I still feel like an asshole.

I know what she's been through, but I just dove straight in. I should have asked if it was okay to touch her; I should have checked that every move I made was okay. I just thought from the way she was being with me that she was okay and that she was right there with me.

How fucking wrong was I?

She was quiet after that, not surprising. I drove us up to this ridge which is covered with wildflowers and has a great view of the canyon. I thought she would like it up there, and I was right. She seemed to perk up slightly, and was back to herself soon after, but not completely back to how she'd originally been with me. The openness from her and the sense of closeness it gave me was gone.

She'd shut down.

We ate, did some more sightseeing, and I made sure not to touch her the whole time.

It was hard, but I said I'd follow her lead and I meant it.

She didn't make any move to touch me.

That was three days ago.

We haven't kissed, touched, or held hands, since.

We've been to the movies, to dinner, just hanging out at the hotel, but it's like we're back to the way we were before – just friends.

Yesterday, we had another unsuccessful trip out to find her mother.

With only two Anna's left, Mia couldn't pick which one to go to, so she'd made me choose. Not easy to do, so I'd just shut my eyes and jabbed my finger at the paper. That was how I'd picked our next Anna to visit. I only wish I had got the other one because this one was the same as the last.

Not Mia's Anna.

At first, I'd thought she was. Blonde and tiny, just like Mia. A really nice lady. When I'd told her why we were there, she took us inside, sat us in the living room and made us tea. Then she proceeded to tell us, in a really nice way, why there was no way she could be Mia's mother.

She couldn't have children.

To say I'd felt like complete shit was an understatement.

We chatted awhile, but I felt Mia slowly slipping farther away. I hated the feeling more than I could begin to express.

Anna offered us more tea, so out of politeness I'd said yes. As Anna got up to go to the kitchen, she'd paused and turned to Mia. *"If I had been blessed with a child, then I would have wanted one as lovely as you."*

It had been a compliment, but it had hurt Mia. I could see it written all over her face…

"Are you okay?" I asked her quietly.

"Yes."

I wasn't sure if she had heard me or not. She was transfixed, watching Anna Monroe with curiosity. And longing. I could see it plain on her face. I knew Mia wished that she were her mother.

It made me hurt for her. And I worried that coming here had been a mistake. I was starting to think this search for her mother was causing her more harm than good, when Mia stood abruptly.

"You okay?" I asked again, getting to my feet and moving toward her.

Her blue eyes came to me, but she wasn't there. She was already some place lost, and buried deep in those beautiful blues was panic. She thought she was hiding it, but I saw it.

Because I see her.

"I have to go," she uttered, her eyes flitting to the front door.

I know when Mia needs to leave, there's no small talk, no pleasantries. She just has to go – I'd figured that out from the visit to the first Anna Monroe.

Nodding, I took her cold hand. "Sure, babe. Let's go."

And I got her out of there.

Mia hadn't talked the whole ride back home, and the instant we'd arrived, she'd just got out of the car, and went straight to her room.

I'd left her be.

I didn't see her the whole night. I knew she needed space, so I gave it to her.

When she came out of her room this morning, she looked weary and drawn, not like herself at all. She told me she was going out, and I was disappointed.

I miss her.

I know it sounds crazy because I see her all the time, but I miss being able to touch her. Miss just being with her.

She's been out all day. I'm starting to think she might be avoiding me.

Honestly, I don't know what to think.

And thinking is all I've done, and it's messing with my head.

I hate not knowing where I stand with her. Are we back to being just friends? Have I fucked it up completely with her? Has she changed her mind about me … us?

I can't just come out and ask her. I'm worried if I do, I'll hear something I don't want to.

I stand up, feeling irritated and frustrated, and angry with

217

myself. It's a fucking hot day, and it hasn't cooled with the sun going down.

Dozer lifts his head and gives a sad sigh. He's missing her too.

Fuck this. I need to cool off.

I strip my tank and shorts off, leaving just my boxer shorts on. I run toward the lake, down the boardwalk, and dive straight in.

The cold waters hits me, making me feel instantly clearer. I swim under the water until my lungs start to burn, forcing me to resurface. I scrub my hands over my face, drying off the water, and push my hair back. Blinking the water off my lashes, I tip my head back and float in the water as I stare up at the sky.

I've no idea how long I stay there like that, but when I decide to swim back, I push my legs down and lift my head to see Mia standing at the edge of the boardwalk watching me.

She looks like an angel silhouetted by the glow of the early evening sky.

Taking a deep breath, I swim to her, reaching a few feet from the boardwalk when I'm stopped in my tracks.

Fingers gripping the hem of her shirt, she pulls it over her head, dropping it to the floor.

The air is knocked out of me, and I can only stare at the gorgeous sight of her. Denim shorts and a white lace bra make for a sexy image.

She looks like a fucking angel. A sexy fucking angel.

Then she unbuttons her shorts and slides them down her legs, stepping out.

She's wearing matching lace panties.

Thank you god.

I'm transfixed. I have never seen anything as beautiful as her.

Sitting on the edge of the boardwalk, she swings her legs in the water. Hands on the sides, she slides down, submerging herself.

She swims close to me. "Hi," she says quietly.

"Hi."

"I'm sorry I haven't been around. I just—"

I shake my head. "Mia, you don't have to explain anything—"

"Yes, I do. And I will. But not right now. Right now, all I want is for you to kiss me … and make love to me."

Fuck. Me.

I suck in a breath.

I want her. *Really* want her.

Half an hour ago, I would have sold my Mustang if it meant I could be with her.

But now … I don't know what this means. She's been gone all day, and now she turns up, strips off her clothes, and tells me she wants me to make love to her.

My cock is telling my brain to shut the fuck up, and just do it, but my head is worried if I do, I'll only end up pushing her further away.

"I need you, Jordan … *please*," she whispers.

Hearing her plead like that … I'm done for. Add in the fact that I haven't had sex for weeks, and she is the most beautiful woman I've had the privilege to know, and my willpower is shot to fucking hell.

My hand goes to the back of her head and I bring my mouth crashing down to hers.

She moans, her arms instantly going around my neck, her legs wrapping around my waist.

Jesus fucking Christ.

I wrap both my arms around her tiny waist, kissing her like there's no breath left in my body. Like she's my lifeline. With our mouths melded together, I lick the inside of her mouth. She tastes like a mixture of candy and mouthwash.

Her hands slide down my arms, into the water and then across my back. Her fingers creep into the elastic of my boxers.

"I want you," she breathes into my mouth.

Then my goddamn brain has to kick back in. I really fucking hate my brain at times.

"Wait." I pull back, breathing hard.

219

The disappointment shows clear in her eyes. I take her face in my hands.

"We don't have to do this now. I'll wait, however long you need. I just want to be with you. That's all that matters. Sex can come later."

Her grip on my boxer shorts increases, and I can feel her nails digging in my skin. "I don't want to wait. I want you *now*. I want to feel normal and complete and whole, and I feel all those things when I'm with you."

My heart sinks.

I shake my head, solemn. "Babe, having sex with me isn't going to change how you feel about yourself. Those things will still be there afterwards."

Who the fuck am I nowadays? Dr. Fucking Phil?

"But they'll be gone for a time."

I shake my head again because I don't know what else to do. To be honest, I'm feeling pretty fucking gutted right now.

Her gaze lowers. "You don't want me," she whispers, starting to pull away.

The tone in her voice almost kills me.

Keeping hold, I force her eyes to mine. "I want you, babe. *Believe* me, I want you like I've never wanted anything before in my life. I can think of nothing else *but* you. What it would feel like to be inside you. I want you because I'm gone for you." I let out a light sigh, my gaze dipping. "But I want you to have sex with me because you want it for the same reasons as I do – and no other reason."

She leans in and sucks my bottom lip into her mouth. "I want you because, since the day I met you, I've thought of nothing else but what it would feel like to have you inside me."

And just like that, my brain is gone.

I kiss her with everything I have. I kiss her like I don't know how long I have left with her. And maybe that's because I don't.

She rubs herself up against my aching cock, and the need to be inside her becomes urgent.

"Fuck, Mia," I groan.

Keeping hold of her, I wade through the water and walk up the bank, not wanting to let go of her for one second, with only one destination is in mind – my bed.

Mia's hands are gripping my shoulders, nails digging in my damp skin. Her wet tits are pressed up against my chest, begging for me to touch them.

Sliding the palm of my hand over the lace of her bra, I rub her already hard nipple through it. Then I move my hand up, around the nape of her neck, driving my fingers into her hair, I take her mouth again in a deep, hard kiss.

She moans a sound so fucking erotic that I almost lose my shit right here.

When I finally reach my room, I kick the door shut, then lay her down on my bed.

My room is in darkness, the only light coming in through the window. I really want to see her, so I reach for the lamp, but she stops me.

"Leave it off."

What? Why?

I want to see every gorgeous inch of her, but because it's her, and I know she'll have her reasons, I let it go and slowly retract my hand.

We can forego the light, but after tonight, I'm going to have every light in this goddamn room on so that I can see every beautiful inch of her.

I stare down at her, letting my eyes adjust to the dark. I see the creamy skinned silhouette of Mia on my bed, and it turns me on in a way I didn't know possible.

I've never had a woman in my bed before. This has always been my space, but I want to share my space with her. I want her here. I want her in every aspect of my life.

Climbing up on the bed, I kneel between her parted legs.

I lean over her, hands pressing into the mattress either side of her head. I dip my mouth down and kiss her once.

Then I trail my hand with featherlight movements down her face, going down her neck until I reach the peak of breasts where her still damp skin awaits me.

"Is this okay?" I check before diving in.

"Yes." She sounds breathy and sexy. So damn hot.

Lifting her hand to my head, she slides her fingers into my damp hair.

I free one strap off her shoulder, letting it fall as I move the cup, freeing her breast.

Her nipple is taut, and so very ready for me.

I dip my head and take her into my mouth, sucking hard. She groans, her hips jerking upward, pressing her pussy hard against my cock. I nearly shoot my load.

"Fuck," I groan. I grip her hip with my hand, keeping her steady. I intend on making this last for as long as possible.

I return my attention to her nipple, laving it with my tongue, then I begin licking and sucking every part of her tit. Not content with the limited access, I ease my hand behind her, reaching for the clasp on her bra. She inclines, allowing me to unhook it, and I slide it down her arms, tossing it to the floor.

She lays back, hands on my shoulders.

I stare down at her naked tits, unable to look away. "Fuck … Mia, you're beautiful."

Her hand goes to her face, covering it. I know she's feeling shy.

I move her hand from her face. "You're beautiful," I reaffirm and press a gentle kiss to her lips.

I shift down her body, allowing me access to her neglected tit. I take it in my mouth, paying it the same attention, sucking and licking while I pinch her other nipple with my thumb and finger.

She cries out. Pushing against me, panting, "Jordan, please. I need you."

"Fuck. You're so fucking hot." I drop my head against her chest. "I wanted this to last, but I don't know if I can."

Getting to my knees, I hook my fingers into the top of her damp panties. I pause, giving her time to let me know if this is too much.

She nods her head, lightly. "Please," she says.

I pull her panties down her legs. She bends her leg, allowing me to slip it off one leg, then the other. I toss them to the floor and look down at her pussy. It's shaved and neat. I bet she tastes as sweet as she smells.

My cock hardens further. I grab it through my wet boxers, sliding the shaft up and down, all the while staring at her pussy.

"I need to taste you." I'm asking, but I don't wait for her answer because I'm off the end of the bed, knees on the floor, spreading her thighs.

I press my mouth to her pussy, sucking on her clit. Jesus, she tastes amazing.

She cries out, making a mewling sound, digging her heels into the bed. I smile, loving her reaction as I run my nose between her lips, inhaling her.

"So fuckin' good," I murmur, knowing the vibration of my voice will only tease her further.

"Please, Jordan…" she moans. "I need…"

I run my tongue down, pushing it inside her, taking more of her sweetness into my mouth. "Shh … it's okay. I got you, babe." I press my tongue against her clit and slide a finger inside her. Then another.

Then I'm pumping my fingers in and out, licking and sucking her. And I don't stop going until she's exploding under my mouth.

While she's coming down from her orgasm, I remove my boxer shorts in the fastest time known to man, and climb up her panting, trembling body, so ready to be inside her it's not even funny.

I kiss her, running my tongue over her lips, letting her taste herself on me.

She sucks my tongue into her mouth. Her fingers dig into my hips, pulling me closer. "I want you," she breathes.

Jesus. She's so fucking sexy.

I reach over into my drawer, and pull out an unopened box of condoms that I'd bought when Mia and I started dating.

223

Call it forward planning.

I'm an optimistic kind of guy. And that was optimistic, not opportunistic.

Turns out I was right to buy them and keep them in here. I used to keep condoms in my car or wallet. But Mia isn't one of those girls I used to go with, and I knew when I did have sex with her, it would be here, happening exactly as it is.

I rip the box open, tear the foil on one, and roll the condom on. Positioning myself between her legs, I press the head of my cock at her entrance. I stop to kiss her—not rough and passionate, but sweet and tender. I want her to know what she means to me. How I feel about her. How much I want this with her.

Her hands grip my ass, urging me forward.

Taking her lead, I slowly slide inside her. "Mia..." I moan her name like a prayer.

Her hips shift under me. "Jordan," she breathes.

Kissing her again, I pull out and slide back in. "You feel so fuckin' good. I've never wanted anyone like I want you."

"Oh God," she moans, digging her nails in my back, scratching over my skin.

The feel of her nails...

Being inside her...

I lose it. I start fucking her like I've never fucked anyone before.

"Don't stop, Jordan. Don't ever stop." Mia's legs lift, wrapping around my waist as I continue to drive into her.

It's too much. She's too much. All these feelings and emotions and sensations...

All for her...

Because of her...

And I have no clue what to do with them.

I take her hands above her head, holding them to the bed. I lace my fingers with hers, thrusting my cock in and out, watching her face, seeing her pleasure, soaking up every moan and whisper of my name that she makes.

It's not long before I feel her tightening around my cock, and

I know she's almost there.

"That's it, babe," I pant over her mouth. "Come for me."

The instant I feel her coming around me, I explode inside her, coming hard like I've never come before.

Catching our breaths, I stay inside her, reluctant to leave her just yet.

I press a soft kiss to her lips.

"Wow," she murmurs.

"I'd say that just about covers it."

She giggles. It's the sweetest sound.

I rest my forehead against hers, breathing her in. "I'm crazy about you, Mia." I need her to know how I feel. How much she means to me. I need her to know everything that I'm not sure how to say yet.

Her fingers touch my face. The barest of touches, but I feel it like she's drumming on my soul.

"I feel the same," she whispers.

My heart exhales, only now realizing how badly I needed to hear those words from her.

"Give me a second to clean up." Easing out of her, I go to the bathroom, disposing of the condom and quickly washing up.

When I'm done, I pull the covers out from under her, and climb on the bed, covering us both. Pulling her to me, I curl my body around her, tucking her into me, and holding her tight.

I'm cuddling. After sex.

And I don't want to run. I don't want to be anywhere else but here with Mia in my arms.

A sense of peace like I've never know washes over me.

I'm drowning in her. And I want every last drop of Mia in my lungs until all I'm breathing is her.

She strokes my arm with her fingers. "I'm happy," she whispers.

I smile against her soft skin. "Me too, babe."

She turns over to face me, a grin on her gorgeous mouth.

"What?" I ask.

She runs her finger down my chest. "Can we, um … do it

again?"

"Now?" I lift an eyebrow.

"Mmm."

"He might need a minute to get some life back in him," I say gesturing to my cock.

She reaches her hand down, wrapping her small fingers around me, and my cock springs to life at her touch.

"Okay, maybe a minute was over exaggerating it," I say, grinning as I push her onto her back. Climbing on top of her, loving the laughter spilling from her lips, which I take into me as I seal my mouth over hers.

Chapter Eighteen

Mia

I can feel warmth on my back. Fingers trailing lightly over my skin. I can't remember every feeling such contentment when waking.

Then I remember where I am, and who is touching my back. Jordan.

I'm in his bed.

Last night comes flooding back to me. A vivid beautiful memory of the sex Jordan and I had.

Then horror hits when I realize I'm naked.

Completely bare. Laid on my stomach.

My body is uncovered.

And Jordan's awake.

He's seen my scars. Probably looking at them right now.

I feel sick.

I meant to wake up before him and put my clothes on. I wasn't ready for him to see them. Not ready for him to question me about them.

This all my stupid fault.

After seeing Anna Monroe number two yesterday … and how nice she was to me, and the disappointment I felt that she wasn't my mother … coupled with the fact that the last Anna left on the list might actually be my mother…

It set off another episode which sent me running to a convenience store, then a motel where I holed myself up for the day and binged myself sick.

"Hey," Jordan said softly as I walked through the lobby.

I knew he was behind the reception desk, I just couldn't bring myself to look at him, knowing what I was going out to do. I was afraid he'd see it written all over my face.

I hadn't spoken to him since yesterday. He'd been so sweet to me about the Anna thing, but I was lost somewhere deep inside my head ... I still was.

"I'm going out," I said. And that was it.

Then I was out the door and in my car, driving to the convenience store on the outskirts of town and buying what I needed to make myself feel better in the only way I know how.

I parked in a quiet spot and started to rip open the food, then realization hit me, quickly followed by panic. What if someone saw me out here? What if Jordan had followed me and knew what I was doing? It was irrational, I knew that, but my head was a mess.

The what ifs were there, and they weren't leaving anytime soon.

How would I explain to him? How would I make him understand?

I wouldn't. I'd lose him.

That was when I saw the sign for a motel just down the street.

Shoving the food back in the bag, I set my car in drive and drove to the motel.

It looked sketchy and rundown, but I didn't care about that. I just needed to be alone, so I got a room.

Once in it, I sat down on the bed and ripped into the food. As the food hit my palette, a discontented peace slid through me that I had needed to feel since I'd left Anna Monroe's house.

I'd hit low. And after I was done, all I'd wanted was Jordan. It was like an urgent panic ... a desperate need to be with him.

He's the only person who has ever made me feel good and whole.

I'd wanted him to give me those feelings back, so I'd cleaned up, then was out of that hotel and in my car, driving back here to him … taking my clothes off … asking him to make love to me…

I just hadn't thought beyond that. The possibility of him seeing me. Seeing my scars.

I need to get out of here.

Moving quickly, I slide out of bed, taking the sheet with me so I can wrap it around myself.

"Morning," he says. I can hear the careful in his voice.

I can't bring myself to meet his eye. "Morning," I say. "I just … need to use the bathroom."

I'm in there a second later, locking the door behind me. Moving to the sink, I stare at myself in the mirror above it. I hate what I see staring back.

I sit down on the toilet, trying to control my emotions, the urges I'm having right now.

I need to get dressed and out of here, but I can't because I left my clothes outside when I was stripping in front of Jordan.

What was I thinking? I don't act that way. That isn't me.

But he makes me want to be that way. He makes me want to be something … someone, better.

And now he's seen the hideous scars I hide, and it's going to be too much for him. I'm going to lose him, just when I'd got him.

A gentle knock on the door. "Mia? Are you okay in there?"

"Yes." My voice breaks. "I'll be right out."

Wrapping the sheet tight around my body, I slowly open the bathroom door.

Jordan is sitting on the edge of the bed wearing black boxer shorts. Nothing more.

If I wasn't in my current messed up state, I would take my time and truly appreciate his fine body which I'm seeing for the first time in daylight.

To say he's toned is putting it mildly. I could happily run my pinky finger along the lines of his six-pack for hours.

His eyes lift to mine. "Hey," he says in a gentle voice. Getting to his feet, he comes over to me.

Wanting him to touch me so badly, yet afraid what it'll do to me if he does, I sidestep him.

"Thank you … for last night." *Thank you? I couldn't think of anything better to say?* "I'm going to go to my room…"

"Wait." His voice comes from behind me. "Don't leave. Talk to me."

I sigh and turn around. "What do you want to talk about?"

"This … you and me." He gestures a hand between us. "The way you're acting now – shutting me out. I thought after last night…" He scrubs a hand over his bed hair. "Look, I think I know why you're acting this way … why you wouldn't let me turn the light on last night … the scars on your bottom and thighs…"

I visibly cringe. "You don't know what you're talking about." I can feel my traitor eyes filling with tears.

"So tell me." He takes a step toward me, holding his hands out.

"I can't."

"Yes, you can. You've told me the other things that bastard did to you. You can tell me this. I haven't laid judgment, and I'm not about to start. Babe, I'm here…"

I shake my head. A tear drips from my eyelashes. "Forbes didn't do this to me."

His face freezes. I see his fingers curl into his palm. "Who?" His word comes out slow.

Fear courses through me. I feel exposed. I wrap my arms around myself, wishing so very badly that I was dressed right now.

"Who, Mia?" I can hear the anger rising in his voice. I know he's not angry at me, he's angry at who hurt me.

Another tear hits my cheek. I rub it away with the back of my hand and take a gulp of air.

"Oliver. My father."

"Your *dad* did this to you?" The disbelief in his voice hurts me. It makes me feel like trash.

"Yeah, well not everyone is lucky to have a great dad like yours, Jordan." I don't mean to sound bitter, but I can't seem to stop myself. "My father wasn't the caring kind of man who loved his child like yours does. Mine was a sick, cruel bastard who used to beat me whenever the feeling would take him, usually with his belt. The scars are from that."

I yank the sheet from my body, exposing myself. I turn my back to him. I'm feeling insane levels of pain, and have absolutely no sense of anything right now. I don't know what I'm doing or where my mind is at. I'm just doing…

"If I'd been particularly bad, as he put it, which wouldn't take much … just leaving the cap off the milk. Or the especially bad crimes I could commit … being a minute late when returning home from school – then he'd use the metal buckle end of his belt. You know, to cause more pain and damage. Helped make his point."

Hot tears are dripping down my face. I leave them burning my skin so that I can feel something. Because I need to feel something. Anything.

"He taunted me with knives and guns. All part of his sick games – letting me know where I stood in the food chain. I've lost count of the number of cracked ribs and broken bones I've had. Broken fingers that I've reset myself. Dislocated shoulders. Popped out knees from his boots stamping on them." I pull in a hard, painful breath. "So that was my life, and now you know all of it, and I'm leaving."

I grab the sheet, covering myself, my self-loathing possessing me like a disease. All I want is to get out of here, but Jordan is quick.

His arms come around me from behind, caging me to him. I don't fight to leave because part of me doesn't want to. I want his care, more than anything.

I don't want to be alone anymore.

I feel the tremble in his body. He presses his cheek to mine. My eyes close on the pain that's burning me from the inside out.

"No, Mia," he whispers. "*No*."

The feel of his arms, his hands … his safe hands that I know would never hurt me…

I break.

Like glass shattering, I go. My legs give out, but Jordan is there, holding me. Lifting me into his arms, he carries me to the bed.

I wrap myself around him, burying my face in his chest as I cling to him and cry out years and years of deeply buried pain.

"I'm here … I've got you … *always*. I'll never let anyone hurt you ever again, Mia. I swear."

At some point, I fall asleep. The sheer exhaustion from crying, and reliving my past pain with Jordan had taken its toll.

When I wake, my eyes are swollen, and my head is sore and heavy.

I lift my head from Jordan's chest, blinking my blurry eyes into focus. His are closed, but his arms immediately tighten around me.

"Don't leave." He opens his eyes.

"I wasn't," I whisper, my voice hoarse.

His hand rubs circles on my back. "How are you feeling?"

Rubbing my eyes, I rest my chin on his chest. "I've felt worse."

He nods in understanding.

"Thank you … for being here, for listening."

"I'm always here for you." He touches my face. "Do you need to talk some more, now you're feeling a little clearer?"

I shake my head. "I feel okay at the moment. I want to keep feeling okay." I lie my head back on his chest and listen to the gentle drum of his heart.

My eyes graze over his tattoo, which covers his right pectoral, goes up over his shoulder, and down his arm, ending at his wrist. It's tribal, with quotes woven through it.

I run my fingertip down his arm, reading the quotes I've seen before, but paying attention now…

Not all who wander are lost.

That's on his bicep.

"I had this tattoo done in three parts," he explains. "That was done while I was traveling. I had it done in Indonesia."

My fingers move down to his forearm…

If you can't live longer, live deeper.

"I got that done after my mom died."

I give a sad smile, then press my lips to the words, kissing them. I sit up, shifting my body so that I'm straddling his waist. His hands go to my thighs.

"You finished checking me out?" He grins.

"I'm checking out your tattoo, and no, I'm not done." I smile, then lean close to read the words on his chest…

I don't go looking for trouble.
Trouble usually finds me.

I let out a laugh. That is such a Jordan thing to say. But why do I know that saying…

"Harry Potter." I jab my finger at the tattoo.

"Ow!" he complains, rubbing his chest.

"Sorry." I smile sheepishly. "That's a quote from Harry Potter, right?"

He gives me a suspicious look. "Yeah, it is. Why?"

I shrug. "No reason … *geek*," I cough, covering my mouth

with my hand.

His eyes narrow, then he's moving like lightening, tackling me back and pinning me to the bed with his body.

"Arrggghh!" I let out a squeal of laughter.

"Did you just call me a geek?" He hovers his face above mine. His face is serious, but I can see the mirth in his eyes.

"Nope." I press my grinning lips together.

"No? I'm pretty sure you did just call me a geek." ·

"Noooo." I give a gasp of shock. "I mean as if getting a Harry Potter quote tattooed on your chest would, in any way, make me think you're a geek. I'd say it's the coolest thing *ever*."

"Smart-ass," he quips. "And seriously, babe, Harry Potter is fuckin' cool. The kid's a wizard for fuck's sake!"

I start laughing. I love seeing this side of him. The one I don't think anyone else ever sees, the stripped down version of him. The real him. The one he hides away, deep inside.

He starts laughing with me, then runs his hand down the side of my face, his thumb pressing against my lips, sending fire shooting through me. The laughter is gone quickly, his lips replacing his thumb.

"I love to see you laughing," he says against my mouth.

My hands slide down his back. "I love that you make me laugh."

Smiling against my mouth, he gives me one last kiss, then lays his head on my chest.

I start playing with his hair. He makes a sound of appreciation, so I figure he must like it.

"I am a geek," he mutters after a while.

I stop playing with his hair. "Yeah, you are." I smile. "But you know what? It makes me like you even more."

He squeezes my hip, pressing a kiss against the peak of my breast.

I start playing with his hair again. "So … what now?" I ask the question which has been hovering in my mind since we first had sex.

I know we've had two dates, a freak out from me when

things first got heavy between us, and now we've had sex followed by an emotional breakdown from me.

Truthfully, I just don't know what's actually happening between us.

I know what I want, but the problem is, I don't know what Jordan wants from me.

His chest lifts on a breath, his hand stroking the skin on my shoulder. "Well, I was thinking that I would leave you in bed, get up and feed Dozer 'cause he'll be wanting his breakfast, and he needs his meds. Then I would make pancakes for my woman, and bring them to her in bed. Afterward, once she's happily fed, I thought we could spend the rest of the day in bed ... only if she wants to, of course?"

His woman. I'll take that as a good thing.

He lifts his head, resting his chin on my chest. His warm eyes stare at me, filled with feeling, feeling he has for me.

I lift my head, placing my arms behind for support, and bring my face closer to his. "She wants," I murmur.

His pupils dilate, eyes darkening with lust.

"Actually, Dozer can wait a bit longer to be fed." His hand moves down my body. Lifting slightly, he puts it between us, slipping his finger inside me.

"Oh, my god," I breathe. I feel him grow hard against my thigh.

"Babe, so wet ... already," he groans.

"It's you ... what you do to me."

"And I plan on doing a whole lot more," he promises before sealing his mouth over mine.

After making love to me, Jordan finally relents and goes to feed Dozer.

I retrieve my panties, and put on one of Jordan's t-shirts that I nab from his closet. It's huge on me, nearly reaching my knees.

I'm wandering around his bedroom, looking at a map of the world he has tacked to the wall. There are pins in it with a drawn line under the pins, marking the route of all the places he has traveled. The last pin is in Thailand, but the drawn line goes onto India, through Nepal, then across China to Hong Kong, up to Shanghai, finally ending in Japan. I'm guessing that's where he would have gone if his trip hadn't ended early.

I look at the photos pinned up around the map, pictures of a slightly younger Jordan in different locations with his friends.

He looks happy; bright eyed.

Looking at these pictures, seeing the fun and adventure in his face when he didn't know what was to come, makes my heart hurt for him.

Beneath the map is his desk. There are a few framed photos sitting on top of it.

One is of a dark haired woman, smiling happily into the camera. She must be Jordan's mom. I pick it up, examining it. She looks quite young in the photo, maybe my age, and she's really pretty. She has the same eye color as Jordan.

Putting it down, I pick up the next picture. It's of a young Jordan, maybe four or five, held in the arms of a man whom I'm guessing is his dad as he looks exactly like Jordan does now. Beside his dad, tucked into his side, is a petite blonde haired lady. She's really beautiful. Oh right, she must be Jordan's mother. Maybe the other woman is an aunt or something.

I'm just putting the picture down, when Jordan comes in with a tray containing pancakes and two cups of coffee.

Could he be any more perfect? I keep expecting to wake up and find out this is all a dream and I'm still in that motel bed back near Boston.

He puts the tray down on the desk, and his arms come around my waist from behind, resting his chin on the top of my head. "That's my mom and dad." He points to the picture I was just looking at.

"Your mom was beautiful, Jordan."

"Yeah, she really was. You remind me of her a bit, you know."

"I do?" I smile.

"Yeah, she always used to speak without thinking like you do."

"Hey!" I exclaim, giving his side a pinch.

"Hey! Knock it off!" He laughs, wriggling behind me. "I'm really fuckin' ticklish!"

I tilt my head back, looking up at him. "Hmm … I didn't know that."

He stares down at me, narrowing his gaze. "Yeah, and I didn't tell you for the very reason that's going through that gorgeous head of yours right now. So don't go getting any ideas about tickling me again."

"As if I would." I smile sweetly.

He shakes his head, giving me a quick kiss on the lips.

I pick up the photo again and examine it. "You look exactly like your dad."

"Well, yeah, he was a handsome fucker when he was younger."

Shaking my head, I laugh as I put the picture down.

"Who's this?" I point to the picture of the dark haired woman.

Jordan loosens an arm from around me and picks up the frame. "Abbi … she's my real mom."

I turn, surprised.

He meets my eyes. "She died giving birth to me. She had an undiagnosed heart condition, and her heart gave out during delivery. She died soon after I was born."

My eyes fill with tears.

God, he's known so much loss. He's lost two mothers.

I reach up and touch his face. "I'm so sorry."

He puts her picture down. "It's okay. I never knew her. It makes it hard to hurt over her loss if you know what I mean. But my dad has told me everything about her growing up, and I have photographs."

"So, the woman you call mom…?"

"Belle. She was my dad's childhood sweetheart. They broke up when she left to go to college. That was when he met Abbi, and they had me. After Abbi died, dad was raising me alone, with the help of my grandpa as dad was already in the force at this point. Then Belle moved back home when I was about three or four. They ended up getting back together, and she raised me as her own."

"They never wanted any kids together?" I ask.

A strange look crosses his face, like he's never considered it before. His lip pushes out. "Nah, I guess not. They already had perfection in me, so what more could they want?"

I roll my eyes and laugh. "Right."

Chuckling, he moves from behind me and gives my butt a pat. "Come on, let's eat before my hard work goes cold."

We sit down at the desk. Jordan gives me the chair and pulls over a stool for him to sit on. I tuck my legs underneath me. It's a subconscious move on my part. Still covering up my scars, even though he knows they're there and exactly how I got them.

Telling Jordan all about Oliver was like opening the door on a dark room and letting the light flood in.

It doesn't fix things or change my memories, but knowing I have him to talk to makes it easier.

Picking up a pancake, I tear a piece off and put it in my mouth. I see Jordan's eyes making work of me, especially the partial leg he can see. He looks like he's remembering what we did half an hour ago. I give him a look.

"What?" he says, eyes wide with innocence. "It's not my fault you look hot in my t-shirt. And you have great fuckin' legs."

A flush shimmers through my body. I can feel myself growing needy for his touch again.

I wonder if I'll always feel like this about him.

I take another bite of pancake. Swallowing, I get an unexpected pain in my stomach. I grip my hand to my stomach. I know where this is from. I went a little rough on myself yesterday, and this is the first time I'm eating since.

Jordan notices. "Hey, you okay?" His brow furrows with concern.

"Yeah, fine." I'm a little breathless as I ride out the pain. I put the pancake down. "Just women's things."

"Do I need to make the most of you while I can?"

I grin, the pain subsiding. "We're good for a few more days, so feel free to take advantage whenever the mood takes."

"Oh, I intend to." He puts his pancake down and pats his lap.

"Now?" I bite my lip.

"Hmm." He nods, that sexual shimmer in his eyes that he gets. The one that tells me he's about to make my body feel amazing.

Getting off my chair, I straddle him, resting my arms on his shoulders and linking my hands behind his head. I can feel him already hard against me. "You're insatiable."

"Only for you, babe." His hands go to my behind and his fingers trace a gentle line over my scars.

My body tenses, my muscles locking.

"Relax," he soothes. "It's just me."

I nod my head, and try to relax.

Standing with me, he carries me to the bed, laying me down.

"You're beautiful." He drops a kiss to the base of my neck. "Every single part of you." He moves down my body, laying on the bed beside me, and turns me to my side, facing me away from him. "Nothing about you is ruined..." His hand gently moves over my behind, down to my thigh. "Or broken, or marred..." He moves down, placing a kiss on my behind. "Just gorgeous, babe."

Jordan moves up my body, curling his around mine with his chest to my back, hugging me to him.

"But nothing on the outside compares to what's in here." His voice comes in my ear, as his hand slips under the t-shirt. He presses his large hand between my breasts, covering my heart. "This is what I'm crazy about, what's in here."

My heart feels replete with him, ready to burst. Needing to be closer to him, I turn in his arms and bury my face in his neck, breathing him in.

239

I've never met anyone like Jordan. He's a miracle to me. My miracle.

He's like breathing fresh air for the very first time.

I realize that I didn't start breathing until him.

I didn't start living until him.

"I breathe you, Jordan," I whisper against his skin.

He tilts his head back, eyes staring down into mine. "I breathe you too, babe."

Chapter Nineteen

Jordan

Running back inside to answer the phone, I grab the receiver off the wall. "Golden Oaks," I answer.

"Hey son, just checking in, seeing how you're doing?"

"Hey Dad. All good here." I hop up on the kitchen counter.

I can see Mia through the window with Dozer. She's feeding him meat treats. Poor fucking dog is going out of his mind with that cast on, so we've been spending time with him.

In-between making out that is.

"How's things?"

"Same." I shrug, grabbing a nut out of the bag I opened earlier, I toss it my mouth.

"No other guests than our current one?"

"Nope." I crunch. "The Perry's are due later on today, though." I lift my voice in optimism, hoping to pass some onto him.

"Christ, is it that time of year already?"

"Yep. I got their room all ready for them, so we're good to go."

Mia insisted on helping me prepare the room. It took a little longer than it usually takes me as we ended up having some fun which began with Mia getting down on her knees and taking my cock in her mouth, and ended with her legs wrapped around my waist, back pressed against the wall while I fucked her to orgasm.

"You're a good son," Dad says.

I shake my head.

No, Dad, I'm not, but I'm trying my hardest to be. And with

Mia by my side, I think I can do it.

He lets out a sigh. "So we've definitely got no other bookings?" He checks this again as if I'm going to suddenly magic some up.

"No … I'm sorry, Dad."

"It's not your fault. Business will pick up soon, I'm sure of it."

Always the optimist, my dad, but I hope for both our sakes that business does pick up.

"How's Dozer doing?" he asks. "His leg healing okay?"

"Yeah, it's healing fine, but he's bored shitless not being able to go out for a run, so Mia's currently keeping him entertained." I look out the window at them again. Mia's laying on the grass with Dozer standing over her, pinning her while he licks her face. She's laughing, trying to push him off. The sight of them has me smiling.

"Mia – as in our hotel guest Mia – is keeping *your* dog entertained?" Dad says, wiping the smile from my face.

Shit. I shouldn't have said that. He's going to know something is going on between Mia and me now, but then he would have as soon as he got back home. I'm serious about her, so telling him now isn't going to hurt anything I guess.

"Yes, Mia as in our hotel guest—"

"Is there anything I need to know?" he cuts me off before I get a chance to tell him about Mia and me. The 'dad' tone in his voice irritates me, so the immature side of me decides to play it out to annoy him.

"Like what?" I say with a casualness to my voice

"Like are you having sex with this girl?"

Okay. Straight to the point.

"Yeah…" I exhale. "I'm sleeping with her … but before you start kicking off, I want you to know this is different. *She's* different."

He's silent a moment. "You've never told me that a girl is different before. Should I take this as a good sign?"

"Yeah." I smile. "You should."

"So you really like this girl, huh?"

Like, is the understatement of the century, but I'm not about to tell my dad that I've fallen in love with Mia.

Yeah, you heard me. I fucking love her.

I've never had feelings for a girl before, but the first time I do, I'm falling in love, and hard. I guess this is what happens to us men who don't love easily. We love quicker and harder.

Now, I just need to find the nerve to tell Mia that, after just a little over a week of knowing her, I'm crazy in love with her. I'm hoping that when I do, I won't sending her running for the hills. She can be skittish at times.

"Yeah, I really like her, Dad," I reply, running a hand through my hair. "I didn't intend to start anything with Mia. I meant what I said to you that time on the phone … but we just got close." I smile at the thought of how good it feels to be close to her.

"She came here looking for her mother, and after she helped me with Dozer when he had his accident, I said I would help her try to find her mom, and we just ended up spending more and more time together. I got to know her really well, and she's pretty fucking amazin', Dad."

"Sounds like you got it bad, boy." He chuckles. "I'm looking forward to meeting this girl who's managed to turn my horndog sons' head."

"Ha! Nice, Dad, real nice." I laugh. "You'll like her though. She's smart, and real beautiful. She reminds me a bit of mom – tiny, blonde, has the tendency to speak without thinking. Actually, that reminds me. I've being meaning to ask you, have you ever heard of a woman called Anna Monroe who lived round here?"

It's a fairly biggish town that we live in, so chances are he might not have, but in his old line of work, he tended to know everyone.

I get no reply.

"Dad? You still there?"

"Yeah. I'm here." He's a little short, and his voice sounds

different … gruff, strained.

"Did you hear what I said? I asked you if you'd heard of a woman called Anna Monroe." I'm pushing now because I know there's something there. He knows something about Mia's mom.

"Jesus Christ…" He sighs. "Jordan, I need you to do something for me. Do you have a photo of Mia that you can send to my cell?"

A hand comes around my throat. "Why?"

"Just do it!" he snaps.

My dad never raises his voice at me – never. Not even when I screwed up with the gambling did he once raise his voice at me. It's just the type of dad he is – a reasoner, not a yeller.

"Jesus! What the hell is going on, Dad?" I say, equally irate.

He exhales. "Look, I'm sorry I snapped. Just … do you have a picture of Mia or not?"

"No, I don't. But wait a minute, I can get one."

I pull my cell from my pocket and set the camera on. I hold it up to the window, and zoom in on Mia's face.

She's smiling. She's happy. And she has no clue that I'm about to take a picture of her to send to my dad for a reason I can only guess isn't good.

The hand around my throat tightens.

I snap the picture.

"I'm sending the photo to your cell now." I watch the little bar sending, then telling me it's been sent.

I hear Dad's message tone beep in the background, then I wait, holding my breath.

"Jesus Christ," I hear him mutter. "It's her."

And this is the moment when I know it's bad, real bad, and that this is going to somehow change everything irrevocably.

"Dad, you really need to tell me what the hell is going on."

He lets out a resigned sigh. "I know. I just don't know where to start."

"Beginning works good for me." I'm getting slightly pissed off, and my heart is beating like a bastard.

"Look, this isn't technically my story to tell, so go easy on me, son."

I sigh with impatience.

I hear the phone rustle, like he's moving, then he starts talking, "You know that Belle lived away from Durango."

"Yeah, she went to college. It was why you guys broke up after high school. Then she moved back home, and you got back together."

"Right. Well the story in the middle is a little different than the one you know. And Jordan, listen, I only found out the extent of your mom's time in Boston days before she died…"

Boston.

Oh no.

Motherfucking, no.

Annabelle – that's my mom's full name. I've always known her as Belle, but her name is Annabelle.

Anna.

Why didn't it click before now? I'm so fucking stupid!

Belle is Anna.

She's Mia's mother. I know it in my gut.

"Belle is Mia's mother." I nearly choke on the words.

Dad sighs a weary sound. And it's confirmed.

My heart feels like it's just been ripped from my chest.

"Yeah, I'm afraid she is."

My mom. The woman who raised me … is Mia's mother.

The mother who abandoned her when she was a baby. Left her alone with that shithole of a father, is the woman who took me on as her own and raised me.

This is a wrecking ball. And it's going to destroy everything in its path.

Mia … us.

My head drops in my hands. "Fuck. Fuck. Fuck!"

"I'm sorry, son. She told me days before she died about Mia. I didn't know. I promise you. All I knew was that while she was in her last year of college, she met this doctor. He swept her off her feet, they got married soon after, but he wasn't the guy she thought he was. The instant they were married, he turned violent.

He hurt her bad. She ended up in hospital a few times because of him. Eventually, she left. Came back here. Divorced him. She *never* told me that she'd had a baby with him."

I feel ill.

I slide off the counter. My feet hit the tiles and feel unsteady, so I sit on the floor.

Knees bent up, I put my head between them and take deep breaths.

"When Belle knew she was dying," Dad continues. "She told me everything – all about Mia. She said that looking back, she thinks she was suffering with post-partum depression. And she was afraid, Jordan. Her ex-husband was a bastard of a man. The scars he left her with…"

I wince at his words, an image of Mia's scars flashing through my mind.

"When I saw them the first time … I wanted to go there and kill him, but Belle wouldn't let me. Obviously, she didn't want me to go because she didn't want me to know about Mia." He sighs.

"Why did she leave her there, Dad? I don't understand?" My voice cracks on the words knowing the life Mia had with her father.

Then I envision a different past for her.

One where Belle brought Mia back here with her. She would have been my sister. I would never have loved her in the way I do now, but rather that, then her have the life she had.

Her life with us would have been good. She'd have grown up happy. She would have had the life she deserved.

Not one filled with cruelty, and pain. Unimaginable pain.

I feel a sick, resentful anger toward the woman who raised me. The woman who patched up my busted knees when I fell off my bike time and time again. The woman who fed me. Bathed me. Loved me.

Jesus. Christ.

I get up from the floor and start pacing.

"Belle's ex-husband was a rich, powerful man, Jordan. He

was a doctor – a heart surgeon. People respected him. He wouldn't let her take Mia. Told her if she tried that he'd have her arrested for kidnapping."

Yanking out a chair at the table, I sit down. "But she could have called the cops – told them what was happening to her. She had the evidence – the scars, her being in hospital because of his beatings."

"You're right she could have. But you know how these things go. She'd have to prove it, and she was up against a man from a wealthy family who ran in high circles. His dad was a good friend of the chief of police. Power and money can make things go away, son. But for all he did to Belle, she knew he wouldn't hurt his own child which was how she was able to leave Mia with him."

I bang my fist on the table, hard. "Are you fuckin' kidding me! I can't believe I'm hearing this shit! He wouldn't hurt her – Dad, I've seen her scars." *I've felt her pain.* "He beat her until the day he died. He made her life a fuckin' misery! And because of him, violence was all she knew, so she ended up in a relationship with an asshole exactly like the one who raised her! Why do you think she left Boston, Dad? The bastard she was with – he beat her – tried to rape her."

"*No.*" His voice is filled with shock and disbelief. He sounds exactly like I felt in the moment when she told me.

"No," he repeats. "I found her – Mia. That was one of the reasons Belle told me about her. She wanted to know Mia, make her peace before she died, but by the time I found Mia, it was too late and Belle had passed.

"But I still went to Boston. You remember when I told you I had that police conference? I went then. I watched her for a few days, not in a creepy way, I just couldn't decide whether to tell her about Belle or not. In the end, I decided against it – I didn't think it was worth hurting Mia by telling her that the mother who had abandoned her as a baby had just died. But I wanted to know she was okay – happy. She seemed it. She was in school, had an application for Harvard. Lived in a great place and drove a nice car. And I saw her with him – her father, Oliver. They seemed to get along well."

"Yeah, well Mia can wear a great mask, Dad. She's a fuckin' specialist at pretending to be something she isn't."

"Jordan, if I'd have known, I would have done something. You know that."

I exhale, heavily. "Yeah, I know. I just ... god, I don't know what to do – how to tell her."

How am I going to tell the girl I'm in love with that her mother – who left her to be raised by that monster of a man – raised me instead of her?

She'll blame me. I'm going to lose her.

I feel physically sick at the thought.

"Just tell her the truth. Exactly as I've told you."

I scrub my hand over my face. "She won't be able to get past this. She's going to blame me. I'm going to lose her."

"No, you won't," he states vehemently.

"Belle left her with him and chose to raise me instead. I know if it were me, it would kill me."

"Jordan, this isn't your fault. I'll come home. I'll explain it to her—"

"No." I pull in a deep breath. "She needs to hear this from me."

"You're sure?"

No. "Yes. I'll tell her."

"Okay. You know Mia best. Call me when you've talked to her. Let me know how she's doing?"

"Yeah, I will."

"Jordan?"

"Yeah."

"It's going to be fine, son. I promise."

I swallow past the burning in my throat, wishing I could be as confident as he is.

"I'll call you later." I hang up the phone, dropping it to the table with a clatter, I let my head follow.

A minute later I hear the backdoor open.

"Hey, you okay?" Mia's soft sweet voice carries through the room, hitting me with a pure agony.

I lift my head, turning to her. The warm smile on her face instantly disappears, turning to worry at my expression.

"Jordan – is everything okay?" She moves quickly toward me.

"I–" The words stick in my throat, and start to sink fast … fast like rocks in water.

"Jordan?"

Oh god. I can't tell her.

I can't.

I get to my feet and take her beautiful face in my hands, forcing a smile onto my deceitful mouth.

"Everything's fine, babe."

Then I press my lying lips to her soft, warm, honest mouth, hating my weak, cowardly-self more and more, with each passing second.

Chapter Twenty

Mia

There's something eating at Jordan. He thinks I don't know, but I can see it in his eyes, and in the way his expression drops every time he thinks I'm not looking.

He's been acting strange after the telephone call he took from his dad the other day.

At first I thought maybe they'd had a disagreement, but now I know it's something more. And the paranoid, sadistic part of me is starting to think it's something to do with me – that maybe, he's changed his mind about us.

A part of me wishes he would just tell me so I would know either way.

I could ask him, but then I'm afraid what his answer will be. So like the masochist I am, I'm taking whatever he throws my way. Granted, he's throwing a lot my way, but there's still something off. I just wish I had more strength than I do. I wish I could just up and leave, and stop being so damn pathetic over a man, who I'm pretty sure doesn't want me anymore.

And the worst thing is, I've realized I'm in love with him.

I know, right?

You think I would have learned my lesson by now.

And it's not as if I can tell him how I feel, or that there's any point. Not while he's working himself away from me.

I just wish he didn't know so much about me. It makes me feel vulnerable to him.

I know what I need to do – pack my things and move out of here, stay somewhere else. It just feels a little easier said than done at the moment.

I also need to grow a backbone and pay a visit to the last Anna Monroe on my list. It just feels a million times harder now I don't have Jordan there to hold my hand.

I guess he really is what he told me he was in the beginning – unable to commit to a girl. And no matter how much wishing on my part for me to have been the one to change him – the signs are telling me otherwise.

Yes, he says he wants me. But each time he's said that, he's either been inside me, or well on his way to it. And I know better than anyone that a man will say things he doesn't mean while he's having sex with you.

Last night was no different. I'd woken up in the early hours of the morning to find Jordan gone from his bed, and in the space beside me, where he'd fallen asleep, was a sleeping Dozer, stretched out and snoring.

In the end, my curiosity and frustration won out. I'd searched the hotel to no success, then eventually found him sitting out on the boardwalk over the lake, drinking a beer…

I walked over and stood between his open legs, staring down at him. Jordan's hands went around the back of my thighs, fingers gripping. His head rested against them, like it was hard for him to look at me.

I slid my fingers into his hair, silently begging him to talk to me … but wishing for only things I'd want to hear.

His hand slid up my leg and took hold of my hand. He tugged me down to sit between his legs. I rested my back against his chest, and he wrapped his arm around my middle while taking a drink of his beer.

"What you doing out here so late?" I asked, my words drifting out over the lake, disappearing into the night.

He nuzzled my neck, inhaling. "Couldn't sleep."

I took the beer from his hand, had a swig, then handed it back.

"What's keeping you awake?"

He placed the bottle down beside him and let out a long breath. "Nothin'."

Nothing!

Angry, tired, and completely pissed off with his lack of communication, I got to my feet.

"If you don't want me anymore, Jordan – this whatever we have – then just say so! Just ... please, stop ... this!"

I swiveled on my heel and ran back to the hotel.

He caught up with me on the porch by the main door.

His hand closed the door I was opening. He came up behind me, pressing his chest to my back.

"I want you," he said, rough, against my ear. "Don't ever think for one fuckin' second that I don't. I want you more than I have ever wanted anyone."

"So, why all this?" I was breathing heavy, feeling confused, my heart thundering in my chest.

"All of what?"

I turned, curling my hands around the door handle as I leaned back against it. "You, being different ... distant with me ... I know there's something you're keeping from me."

His eyes closed as if he were in pain. "It's nothing for you to worry about."

I reached for his hand, curling my fingers around his. "I just want you to talk to me." I tugged on his hand, trying to encourage speech.

His eyes opened, staring down at our entwined hands.

A long breath. "I will..." He shook his head. "But not right now ... not now." It felt like he wasn't even talking to me by this point.

Then his hands went to the door, either side of my head, and his lips came down hard on mine, no hesitation.

I wanted to push him away, tell him to talk to me now, not later. That kissing me wouldn't solve whatever was eating at him.

But I didn't. Because I didn't want him to stop kissing me – ever.

He broke the kiss to pull my pajama tank over my head.

252

Bending his mouth down, he took my nipple into his mouth.

My head fell back against the door with a thud.

I reached for him, unbuttoning his jeans. I slid my hand inside his boxer shorts, grabbing his hot, hard cock.

"Fuck, Mia," he groaned, pushing himself into my hand.

Then things got heated and urgent and fast.

My pajama bottoms and panties were off, and before I knew it, I stood naked on the hotel porch, and Jordan – still fully clothed, was lifting me off my feet and slamming his cock inside me.

I cried out from the quick invasion and the instant pleasure. Wrapping my legs around his waist, I dug my fingernails hard into his shoulders.

This only set him off further.

He was hitting me with sure, hard thrusts, his jeans chaffing painfully against me, but I didn't care. All I cared about was having him inside me. Nothing else mattered at that point.

We were outside, having crazy, furious, make-up sex in the early hours of the morning ... all those things fueling it a hundred times hotter ... a thousand times more intense.

"You're mine, Mia," he ground out as his hips pinned mine to the door, making love to me with a fierce intensity. "I'm never losing you. Never."

"You're not going to lose me," I panted out, confused and turned on like never before. "Not ever."

That was a handful of hours ago. And now I've woken again to find myself alone in Jordan's bed.

I let out a sigh, swing my legs over the edge of the bed, and pay a visit to the bathroom.

I put the clothes I was wearing last night back on as I hadn't brought any clean ones from my room. Not even ready to talk to Jordan at the moment, I decide to go back to my room so I can shower, brush my teeth, and change into clean clothes. I grab my room key from his desk and head through the house of the hotel.

When my foot is on the first step to take me upstairs to the hotel, I hear two male voices. One is Jordan. The other I don't recognize. They're upstairs in the office.

I debate what to do.

I don't want to go barging into the office if he's talking with someone important. I'll just go out through the back door, and walk around the hotel and come in through the lobby to get to my room.

I turn on the step, but stop when I hear my name spoken. It's not Jordan who says my name. It's the other man.

Curiosity getting the better of me, I walk up the stairs quietly, the voices becoming clearer.

"... can't believe this, Jordan."

I hear him sigh. "I know, Dad. I've fucked up."

His dad's home? I smile at the thought of meeting his dad, but when Jordan continues talking, his words wipe the smile off my face.

"I was going to tell her, but ... I just couldn't bring myself to do it. I couldn't find the words to start with."

"The truth, Jordan. You start with the truth. I knew I should have come home the day I told you. It's why I've come home today because you've been avoiding my calls. I knew there was something up." A sigh. "I thought maybe you and Mia, had argued about it ... I just didn't want to believe you hadn't told her because it's not how I raised you. I know you really care about Mia, but you can't just carry on with her, all the while keeping the truth from her. It's not right. How do you think she's going to feel when she finds out that you've known the truth about her mother for days and not told her?"

My heart stops dead in my chest, my stomach clenching in painful, sick inducing knots. I curl my fingers into my hand, digging my nails into the soft skin.

"Shit..." Jordan says, sounding like he's in pain. "I've fucked up badly. I thought she wouldn't forgive me before ... she'll never forgive me now. She knew – she knew something was up, and I just kept telling her everything was okay."

"Do you want me to be with you when you tell her?"

"No." Jordan sighs. "I'll tell her alone. I don't want to bulldoze her with the two of us. I'll go speak to her now." The determination in his voice, and his heavy footsteps across the floor, have me turning to run back down the stairs.

I know I have no chance of making it, but still I try.

I hear the door open and Jordan say, "Mia," in a tone that can only be described as fearful. I have no choice but to turn around.

The fear in his voice matches the fear on his face, but it's the look in his eyes that's the worst. He looks hopeless. Like he's about to lose everything. Or maybe it's me that's about to lose everything.

And the sick I was feeling worsens.

Chapter Twenty-One

Jordan

When I was fourteen years old, Maisy Richards kicked me in the nuts at Ben Castle's birthday party because she'd given me a handjob in the hall closet, then caught me making out with Sophie Jenkins an hour later.

It literally feels like your testicles have exploded and the flying debris is obliterating your insides like a dirty bomb, leaving you feeling pain of the unimaginable kind.

Up until exactly thirty seconds ago, I'd believed that was the most painful thing I would ever feel.

I was wrong.

Because standing here, seeing the crumpled look of devastation on Mia's face after telling her that her mother—the mother who left her behind to be raised by a father who repeatedly beat her—is, in fact, the woman who raised me.

"I-I don't understand…" She stumbles back, her knee making contact with the office desk with a sickening thud.

I reach for her, but she doesn't even seem to have registered the pain, which only aids to show me how bad this is.

How badly I've screwed up.

"I'm so sorry." I shake my head, disconsolate.

"She's … my … your mom … *dead*." Her hand grips her stomach as if she's in actual pain.

"Mia…" I step toward her, needing to be close to her.

Her hand goes up, stopping me.

"Mia," my dad says in his gentle 'cop' voice. "You should sit down. It's a terrible shock you've had … sit. Let me get you a glass of water."

She looks at my dad with a confused look on her face. Then her eyes slice back to me, and the way she looks at me … through me. Her eyes are ice-cold. The pain slides through me as easily as a hot knife in butter.

Then her eyes drift across the room to the wall, and I know what she's looking at without me even needing to turn.

She's looking at the framed photo of me, Dad and Mom. It was the last picture we had taken together before she died. The day I was leaving to go traveling.

Her face crumbles, and tears fall from her eyes.

She covers her face with her hands. I hear a sob emit from her, so painful it shatters my heart, leaving nothing but dust in its place.

I can't stay away.

I cross the room in quick strides, and wrap my arms around her.

It's only a second before she's pushing me off with a strength I didn't know she had.

"Don't touch me … don't *ever* touch me again." She dries her face on her sleeve, turns and runs out the office.

I look at my dad for guidance because I literally don't know what the hell to do.

"Go after her," he urges.

I'm out of the door a second later.

I catch sight of Mia disappearing into her room. I run down the hall, expecting her door to be closed, but it's not. It's wide open.

I don't go in the room out of respect for her space. So I stand in the doorway, gripping the frame to keep myself from going to her.

She's pushing her feet into her sneakers and grabbing her purse.

"Mia?"

She ignores me, pulling her jacket on.

"Mia, please. Talk to me."

She grabs her car keys, swings her purse over her shoulder, and without a word she pushes past me and walks quickly down the hall.

I'm at her heel, following, trying to talk to her.

"Please don't go … just wait … I know how hard this must be for you … how much you're hurting right now … but if you'll just let me explain…"

She stops outside on the porch—the porch where I made love to her only a few hours ago, when I lied to her *again*—and slowly turns around.

The cold in her eyes, and the dead look on her face, tell me what I already fear.

I've lost her.

There is no getting past this.

I lied to her. I let her down. Men have been letting Mia down her whole life, and now I've just added my name to that list.

"Explain? You want to explain now? You've had DAYS TO EXPLAIN!" she yells. "DAYS TO TELL ME THE TRUTH, BUT YOU LIED … *you lied*." Her voice drops to a whisper. "She loved you … not me – *you*. She left me with him. God, she must have hated me…"

"No, Mia. *No*. You need to hear everything, you need to let me explain."

"I DON'T WANT TO HEAR ANYTHING MORE!" she screams. Tears are streaming down her face, and her hand is clutching her stomach again.

My eyes are stinging from her pain. I rub them roughly with my hand.

"I have to go," she says in an eerily small voice, her eyes sweeping to her car. "I have to get out of here."

A fist of absolute agony twists in my chest.

She runs for her car, unlocking it on her approach. I scramble after her, grabbing her arm, trying to keep her with me.

"Don't go," I plead. "Not like this. Please, Mia. Just stay, talk to me. I can fix this. I *will* fix this."

Her empty eyes lift to mine. "This isn't fixable … *I'm* not fixable. I was broken a long time ago beyond repair."

She yanks her arm from my hand, climbs in her car, and drives away, leaving me in a cloud of dust and agony.

I don't realize I'm sitting on the gravel until I feel Dad's hand on my shoulder.

"I'm so sorry, Jordan. I'm sorry that you're paying for the mistakes Belle made a long time ago."

I scrub my face with my hands, then get to my feet.

"No ... I just ... I can't lose her. I have to make this right. I'm gonna go after her—"

"No." He places a firm hand on my shoulder, holding me in place. "That's not a good idea. If you go after her now, it could only make things worse. Give her time to cool down, process her hurt."

"But what if she doesn't come back?" The pain in my chest twists to pure fucking agony. I rub at the ache, feeling breathless.

"Her things are here, Jordan. She has to come back for them."

"No." I shake my head, knowing how she left everything she owned behind in Boston when she ran. "Material things don't matter to her. She left everything behind in Boston, so a few clothes left behind won't make her come back here."

A look of concern twists his expression for a moment. Then he pats my shoulder. "She cares about you, a lot. She'll come back. If she doesn't, then we'll find her."

"How?"

He puts his arm around my shoulders, and starts to steer me back inside. "Have you forgotten that your old man used to be a cop? Finding people is what I'm good at." He smiles, trying to be helpful, positive, encouraging.

I nod, not really feeling it because my fear isn't *not* finding her. I'll track the earth until the day I do.

No, my fear is what will be waiting for me when I do see her again.

Chapter Twenty-Two

Mia

There's nothing.

No thoughts in my mind.

No pain in my body.

No ache in my heart.

Just one focus. One aim.

I slam on the brakes in the grocery store parking lot.

Sliding my sunglasses on, I grab my purse and head inside.

I get a cart. Then I hit the aisles.

There's no conscious thought. Just need. Only need.

My cart is filling quickly. I'm eating already. A bag of chips already torn open and gone. A pack of candy half-eaten.

If people are staring, I don't care to see.

The cashier attempts small talk. I don't reply.

I bag my food, pay and leave.

Then I drive my car to the motel at the edge of town, the one I came to the other day.

Most people come to motels during the day to have affairs. I come to eat. To hide my shame.

Yet, in this moment it doesn't feel so shameful anymore.

Just necessary.

A means to an end … an end I can't currently see.

I check in at the desk. One night. I don't need any more than that.

I just need to get this out of my system. Then I'm leaving town.

Once I have the key to my room, I go back to my car and get my bags of food.

I let myself in the room and dump the bags on the bed.

It's not the room I was in the other day, but it looks exactly the same.

The same cheap, dirty, stale overused room. It feels right to be here.

That's what I am. Cheap, stale and overused.

I foolishly let myself think otherwise. Let myself think I was worth something … that I meant something to someone … him.

Jordan.

It hurts to think his name.

I bang my hands against my forehead, forcing him out, but he won't go.

So I go over to the age old television and turn it on. I want to drown out the pain in my head with meaningless, but the knowledge still creeps in and cripples me.

Music from the television flows into the room, filling every empty corner with Rihanna's "Diamonds".

Pain lances through me. I catch a sob with a fist to my mouth as I sink to the floor.

How could he…? How could she…?

Stop, Mia. Stop now.

You know how to take the pain away.

I crawl over to the bed and rip open the first thing I lay my hand on.

Shoving it in my mouth, I chew quickly, swallowing. There's no taste. Just relief. The relief that always comes with this.

I drag a bag down from the bed, emptying its contents to the floor.

I tear open another packet – cookies. I shove them in my mouth, chewing, trying to eat as many as I can as quickly as possible.

But the food is sticking, like my body is ready to reject already.

I swallow hard, forcing it down, and grab the bottle of soda I bought, downing some, lubricating my dry throat.

Then I start in, eating harder than I ever have before.

I'm laying on the dirty floor of the room, staring up at the cracked ceiling. Nearly all the food is gone, my body is drenched in sweat, and my stomach hurts like I've never known before.

I've eaten more than I ever have before.

But the feeling is soothing because it's better to feel the painful ache of the food in my stomach, than to feel the crippling agony threatening to shred my heart to pieces.

My mother abandoned me to raise him.

Jordan.

The man I'm in love with.

I'm truly *that* worthless.

I struggle to my feet. I'm going to be sick. But I hold it back.

I need the relief of doing this to myself.

Struggling my way to the bathroom, I kneel at the toilet. Fingers pressed together, I push back in my throat, and rid myself of the pain trying to consume me.

It's still here. It didn't work.

No.

They've taken this from me too.

My ability to stop feeling. To stop the pain from taking me over. And now it's here, and my ribs feel as if they're going to crack from the absolute agony that's tearing through me.

No. No. No. No!

I hate him.

I hate her.

I'm glad she's dead.

Crawling out of the bathroom, I struggle to my feet. My legs feel numb, my head woozy.

I stagger over to the bed. Scouring through the mess of empty bags and wrappers and containers that litter the bed and floor, I find some food. A bag of popcorn and some peanut butter cups.

No! I need more than this.

I check the bed for more food, but nothing.

Ripping open the popcorn, I shove it into my mouth, handfuls at a time, retching as I swallow, but I don't care, I push through. Then I switch to the peanut butter cups. When they're gone, I get down on my hands and knees, rummaging through the trash on the floor.

I find a jar of chocolate spread which had rolled under the bed. I crack it open and start scooping it out with my hand, shoveling it in my mouth.

Then the food's gone, and I'm nowhere near full, but it'll have to do. I stumble back to the bathroom, stand over the sink, and force the food back up.

Running the water, I try to wash the sick away, but the plug is blocked. There's chocolate all over my hands and arms. Vomit in the sink. I lift my head and see myself in the mirror above it.

Disgusting.

Food is smeared across my mouth, my face … in my hair. There's vomit on me.

I'm disgusting.

I don't hate them – Jordan. Anna.

I hate *me*.

Anger that I've never allowed myself to feel tears through me. I slam my fist into the mirror.

It shatters, small shards falling into the sink.

Blood drips down from my hand landing on the white tiles beneath my feet.

But I don't feel the pain in my hand, only the pain in my heart.

I close my eyes on the flood.

The self-hate. The disgust. The loss. The helplessness.

263

The gates open up, and it all comes washing in – fierce, like the force of a tsunami.

I grip the sink, opening my eyes, but I can't see for the hot, burning tears.

I need to get out of here. I need more ... something, *anything*.

Moving too quickly, shadows dance before my eyes, blinding me, taunting me. I stumble around the bathroom, searching for the doorway.

I've overdone it.

I'm going to black-out.

Fuck.

I reach my hand out for support, finding none, and it's too late, I'm going down ... hard.

Chapter Twenty-Three

Jordan

"I can't take this any longer," I say, grabbing my car keys off the table.

I've waited all day, but there's been no sign of Mia.

And now it's getting late.

And I'm beyond fucking worried.

I tried calling her cell a few hours ago. I got her number from the booking in sheet. How bad is that – I didn't even know her cell number. But then I've never needed to call her, and I've not once seen her with a cell in all the time I've been with her. Still, I had to give it a try.

It was a dead end. It was switched off, and I couldn't even leave a damn voicemail because her mailbox was full.

I'm frustrated, and I feel fucking helpless, so now I'm doing the only thing I can. I'm going to look for her.

"I'll come with you." Dad gets to his feet.

"No, stay here in case she comes back. If she does, call me right away."

"Where are you gonna look?" he asks as I pull the front door open.

I pause. I have no fucking clue. I was just going to drive around Durango until I got an idea.

Turning back to him, I ask, "Where would you look?"

He rubs his hand over his short, greying hair. "If I were Mia and I was in a town that wasn't home and not familiar, and after what she just found out … if it were me, I'd want a bar and alcohol … but I don't think she's that kind of girl," he adds as I shake my head no.

"She's not."

"Then I'd want somewhere quiet. Somewhere I could be alone."

"Where's quiet?"

"Here," he says.

"Another hotel?"

"I'd say so."

"Thanks, Dad."

I run out to the Mustang and tear up the gravel, speeding out of there.

I've checked the parking lots of ten hotels so far looking for her car, and nothing.

I don't know if I'm wasting my time here. She could have left town, but I have to keep looking.

I pull up at the stop sign at a junction. Feeling lost, not sure which way to turn, I rest my forehead against the steering wheel.

A second later, a horn blasts out from behind, frightening the shit out of me. My eyes hit the rear-view to see a car behind.

"All right! I'm moving!" I call out. I shift into gear and take a right.

It's not until I'm half-way down the street, I realize I'm on my way out of town. Maybe she has left, and this is my sub-conscious telling me.

Feeling disheartened, and like a complete failure, I start to make a U-turn, taking one quick glance around to make sure all is clear, and that's when I see her car. It's parked outside a seedy looking motel.

My heart stops.

Then restarts with a thundering gallop.

Swallowing my nerves, I spin around and drive into the motel lot, parking by the office.

The guy behind the desk looks like a complete stoner. He doesn't even look away from the TV when I walk in.

I hate that Mia felt she had nowhere to stay but here. She doesn't belong in a place like this. She belongs with me.

"Hey man." I rest my hands on the counter. "I was wondering if you to do me a favor. My girlfriend and I had a fight—" *Girlfriend. That's the first time I've called Mia my girlfriend. Funny when I'm not even sure what we are anymore.* "—and it was a real big one. I really need to talk to her, but she's not answering her cell."

"Then I'm guessing she don't wanna talk to you," he says flatly without taking his eyes of the TV.

I curl my hands into fists.

Ignoring him, I say in a clipped tone. "Look, her car's parked up front. I know she's staying here. I just need you to tell me what room she's staying in."

Technically he can't, I know this. But this isn't the most reputable of establishments. So he'll either tell me, or be a complete dick. From the look on his face, I'm figuring the latter.

His lips curl as he smirks. "You're talking about the cute blonde with the tight ass, drives a car as hot as she is? Was here the other day as well – stayed for just the day."

She stayed here the other day?

All my muscles lock, rigid tight.

"I'm guessing for a nooner," dickface continues. "And going by the look on your face, it definitely wasn't with you." He laughs. "Yeah, man. You're not getting shit from me."

I reach over the counter and grab hold of his shirt, dragging him off his chair. "You will tell me what room she's in, right fuckin' *now*," I hiss in his face, "or I'm gonna kick your ass, then I'm gonna bang on every fuckin' door of your scummy motel, dragging out all your regular business – the ones who don't want interrupting 'cause they earn by the hour – until I find her."

He opens his mouth, but I stop him before he starts.

"And before you cry about calling the cops, my dad is the

cops—" *Okay, so that's a lie. But I'm playing all I got here.* "—
so don't waste your fuckin' time 'cause they ain't coming out for
your low rent dive, or a piece of shit like you. Now tell me what
fuckin' room she's in!"

He grabs his shirt, pulling it from my hand, freeing himself.
"Fine!" he huffs, breathing heavily. "Whatever! Like I give a shit!
She's in room 106."

"See, now that wasn't so hard, was it?"

I slam the door, and head down the walkway toward her
room.

One-oh-six. I rap on the door and wait.

Nothing.

I look through the crack in the curtains. The room's dark
except for the flickering TV, but no sign of Mia.

I knock again, louder, calling her name through the door.

Waiting, I listen for movement.

Still nothing.

"Mia!" I bang again. "I know you're in there. Your car's out
front. I just need to know you're okay."

I press my ear to the door, listening for noise. Then I hear her
… faintly.

"Mia!" I call again, my heart pounding.

"*Jordan.*"

Without a second thought, I rear back and slam my foot
against the lock. It gives in one kick.

I tear into the room, and I see mess everywhere. Food
wrappers, containers … just trash, everywhere.

I hear her groan. Bathroom.

She's on the floor. My stomach bottoms out.

My eyes take in everything in less than a second. Dried blood
on her forehead matted into her hair. What looks like chocolate,
smeared on her face.

Then the smell hits and that's when I see the vomit in the
sink … and the smashed mirror above it.

I drop to my knees beside her. "Mia. It's me, I'm here. Jesus,
baby, what happened?" I take hold of her hand. Her knuckles are

torn up, dried with blood – the mirror.

Fuck. *What have you done to yourself, baby?* Tears sting my eyes.

"*Jordan...*" she groans, her eyes flicker open, looking out of focus.

"I'm here." I press my hand to her cheek. "I'm gonna get you some help."

"No..." she mumbles. "... be fine. Just give ... min-ute..." Her eyes close.

"Mia, baby. Stay with me. Stay awake." I gently pat her cheek.

"*Tired...*"

"Mia." I pat her a little harder, but she's out, and then I'm dialing 9-1-1, telling them I need an ambulance immediately.

"How's she doing?"

I stand as Dad approaches. I'm in the waiting room where I've been for the past half-hour since we arrived and they left me here, rushing Mia straight off.

"They're not telling me anything because apparently, I'm not family." I throw my arms in the air, darting an angry look at the receptionist.

Dad puts his hands on my shoulders, bringing my attention to him. "Technically, we are *family*." He gives me a firm look before turning and walking over to the reception desk.

The last thing I want to do is refer to Mia as my step-sister, but if it'll get me any news on her, I'll tell them whatever the fuck they need to hear.

I pace around as I watch my dad talk to the receptionist.

He gives a few nods. Says a few things. Another nod. Then he's walking back toward me.

"What did she say?"

"Just that Mia is currently undergoing tests, and they're extremely busy tonight so we could be waiting hours before we hear anything."

"Jesus." I press my fingers to the bridge of my nose, closing my eyes, trying to settle my rattling emotions. "I just need to see her. Know she's okay."

"She's gonna be fine, son." His hand squeezes my shoulder. "Looks like we're gonna be here a while, so I'll go get us some coffee."

I nod, and lean back against the wall, my eyes still closed.

A few hours later...

"Mr. Matthews?"

My head jerks up. A woman, mid-thirties, hair tied in a bun and wearing a white coat, stands before me.

"I'm Dr. Packard. You're Mia Monroe's family? You came in with her?"

I get to my feet. "Yes. I'm her ... her..."

"I'm her step-father," Dad cuts in, standing beside me. "How is she doing?"

Dr. Packard turns her attention to Dad. I give him a grateful look.

"Mia suffered a small contusion to the head from her fall, nothing too serious, but what was of concern to me after initially examining Mia was that she was showing signs of severe dehydration, and her blood pressure was dangerously low—"

"Severe dehydration?" I say, confused. "What would cause her to be severely dehydrated?" I'm no doctor, but I know severe dehydration isn't something you just get.

She gives me an uncomfortable glance. Then turns to Dad.

"Mr. Matthews…"

"Jim, please."

"Jim, has Mia ever had any issues in the past? Any *problems* with food … of any kind?"

"What do you mean – problems with food?" I ask.

Her eyes dart to me again. "You are Mia's…?"

"Step-brother." I nearly choke on the words because it couldn't be farther from the truth. "Jordan. I'm Jordan."

She clears her throat, turning to me. "Jordan, after examining your step-sister, a few things I discovered brought up a concern."

"What concern?" My heart leaps out of my chest and starts to sprint down the hall.

"I'm not at liberty to discuss in length, not before speaking to Mia."

"You asked us for a reason? What is that? You think Mia has a problem with food, so let's talk about it—" I'm being a dick, I know, but something about this is bothering the fuck out of me. "—what kind of problem? Allergies? A food intolerance? An eating disord—" The words are out of my mouth before I even realize what I'm saying.

And then I realize.

And my eyes close under the wrecking ball of that realization. The way I found her in that motel room stilling my mind into a freeze frame of events. The excessive amount of empty food wrappers. The way there was chocolate smeared on her face as if she'd been gorging on it.

And she'd been throwing up.

She'd been throwing up.

Excessive eating. Throwing up.

Think Jordan. Think…

Bulimia.

Fuck, no.

I open my eyes. "You think Mia is *bulimic*."

Dr. Packard pushes her hands in her pockets, releasing a slow breath. "There are many signs pointing to that possibility, yes, but like I said, I can't be sure of anything until I've spoken to Mia."

And my heart leaves the building.

"So talk to her – now." I gesture down the hall. "I'll come with you."

She shakes her head. "That's not possible at the moment as Mia is sedated, and I—"

"Sedated?" I frown. "Why?"

"Jordan, when Mia came around, she became quite upset. And through the stress of the situation, some other issues arose." She stops talking as someone passes by.

"What other issues?" I press, wrapping my arms around my chest, trying to hold it together because I'm two seconds away from sprinting down this hall and searching every fucking room until I find her.

Dr. Packard draws her hands together in front of her. "Mia became extremely upset during examination, and due to the stress she was already under, and the dehydration combined, she suffered a seizure."

"A seizure. Jesus fuckin' Christ." I close my eyes on a painful breath, my hands covering my face.

I feel my dad's hand go to my back for support.

"Once we had the seizure under control, I felt it best to sedate Mia. Allow her body time to rest, and give us time to get her rehydrated intravenously as Mia was continually rejecting our efforts to help her while awake."

Rejecting their help? She didn't want to get better?

Her phone goes off in her pocket. "Excuse me." She pulls out the phone, looking at. "I'm sorry, but I have to go." She begins backing away.

"When Mia's awake—"

"I'll come and tell you right away." Then she's gone.

I slump down in the nearest chair. Head in my hands.

Dad sits next to me. "She'll be okay, son. We'll help her. Whatever she needs."

I lift my head a little, and look at him. "But what if she doesn't want *my* help?"

He gives me a sad smile. "We'll figure it out. Don't worry."

Dad and I spend the night here in the hospital waiting room. We hear nothing more, no matter how many times I check with the receptionist, the answer is always the same – no change yet – Mia is still sleeping.

So I spend most of my time running everything over and over in my mind. Trying to figure out how I missed it. Were there any signs?

But I come up dry.

In the end, I'm still no clearer on it all, so I give into sleep, stretching out across three seats, letting Dad have the bench. I close my eyes, and I'm out.

When I open them again, daylight is pouring in through the large windows, and a glance at the clock tells me it's seven-thirty.

Dad is already awake, watching the news on the TV up on the wall, drinking more of that shit vending-machine coffee.

"How long you been awake?" I ask, sitting. I stretch my back out, and every bone in my body cracks.

"Not long."

"Any news?"

"No. I got you a coffee. Might be a bit cold now." He hands it to me.

"It'll do. Thanks." I take two large gulps of the luke warm coffee and put it on the table.

"I spoke to Paula, she's on her way to the hotel now, she'll see to Dozer."

Thankfully the Perry's left the other day, so there's only Dozer that needs taking care of.

I get up to stretch my legs. "Thanks."

The main doors whoosh open, throwing a cold blast of air through the room. It actually helps wake me up.

I see coming in through the doors, a guy about my age. I

notice him because he's *clearly* money. Walks with that air of arrogance that only pricks with money do. He strides over to the reception desk.

"I'm just gonna go take a piss," I tell Dad.

I'm walking past the reception desk, heading for the bathroom, when I hear that money guy talking with the receptionist.

"… name is Forbes Chandler. I received a call last night telling me that my girlfriend Mia Monroe had been brought it. I want to know how she is, and when I can see her."

Blood rushes straight to my head. I stop and turn back, slowly.

"Yes, of course," the receptionist smiles. "Just let me check."

She's starts typing. Clicking on the keyboard.

He checks his watch.

That's him. This blond, prissy ass motherfucker, is the one who hurt Mia.

Why is he here? Who called him? Did Mia ask for him – did she ask them to call him?

Pain lances through me, quickly morphing to rage and despair and frustration.

Forbes turns his head in my direction. He sees me staring.

My fists tighten at my sides.

He gives me an odd look, then looks away, but he knows I'm still staring at him, so he looks back.

"Can I help you?" he asks with a smug look on his fuck ugly face.

I take a step toward him. "You're Forbes?"

"Yeah. I am. Who's ask—?"

He never finishes that sentence.

Because I punch him in the face. Hard.

He goes down from that one hit. Pussy. But I'm not stopping there. I'm on him, on the ground, punching him repeatedly over and over, and I can't fucking stop.

Because all I can see is Mia's black eye.

Him trying to rape her.

Her forcing herself to be sick. Passed out on that bathroom floor.

Me loving her. Wanting her.

Just pain. Fucking pain.

It's endless, relentless. And I just keep plowing my fist into his face, trying to rid myself of it.

I don't know if I'd have ever stopped, or if I'd have kept going until I killed him, but I don't get the chance to find out because I'm pulled off him by Dad and the hospital security staff.

It takes three of them to get me off him. That's how far gone I am.

"What the fuck!" he splutters through the blood in his mouth. "Are you insane? You've broken my nose!"

"That's the least of your worries," I growl. "You go near Mia ever again, and I'll fuckin' kill you!"

He stills. Just a moment. Hands covering his bleeding nose, his eyes meet mine. Something in them moves. I don't know what it is, but I sure as hell don't like it.

Then his hand drops. And he smirks. "Mia's suckered you in good and proper." He lets out a clipped, bloody laugh. "She's good at that ... playing the victim. And I'll take it from the look on your face that you've been fucking her. Sorry to tell you this, but you're not the first, won't be the last."

"You're a fuckin' liar!" I launch myself at him again, but I'm still being held by Dad and the burly guards, so I get nowhere.

"Let. Me. Fucking. Go!" I yell, trying to fight them off me.

"Calm the hell down!" Dad hisses in my ear. "Keep going like this, and they'll call the cops if they haven't already. Then they'll throw your ass in jail, and you won't be able to help Mia from there."

The instant his words hit, hearing her name in that context, I start to slow down. "Okay." I'm breathing hard. "Okay ... you can let me go. I won't hit him again." I pin him with my eyes. "Not yet, anyway."

"Jordan," Dad scolds.

"What in the world is going on here?" I turn my head to see

Dr. Packard walking toward us. Her eyes flick to Forbes, then back to me. She does not look happy.

"Dr. Packard, this man just attacked this gentleman here for no good reason." This comes from the receptionist, who is still looking a little shocked by the whole thing.

"No good reason my ass!" I yell. "This motherfucker is the reason Mia is in here!"

"I haven't seen Mia in two weeks—"

"Yeah, and why is that?" I take a step toward him. Dad's arm comes in front of me, stopping me.

"Jordan," Dr. Packard says. "You assaulted this gentleman?"

I scoff at the term. "Yeah, and I'd do it again – with pleasure."

She turns to Forbes. "Mr....?"

"Chandler." Blood is still running down his ugly face and onto his pristine hundred dollar shirt.

"Mr. Chandler, I'll get a nurse to clean you up. Do you want us to call the police to report this attack?"

His eyes drift to me.

"Do it." I step forward, pushing against Dad's arm that's still pinned across my chest. "I'll happily do a stretch. And while I'm with the cops, I'll tell them *exactly* what you did to Mia."

His eyes flash with fear.

Yeah, I know what you did, motherfucker.

"No." He clears his throat, wiping his mouth on his sleeve. "I don't want to press charges. I don't need the hassle. Just keep that psycho away from me."

"Nurse Callaghan, can you tend to Mr. Chandler, please," Dr. Packard calls to a nurse.

"Of course." The nurse comes over and leads him off down the hall.

I keep my eyes pinned to his back the whole way.

Dr. Packard stands in front of me, blocking my view. "I don't know what that was about," she says in a lowered voice. "But if you *ever* behave that way in my hospital again, I'll call the cops myself, and you'll *never* get through the door again. Do you understand?"

I exhale. "Yeah, I understand."

"Good. Because Mia is awake, and she's asking to see you."

My head snaps up.

"She is?"

"Yes, so you best come with me now." She starts to walk away.

I look at Dad.

"I'll wait out here," he says.

I mouth thanks to him. He gives me an encouraging smile.

I catch up to Dr. Packard. "How is she doing?"

She looks across at me. "Better. She's been talking."

I shove my hands in my pockets. "That's good."

"Yes, it is. Funny thing though, when I said to Mia that her step-brother was waiting to see her, she told me she doesn't have a step-brother. That she doesn't have any family actually." She slides a look at me.

I smile sheepishly. "It's complicated." I shrug.

"Life always is." She stops near a door. "Mia's in here. Now, Jordan, I've spoken at length with Mia regarding the concerns I have about her problem, and I feel it's best if you don't mention anything."

"You mean don't tell her I know about the bulimia."

"Exactly. Let her tell you – I'm sure she will. She's very aware of her problem, but she's also had a massive shock to bring about this realization. It's an upsetting subject for her. I don't want her upset any more than she already has been."

I nod. "I hear you, doc. I'll do whatever it takes to help her."

She smiles. "Yes, I can see that."

I turn to the door.

"Jordan."

I look over my shoulder at her.

"You might want to clean the blood off your hands before you go in."

I glance down at my hands. I've got that fuckers blood all over them. "Shit, yeah."

She pulls a handkerchief from her pocket, then walks over to the water dispenser a little farther down the hall. Pressing the tap, she wets the handkerchief underneath, then brings back to me.

"Thanks." Taking it, I scrub the blood from my knuckles, then offer it back to her.

"I'm good." She holds her hand up, smiling. "Keep it."

I let out a small laugh. "Thanks." I shove the handkerchief into my pocket. Then taking a deep breath, I push the door to Mia's room open.

Chapter Twenty-Four

Mia

One look at Jordan and I know.

I can't be with him anymore.

Not because I don't love him, I do, but all I see when I look at him is my mother's betrayal. She chose to raise him, not me.

It hurts to be near him.

I don't want to end up resenting Jordan for everything he had, everything that should have been mine. This isn't his fault – what my so called mother did wasn't his fault. My rational side knows this, but it doesn't change the way I feel. She wanted him. Not me.

I can understand why. He's such a beautiful, amazing person. He shines so bright. He is so much more than me.

And he deserves better than I can ever give.

He deserves better than I am.

I'm broken. Damaged.

Dr. Packard thinks I'm repairable. I'm not so sure about that. Look at me – where I am right now. What I've done to myself.

I've hit bottom. Now, I need to figure out if I can ever climb back up, but I have to do that without Jordan.

"Hey." He closes the door behind him.

"Hi."

I can barely bring myself to look at him. It hurts, knowing that this will be the last time I'll see him.

I've known him such a short time, but the time feels irrelevant. It's as if I've known him always. And never seeing him again will be the hardest thing I'll ever do. Harder than living through Oliver. Harder than getting away from Forbes. Harder than combating my illness.

Jordan takes the seat by my bed. The seat Dr. Packard recently vacated, after spending a good hour talking to me about my illness. I didn't go to in depth about my issue with food, but it was hard to avoid the bulimia conversation as being a medical professional, she knew. I tried to deny it at first, but the signs were all there for her to read.

After I confessed to her – the first person I have ever told – and how long I've been eating and purging—ten years—she went on to tell me everything I already knew, about the damage I'm doing to my body, the health risks – liver or kidney failure … possibly death.

You'd think already knowing these things would have stopped me a long time ago, but I didn't want to think of those things. I just wanted the pain to stop, and for a long time it helped. And maybe, deep down, I did want to die.

But after being in here, talking with Dr. Packard … but mainly from knowing Jordan and my time with him, I've realized that what I want is to live and be happy.

And to do that, I need help.

Dr. Packard told me of a specialized clinic that can help me, and that she would refer me to them, but for the treatment to work, I have to want it – I have to want to get better.

And I do. I'm ready to get better. I *need* to get better.

Dr. Packard is calling the clinic now to see if they have a place for me, so all that's left for me to do is tell Jordan that I'm leaving.

"How are you doing?" he asks, his voice soft.

"I'm okay." I glance at him. His eyes are on my face, deep and dark and searching.

It hurts so badly to look at him. Each time I do, I'm confused by the love I feel for him and the past he represents. The past that should have been mine.

Looking down, my fingers trace patterns over the comforter. "Jordan … I need to apologize for how you found me in that motel room."

"I'm gonna stop right you there. You don't have anything to be sorry for. I'm just relieved that I did find you and that you're okay." His fingers rub at his chest. "I'm the one who has *everything* to apologize for, babe. You wouldn't have gone there … been alone if it weren't for me keeping…" He runs his hand through his dark hair, blowing out a breath. "God, I'm just so fuckin' sorry that I didn't tell you about my mom—" He stops short.

His mom. He's right, she was his mom.

His eyes flash to mine. They're filled with apologies, and sorrow. He feels sorry for me. Pity.

I hate pity.

"I just…" He exhales. "I should have told you the moment I found out that Belle was Anna … *your* mother," he highlights this, his voice deep and low with meaning.

I turn my head and stare out the window. "It doesn't matter anymore."

"Yeah, it does. And I want you to know I'm sorry … for everything. I know it doesn't seem like it, but I would never do anything to hurt you. I was just afraid to tell you. That if I did, I'd lose you." He slides his fingers over my hand.

"Don't." I pull my hand away.

I have to shield my heart from the look of hurt on his face.

The silence between us is blistering.

He scrubs his hands over his face. "Have I lost you?" His words are so quiet, but they hurt with the intensity of a scream.

I close my eyes on the tears burning them. "I'm sorry, Jordan."

"Jesus…" He shakes his head. "Just tell me one thing – is it because I kept it from you, or because of Belle?"

"It's not because of you, it's because of me—"

"Don't give me the 'it's not you, it's me' bullshit!" He stands, moving away from the bed.

He's angry. Anger I can work with. Anger I understand.

"Just give me the truth, Mia. You might not think I deserve it,

281

but it's all I'm asking of you."

My eyes snap to him. "Fine." I sit up on my haunches. "You want the truth? The truth is every single time I look at your face, I see everything I never had – what *she* should have given me, but instead chose to give to *you*. Do I blame you for that? No. But it doesn't change the fact that the woman who gave birth to me— who was supposed to be my mother—chose to be yours. She left me with him!" My voice is getting louder, and my hands are shaking, but I can't seem to stop. "And I hate the way that makes me feel – knowing that she chose you over me!"

"She didn't choose me!" He bangs his hand against his chest. "*I* wasn't anything to do with her decision – you need to hear me out, so you can understand—"

"No!" I press my hands to my head. "I can't hear anymore!" I know what I feel is irrational, but I can't think straight in this moment. All I can do is *feel* – and I feel irrational.

"I hate this! I hate everything! I hate me!" I'm crying now.

Jordan crosses the room in a few strides and pulls me into his arms.

The feel of him…

His heat and strength…

I curl my fingers into his shirt. "Everything's a mess. I'm a mess." I sniffle, pulling away, unable to be this close to him knowing that I'm leaving.

Not willing to let me go, he takes my face in his hands.

"You're not a mess." He sweeps his thumbs over my cheeks, drying my tears. "Just talk to me, babe. Let me help you."

A crushing feeling in my chest takes my breath with it. "After everything I just said to you … you still want to help me. Why?"

His grip on my face increases. His eyes darkening. "Because I fuckin' love you, Mia." His eyes close, almost as if he's in pain.

He loves me.

Jordan rests his forehead against mine, his hand sliding around to cup the back of my neck.

"That didn't come out exactly as I'd planned, but it is the truth. I'm in love you with." His breath fans my skin. His words

282

crush my heart. "I know it's probably too soon, and I know you have a lot to deal with right now and that I'm the cause of some of it, but I just want you to know the extent of my feelings for you before you throw us away. I love you, Mia. Every part of you. The best and worst. The broken, the perfect. The bad, the good. You're it for me, babe. I see only you."

He loves me.
Jordan is in love with me.
Me.

I love him too. So much.

But it won't work.

I'm too broken. Too hurt. Too resentful.

And I can't see any of that going away anytime soon.

He deserves so much more than I can give him. And to tell him that I love him would be wrong and selfish of me.

I open my eyes. "I'm leaving Durango."

He pulls back from me, hand still curled around my nape. "Are you going back to Boston?"

I frown. "No. That's the last place I'd go. Why would you think that?"

He shakes his head. Eyes down.

This is it. I have to tell him about my illness. "Jordan, there's something you don't know about me…" I stall, blowing out a breath. "When you found me in the motel room … I don't know if you saw all the empty food wrappers?"

"I saw them."

"Well … I have this problem." I dig my fingernails into the bed of my hand. "When I'm stressed or upset, I, uh … I eat … a lot of food, then I, uh … I make myself throw it back up."

He doesn't react. Doesn't move. He just stares back at me with the same emotion that was there moments ago.

"I have an illness called bulimia, Jordan. I don't know if you've heard of it before."

"I've heard of it."

"Okay. Well, it's not – for me, anyway – about being thin," I clarify. "It's about the problems up here." I touch my fingers to my head. "When things in my life are too painful, or out of my control, or just too much for me to deal with, I take the pain away using the comfort of food. Then to get the control back, I guess you could say, I make myself throw the food back up."

"How long has it been going on for?" he asks softly.

I take a deep breath. "Ten years, on and off. Worse in the last few."

"How do we fix this?"

I meet his determined eyes. "*We* don't. *I* have to." Blowing out a breath, I tell him, "There's a specialist facility in Denver for people who suffer with eating disorders like mine. I'm going there to try and get better."

"How long will you be there for?"

I lift my shoulders. "I don't know … however long it takes, I guess."

His eyes lift. I see a flicker of hope in them. "Denver's not far, Mia – like a six hour drive, max – I'll drive out every weekend to visit—"

"No," I say, squashing his hope.

"No," he echoes.

"I have to do this alone." I pull on my lower lip. "I don't want you to come visit me."

"Okay…" He rubs the bridge of his nose with his finger. "What about when you're better … can I see you then?"

I look away from him.

It makes no difference because I can *feel* his eyes on me. It hurts. So much.

I shake my head slowly.

"Ah … right. Okay … so you really meant it before when you said I'd lost you." He sounds in pain, hurt, and it's awful.

But I am doing the right thing – I know I am.

The resentment I feel isn't going anywhere. And eventually it would eat at me … *us*, and in the end there'd be nothing left but hate and hurt.

I've had enough hurt to last a lifetime. Better to end things now, than later.

I feel the bed shift as he stands. "Will you do one thing for me?"

I lift my eyes to him, but I'm unprepared for the pain than slices through me when I see the pure look of it on his face.

"Don't shut out the next person who tries to get close to you. Tell them everything. Don't worry that they won't love you because they will. It's impossible not to love you, Mia." He lets out a resigned sigh. "I know that better than anyone."

I slide my hand across my chest, gripping at the place where my aching heart is. And in this moment, I crumble, changing my mind, ready to tell him that I love him. That I'll find a way to get beyond how I feel.

But before I get a chance to part my dry lips, he's gone, the door banging closed in his wake.

Panic claws at my chest. I want to run after him. Tell him I was wrong.

But my legs don't move. And I know why.

Because deep down I know letting him go is the right thing.

I slide down the bed, turning on my side as I pull my knees to my chest, hugging them.

I'm wiping at my tears when I hear the door open.

Jordan.

My heart leaps.

I turn around.

Forbes.

Oh god no.

No.

I can feel my body turning in on itself. Like a snail, retreating into its shell.

What is he doing here? How did he know I was here? What happened to his face?

His nose is taped up. His face cut and bloody.

He shuts the door behind him, and my blood turns cold.

My eyes start scanning the room looking for an escape, but my only current escape is the door he's standing in front of. I could always make a dash for the bathroom and lock myself inside.

"F-Forbes," I finally manage.

"How are you feeling?" he asks perfectly normal, as if the last time I saw him didn't involve him beating and attempting to rape me.

"H-how did you know you know I was here?"

He smiles, and it makes my blood run cold. "I'm your emergency contact on your medical insurance, remember? The minute they brought you in, I got a call. I came straight away. I was worried about you, baby. I've been worried about you for the last two weeks. Not knowing where you were … it's been torture." He takes a step closer to me.

I scrabble back in bed, covering my legs with the hospital gown I'm wearing. It's my natural reaction.

And I hate that it is.

He holds his hands in a placating manner. "I'm not going to hurt you, Mia. That's not why I'm here."

I don't believe him. I've heard that from him so many times before.

I slide my hand behind my back, searching for the emergency buzzer.

"I just want to talk to you." He sits down in the chair by the bed. I stop moving my hand, shifting my body a little to hide what I'm reaching for.

"W-what do you want?" I try to hold my voice steady.

"I want you to come home."

I can feel my head shaking before I even have a chance to think through what I'm doing. I know it's the wrong thing, and even more so when I see the flare of anger in his eyes.

I swallow past the dry in my throat as I creep my fingers outward, trying to find the buzzer.

"Mia…" He sighs, rubbing his temple, shaking his head. "That's not the answer I want to hear."

"What happened to your face?" I ask. A diversion tactic until I can figure a way out of this.

His face darkens. "It's irrelevant."

I bind my hands together.

"Mia, I came all this way, and I'm not leaving without you. And really, what do you have here? *Nothing.* You're all alone. You need me. You can't survive without me."

I wrap my hands around my cold body.

He's right. I am alone, but alone is better than with him.

Forbes stands. "Where are your things?"

"I don't have anything here with me."

"Good. That makes it easier." He picks my folded up, dirty clothes from the side. "What the fuck are these?"

"My clothes."

The look of disgust on his face is so familiar to me.

He's so familiar to me.

"We'll pick you some clothes up at the airport, but for now, get dressed." He throws the clothes on the bed in front of me.

"Why?"

He looks at me. Anger is dominating him now. "Because we're leaving this fuckin' hick of a town and going home. So get your ass fuckin' dressed!" he hisses.

This is the Forbes I know so well.

Fear controlling me, and unsure what else to do, I obediently climb off the bed and pick the clothes up to change in the bathroom.

"Where the fuck are you going?" he snaps.

"To change," I answer in a small voice.

"Change here." He moves across the room toward me, predatory in his step.

My heart stops. I hold still to the spot, fear still controlling me like a sickness.

Running his finger down my bare arm, he leans close to my mouth. "I've missed you, baby … I *want* to see you."

His touch ignites painful memories of all the times he hit me, kicked me, punched me … *violated* me. His hand feels like a disease of the worst kind. A sick, awful disease I want off me, and away from. *Now.*

My heart kickstarts, and begins pumping hard in my chest.

I *won't* leave here with him.

I *can't*.

Holding the clothes to my chest, I lift my chin. "I'm not going back to Boston with you."

There's no hesitation. He grabs me by the throat. Pushing me down onto the bed. "You will do as I fuckin' tell you! You will get dressed. Then you will leave this hospital, and get on a plane home with me."

"No," I croak out.

His hand grabs at my gown, lifting it. He grabs the fabric of my panties and tears them off my body. His knee comes between my thighs. I press my legs together, trying to keep him out, but he's too strong, and he pries them apart.

With his knee pressed painfully up against the most intimate part of me, he leans into my face. "Do I need to teach you another lesson, Mia?"

Fear and memories start to take hold.

And I stop them as soon as they start. I will not be controlled.

Not by him.

Not by anyone.

Ever again.

I hate Forbes more in this moment than I ever have. And it gives me strength. Strength I need.

Slowly, I shake my head.

He smiles, a winners smile. "Good girl." Then he pulls my gown aside, revealing my naked breast. "So fucking beautiful," he says, pressing his hand to my chest, moving his disgusting fingers over my nipple. He squeezes.

I close my eyes on the pain. Tears press from the corners of my eyes.

Jordan. It's a silent scream in my mind. A plea for him to come back. To make right on his promise when he said that he would never let anyone hurt me, ever again.

But Jordan's not coming because I sent him away.

This is for me to do. And I *can* do it.

Slowly, I lift my hand to Forbes' face. His eyes fire with

288

triumph, and I know I have him.

Tilting my chin, I offer my mouth to him.

His eyes flare. "Tell me you want me, Mia. Say, 'Fuck me, Forbes. *Please*.' I want to hear you beg, baby."

I swallow down all the words I want to say, and do as he says, "Fuck me, Forbes. *Please*," I say in a steady voice.

"There's my, girl." He smirks, lowering his face to mine.

The instant his lips touch mine, I moan, knowing it will turn him on to deepen the kiss. And that's the moment when I go back to the tactic I used the last time, and bite down on his lower lip. But this time, I bite like I mean it.

His blood floods my mouth, along with his yell of pain.

"You fuckin' bitch!" He hits me hard.

Pain explodes in my head. His grip on my throat tightens. Breathing quickly gets hard.

I need to get out of this, but I can't move my body, so my hands slap him, scratching, pushing, just trying anything I can to get him off me, but he's unmoving.

It's when he's rearing back to hit me again, fist clenched, that I turn my head away.

And that's when I see my escape, on the table by the bed.

Without another thought, I grab the glass water jug and using all the strength I have, I hit him with it.

I make contact with the side of his head. I feel and hear the dull thud of the glass as it strikes his skull.

Water spills out, soaking my face and hair.

Forbes looks stunned. Like he can't believe I really just hit him with it.

He wobbles, but he's still upright, and I need him down.

So I pull back and hit him again. Harder this time. And that's when he goes down, falling right on top of me.

The jug drops from my hand and hits the floor with a loud shatter.

I'm panicking, coughing up his blood mixed in with my own, just needing him off me. Terrified that he's going to wake up and then it's game over for me.

With unknown strength, I manage to struggle out from underneath him. Sliding off the bed, my eyes trained on his unmoving body, my bare feet hit the floor.

Glass shards cut straight through the soles of my feet, I bite my lip on the cry of pain I want to make.

Not taking my eyes off Forbes, I grab the emergency buzzer by the bed, pressing it multiple times. Then as quietly as I can, I move across the floor, stifling my urges to cry out as the glass continues to cut mercilessly, into my feet.

I'm steps from the door, when I hear running footsteps down the hall. Then the door bursts open. It's Dr. Packard with a security guard flanking her.

Thank god.

"Mia, what on earth has happened? Are you okay? We heard glass breaking, then your buzzer was going off frantic!" Her eyes sweep the room taking in the state of me and Forbes out on the bed. "Oh, my god, are you okay?"

I take a few steps toward her, stumbling, I collapse, relief taking me down.

Dr. Packard catches me, holding me in her arms. "It's okay, Mia," she soothes, holding me to her. "You're going to be okay."

But in this moment, her words aren't so easy to believe. And all I can think is how much I wish it were Jordan's arms around me right now.

But they never will be again.

And I only have myself to blame for that.

Chapter Twenty-Five

Jordan

Day two: post-Mia...

"Jordan."

Dad knocks on my door.

I ignore him. I'm not in the mood to talk to anyone right now.

The only one I want to keep company with is the one who understands my pain best – Dozer. He's missing Mia as much as I am.

I hear the door open.

"Go away," I mumble into my pillow.

Dozer lifts his head, looks up, then lays back down.

"You really need to open the window, let some air in. It stinks in here," Dad says, ignoring me.

"I like the stink."

Truth is, I don't want to open the window in case the fresh air takes the scent of Mia from my bedding, disappearing just like she has from my life.

"You really need to leave this room, Jordan." He sits on the edge of my bed. "It's been two days. This isn't healthy. Let's go to the movies or something."

I tilt my head, moving my mouth from the pillow. "Not in the mood."

"Well, can you at least consider taking a shower because the stench in this room isn't Dozer, it's you."

"I'll shower when I'm ready." I press my face back into the

pillow.

"Look, son. I know you're hurting right now, but it will get better."

I snort. Then get another lung full of Mia. It makes my chest burn.

"I have been through this myself … when I was younger. With Belle—"

My muscles knot. I lift my head. "I don't want to talk about her right now."

"I know you're angry with your mom—"

I roll onto my back. "Angry doesn't ever come close … I just … I don't understand her. Why she did what she did."

He sighs. "I didn't either. But it's not for us to judge. We weren't there. We don't know where her mind was at, or how limited she felt her choices were."

"I just wish…" I sigh. "I just wish Mia could see the bigger picture. I wish she … I don't know what I fuckin' wish!" I throw my hands up in the air, feeling helpless.

What I want is to not feel this way. Like I'm fucking dying – slowly.

I turn over, putting my back to him.

"You wish she'd see past it and come back."

Tears sting my eyes. "It's too late now. She's gone."

"It's never too late. You know how Belle broke up with me after high school, when she'd left for college. I was pretty much like you are now. I was low and didn't want to talk to anyone. I guess I was lovesick. I just wanted to reach her … so I wrote her a letter and made her a mix-tape."

I let out a small laugh. My first in days. "That's pretty lame, Dad."

"Yeah, it was." He runs his hand over his hair, smiling lightly.

"Did you hear from her after you sent the letter and tape?"

He shakes his head. "No. I didn't hear from her until she came back after I'd had you."

I sit up, back against the headboard. "So you're saying I

should write Mia a letter and make her a lame ass mix-tape when it didn't even work for you. Mom married someone else and didn't come back to you for years."

"No, it didn't work for me … not right away. Doesn't mean it won't for you. But I'm telling you this because whether it worked in a day, or years later – it worked. She never got rid of that letter and tape, Jordan. She kept them for all those years. She never let me go, not fully. And when she needed help … needed me most, that's how she knew she could come back. That letter and tape reminded her that she could. Reminded her of what we once had. That I'd always be there for her, no matter what."

He gets to his feet and pats Dozer's leg. "Come on, boy, it's feeding time."

Dozer climbs down from the bed, standing by Dad's legs.

"Just think about it. You've nothing to lose by reaching out to her. Write and tell her everything she doesn't think she wants to hear, but needs to. Tell her how you feel."

"Basically make a fool of myself."

"Men generally are fools in love."

"Yeah, well I'd definitely look a fool if I send her a lame ass mix-tape." I know I'm stepping out of line and he doesn't deserve it, but I'm feeling bitter and angry, and I don't want to be alone in my pain.

"Well, I think it'd be a mixed CD for you, son, or even an iPod if you're feeling flashy, as they don't make tapes anymore."

I give him a look and a grunt.

Yeah, I've turned back into a fully-fledged teenager.

"Look, son, all I'm saying is, music can evokes memories and feelings. It can enhance those words you write to her. It's just knowing which memories you want to trigger, what words you want her to hear, and which song will do that for you."

He leaves my room with Dozer, his words lingering long after he's gone.

293

Day three: post-Mia…

"Jeez … you're listening to Damien Rice. This is worse than I thought." Beth drops down onto my bed beside me.

"Can't you people just leave me the fuck alone?" I pull the duvet over my head.

Beth pulls it off and sniffs the air. "It smells really bad in here, did you know?"

"I've been told."

"I don't think its Dozer." She leans over and sniffs me. "Jesus Christ! It's you – you smelly bastard! When was the last time you showered, or brushed your teeth?"

"At three o' fuck off a clock."

"Funny." She pokes me in the back. "So to what extent am I going to have to annoy you to get you out of this bed and into the shower? Or at least get you to visit with a toothbrush?"

"You're already annoying me and it doesn't look like I'm moving, does it?"

"Come on, stinky breath." She tickles my side.

I push her hand off. "Beth, seriously, knock it off. I'm not in the mood."

Her silence has me feeling guilty. "Look … I'm just not up for company right now."

"But I brought your favorite pie – Key Lime." I can practically see her pout from here. "And some movies with tons of action, killing bad guys, all that gory type shit you like. I even think a chick gets blown up in one, or at the very least she gets her ass kicked."

I twist my neck to look at her. "Watching a chick get her ass kicked? That's how you intend on cheering me up?"

"Hey, I'm no expert. I'm just doing what my best friend did for me a few years ago when my heart got ripped in two."

I roll onto my back and look at her, remembering how I sat in Beth's room with her for a day and a half straight after that bitch

Monica Teller had broken her heart.

Beth was crazy about her—kind of how I am for Mia.

And that bitch Monica told Beth she was in it with her too, wanted to be with her, but when it came down to it, she was too chicken shit to tell her religious folks that she was a lesbian, so she dumped Beth and married the douche they wanted her to marry.

Beth cried for a week straight after Monica got married.

And now she's here, trying to help me like I did for her.

I feel a pang in my chest for my best friend. Sitting up, I take her face in my hands and kiss her forehead. "Thanks, Beth."

"Eww! At least use mouthwash or something before you kiss me. I could catch cooties from that days old breath!"

I chuckle, climbing from the bed and turn my iPod off, silencing Damien Rice.

"Get the bitch ass-kicking movie ready while I take a shower." Reaching the bathroom door, I pull my t-shirt off and toss it in the laundry basket.

"Beth?"

"Hmm."

"You know how much you mean to me, right? That you're not just my best friend, you're like my sister?"

She glances at me, smiling. "Are you getting all emotional on me, Matthews?"

I shrug. "Maybe. A little. I just wanted you to know that I love you is all." I close the door on her shocked expression.

Beth knows I love her, I've just never told her before now. It felt good to say, and kind of awesome to see the happy it put on her face.

I make a mental note to tell her more often from here on now.

I guess I have Mia to thank for opening this up in me. She got me feeling again … maybe more than ever before.

"I thought there was no romance in this movie?" I complain, licking the pie off my fingers.

Fuck that was some good pie.

Beth grabs the case, reading over the back. "It said there wasn't. Just, and I quote, 'plenty of high action ass-kicking'.

"Well the only ass-kicking going on right now is from her stilettos, digging in his ass while he screws her."

"I guess maybe sex isn't classed as romance nowadays." Beth tosses the case to the floor and tilts her head at an angle, watching the two getting it on, on screen. "Seriously, I'll never understand a woman who likes cock."

I let out a laugh. "That's because you've never had it."

She look across at me grinning. "And I intend on keeping it that way, thank you very much."

"I wasn't offering."

She jabs me in the arm.

"You hit like a girl."

"I am a girl." She folds her arms.

I look back to the TV. They've finally finished going at it, but now we're into the post coital bliss where they're cuddled up in bed.

Fucking excellent. Just what I want to see. A happy couple together.

I grit my teeth, thinking of Mia in my arms. How soft and warm her body felt against mine.

I miss her.

Jesus.

I close my eyes on the ache in my chest.

"This movie sucks," I grind out.

"The movie does suck, you're right, but it's not the movie that's bothering you."

I let out a resigned breath. "I miss her." I open my eyes and turn my head to look at Beth. "Is it fucked up that I miss her this much after knowing her for such a short time?"

"No. Who's to determine what's wrong or right. You feel

what you feel. Time is irrelevant in my opinion. And I'm always right, before you have a comeback."

I can't muster the energy to find a comeback. And honestly, I think she's right. Though I'd never tell her that.

I glance back at the TV, drumming my fingers on my thigh.

"Dad thinks I should write Mia a letter," I say quietly.

Beth sits up, putting herself in my eye line, blocking my view of the TV. "I think that's a really good idea."

"And he also said I should send her a mixed CD."

A grins slides across her face. "Okay, so maybe leave the mixed CD out of it. What would you say in the letter?"

Sliding down the bed so I'm flat on my back, I rest my arm over my eyes. "I don't know…" I shrug. "I guess I'd tell her that I miss her. That it's getting harder and harder to breathe without her. For every day she's gone … every day that I don't get to see her face or hear her voice, takes me a step closer to insanity." I hear the break in my voice, and it stops me talking.

I swallow past the pain.

Beth lies down beside me and rests her head on my shoulder.

"I think you should write her a letter saying exactly that." She sniffles.

"Are you crying?"

"Of course I'm fucking crying! I'm a girl, aren't I?"

Trust Beth to find the way to make me smile through the pain.

Day seven: post-Mia…

I seal the envelope. The envelope that contains the letter that's taken me four fucking days to write. If you saw the letter, you'd be confused as to why it took me four days to write.

Basically, the letter is shit. Because I can't write for shit.

And that's the reason for the CD inside this envelope.

Yeah, I've become *that* guy.

The kind of guy that makes a CD with one song on it to tell the girl he loves how he feels.

I've come to terms with the fact that I lost my balls ages ago. I figured it out when I couldn't get out of bed for three days over Mia leaving me.

So now me and my ball-less self is hoping that this song will tell her everything I'm failing to. Worst case, she'll think I'm lame and laugh her ass off, and I'll never hear from her again. But one thing I know for sure; whenever she hears this song, she'll always think of me, because there are a handful of songs that I can't listen to now without thinking of her. The first time I heard her singing in my car to that Taylor Swift song that I hate, but now listen to all the time … and the Will.i.am song that was playing the first time I kissed her.

Dad was right when he said music evokes memories.

This song might not evoke her memory, but it will tell her where I'm at right now, and hopefully bring her back to me. And that hope is all I've got left now.

I take a deep breath and drop the envelope in the mailbox.

Chapter Twenty-Six

Mia

Two and a half months later…

"You still haven't opened that?"

I glance over my shoulder to see Danni standing in the doorway. Danni is a patient at the clinic, like me. Except Danni suffers with anorexia. It's her second time back in. Not here. She was at a different help facility a few years ago, got better. But she relapsed recently. We met here on my first day. She's a great friend to have as she understands everything I go through.

I've never had a female friend before, and it's been wonderful to have one who understands me as well as Danni does. I've told her everything about me. Jordan's words haunted me when he said I should open up to the next person who tries to get close to me, so I took that chance on Danni, and I'm glad I did.

She's helped me so much. We've helped each other.

After what happened at the hospital, after Forbes' attack, Dr. Packard encouraged me to press charges, so I did. Having Danni to hold my hand through it really helped.

Thankfully I didn't have to go to court as I was here in the clinic.

Forbes didn't get jail time for assaulting me at the hospital. I'm not sad about that as I never thought he would. He got a twelve month suspended sentence, and was forced to attend anger management classes.

I also took out a restraining order. Not that it would do any good. If Forbes wanted to get me, he would. But honestly, I don't think he will. I think we're finally done.

"No, I still haven't opened it." I sigh.

She comes over and sits on my bed. "You've spent so long staring at that thing, I'm surprised you haven't burned a hole in it. Why don't you put us both out of our misery and just open it because the suspense is just about set to kill me."

Danni knows all about Jordan. How I felt … still feel about him. You think my feelings for him would have lessened, but they haven't.

And now that I'm close to better, I'm finding regret a bitter pill to swallow.

I miss him so much.

My trembling fingers run along the line imprint, of what my extensive examination, has figured to be a CD case.

Why would he send me a CD?

She reaches over, her slender fingers touch my arm. "Open it. See what's in there. It could be a DVD of him telling you how desperate he is to see you." Her hands clutch her chest in a dramatic manner.

Danni's a romantic. Even though she's been burned in the past, she stills believes in love.

"I don't know." I shake my head. "Whatever this is – he sent it over two months ago. A lot can change in that time. He'll have moved on, I'm sure."

She shakes her head. "No way. Love doesn't just disappear that quickly, especially not the kind of epic love you both have for each other."

I raise my eyebrow. "You got epic love from what I told you about Jordan and me?"

She gives me a gnarly look. "What he said to you in the hospital, about how he's in love with you … guys don't just say that stuff easily, Mia, not guys like him. *Epic*, I'm telling you."

With a heavy heart, I look back down at the padded envelope in my hands.

"What have you got to lose? Your treatment is almost done. You have a week left. Whatever is in here could determine where you go when you leave here."

Nodding, swallowing down my fear, I slide my finger under the seal and tear it open.

I can almost hear Danni holding her breath as I put my hand inside the envelope.

My heart is beating a mile a minute.

I pull out a piece of paper folded in half, and a clear CD case with a disc inside it. On the front of the disc written in black pen is 'Mia'.

I glance up at Danni. "Read it," she encourages.

My shaking hands open the letter.

Mia,

I've tried for four goddamn days to write you a letter ... trying to tell you how I feel about you - how much I fucking miss you. But everything I write just sounds inadequate. All I know is, being away from you ... makes it hard to breathe. I miss you so much.

So, I'm sending you this song. It says everything I want to and can't. And if you feel any differently about me ... us, after reading this, then you know where I'll be.

I'll always be waiting for you.

Jordan

I wipe the tears from my face.

"God, you're killing me here! What does it say?" Danni looks like she's about to burst, so I hand the letter to her.

I watch her eyes scan over the letter. She reaches the bottom and looks up at me. Tears are glistening in her eyes.

"Holy hell … that was…" She presses her hand to her chest. "You have to listen to the song." She thrusts the case at me.

"I don't have a CD player – just an iPod," I say defeated.

Her eyes scan my room. "Television!" she exclaims. "It has a built in DVD player – you can listen to it through that."

My heart lifts. I jump to my feet, taking the disc with me.

I turn the TV on, and wait for it to come to life. My whole body is trembling.

"You're a genius," I say to Danni as she comes to stand beside me.

"It's a gift." She shrugs.

I take the disc from the case and insert it into the player.

Waiting for it to load feels like an eternity.

Then the song Jordan sent me starts to play, and the soft guitar intro to The Scripts "Man Who Can't Be Moved" fills the room.

My heart picks up pace, and my eyes close on the lyrics. I absorb them. Hearing exactly what Jordan is trying to tell me.

'I'll always be waiting for you'

He's waiting for me.

Danni grabs my hand at my side. I look across at her.

"Don't wait the week. Go to him. Now."

Chapter Twenty-Seven

Jordan

It's been three months since she left. Two and a half since I sent the letter and song.

I haven't heard from her.

The song didn't work.

It was lame and stupid of me to think it would.

After waiting a few weeks to hear from her, I accepted she wasn't coming back … and then I got pissed.

I guess it was one of the stages I had to go through. I'd done the depression. It was time for angry, so I went out and got trashed.

And I hooked up with a random chick.

Not my finest moment.

But it only got as far as her hand down my pants, jerking me off before I stopped it, because in that moment I'd realized that I could sleep with this girl, but I'd only feel the same, probably shittier, when I woke up the next morning. I'd still be in the same position. Mia still wouldn't be here with me. I'd still fucking miss her. I'd still have this gaping hole in my chest that only she can fill. Screwing some random chick wasn't going to fix that. It wasn't going to fix me. So I removed her hand from my pants, told her I was sorry, and left.

Since then, the only action my cock has seen is from my hand.

I think about Mia. And I don't mean when I'm jerking off. But while the subject is here, of course I think about her while I date my hand.

She's the only thing I think about.

I figure at some time in the future, I won't think about her so much. That I'll eventually get there. Just maybe not right now.

So I'm keeping busy. I've been doing more tours for Wade. The first time I went back up to *La Plata Canyon* after being there with Mia was hard, but I swallowed past it, and now it's getting a little easier each time I do a tour up there.

The hotel is still quiet fairly, but we're chugging on and I'm working on a website for the hotel, signing up to tourist and travel agent sites, getting our name out there. My mission is to have the hotel busier than it's ever been by next summer.

Dozer comes over and plants his face on my legs. "Hey, buddy, whatcha up to?" I say, pulling my eyes from the computer to look down at him. He got his cast off a while back, and he is totally back to himself.

Except he still misses Mia.

At times, I feel like there's only him who understands me.

He nudges my leg with his head, and brings his paw up batting me with it.

"What? You hungry?" I reach onto the desk and grab one of the cookies I was eating.

I give it to him, and he takes it, laying down to eat it.

I rub my tired eyes, and look back to the spreadsheet I'm working on. Accounts. Fun times.

I know it's bad when it's a Friday night and even my dad is out on a date, but I'm sitting here with my dog, working the accounts.

I really need to get a fucking life.

The hotel phones rings.

"Golden Oaks," I say, leaning back in my chair.

"You're home on a Friday night? You really are turning into a sad case."

"Thanks, Beth. You really know how to boost a guy's confidence."

She laughs. "Confidence is one thing you will never lack in, Jordan."

"Yeah, yeah, whatever. Anyway, you're giving me grief, but it's not like you're out, hitting up the town."

"Um, working girl here."

"Your mom isn't paying you enough at the diner, so you've had to turn to being a hooker. Sounds like a *Lifetime* movie in the making"

"Ha. Smart ass. I called because I thought I'd let you know I'm sending a tourist up your way. Thinking I should change my mind, tell her to go somewhere else…"

"Okay. I take it back. Only, as long as this tourist isn't like the last one you sent me. Kinda got my heartbroken the last time you did that." I try to come off as jokey and light, but it doesn't work.

She goes quiet down the line. "Nah, this one is different to the last … I'm sure of it. And she's not that good-looking. You wouldn't go for her."

I let out a laugh. "Okay. Good to know. Should I take it she's more of Pine room kind of girl?" Pine is our cheapest room.

"Nah, this one is definitely a Lakeview kind of girl. She might be unfortunate looking, but she's definitely got good taste."

I swallow down. No one has stayed in there since Mia. I just haven't been able to bring myself to let anyone sleep in there yet.

Stupid I know.

"Okay. Cool. She on her way now? I'll go get the room ready."

"She's setting off in a few."

"Thanks, Beth. And I mean that."

"I know you do. And thank me later."

I hang up and push out the chair. I grab the keys for Lakeview, and head down the hall.

I switch the light on, avoiding looking anywhere that will remind me of the times I had in here with Mia. I switch the heater on to warm the room for our new guest, turn the bed down, and put fresh towels in the bathroom.

I turn the light off, lock the door up, and go back to the office.

Twenty minutes later I hear a car pulling up the gravel. Dozer jumps to his feet, ears pricked, sniffs the air, and he's out of the office. Guess he's smelled something he likes.

I follow to get him back in the office before he scares the living daylights out of our new guest, but I'm too late, and the door opens on the chime. I look up and my heart stops.

It actually fucking stops.

"*Mia.*"

I'm not sure if I say the word, or just breathe it through my aching lungs.

"Hi," she says. Her voice sweet and soft … and painful.

I feel a surprising jolt of anger toward her.

Nothing for three fucking months, and she just shows up here unannounced. Screw the fact that I've been dreaming about this very thing happening for three months, I'm still fucking pissed. I'm beyond pissed.

I turn and walk away, putting myself behind the reception desk.

I need a barrier between us to stop me from doing something stupid. *Like getting down to my knees and begging her to take me back.*

She stays by the door, unsure eyes on me. She looks so tiny and fragile. It makes me want to go to her … hold her.

I grip hold of the desk to steady myself.

Dozer is on her, nudging his head at her leg, desperate for her attention.

"Hey buddy." Her eyes leave me, and she bends down to stroke him. "Look at your leg, all healed."

Yeah, well it has been THREE FUCKING MONTHS!

She wraps her arms around his neck, hugging him. "I missed you," she whispers to him.

She missed him! What the fuck about me?

I scrub my hands over my face, exhaling through my feelings. "Why are you here, Mia?"

She looks up at me, slowly rising to stand. The crestfallen look on her face is like a knife to my chest.

Her hands are shaking. She wraps her arms around herself.

"I read your letter, and the song ... I listened to the song. All the way here, in fact," she adds quietly.

I cross my arms over my chest. "You mean the letter I sent two and a half months ago."

She bites her lip. "I only read it this morning. I was afraid ... afraid there would be something in it that would bring me back here. And I couldn't come back then. I had to figure a way to get past everything I was feeling, complete my treatment. In hindsight, I wish I'd read it straight away. But the moment I did ... the moment I heard that song ... I checked out and drove straight here."

"Why?"

She takes a step closer. "Because ... I *hoped* you'd still be waiting."

I tighten my arms, and my stance. Every muscle in my body locked. "Why?"

She closes her eyes. "So I could tell you the one thing I didn't when we were at the hospital."

I stare at her expectedly.

"That I love you ... I'm *in* love with you, Jordan."

She loves me?

I can't speak. Or think. Or move.

You know when you've been waiting to hear the one thing from the one person who matters most, and then they say it and it freezes you to the spot with fear.

Yeah, I'm about there right now.

The silence between us is blistering with pain and confusion and want.

Then I find my voice. "So you came here to tell me you love me?"

I watch her wipe a tear away with her hand. She nods, tugging on her lower lip, twisting it nervously. "Yes. I needed you to know that. And ... also ... to see if you have a room ... for me?"

And there it is. I should have fucking guessed.

"You're the tourist ... you went to see Beth first?" I don't know why, but knowing that is really pissing me off.

Her eyes drift from me. "I got here and I was afraid. I thought maybe you might have changed your mind ... that your feelings for me might have changed after all this time, maybe ... there was someone else..." Her eyes come back to me. "I guess I panicked, so I went to the diner in the hope Beth would be there and I could ask her."

"And what did she tell you?"

She runs her hands nervously down her clothes. "That you ... you haven't moved on."

"Yeah. Well, Beth was wrong. I have moved on. Moved on majorly, in fact. And I'm sorry, but you can't stay here."

I don't mean it. But I'm hurt and I'm not thinking clearly. And I'm an asshole.

The pain on her face lances straight through me. Her shoulders pull in as she wraps her arms around her stomach. "Oh. Right. Okay. I'm sorry..." A tear runs down her cheek. She swipes it away with her finger. "... I shouldn't have come." Then she's gone, out the door.

Dozer growls at me, giving me a 'you fucking idiot' look, then he starts pawing and butting his head against the door, trying to get to our girl.

"I know, I'm a fuckin' idiot!" I grip my hair, angry with myself. "Shit! Motherfucking shit!" I kick the desk. Then without another thought, I'm burning out of the hotel, chasing after her. "Mia! Wait!"

She stops by her car, face away from me, but I don't stop. I stride right over to her, standing before her, I take her tear streaked face in my hands.

It hurts so much to know I put those tears there. "I'm sorry. I didn't mean that ... I was angry, like three fuckin' months worth of angry. But I don't want you to go ... fuck! ... Mia, I just ... I just want *you*."

Her eyes flash up to me with surprise. "You want me?"

"I'll always want you."

Then I kiss her. I kiss her with three months worth of pain and hurt and want and need.

"I love you," she breathes over my mouth.

It makes me kiss her harder. My feelings for her consuming me.

"I love you…" I say, holding her to me. "So fuckin' much."

She stands on her tiptoes, wraps her arms around my neck, and buries her face in my shoulder. I hold her tight. Afraid to let her go. Afraid to *ever* let her go again.

"Does this mean you have room for me?" she whispers.

I tilt my head back staring in her eyes. "I think I could make space for you."

"For how long?"

I shrug. "How does forever sound?"

She puts her hand to my face, the smile on her own real, but tentative. "It sounds too good to be real," she whispers.

"Oh, it's real, babe." I squeeze her ass, lifting her off her feet, loving the feel of her legs as they go around my waist. I turn, walking back to the hotel with her. "And it's gonna be as good as I'm about to make you feel – this is *me* we're talking about here." I lift an eyebrow.

Her laughter fills me. Her kiss soothes me.

And I feel a peace I haven't felt in months.

Epilogue

Mia

"So what happened to us going out for dinner?" I trace patterns on Jordan's bare chest.

"You happened. I was just innocently coming out of the bathroom after my shower, all clean and ready to get dressed, and there you were standing by our bed, wearing your new sexy underwear, looking smoking hot, and of course I got hard because … well, it was *you*. In underwear. Then we had some seriously fuckin' awesome sex, babe, and now I'm in post coital bliss with my girl, and moving just isn't an option."

Laughing, I tilt my head up to him, offering my mouth.

He captures it in a delicious kiss which send shivers right down to my toes.

"See, and that's why moving isn't an option because I intend on doing this with you for the rest of the night."

"Works for me." I smile, stretching my arms up.

Jordan slides his fingers around my neck, playing with the locket around it.

The locket was Anna's. Jordan gave it to me a few months ago.

After I came back, Jordan and I spent time getting *reacquainted* with one another. Then we spent a lot of time talking through the issues that were sitting between us.

I was no longer in the place where I saw the betrayal of my mother when I looked at him.

But the fact was still there.

She had left me behind and raised him.

When Jordan told me everything about her situation with Oliver, it didn't make things better, but it gave me a semblance of understanding.

It's taken me a long time to process my feelings about my mother, but I'm almost there.

Pain of the past never goes away, you just find a way to deal with it. And the future … all the promise it holds … that's what keeps you moving forward, and out of the darkness.

Jordan. He's my future. My promise. My light.

He keeps me sane. He keeps me safe.

When I struggle to breathe, he gives me the air I need.

Some days are hard. Some days when my mind blackens and all I want to do is hide away and eat and purge. He's right there with me.

I'll always be recovering from bulimia.

But now those days when I feel the urge for control and the need to hurt my body are few and far between. I can't even remember the last time I felt that way.

I'm still seeing a therapist. When I left the center, my doctor there referred me to a therapist here in Durango – Dr. Peterson. She has been really great and has helped me work on all my issues.

I still have a long way to go when it comes to dealing with the life I lived with Oliver and Forbes, and the mental scars it left me with, but I'm getting there.

And I still have Danni. We talk regularly on the phone, and she came to visit a few months ago. She stayed for a week, which was awesome. It was great to have some time with her as I'd really missed her. Jordan took us out on a Jeep tour to the canyon. Beth and Toni came along as well. It was a really great day.

Beth and Toni are still dating. It's getting pretty serious from what Beth says, and she told me the other day that Toni and her have been discussing moving in together.

I'm so happy for her. Beth is amazing, and we've grown close. It's great to have a female friend here, especially one as fun and cool as Beth is.

She takes me out shopping and to the beauty salon. All things friends are supposed to do, but I was never allowed. It's novel for me, even now. I don't think I'll ever take being able to do these things for granted.

I'll never take my freedom for granted.

And being in the good place that I am now, settled into my new life … I think that was why Jordan felt I was ready to have my mother's locket. He was confident it wouldn't push me back a step. He was feeling my peace. And he was right. I can't say it was easy to see the locket which Jim had kept of Annabelle's.

It had hidden inside of it, a tiny picture of baby me.

Even though it pained me to see, it also gave me a sense of peace in some way to know that in her own way she had always been thinking of me.

Would I ever do what she did? No.

But it's easier to judge when you're on the receiving end of the hurt. And I know too well what it's like to be with a controlling, abusive man.

I know what it was like to live with Oliver.

I sold my apartment in Boston and all the furniture in it. I never went back. Jordan handled it all for me. And I moved into the hotel with Jordan and Jim, and of course Dozer. Too soon, probably, but I spent a long time living unhappily. Jordan is my happy, so I was grabbing it with both hands.

I invested some of Oliver's money into the hotel. Both Jim and Jordan protested – Jordan the loudest. He was having none of it at first, but it was also my mother's hotel, and now my home.

I want it to succeed.

So after a few well timed seductions, I got my own way. Jordan finds it hard to say no to me.

The hotel is doing amazingly well. Jordan really got the business moving. The website and links he built have helped immensely. Also, he set up a business deal with Wade, and they tied the jeeps tours into the hotel. People can stay at the hotel, and the tours go from here. Using some of the money I put in, Jordan had a garage built to store the jeeps.

It's really helped things. I'm so proud of him.

I'm proud of me too.

I left Harvard, but I haven't left behind medicine completely. I'm just moving in a different direction. I've enrolled in Veterinary school to start this term. I'm hoping Dozer will let me practice my examining and bandaging skills on him. I'm sure he will; he's pretty soft on me as I am him, much to Jordan's annoyance.

But school is a little way off starting as it's summer break, and today is a year to the day since Jordan and I first met.

We were supposed to be going out to dinner, but that's off the menu now.

I have a gift for him that I can't wait any longer to give to him.

I start to get out of bed, but Jordan catches my hand. "Where you going, babe?"

"I thought as we weren't going to dinner now … you might want your gift?"

His eyes light up. "Well if you're giving me mine, then I guess it's only fair you get yours."

My heart does a somersault in my chest. He got me a gift! Not that I thought he wouldn't. I've just never received a gift in this context before – not one where there's no pain before it.

Going to my closet, I get out the envelope containing Jordan's gift. I put a lot of thought and effort into his gift. I think he'll like it … I think … I'm not sure.

Shit, I'm so nervous! I've never given anyone a gift like this before.

I meet him back on the bed. We sit facing each other. I keep the envelope containing Jordan's present behind my back.

"Who's going first?" he asks, looking excited, like a little kid on his birthday.

I'm excited too. Trembling with it.

"We could open together. Or you first. Or me," I say.

He raises his eyebrow.

"What? I'm just excited!"

"Not together," he says. "'Cause I want to see the look on your face when you open mine."

"Okay. You go first."

"You sure?"

"I'm sure."

My nervous, trembling hand brings the envelope around to give to him.

His eyes meet mine, a puzzled look in them. Then he takes it from me, and tears the envelope open. Hand in, he pulls the papers out.

I watch his eyes reading over it, then widening as he takes the details in.

His eyes lift to mine. Awe and love in them. It squeezes my heart. "Did you really do this?"

I nod. "Not on my own though, the agent helped me … is it too much?"

His eyes go down to the papers, then lift back to mine. Now they're glistening, and I can feel my own welling up. "No … it's just … fuckin' amazing, babe … I can't believe you did this."

I tug on my lip. "I was thinking of what to get you, and I remembered how you sounded that day when you said you'd never go traveling again. The sadness in your voice. I didn't want that to be the case. I know how much you love traveling … seeing the world, so I thought I'd finish off the trip you started with your friends."

The gift I bought Jordan was the rest of the trip he never got to finish when Anna got sick.

I bought a three week vacation, leaving in a week, taking us to India, then Nepal, onto Hong Kong, then Shanghai, and ending in Japan.

It's a gift for me too as I've never travelled before. And who better to break that virginity with than Jordan?

His face breaks into a grin. "Looks like we're on the same page with our gifts."

"What do you mean?"

He pulls out an envelope, similar to mine from behind his

back. "Open it." He smiles, handing it to me.

I tear the envelope open, and pull out the contents.

Holy shit!

"A trip to Paris at Christmas!" I yell, then cover my mouth with my hand.

He chuckles. "I knew you'd never left the country before, and I've never been to Europe, so I thought we could go over for Christmas. Looks like we're gonna accrue some serious air miles this year." He grins.

I launch myself at him, kissing him deeply. He takes us down to the bed, rolling me underneath him.

His hand slides down my thigh, cupping my butt, covering my scars, holding me. "Love you, babe."

"I love you too."

I came here to Colorado, looking for my mother, trying so hard to escape my past. Trying to find a purpose, a reason to live.

I might not have found my mother in the way I'd first hoped, but instead I found so much more.

I found something I've never before had—never dreamed I would have … a *real* family.

Jordan, Jim, Beth and Dozer.

But best of all … I got love.

Not love under fear or condition. Not love that comes with a price. I got real, honest to god love in all its purest forms.

Family love. Friend love. Unconditional love. And the best love of all…

Jordan.

He gave me the one thing he's never given to anyone before.

He gave me his heart, and his trust.

And in return, I gave him the same right back.

The End

Acknowledgments

To my beautiful family, thank you for your never-ending support. I live *my* dream, every single day with the three of you. I'm blessed to have all your love, and know I love you right back, immensely.

A massive thank you to Sali Benbow-Powers, you went that extra mile for me, talked me off the ledge, encouraged me to push my boundaries … you helped me step out of my comfort zone on this one, and for that I'll be forever grateful.

Jenny Aspinall, thank you for the nudge in the right direction. You truly are the book whisperer.

My girls, Trish Brinkley, Rachel Maybury and Rachel Fisci – I have the most fun with you girls! Love you three, very muchly.

Jennifer Roberts-Hall, you're a dream to work with. Thank you for waving your sparkly magic wand and spreading your fairy dust.

To every blogger who reads and shares and talks up my books, I can't thank you enough.

And to you, the reader, an endless amount of thank-you's and that still wouldn't be enough to express the gratitude I feel.

About the Author

Samantha Towle began her first novel in 2008 while on maternity leave. She completed the manuscript five months later and hasn't stopped writing since. She is the author of THE MIGHTY STORM and the Wall Street Journal Bestseller WETHERING THE STORM.

She has also wrote paranormal romances, THE BRINGER and the ALEXANDRA JONES SERIES, all penned to tunes of The Killers, Kings of Leon, Adele, The Doors, Oasis, Fleetwood Mac, and more of her favourite musicians.

A native of Hull and a graduate of Salford University, she lives with her husband, Craig, in East Yorkshire with their son and daughter.

For more info on Samantha visit: www.samanthatowle.co.uk

You can also find her on Facebook: Books by Samantha Towle
Twitter: samtowlewrites